Head o' W-Hollow

JESSE STUART

Head o' W-Hollow

With a Foreword by

Robert Penn Warren

THE UNIVERSITY PRESS OF KENTUCKY

To
Merton S. Yewdale

Scholarly publisher for the Commonwealth,
serving Bellarmine College, Berea College, Centre
College of Kentucky, Eastern Kentucky University,
The Filson Club Historical Society, Georgetown College,
Kentucky Historical Society, Kentucky State University,
Morehead State University, Murray State University,
Northern Kentucky University, Transylvania University,
University of Kentucky, University of Louisville,
and Western Kentucky University.

Editorial and Sales Offices: The University Press of Kentucky
663 South Limestone Street, Lexington, Kentucky 40508-4008

99 00 01 02 03 6 5 4 3 2

Library of Congress Cataloging-in-Publication Data

Stuart, Jesse, 1907–
Head o' W-Hollow.

Reprint of the 1st ed. published by Dutton, New York.
1. Kentucky—Fiction. I. Title
PZ3.S9306He 1979 [PS3537.T92516] 813'.5'2
ISBN 0-8131-0142-5 79-11240

This book is printed on acid-free recycled paper meeting
the requirements of the American National Standard
for Permanence of Paper for Printed Library Materials.

Manufactured in the United States of America

CONTENTS

ACKNOWLEDGMENTS

The author expresses his thanks to the editors of *The American Mercury*, *The New Republic*, *The Yale Review*, *The Southern Review* and *Story*, for permission to reprint certain stories.

FOREWORD

Head o' W-Hollow, by Jesse Stuart, is a unique book, bound for its own kind of immortality. It is unique, and highly personal, but we can readily see that it belongs to a certain genus—a genus that includes *Sut Lovingood* by George Washington Harris, *Georgia Scenes* by Augustus Baldwin Longstreet, and the ramshackle epic of *Davy Crockett*. Such works have, of course, a special historical value, giving pictures, sometimes creatively distorted, of the way life was lived in the American backcountry in early days, or more recently in isolated regions. But the gift of observation, poetry, and humor runs through all of them, and provides a dimension of literary value.

Certainly *Head o' W-Hollow* has a permanent if modest historical value. Jesse has a rattrap memory for turns of speech, and he has given a sociohistorical record of daily life in his remote world—now so much less remote and more changed. But if that were all, the value would be infinitely less than it actually is. The book is a work of true literary talent—part of the human record in that dimension.

Jesse's range of effect is wide—including the pathos (and grim humor) of "Mountain Poorhouse"; the Gothic (and sometimes comic) gruesomeness of "Brother Groan," in his robe of flowing sleeves, like Jesus on a Sunday school card, and his "Disciples" digging up his dead (and even in life hideously ugly) wife after a year in the ground to encounter in the dark digging a nest of copperheads; the comedy of Anse's losing the "pretty girl-preacher" he loves, by arranging that, when she sets out to demonstrate her faith and sanctity by accepting a copperhead's bite, the snake in hand is one from which Anse has secretly extracted the fangs by a "pair of shoe brad pullers"; the farce of "Governor of Kentucky"; and the celebration of endurance and courage in "Dark Winter."

Earlier I have remarked that the gift of observation, poetry, and humor runs through the genus to which *Head o' W-Hollow* belongs. But the fact is even more marked in that book, and in much of Jesse's other work. The wilted corn blades "flap-flap with the wind and talk to the soap-slick poplar leaves by the pig pen." Eyes have "a steel glint of mountain-river blue." At sunset there is "a red ember spot on the sky above the chestnut tops." A man has "one of them old sour drunk man's frowns on his face." A character in "Woman in the House" is "drunk as the Devil wanted him to be." When another man refuses a drink from religious scruples, Hankas says: "I'll be dogged. Lord has saved him and he promised not to drink any more licker to the Lord. Wonder what the Lord wants fer nuthin." Mom, in "Dark Winter," is "tall, sinewy, dark as a pawpaw leaf bitten by frost, . . . her white teeth there in the dim-lighted room." A boy lies on the ground "full of pain as a water barrel full of wiggler tails." Striking a match in a dark room of people is "like turning the lights on in Hell to see what your next door neighbor is." In fact, one of the pervasive effects—one of the most difficult effects for a writer to achieve—is the sense of language speaking off the page, and that is a gift Jesse has, a gift based on years of astute listening and watching. It is a gift that goes far toward creating a world.

Long ago, at Vanderbilt University, when I had just begun teaching, Jesse Stuart appeared as a graduate student. He was an impressive youth, tall, powerfully built, dark-haired, keen of eye, full of all sorts of curiosity, intellectual and otherwise. But he was already a compulsive writer, as though all the life he had absorbed was struggling to find a way out, and perhaps to achieve its meaning. For instance, a term paper in one course (not my own) turned out to be not a paper at all but a book-length autobiography—later published as such. In poetry and prose, the flow continued unabated, always a reflex of his mountain youth when he had absorbed all and missed nothing. He was wise enough—or perhaps he could not have done otherwise—to go back to the country where his gifts had been formed. But long before that we had become friends. It was to be, unhappily, a friendship largely of recollection, for I saw him only a few times after the Vanderbilt period, once in Washington, where, on leave, he was wearing the blue of a naval officer, and once or twice on his rare trips to Nashville. Years, distance, ill-health intervened after that, but I am happy to say that now *Head o' W-Hollow* has renewed recollections, and that, though I have reread the book several times over the years, this reading has given me more pleasure and admiration than any before.

ROBERT PENN WARREN

Head o' W-Hollow

YOU can take the road you please. You can go take the way a crow flies or the way the wind blows. And you can follow your nose. But the road that leads you to W-Hollow is a wagon road, the first three miles of it. For the rest, it's a cow path, a goat path, a rabbit path, a fox path, a mule path—it is whatever you want to call it. But the drum of the automobile is far away. The clockin of the horses' hoofs used to beat hollow on the earth—and does still. The road is the color of a sand rock, a pied copperhead turned on its back in the sun.

You can follow the wind, for the wind blows west from the old E–K–Railroad, where the mail used to start out once a day and then twice a day; but if a tunnel fell in, there was no mail at all. Or if you come from the muddy Little Sandy, where people do their fishin and their baptizin in the springtime—come to the covered bridge, turn east and follow your nose. If one stranger comes from the old E–K– and another comes by the covered bridge, where the half-darkie used to sleep all day with the pigeons because he couldn't go to a white school since he was half-colored and couldn't go to the colored school because he was half-white—let one turn west followin the wind and the other turn east followin his nose, and they'll meet somewhere in the bread pan of W-Hollow.

W-Hollow is a place under the sun—the sun creeps into the low spots at midday—and used to be when there was big timber and hoot-owls—the hoot-owls would who-who at the sun hurtin their eyes at midday. Now there is plenty of brush in W-Hollow, enough to hide in when someone is huntin for you, enough to hide in if you owe debts and are tryin to get away from them—it takes a lot of wind and gasoline to find you. And if you are a rabbit or a blacksnake, or a fox or a possum or a polecat, it's a fine place. If you are a copperhead you had better stay out. Fire runs through W-Hollow, and a copperhead is like to lose his temper and die—a white whip lash of ashes on dark burnt ground. If you are a terrapin, you are too slow to get out of the way of fire, and you'd better stay out of W-Hollow, too. Haven't I seen the terrapin shells piled up like stalks from a sweet potato patch, after the fire went through the new ground! I have seen the copperheads white whips of ashes on the new ground. I have seen the crows come over and hunt the ground for the half-burnt terrapins. They picked the shells out clean and left them in the wind and sun to dry.

W-Hollow is a place under the sun, fenced in by the wind. It knows more things than it can ever tell. Its earth cannot speak, or its brush. And that is fine, too. Let them be dumb. And if two strangers meet there, one from the East and one from the West, let them take off their hats to each other in the bread pan of W-Hollow—it's just a place with four seasons, wind, sun, rain, snow—with scrub oaks and old log houses and new plank shacks—a place that's somewhere for some and nowhere for many.

How did it get its name? Who cut the big trees in W-Hollow? Who made the slippery wagon road in the long ago? Who built the old house at the forks of the road?

Do not ask me so many questions at once. I am sure I don't know who named W-Hollow. It was named for the letter "W," so I have heard, as I have heard so many more things that are true and untrue—that are words useless as the wind, blowin about carelessly as the wind blows. Ask the dead on the Three-Mile Hill who named W-Hollow and who made the slippery wagon road—a road that is good now as it ever was and not a bit better now than it ever was. Ask the dead who cut the trees in W-Hollow. Ask them if they did it. Ask them if they would do it again, if they had it to all do over again and could see the W-Hollow we have today. Ask them if they didn't build the house at the forks of the road. I'm sure some of them could tell you.

You see, it is fall now. Dead leaves are flyin. It has always been fall on the Three-Mile Hill and the Plum Grove Hill—W-Hollow gives up its dead to Three-Mile Hill. There is not a graveyard in the Hollow. There used to be one for dead horses, when men drove them into the chestnut thickets and took their hides for a few dollars and left their carcasses to the hound dogs, possums, buzzards, and crows. There was such stench then on the summer dry-wind that the people comin up the Hollow had to hold their noses when the wind blew. Now there is not even a horse graveyard. There is not anything but some old jaw bones and some knee bones. Children are born in W-Hollow, but the Hollow gives up its dead like the tree sheds its leaves in fall.

In or out of the Hollow, you can take the road you please. You can take the way the crow flies, the way the wind blows, or you can follow your nose. It is just two pipes of taste-bud whichever way you come or go. Sometimes the ragweeds are growin in the road and they'll make little sulphur-colored streaks up and down your pant legs. Of course, when the fall comes and the rabbits and birds and possums get ripe, the ragweeds will all be dead, and there will be a lot of dead sycamore leaves in the road and dead leaves a-floatin on the little blue dwindlin holes of water in the creek.

In the spring you can hear the beetles and the whippoorwills if you come. You can hear the birds a-singin new songs. In the spring you can hear the wind slushin around in the leaves. In the summer you can hear the wind and the corn blades parleyin around. You can hear the grasshoppers and the crickets. You can hear the lazy wind. You can hear the baa-baas of the sheep and the lambs up on the hills. The whole Hollow looks lazy in the summer sun. And the sun allus shines on W-Hollow in Kentucky. It never reaches some of it till noon. But it gets there.

In the fall you can see the brown leaves along the path, and you can see them flyin in the wind. You can hear the beetles in the bean patch—and down in the old cornfields. Falltime is good to hear in W-Hollow. It is kindly sad, and if a body remembers the old-timers that used to be in W-Hollow in the falltime and remembers the frosty weed fields and the way they used to hunt—a body sorty wonders if the owls who-who for them in W-Hollow—them that used to be there and them there now. For it is a place under the sun, walled in by the wind and the hills—nowhere for many—somewhere for some.

I

BIG EIF said: "Go ahead with the work this mornin, Gleen—you and Everett and Little Eif. I'll not be out with you this mornin. Take the wagon and go to the far-field and haul in the cane-fodder blades and stack them in the loft. You will need them this winter for the cows."

"What is the matter with you, Pap?" says Gleen. "Why ain't you goin to the field with us? This is a mornin good to work. The wind makes a body feel fine. It kindly tastes of frost. Rabbits are ripe. It is a pretty mornin. Why ain't you goin with us?"

"My boy," says Big Eif, "it is a long story to tell you and there is no need to tell you just now. I'll tell your Ma atter while. You go ahead with the work. Take the wagon and do as I tell you. Mind them bad ruts on the other side of Pine Hill. The wagon tires are liable to come off there. Drive the wagon in the creek and let it set a little while to swell the wheels. Be sure and do that. Be sure to bind the bundle of cane-fodder blades down with a good stout bindin stick. Use one of the old trace chains for a bindin chain. You had better hurry along, for the sun is comin above the Perkins' hill and the frost is drivin off'n the half-dead leaves. Be sure to warm the bridle bits before you put them in the mules' mouths. Put 'em in cold, you know they'll take all the hide off'n the mules' tongues."

"All right, Pap," says Gleen.

"Why ain't you goin, Pap?" says Little Eif. "I can't remember the time when you didn't go to the field with us and drive the team and wave your hand and tell us what to do. And you could allus do more work than us three put together. Have you et somethin that don't agree with your stomach?"

"Now, never mind," says Big Eif. "Do as I tell you. Go ahead to the field. The farm must go on even if I do set by the fire and smoke my pipe. The farm must go on, my boys, even when I am gone."

Everett goes to the barn and he piles up some cornstalks. He goes to the harness rack, an upturned sourwood limb nailed to one corner of the mules' manger. He takes down the two bridles looped over this sourwood limb and brings them out in front of the barn jungling in his hand. He strikes a match to the cornstalks. A red tiny blaze oozes up through the bright cool autumn wind, a blaze nearly as red as the black-oak leaves back on Graveyard Hill. He holds the bridle bits over the blaze, and puts his fingers on them. Then he walks toward the barn.

Everett brings the mules from the barn, harnessed and curried. The trace chains are jingling. The mules' heads are high, wind in fog-streaks is coming from their nostrils. Everett takes them to the jolt wagon in the shed. The harness jingles as they prance and breathe the air of October. "Whoa, Barnie—whoa, Jack—back 'em—back 'em up! Whoa back!" Now Everett has hooked the trace chains. He fastens the breast-yoke and girds the checklines through the loops on the harness, a red tassel on each mule's bridle, a red tassel flying in the crisp autumn wind. With the creaking of wagon and the whirr-whirr of the cornstalks and dead leaves under the wagon, Everett drives down to the sawdust pile.

Little Eif and Gleen climb in the wagon, throw down their pitchforks on the wagon-bed floor, put their arms on their brother's shoulders and away goes the team, the axles creaking against the hubs, over the dead leaves and the road rock, under the bright autumn sun and through the mist of frost that is melting from the dead and half-dead blades of corn.

"I like to see pretty farms, big barns and nice geared-up mule teams," says Big Eif Porter. "I hate it that I can't be with the farm, the team, and the boys any longer. It breaks my heart and my soul. I hope there is a farm in Heaven where I can work and I hope they have winter, summer, springtime and fall there just like we have here."

Big Eif walks toward the wash kettle where Treecy, his wife, is tending a fire. Big Eif is tall as a stalk of corn, sturdy as a young poplar in an ash cove, the color of an autumn leaf, with eyes blue as the sky and with a far-away look like an eagle's. His hands are made rough as sand rocks from work in the fields, his two hands are nearly as big as a brown churn dash.

"Why ain't you at work with the boys this mornin, Eif?" asks Treecy. "You ain't missed a mornin since I can remember bein married to you. You ain't missed a day that you could work in the field in the last twenty-nine years. Why are you off this mornin? Ain't you a-feelin good? Didn't that berry cobbler you et for your supper last night agree with your stomach?"

"I ain't sick," says Eif. "I feel all right. I just want to take today off and be with you."

"Anythin happened to you, Eif, in any way?" asks Treecy. "Tell me what is wrong and if I can be any comfort to you in any way I will."

Treecy takes her clay pipe from her apron pocket and fills it with taste-bud tobacco. She shoves the tobacco down firm and crumbles it with her forefinger. She looks at the ashes by the side of the kettle. Then she stoops and dips her pipe in the red brands under the kettle that the wind keeps kindled. She sucks the long stem and blows out smoke bluer than the October wind.

"Does that 'backer bite your tongue, Treecy?" asks Eif.

"Not a bit," says Treecy. "It is the best 'backer I believe I ever smoked."

"Give me a chaw of it then," says Eif.

Treecy is not pretty as she was twenty-nine years ago. She does not have the color of peach petals on her cheeks, and teeth white as elm bark. Her fingers are rougher now than they used to be, once slender as the stems of the lady-slipper. Her eyes are faded too, eyes once blue as the wild larkspur petals. Time has brought these things. But she has kept pretty for a woman of her age, she who has played with time, childbirth, and work in the house and in the field. Treecy has turned the color of a faded October leaf. She is lean as a black-jack sapling, and her flesh is as hard as the flesh of a young chestnut.

"Let me mend up the fire for you, Treecy."

Eif picks up the brands and mends the fire under the wash kettle. The bright flame with blue tips laps around the black kettle like so many forked tongues and the water in the kettle boils. One can see a pile of white clothes in the kettle. Treecy has the wash tub under a beech shade. The tub is sitting on a stool chair. She takes both hands, gets a white shirt and rubs it up and down over the ridges of the brass washboard, her weight bearing down on her hands, down upon the shirt dripping with foamy water. The bubbles, blue, red, white, purple, follow on the ridges of the tub.

"Wonder how the boys will make it over the rough road after the cane-fodder?" says Eif.

"Big enough they ought to be, able to go after a load of fodder if they are ever goin to be able to do anythin," says Treecy. "They ought to be able to go on with a farm—worked on it all their lives except the five months they go to school every year. Why can't they haul cane-fodder to the barn and dig taters, make 'lasses, cut cane wood? Why can't they raise corn, wheat, oats, rye, 'backer? They ought to be able to do anythin on a farm any man can do. W'y I believe them two girls in the house can run this farm."

"I'm glad to hear you talk like that," says Eif.

"What are you drivin at, Eif?"

"I like to see big pretty farms and fat barns," says Eif. "Pretty mules with pretty harness on their backs to jingle and red tassels on their bridle rings. I love to see wagons loaded down with plenty of corn, 'backer, 'lasses, pumpkins layin all among the corn and fodder. I love to see plenty of fat hogs around on a big floored pen. I love to go out by daylight and work all day, take my dinner bucket and hang it in a tree so the ants can't get in my dinner. I love to drive in atter dark and feed the mules and the fattenin hogs. I love every foot of my three hundred acres. You know how we have come by it, a little at a time. Atter I sold a good 'backer crop I allus bought another little strip of land. But I ain't goin to farm anymore, ain't goin to buy no more land."

"What are you talkin about, Eif Porter?" says Treecy, and she stops rubbing a shirt and looks at him. The blue smoke dances about her face in tiny swirls. The wind blows through the beech top above their heads and sighs through the hanging leaves. "What are you talkin about? Nothin ain't happened to you, has it?"

"Nothin exactly—nothin only what is natural. Listen to me now, Treecy. You want to cook a big goose for supper. Make plenty of dumplins. Have a big supper tonight. Have milk, corn-dodger bread, hot biscuits and butter, and all the things I like to eat. I'll go out and knock down a couple of rabbits atter a while and a mess of quails. I want you to make brown gravy with them. I want a real supper tonight, and fix up the table so about twenty can eat besides the family. Put all them extra leaves in the table we use when we have workins."

"What do you mean, all of this of a sudden?"

"Now a good wife never asks a man what he means. You are a good wife and you listen to me, Treecy, and do as I say and ask the questions later," says Eif.

II

He goes into the house and gets the gun, calls Leaf and Loap, the dogs, and walks up the hill above the house into the brown broom sage where he starts throwing rocks and pieces of stumps into the briar thickets and old brush piles. Loap wiggles his spotted tail and hunts the thickets and the ditches where the brims of tufted sod hang over. Under such places the rabbits hide. Leaf tries to find a quail. She wiggles her gray and blue speckled body through the briars and wags her tail. She hunts faster than the hound Loap. After a while Treecy hears the dog yelp and then "pow-pow!" And "pow-pow-pow-pow-pow-pow—" again. And she hears the dogs run. She hears again and again "pow-pow" and "pow-pow." She hears the dog whine, yelp, bark and run through the dead leaves.

Treecy finishes the washing. She carries the clothes in a big crock and pins them on the line. She has put bluing in the white clothes and they look whiter than the small October cloud that floats across the heavens above the house. The clothes flutter on the line, the white clothes in the wind, the blue clothes in the wind. The girls are getting dinner. Clara Belle is putting the steaming corn-dodger bread on the table and Barbara is putting down the knives and the forks and spoons and plates. It is getting nigh onto twelve o'clock.

The wagon comes creaking up to the barn door. The mules blow and their sides go in and out, sides slick and pretty, the color of a brown hairy carpet.

"Thank God, we made it all right over that awful road. Thank God, that trip is done, but think of the seven more to make even if the wagon holds up over that rough road!" says Everett.

Big Eif Porter comes down off the hill now. Loap and Leaf come behind him with their tongues nearly to the ground, red thin tongues with little white flakes of foam on the tips. And Big Eif begins to throw birds down beside Treecy where she is sitting on the porch stringing October beans for the supper tonight. He throws down thirty-one birds, quail with blotches of blood on their feathers and with pretty feathers around their necks. He goes back into his hunting coat and pulls out seven rabbits, rabbits with new sets of winter fur, bright, fluffy, the color of the dead leaves and the sunlight.

"Them looks good enough to eat, don't they, boys?" he says.

"Shore do, Pap," says Everett.

Big Eif gets the wash pan, fills it with cold water, and washes his hands and face. He dries his face and hands, and sits down at the table. Treecy throws the beans from her apron, and comes and stands over the table, and blesses the food.

"Help yourselves now everybody," says Big Eif. "Eat, my children, eat."

Everett, his mouth full, says: "Now that road is at its worst right over there before you get to Harkreader's place. Them ruts are nigh waist-deep there, nearly up to a mule's belly."

"You boys can take the evenin off this evenin," says Big Eif. "I want to set around and just talk to you boys."

"W'y, Pap, w'y are you actin so funny? You went huntin this mornin, never went out to work, told us what to do. Now you are tellin us not to work. Liable to be fallin weather on the cane-fodder and a couple of good rains, and them cane blades would be ruint. You know that. We'd better make hay while we got a sun like we got. We ain't got time to lay off from work like this."

"Listen to me," says Eif. "I'm glad to see you so much like your old Pap. But I am still boss around here long as I am here. Now you boys unharness the mules and turn them in the lot. Day after tomorrow you'll use them for somethin else than haul cane-fodder with. You'll be haulin another kind of load."

"We don't understand you, Pap," says Everett.

"You'll understand me by and by," says Eif. "You know I wouldn't stop workin without a reason. I have a very good reason for bein off and I'll tell you later. You know, Everett, you are the oldest of my children and you sorty got man-ways about you. You can run a farm. I want to see you do it. I am not goin to run one always. I want to see you carry on. You are somethin like an oak tree. You are solid. It takes solid men in this world to carry on. Mark that down. We need solid men. It takes a solid man to help build a nation: a man not afraid of hell itself in the time of trouble, a man that has the courage of a oak tree in the storm, a man deep rooted in his own clay. I want you to carry on when I leave this farm."

The mules wallow in the barn-lot sand. The harness hangs on the sourwood limb by the manger. The October sun is high in the blue sky. The crows fly over the land of plenty, the land of brown fodder shocks, old stubble fields where the pumpkins lie thick and brown, holding to their old dead roots of life. The crab grass is seeded and the birds fly in droves, the blackbirds and the cowbirds. They peck, peck their tiny bills and get the grass seeds to fill their tiny craws. The trees are getting balder every hour, the wind sweeps off their brown leaves and does nothing more than throw them on the ground for the rabbits to hide in and the snakes and lizards to sleep under.

III

Clara Belle and Barbara come walking out where Big Eif, Everett, Gleen and Little Eif are sitting under the apple tree.

"Get you a couple of chears off'n the porch and come and jine us—have your Ma to come too," says Big Eif. And when they do he says: "Now all of my family is here. Here is my family—my three boys and my two girls—all but the three dead ones, asleep back up yander on Graveyard Pint. And Treecy, didn't I tell you when one of the children was a-goin to die? Didn't I allus warn you? You was one of them Free Willed Baptis. I have allus been a Forty-Gallon Baptis. I tell you we know when we get a token and that is more than any other church on earth ever gets—that is, a token. Now let me tell you, I got a token!"

"A token?"

"My God!"

"A token, Pap?"

"Yes—now you keep your hats on, I got a token."

"What was it? What did it say?"

"It said I was to leave you tonight at ten o'clock."

"My God!"

"A token!"

"Now take it easy. I am goin to change worlds tonight at ten o'clock. I can show that I am right. I have allus told you that the Forty-Gallon Baptis was right. You can't get a token among the Free Willers. Now I want all the Free Willers in this neighborhood in here tonight. I want to show them somethin that I can't tell them. They won't be Free Willers atter tonight when they see what I have told them is goin to come to pass. I want them to be my neighbors in Heaven and live on adjining farms. So I want you to get on a mule, Little Eif, and invite the neighbors in for supper tonight. I want you to ask Hull Hillman, Bunion Thacker, Hillman Taylor, Vice Wormwood, Liebert Collingsworth, Harry Black, Jonas Jurdan, Flint Thompson. They are all Free Willers. Have them bring their wives and oldest children. Don't want too many babies a-cryin on this precious night. Go up Sand Suck and invite Ian McCleary, Cheery Williams, Foxey Smith, Hal Smith, Bob Hunt, Alexander Sims, Eif Cowley and Ben Frazier. Hurry up now—tell them we've got a big supper and we're goin to have a little church over here. Get Brother Issiac Flint and have him bring over a couple o'dozen of them song books with the old songs in them."

"All right, Pap."

"Now dry up them tears—all of youns."

"A token——"

"I can't stand it," says Treecy. "I'm glad we got most of the cookin done already."

"Dry up your tears," says Eif. "This is somethin that happens in every man's and every woman's life. It is just a-changin worlds—somethin like a-goin from my farm over into Wormwood's farm. It is just a little change. It is better to get a token and know about it and get things fixed up about the place than it is to kick the bucket all of a sudden. You know that, Treecy."

"I don't know," says Treecy. "It's hard any way you take it. It's hard to give up a loved one. How can I go on without you? The children will all marry off and leave me alone—all alone and without you."

"Don't worry about that," says Eif. "You are crossin bridges before you come to them. Take it easy and dry your tears up."

"But how did you get the token?" asks Treecy.

"I got it this mornin when I went to feed the fattenin hogs. A voice come to me and it said: 'Prepare to meet thy Maker at ten o'clock tonight.' And it come out'n a clean breath of wind. It wasn't no movin dead leaves neither. I know I heard that voice—that little voice a-cryin—and I'll show you tonight."

IV

Clara Belle and Barbara are putting the steaming food on the big table. Sweet-smelling food: cooked hams with brown gravy; goose, cooked tender and brown, and a pot of dumplings; there is corn-dodger bread and hot biscuits—steam going up from the bread, and mingling with the steam from two pots of coffee; buttermilk, sweet milk, to drink; apples, peaches, pears, apricots, apple jelly, peach jelly, blackberry jelly, and wild grape jelly; quail on a heaped-up platter with another plate of brown quail gravy; rabbits on a heaped-up platter with a dish of rabbit gravy; five stewed hens and a couple of roasted ducks; pies, cakes, and wine; blackberry cobbler, cider, potatoes, fall beans, soup beans, and leather britches. Food on the big table ready for Big Eif Porter's last supper.

Now the crowd is coming. They tie their mules to the paling fence and to the apple trees and to the fence posts in the barn-lot fence. A few more men come riding on their mules—men in the saddles and their wives riding behind them on quilts spread on the mules' backs. A few come over the rough roads in buggies. It looks like church to see the crowd. Here is Brother Issiac Flint with about twenty song books. The whole crowd invited must be here and many more from the looks of the mules tied to the palings and the posts in the barn lot. The mules snicker to each other and the dogs bark at the strange animals tied about the place.

"Come in all of you," says Big Eif. "Come right in. Supper is ready right now. Hope you are all empty and hollar as gourds. Want you to clean up this table of grub, want you to eat and be happy, and atter we eat we want a little prayer meetin and a few testimonies."

There is much speaking and shaking of hands. Neighbors five miles apart haven't seen each other for two months or perhaps longer. Then they begin to drop round the big table in the long log kitchen with its rough walls and puncheon floors.

"Fill up these chears right here, boys," says Eif. "And right over here there is a big bench that will seat about twenty of you. We got room here for fifty more. Now don't be bashful. I want you to help yourselves. Brother Issiac Flint will ask the blessin."

And then he says, "Let's stand please and sing one verse of 'Lord, I'm Comin Home!' "

And then, "Be seated now and partake of the grub."

"Just why all this good supper of a sudden, Brother Eif?" asks Bunion Thacker. "Why call us in so sudden like? W'y we're busy as bees gettin in our crop, but when Big Eif Porter calls somethin we allus come."

"Let's eat now," says Eif, "and I'll tell you atter while. Eat now with me. Eat and be merry, for the Book says, 'Tomorrow ye may die.' Now I want you people to eat and be merry. Help yourself."

"Pass me them quails down this way."

"I do like ham and gravy."

"Carve me off a piece of that stewed hen."

"I'll have a biscuit, please."

"Yes, blackberry jam, please."

"I'll take coffee to drink."

"Buttermilk for me."

"More bread—corn-dodger bread, please."

"Beans around this table are a-goin beggin, ain't they?"

"Not these fall beans. Never tasted anythin better'n my life."

"You know I like a good old table filled with grub and I like to set down and eat and eat until my stomach is tight as a banjer head. Then I wish that I had another stomach."

"Boy, this is the best grub I ever tasted and the fullest table that I ever put my feet under."

"Pass me the stewed hen, please."

"I'll take a little of that roasted goose. Move that dish o' beans there. Ain't it in the way of your elbows?"

"Pass me some sorghum 'lasses down this way."

"I'll take some maple syrup, please."

"Now reach and help yourselves everybody," says Eif. "Don't no one go away from my table peeved or hungry. Got plenty of good old taste-bud 'backer for you to smoke when you get through here."

"Don't worry—we ain't goin to leave a table like this feelin hungry."

"A little rabbit this way, please. Law, but I do love them brown rabbit legs."

"Ain't half as good as roasted goose."

"Pass the taters, please."

"A little wine to taper off on."

"I bout had all I can put away. Hate to go away and leave all this grub."

"I got to unloose my belt three holes."

"Yes, I'll take one of them old-fashioned taste-bud cigars.

Lord, they are good. That smoke is good for a body to inhale."

V

"Well, people," says Big Eif at last, "I just want to tell you that I don't have much longer to be with you."

"What do you mean, Brother Eif—not much longer to be here?"

"You ain't stole no chickens, have you, Brother Eif?"

"No, ain't stole no chickens and ain't harmed no women. Ain't goin to no scaffold," says Eif. "Just goin to change worlds at ten o'clock tonight."

"Change worlds?"

"My lands, change worlds!"

"Yes, I am goin to change worlds."

"How do you know that, Eif Porter?"

"I got a token."

"A token!"

"When did you get a token?"

"This mornin before daylight."

"Where did you get a token?"

"At the pig pen."

"How did it come to you?"

"A voice in the wind," says Eif. "I heard it plain as my wife Treecy speaks to me when she wakes me in the mornin. I know I heard it. You will see tonight what I am tellin you is the truth and is not anythin but the truth."

"I never believed in tokens," says Hull Hillman.

"That is because you are a Free Willer," says Eif. "I ain't got nothin against your church, Hull, but I want to show you the power of mine. Wait just two more hours and you will see what you will see. Now I want my children to come right up here close. I want to tell them about the land in the presence of all you neighbors.

"I want Clara Belle to take this strip of land over here back of Wormwood's that runs with the beech hollow down the hill by the old rail fence to where the old beech tree stands above the slate-bottomed swimmin hole. I want Barbara to take that piece back yander next to Hillman's; it will top up there in a peak by that squirrel-hickory. I want Everett to have this piece with the house on it and the barns and little creek bottoms. I want him to keep his mother Treecy long as she will stay with him. Keep all the family together like a father, long as they will stay with him. I want Little Eif to take the upper house on this place; his boundary will be Cheery Williams' place on the north and the strawberry-shed creek on the west. Gleen, you are to get the rest of the place.

"Now you get about sixty acres of land apiece. It is elbow room for you children and I don't want no fussin and fightin around when I change worlds tonight at ten o'clock. You people are witnesses to this will. It ain't a written will, for I don't believe in that among children. Now if you ever have any trouble, meet back there under the squirrel-hickory where your land jines: get it settled under that tree. I want you to take care of your ground. You know how I got it—I worked for it. I come by it honest."

"Ain't you fooled about changin worlds tonight, Big Eif?" asks Flint Thompson. "What if you don't go? This will be a joke on you."

"You are of little faith, Flint," says Eif. "You are a Free Willer. If you was with me and in the church I'm in, you would not ask that question. Tonight, when the clock strikes ten, I'll be partin from this world. I'll be on my way to the next. That is as good as the Word itself."

"What do you hate to leave most?" asks Harry Black.

"I hate to leave all the things that belong to me," says Eif. "I hate to leave my family, for no man has a better set of youngins than I have, nor a better wife. My wife will get up for me at the blackest midnight and make me a biler of coffee —how many women will do that nowadays? I hate to leave my dogs. When I've come in from fox huntin and am plantin corn the next day or a-plowin, and if I happen to fall asleep, them hounds of mine and my bird dog will lay right down beside me and watch over me. I love my dogs and they love me. All the live stock on this place will follow me. I feed it. I won't allow a brute whopped around in my presence, for I feel like they allus wanted to speak and tell me their troubles. I'd whop a man quicker than I would a brute. I hate to leave my land. Just think how I have worked to build that land up, worked to own it, bought a little strip here and a little strip there and at last I own three hundred acres—just enough room for a body to get proper elbow. Now I have to leave it all. But I'm goin to another farm, don't you doubt. All I hope is that I get the joy of livin there that I got on this farm."

"I've heard it said there was tokens that told people things," says Hillman Taylor. "They come like headless men or in the forms of a light, and they speak to people. I've heard of them comin in the forms of a shepherd dog at night or a pig that run across the road and squealed. But I never heard of one in the wind before."

"Well, people," says Eif, "you'll believe me, won't you, when I tell you that I was wide-awake feedin the hogs and heard that voice in the wind? It wasn't no dead leaves neither. It was the voice that summons a body. I ain't an hour here now."

"Where are you goin to be buried, Brother Eif?" asks Bob Hunt. "And who is goin to preach your funeral?"

"I am goin to be buried back on Graveyard Pint," says Eif. "Buried back there by my little ones, my Pap and Ma. Treecy's Pap and Ma is buried back there too. Brother Issiac Flint is goin to preach my funeral. He believes that I'm goin as I said I was goin at the appointed time that I'm called. I don't know why they want to rush me to Heaven at that certain time unless it is to plow some ground or clear some land of brush and briars. The Lord will find me a good worker and a honest man. I am a solid man too. That is why the Lord wants me, I guess. They ain't no use to shed any tears, youngins. Take it easy these minutes I've got to be here with you. Don't make my life miserable here these last few minutes."

"It is time for you to dress yourself and shave, Eif," says Treecy. "I've laid your clothes out. You told me to warn you when nine o'clock come. Your clean clothes are layin in there on the bed where I've allus put them for you."

VI

Big Eif pours hot water from the teakettle. He makes a lather on the soap in the mug. He puts the lather on his saw-briar beard. He uses the long black-handled straight razor with ease. His whiskers rip-rip and he puts them on a piece of brown sugar sack and throws them in the kitchen stove. He puts on his Sunday suit, his black derby hat, his clean blue shirt open at the collar. He never wore a necktie in his life. "I never wore a necktie here on earth and I won't need one in Heaven." He puts on his Sunday shoes. He walks back out before the crowd gathered at his home.

"It won't be long now, will it, Brother Eif?" says Brother Issiac Flint.

"Only a matter of minutes now," says Eif.

"Do you really want to go?" asks Flint Thompson.

"Yes, Flint," says Eif, "it is a part of my duty same as bein born was a part of my duty. I am ready. I have no apologies to make; no confessions. I have lived till I could go to bed at night and sleep. I never bothered anybody's chicken roost. I have never bothered my neighbor's wife. I never stole from my neighbor. I've prayed to the Master often and when my summons comes I am ready. I never got into anythin that kept me away from the Master. I'll see the Master by eleven tonight. I guess it'll take me about a hour to get up that long ladder a body's got to go up before he gets to Heaven."

"Pap, I'll do the best I can with everythin," says Everett. "I see now why you didn't work this mornin. The best luck to you, Pap, on your long voyage."

"So live, my son, that you won't dread it," says Eif. "Be good, Barbara, you and Clara Belle. Gleen, you and young Eif help Everett to carry on. Be good solid men. Be honest. Treecy, it won't be long till we'll be together again."

"Five minutes till ten."

"Let me tell you somethin before I go," says Eif. "My Pap was called by a token and changed worlds at the appointed time. My Pap's Pap was called by a token and he changed worlds in the appointed time. I have no fear. Now I want you all to be my neighbors in Heaven and I want all the Free Willers to step in this room with me and wait for the clock to strike ten."

The silent men get up and walk into the bedroom where the bed has a goose-feather tick on it and has just been dressed with clean sheets and clean pillow cases. Big Eif stretches full length on the bed. He is long as the bed is long. He looks at the ceiling.

"One minute."

"I hear the death bells," says Eif. "I hear them singin. I see my Pap and Ma. They are atter me."

"It is all over," says Hull Hillman. "I never seed anythin like that in my life or heard tell of it."

"Is this a dream?" asks Harry Black.

"No, this is not a dream," says Hull. "Everythin is real. See the man there dead. See him on the bed. See the bed post. See the pillows with the white slips. See the clean sheets. Feel the wind comin through the window. See the moon outside the window. Feel of my hand. I am real. This is Hull Hillman. I come in here to see what would happen."

"I never knowed of this happenin in my life before," says Treecy. "I never believed in tokens nor that Baptis Church Big Eif belonged to. Must be somethin that the great Master's got in this church. Calls them right to Heaven. Beats anythin I ever saw."

"Never mind, Treecy," says Hull. "We'll be of any help to you. We'll take care of the grave and the coffin. Never mind now. Take it easy. We'll see to everythin. Big Eif was one of the best men that ever lived in these hills. He's mightier than a oak. He was solid as the rock-cliff over there above his cornfield. We'll miss Big Eif. But he's better off than we are here. Take it easy."

"Just to think," says Treecy, "we planned to buy more land next spring and raise bigger crops. Big Eif is gone. Ain't nuthin for me to live for with him gone."

"Take it easy now, Treecy," says Hull. "And I guess some of us had better set up here tonight. All of such a sudden it left you tore up a little."

There is a noise of talk in the house.

"Beats anythin I ever heard tell of."

"How did he know he was going to change worlds?"

"I tell you there is somethin to them Baptis. They ain't to be made fun of around where I am no longer. They are God-fearin people. They are good people. They must have direct communion with the Spirit."

VII

The people are leaving. They are getting on their mules. The mules whinny to each other and the wind blows through the apple trees and the dogs bark. There is weeping in the house.

"Day atter tomorrow the mules will haul a different kind of load over the rough roads," says Everett. "Yes, I understand. The mules with their feet diggin into the earth will haul a wagon up the Pint with a box in it and a whole crowd of people will be followin. It will not be a load of cane-fodder. It will be my father. My Pap. Yes, I understand."

Yes, the harness will jingle. The mules will steep their shoe toes into the hard earth. The driver will say, "Get up there, Jack! Whoa back there Barnie! Whoa, boys! Whoa-whoa–" The wind will blow. The dead leaves will keep falling, falling like the rain. There will be a fresh hole where the dirt is piled high. There will be a crowd and they will read a line of "Lord, I'm Comin Home." Then they will sing that line and Brother Issiac will crumble in some dirt and say a few words and the leather checklines will be pulled up and the spoons filled with dirt will fill the hole. The mules will go back down the hill, holding back the creaking wagon. Their red tassels will be flying in the bright October wind.

UNCLE CASPER

I

UNCLE CASPER comes to town on Saturday. He is running for State Senator. His eyes are two black sparkling slits. His mustache is a tuft of dead bull-grass, neatly pruned, and his nose is the sawed-off root of an oak tree. His hair is two spoiled waves of sickled timothy parted in the middle—the east wind blew a swath west and the west wind blew a swath east. There is a cricket ravine between the swaths.

If you could see Uncle Casper. There are white milkweed stems among the dead-timothy hair. If you could see the long arms and the age-spotted hands like the spots on the body of an aged sassafras. His black suit fits his body like the winter bark on an oak tree. The toes of his black shoes have fought the rocks and stumps on Kenney Ridge. His socks fall over the tops of his shoes to hide the scars.

Here comes Uncle Casper on the courthouse square. His black eyes dance, his arms swing like a willow wand waving in a swift wind of Spring. "What is your name, son," says Uncle Casper, "and are you old enough to vote, my son?"

"Press Freeman is my name, I have had the seven-year 'each' three times. If I hadn't I'd be over twenty-one on Election Day all right."

"Which ticket do you vote, my son?"

"I vote on the side of the Lord."

"That is the ticket I belong to," says Uncle Casper, "and, my son, I am runnin for State Senator. I aim to give the poor people a chance since I am a poor man. My family has broke me up. Sent a boy to college—borrowed the money—mortgaged my home. Found him on the bank of a river in Michigan a-fishin. Sent another boy out to college and he didn't do no good, took to a pack of cards and a bottle. I went to the eighth grade, son, in the old school and I've teached for fifty-nine years. Now, I'm a broke-up man. Set out of a house and home. Can't get a school anymore since we ain't got school trustees. I used to run my trustees and get my schools. I could a got four or five. Things has changed anymore. Not like they used to be. Vote for me in November and I'll make them like they used to be."

Uncle Casper's eyes blink. His hands talk.

"A vote for me means better roads, better schools, better schoolhouses, feather beds for men when they get drunk instead of ditches, homes for the widows and the orphans, no totin pistols nor bowie knives. I'll put two pieces of bread in your safe where you ain't got but one. Pensions for the old broke-down men like myself and your Pap, and I'll put the school trustees back—three to every deestrict. A vote for me means a help to you. Son, I am a poor man and I'll help the poor people."

"I'll be there, Uncle Casper, to vote on the ticket the Lord and me and you is on. I'll be there and I'll finish the third spell of the seven-year 'each' by then."

Uncle Casper goes down the courthouse square. He talks with his hands. He talks to this one. He talks to that one. Men gather around Uncle Casper to hear him talk. "I lived on corn bread and onions to get my education, and wore shirts made out'n coffee-sacks and muslin and calico. My boys has broke me up. I've preached the word of God and teached school for fifty-nine year. Brothers, I ask you in the name of the Lord to help me in November and I'll guarantee you every vote you cast for me will mean two slices of bread in your safe where you ain't got but one, and one slice of bread in your safe where you ain't got any. Two hams of meat in your smoke house where you ain't got but one, and one ham of meat in your smoke house if you ain't got any."

Then Uncle Casper goes down the square and he meets Press Freeman. Uncle Casper says, "And what might your name be, my son?"

"You just met me awhile ago," says Press, "I am Press Freeman. Don't you remember me? Remember we talked about who was on the Lord's side and who wasn't?"

"Yes, I remember you now, son. We talked about the old times. I just want you to remember me in November. Did I ever tell you the story about the snake?"

"No you ain't never," says Press.

"Set down in this bandstand," says Uncle Casper.

"Okie-dough," says Press.

"I was sittin in the yard," says Uncle Casper, "with my feet propped up on the side of the house when I saw it. I was smokin my pipe and lookin toward my potato patch to see if I couldn't just about see my potatoes grow. When all of a sudden, I saw a big black-snake's head bobbin up and down out of the ragweed patch beside the potato rows. That snake, bigger than a baby's leg, went tearin right out of that ragweed patch and took down across the potato ridges fast as a horse could run. I thinks to myself, 'What now!'

"The snake sorty halted in the garden between two rows of cabbage heads. I saw him bob his head up and down. He looked like a scared rabbit. I kept my eye on him. There was a little patch of briars beside the cabbage patch–in the old fence row beside the garden. That black snake, big around as a baby's leg and long as a rail-fence rider, made a headlong dive into that briar patch like a cat divin for a mouse. It acted like a cat that smelled a mouse and jumped to get it. And then I saw what I saw. I stopped smokin my pipe and forgot about my leg bein left lame from that bullet I got on Brush Creek at that Revival Meetin.

"That black snake wropped around that big rattler so quick it would make your head swim. I saw it all right there in that briar patch. That black snake wropped that big rattler up like a love vine wrops a ragweed. Then the black snake started to clampin down with all its strength and bitin the rattler's throat. Then he squeezed. I let them fight. The old rattler was squeezed so tight he couldn't rattle. Think about me a-sittin that close to a rattler and not knowin it!

"That black snake worked hard–squeezin, bitin, beatin with its head. Then it uncoiled a wrop at a time until it got down to the last wrop–then it uncoiled the last wrop and sprung way out in the cabbage patch. It bobbed its head up and looked back. It saw the rattler was still movin. Then it took right back into that briar patch. It wropped that rattler up tighter than ever. It bit it harder than ever. It whipped it with its tail like it was a buggy whip. The old rattler couldn't take the last beatin. It give up the ghost and turned over on its back and died. Its belly was turned up to the sun. The black snake took out of there and run out and bit him off a little chew of a weed. It munched it in its flat jaws like a rabbit munches clover.

"I hopped up on my lame leg and parted the briars with my cane. I pulled that dead rattler and took it in and showed it to Liz, my wife. It had twenty-seven rattlers and nine buttons. W'y Liz wouldn't believe what I told her about that fight and the black snake killin the rattler. I skinned the rattler and made me a belt out of its hide and Liz a pair of garters."

"I'll be dogged," says Press.

II

"Somethin kept catchin our chickens. Every mornin we would go out to the barn and count the hens. There would be one missin. So I looked under the roost and found a lot of loose feathers and part of a old white hen. Chuck Winters said to me: 'W'y Casper, that is one of them little chicken owls doin all this. They can hold more chicken than a fox. I'll show you how to trap him.' So I took Chuck at his word.

"We took a dozen steel traps down to where the white hen was layin on the ground. Her head was eaten off and some of the meat was gouged out from under her wing.

"Chuck said: 'Now dig a little ditch around the hen. Throw the loose dirt away. Set the traps in a circle around the hen. Put feathers over the traps. Drive a stake down through the body of the hen so when the owl pulls he can't move her. And in the mornin we'll have the bird that caught that hen. When a owl eats no more of a hen than this he always comes back for the second mess.' And we set the traps, covered them with feathers and staked the steel-trap chains to the ground with little wooden pegs. We staked the hen down.

"Behold the next mornin if there wasn't one of them old barred hoot owls bigger 'n a turkey gobbler a-settin right on the hen with his neck feathers all bowed up like a rooster ready to fight. He was caught by one toe. But we had the chicken thief that had caught over thirty hens.

"And I said to Chuck, 'Chuck, what kind of punishment are we goin to give this bird?' Chuck studied for a minute and he said, 'W'y Casper, let's saturate him with coal oil, set his tail feathers on fire and turn him back into the elements.' Chuck has always been quick to think of things like that. So, I went to the kitchen, got the coal-oil can and a match and went back to the owl under the chicken roost. I throwed the coal oil on him. We could not get very close to him. Chuck got broom sage and tied it to the end of a stick and set fire to it. I pulled the peg out of the ground that held the trap and Chuck set the fire to his tail.

"Gentlemen, right up into the elements with that steel trap janglin from his toe—that fire to his tail—he soared a red stream of blaze through the elements. Fire from that owl fell onto my meadow. It was in late March when the wind was blowin steady and everythin was so dry. Fire popped up all over the meadow at once. It looked like the red flames of hell and the wind was a-ragin. That owl went right on through the elements.

"I hollered to Chuck to shoot him with a pistol before he fired the whole country. Chuck put seven hot balls of lead at that owl. But it soared right on through the elements. It went right over Mart Haley's timber. The blaze shot up like flames from hell. Flames lapped right up through the dead saw briars and leaves. 'All my timber is gone,' shouted Chuck—'timber lands jines Haley's timber lands. My rail fences are all gone. That owl will set the world on fire if somebody don't shoot him from the elements or the fire don't consume him.' I tell you, gentlemen, that owl set fire to the whole country. My land was ruined. My timber was burned to death. That fire burnt up one thousand panels of rail fence for me. It ruined my meadows. It ruined my neighbors. We had to get together and have workins and put the fence back. We had to put some barns back and two houses. It ruined the whole country. If I hadn't a had good Baptis neighbors I would a been sued over that owl and would be a broke-up man today."

"Well I'll be dogged," says Press. "Grandma said to burn owl feathers you'd have bad luck among your chickens for seven years."

"Not so, I ain't had a bit of bad luck since then," says Uncle Casper.

III

"One day Chuck and me was out diggin ginsang. Chuck and me used to run together a good deal and this is the way we made a little spendin money. We had our sacks nearly filled with two-prongs, three-prongs, and four-prongs. Chuck looked down in the weeds and saw a big rattlesnake. 'Come here, Casper,' he said to me. I went over where Chuck was and by the eternal God I never saw such a rattlesnake in my life. It was big as a cow's leg. 'I can handle that snake,' says Chuck. 'I never was afraid of a snake—not the meanest snake that ever growed.' Chuck was drinkin some brandy—some persimmon brandy. So he jumps right in a-straddle of the rattlesnake and brakes it down in the back with his fist. Then he begins to choke.

"It scared me to see Chuck a-straddle of that rattlesnake. So, I says: 'Chuck, get off that rattler's back. It will bite you shore as God made little apples.' Chuck just looked up and grinned at me. Then he said: 'You hold it down and I'll pull its teeth and we'll take it home and show it to Ike Wampler. He'll never believe we captured a snake this big.' So I gets down a-straddle of this rattler's neck. 'Choke it,' says Chuck. I choked it till I was black in the face. Chuck says: 'I see its fangs and a little gall bladder of pizen back in there. Wait till I twist a withe and I'll yank them teeth out 'n there before you can say Jack Robinson.' My grip kept givin out. My hands got so tired a-hold of that big rattler's neck. And when my grip was goin Chuck hollered out that it had shot a stream of the pizen from the gall bladder through the fang into his eye. He said: 'I'm stingin in the eye like a barrel of red pepper had been dumped into my eye. I'm pizened in the eye by that rattlesnake.' I jumped off 'n the rattlesnake's back and got hold of Chuck and drug him down among the nettles and the pea vine.

"The first thing I thought of when Chuck was glombin and clawin at this eye, was my twist of taste-bud tobacco. It is that old-time tobacco that used to be growin around the barn on old manure piles. Well, that is where I got this. The twist was bigger 'n my forearm. So I bit me off a big chew and I chawed it. I got Chuck down, for he was smartin a right smart by now. I put my feet on his chest and held each one of his hands in a hand of mine and I chawed that chew up and squirted every bit of it in his eye. He squalled a little, but I knowed it was a case of life or death. Then I took off another chaw and chewed it and squirted that in Chuck's eye. I kept on till I chewed up the whole thing and squirted it into Chuck's eye. And when I let Chuck up Chuck says to me, 'I'd rather have the disease as to have that remedy.' "

"Well, I'll be dogged," says Press.

"I went upon the hill one day to cut a pole of stove wood. I saw a dead sourwood pole and I took my ax and thought I would cut it. It looked dry, hard and seasoned. I saw a knot hole upon the side and the sour gnats were comin out and goin in. Before I got to the pole a racer snake sprung at my throat and I struck at it with the double-bitted ax. It saw I was going to put up fight so it started to scramble. I took after it with the ax. It went straight to the pole and wropped right around it–right up that pole like a black movin corkscrew. Then it ducked down in the hole where the sour gnats was. It stuck its head out and licked out its tongue at me. I thought, 'Old Boy, I'll fix you.' So I climbs up the pole with a wooden glut in my hand that I whittle from the butt of the pole. I stuck that glut down in the hole and drove it in with a stick. 'I'll let you stay in this tree awhile,' I says.

"Well, I went on and cut some dry locust poles for stove wood. I took them into the wood yard and cut them up for stove wood. One year after that I was back on this same hill gettin stove wood and I happened to see this sourwood pole with the glut stickin in the hole. So, I remembered the snake. I went up and whacked down the sourwood pole. The tree was hollow down to the roots and when I cut into the hollow, out popped that snake poor as Job's turkey. I could a-counted its ribs if I'd had time. But that racer remembered me. It coiled around my leg like it was a rope around a well-windlass. It grabbed me by the ankle. I took off the hill hollerin. I just couldn't help it. Its sharp pin teeth stuck into my ankle bone.

"I run to the wood yard hard as I could go. That snake tightened down on my leg and cut off the blood from circulation. I'd about give up the ghost when Liz come out and she said, 'Casper, what is the matter with you? You are white as a piece of flour poke.' And I says, 'See what has me by the leg, don't you?' And Liz went in and got a butcher knife. That snake still held me by the ankle. It tightened its holts. It bit me harder. Liz just reached down with that butcher knife and she cut that snake into ten pieces. It was wropped around my leg five times if I am right. Its head still held to my leg. Its teeth held right into my ankle bone. Then Liz pulled at its head and she yanked its teeth out, but they brought a hunk of meat.

"When our baby boy Frons was born he had the prints of the prettiest little racer black snake right over his heart."

"I'll be dogged," says Press, spitting at a knot hole on the bandstand. Uncle Casper spits at it. "Center as a die," says Uncle Casper. "That's a sign I'm goin to get elected Senator."

IV

"Chuck took a notion to run for Representative of Greenbriar County. Chuck preaches some, you know, and one Sunday afternoon when he was preachin Abraham Fox's funeral he said to the people, 'Did you know, folks, that you was a-lookin square at Greenbriar County's next Representative? If you don't know it, I'll tell you that you are lookin square at him.' And Chuck Haley goes out and tells the people that he is goin to pass a Law that the people will get a bounty for every fox hide they bring in to the County seat town of Greenbriar. He told the people that if they didn't clean out the foxes that they was a-goin to clean out the chickens and there wouldn't be enough yaller-legged pullets left for a Baptis preacher a mess. Well, as you know, Greenbriar County has a lot of Baptis and they elected Chuck, though he was on the wrong Party. They went for their religion before they did their Party. Chuck was elected, but not by the fox hunters. They stuck by their foxes.

"Chuck told me all about goin to Frankfort. He said they let him talk in a little thing that looked like a fryin pan. He said it was over behind the pianer. He told them about his bill on the bounty of fox hides. Some said they fooled old Chuck about talkin over the air—said he talked over a old broke-down telephone without any wires to it. Then he did talk over the air. But he give his speech about foxes. I knowed Chuck was goin to get into it with the fox hunters. When he come back from Frankfort and the news got into the *Greenbriar Gazette* about his big speech over the air on foxes and him actin like that and belongin to the wrong Party too, w'y the fox hunters had done had their meetin and they was a-layin for him. Chuck hired a hack and started home smokin a cigar he'd rolled out 'n twist-bud tobacco and plump went a hole through his black Stetson hat. Chuck whipped the horses fast and got away from that bunch of rocks upon the Winsor place. That is where they waylaid Chuck.

"Some said it was old Tiger MacMeans that waylaid Chuck. Old Tiger is a big fox hunter. One time he run a young fox around one pint and up over another pint and into a dirt hole and he dug it out with a stick. Another time one of his Blue Tick hounds got hung up in a rock cliff and he blasted rock down with dynamite for eight days and hired everybody in the neighborhood to help him get old Queen. And old Tiger got her too. She was so nigh gone she couldn't stand up, but when they found her she had the fox right by the tail. He took Queen home and fed her goat's milk and she got all right. Well, he is the fellow we thought put the bullet through Chuck's Stetson hat.

"Gentlemen, by the eternal God, them fox hunters I guess it was got after the Baptis and we had a regular war in Greenbriar County. Barns filled with tobacco burnt all over Finish Creek and Laurel Creek. Cattle barns was burnt to the ground with all the live stock in them. It was a time. I never heard tell of anythin like it. And out on the hills a body could find Irish taters with rat pizen on them—fried taters and dead hound dogs dead along the ridges. They was dead along the creeks where they had tried to get water when the pizen struck them and their insides went to burnin. Chuck couldn't get to church. People looked for him—men that had had their hound dogs pizened. The fox hunters waited for him when they tooted their horns for dogs that never come home. Of course, Chuck never put the pizen out. But friends of Chuck's put it out when Chuck's Stetson was plugged from a rock cliff.

"And Tid Redfern picked up a coffee-sack full of pizened biscuits put out to get the dogs. We don't know who put them out. It might a been the shepherds on the hillsides that had been losin sheep, and when the Baptis and fox hunters got into it they put their noses into it for the time was right for them to get the dogs. They wasn't a hound dog left in that country big enough to run a fox or to teach the young pups how to start a cold trail. They said old Tiger could get down and smell where a fox had been and put the young hounds on a cold trail. They wasn't a barn left on Tiger Creek or Laurel Creek big enough to house a yearlin calf. Bloodhounds were used to track men that done the burnin, but they used red pepper on their shoe soles and when the bloodhounds sniffed that they didn't sniff anymore. So, no one was caught. And people just cooled down in three or four years themselves.

"Bert Flannery said he never could get over it when his milk cows burned in his barn. His barn doors were left open, but the cows would not come out of their stalls. He said he heard the cows bawl so pitifully that it made him cry. He said he couldn't forget that dreadful night and it would stay with him as long as there was wind in his body. Bert Flannery is a good man. He is a good prayin man and he tends to his own business, but he was just drawed into the fracas like a lot of us innocent men. Fudas Pimbroke said he could never forget seein his old Fleet turned on her back on the ridge road where she had been leadin a fox when the pizen got her down. He said she was stretched there bloated with wind. He said he could never forget the look on that dead hound dog's face.

"When the next session of time come around for Chuck to go back to Frankfort, they hauled him to the station one night under a load of fodder. He took the train straight for Frankfort to get his Law about bounty on foxes repealed. And Chuck told them about the dogs pizened and the barns and church houses and homes burnt in Greenbriar County and about the war still ragin there—and they wiped that Law right out. Got rid of it root, leaf, and branch. But that got all the Baptis mad at Chuck. Now they was all mad at him—the Baptis and the fox hunters. He didn't have a side to cling to. So, he went home to stay and one mornin when he was milkin the cow, flop went another bullet through his hat. So he got under another load of fodder and went to Greenbriar. He caught a train for West Virginia. He's never come back to Greenbriar. I was readin the paper where he had been killed for givin a West Virginia hound arsenic. The fox hunter hit him in the head with a coal pick. He wasn't any count for a Representative anyway, for he couldn't read nor write nor cipher. And besides, he didn't belong to the right Party. When a man goes out of the bounds of his Party to elect a man of the wrong Party, then you can take care. Things are a-goin to pop. People in Greenbriar County has kindly come back together agin after a time."

"I'll be dogged," says Press, "I'll be right there to vote for you, Uncle Casper, in November." Press spits at the knot hole. He misses. Uncle Casper spits from his wad of homemade taste-bud. "Center as a die," says Uncle Casper, "sign I'll be your next Senator of Kentucky."

EMORY HARE turns the shelf of the hill from the deep beech woods, around the toe-path by the new-ground corn on the steep bluff. He has a coffee-sack on his back. It is tied with a sea-grass string in a bowknot and is frizzled on the ends like a twisted hickory withe used to tie bundle fodder. Emory's black felt hat is slouched to one side to keep the July sun out of his left eye. His face is turkey-wattle-red and the beard on his face is long and set far apart on his face like briar stubbles left on a new ground after the vines have been swathed by a briar scythe. His lips are amber-colored. He walks to the rhythm of the lazy wind, picking his feet up with ease like a mule and setting them down methodically as a mule on firebranded new ground.

"Oh, I see Pap comin," says Ella Mae who is playing in the creek below the house, her light stringy hair flashing like a rift of dead cut wheat in the July sun.

Emory pricks his ears, stops and looks like a hound dog and then steps on like a mule, the sack swinging in rhythm to his stooped body wrapped in his gluey overalls like a slipper elm in its bark. The brown-backed butterflies flit on the tops of the iron-gray milkweed blossoms that line along the lower edge of the new-ground corn on the bluff. The bumblebees hiss in the alder tops and the honeybees fuss on the gold-fringed buttercups that spring from the wet-hot earth beside the creek.

"What are you doin in that creek over there, Ella Mae? I thought I heard somethin a minute ago and that was you. I thought it was the wind in the corn and it was your voice I heard. Get out of that creek! Ain't you afraid of a pizen water moccasin?"

"I got a turtle here, Pap—a soft-shelled turtle big as Mama's butter crock. Come and get it before it gets away. It's a lot bigger than that old blue-backed hard-shelled turtle that we had for dinner last Sunday."

"How are you a-holdin that turtle?"

"Got it in the mouth with a forked stick. It can't get loose. Hear it pop its teeth––"

"Watch that turtle, Ella Mae, if it bites you it won't let loose till the sun goes down. Come away and leave that turtle," says Emory as he shifts the position of his feet on the grass and holds to a sprig of sourwood to support himself beneath the coffee-sack load on his back.

"Leave this turtle, Pap! W'y that is the first time in your life you ever left a turtle in the creek. It will be good eatin. What will Mama say to leave a turtle like this when we can eat it–and if we leave it the turtle will catch all Mama's ducks and geese," says Ella Mae as she holds the snapping turtle in the muddy hole of water under the greenbriers and the sycamore sprouts whose broad leaves fleck little dots of July sunlight on the muddy water when the wind lazy-as-a-mule blows up the creek.

"You do as I say, Ella Mae, before I come over there and take a withe to you about five yards long and cut the little dress right off'n your back and switch them legs of yours till they are red. Come on over here! Don't you halt a minute or I'll be right over there after you."

"Pap, don't you like turtle eggs as well as any of us and the seven kinds of meat there is in a soft-shell turtle? Let me hook him out and take him home. Let me do it, Pap," says Ella Mae, her lips puckering and her blue eyes squinting–her hair tangled like sickled wheat and the color of wheat blowing free in the July wind.

"You do as I say. A youngin that won't mind a word I tell her. I'll thresh the shirt right off'n your back. You get over here and leave that turtle alone and you get over here damn quick!"

Emory throws the sack from his back. He bends the sourwood with one hand and with the other he fumbles his knife from his pocket, takes the blade with his teeth and with his free hand he opens the blade and cuts a limb from the sourwood. Ella Mae sees him cut the limb. She frees the turtle and comes jumping like a rabbit, her white head going up and down, her arms outstretched, her thin brown legs and bare feet working nimbly.

"Don't, Pap—don't! Oh, Lordy! Don't, Pap! I'm comin—Don't whop me this time! I turned the turtle loose. Let me alone this time. I don't want to be whopped," Ella Mae screams as she runs down through the milkweed blossoms and scares up the brown-backed butterflies and the big golden butterflies—her free wind-flung hair dragging on the tops of the buttercups.

"I don't want a youngin o' mine anymore givin me any of their jawr and I don't aim to have it. From now on I am man o' my own house, little lady, and when I speak to you I want you to move. Don't you ever tell me you won't do this and won't do that. You are my youngin and you'll listen to me. Don't ever give me anymore of your back sass—a girl eleven years old tellin her Pap what to do," says Emory, and he walks up the path, swaying this way and that under the load of coffee-sack, under the July sun that leaves a blue glimmering above the meadow by the woods and the pig pen.

"That is the way nowadays," says Emory talking to the wind, "that the little pups try to treat their Pappies and Mammies that kill theirselves a-workin for them—Mammies punish themselves, bring them into the world, and then they up and sass them. I'll run my house from now on. I am the man o' my house long as I am able to use a club. I'm goin to clean my house and make it fit for a man o' my age to live in peace. I don't wear the pants anymore. My wife Symanthia and my boy Issiah wears the pants. I'll show 'em by-hell, I'll show 'em who wears the pants from this day on."

"I'm goin to tell Mama on you, Pap, for not let me catch that soft-shelled turtle and bring it to the house," says Ella Mae overtaking Emory and running past him—her lips puckered like a child eating sauerkraut and her hands outstretched in the wind and her fingers trying to get a-hold of the wind.

"Go and tell your Mama! That is what I want you to do! Go tell her! Tell her I wouldn't let you get that damned snappin turtle and them eggs. How do I know I ain't et a few snake eggs among all them turtle eggs you brought in here anyway when you said you found the old turtle settin and shoved her off the nest and got the eggs. Likely as not they've been snake eggs I've been eatin. Black-snake eggs. Get on up that road and tell your Mama and you'd better tell Issiah too—that young swine that is as much like his ma's people as two swines."

The shingle roof of the shack is now in sight. The corn is in front of the house, in back of the house and to the north of the house. Its wilted blades flap-flap with the wind and talk to the soap-slick poplar leaves by the pig pen. The long twisted rows are pretty in the wind. They bend to the right first from where Emory sees them and then they swerve back to the left behind the pig pen—rows of corn that go out of sight. Behind the house is the pasture field where the mules do not keep the stubble grass eaten close to the ground like the cows did and the sprouts have left short stubby tough leaves that the mules won't eat—sprouts sprinkled with mats of purple ironweeds.

"A man's own home—pretty as a picture—pretty as a paper doll and he ain't got no say-so of his own home. My corn out there—pretty as any man ever saw—my spotted cows over there on the hill and I can't sell one but what the old woman puts her jib in and tells the fellow that I trade with that the cattle belongs to her. My sassafras up there by the well box and hickory trees back of the smoke house. My own home. My house that I cut ever log that went into it and rive with a fro ever shingle that is on that roof and blacksmithed ever nail that holds the boards on, and then I ain't boss of it. I ain't more than a dog. I ain't more than a dog because I let them get the upper hand of me, trustin my business to them because I can't write my name. That's where they got it on me. Man is made to rule the roost, at least to carry the grub to the roost. Don't the bull rule his cows, the ram rule his ewes and the turkey gobbler keep his flock in line and the rooster calls his hens and they come! But you crap the rooster's wings and watch him drop his feathers and you dehorn the bull and watch him, you pluck the turkey gobbler's tail feathers out one by one and watch him get humbler every day and give in to the hens. That's what the matter with me—my tail feathers have been pulled one by one. I have lost my pride. I'm a whipped rooster!"

"Mama," says Ella Mae, "Pap's comin up the back with a coffee-sack on his shoulder and he's mad as a hornet about somethin. He's just a-puffin and a-blowin. I was over there by that bunch of sycamore sprouts and greenbriers and I had a turtle hooked in the mouth with a forked stick. And Pap come up that road out of the beech trees and I hollered at him and told him I had a turtle so big I couldn't pull it out of the creek —a soft-shelled turtle and he told me to leave it alone and I just kept on pullin at that turtle and he said if I didn't loosen it he'd come over there and cut the dress off'n my back. I didn't come right then and he throwed the sack off his shoulder and started cuttin a switch long as your leg. I let the turtle back in the water and I come a-runnin and passed him on the hill."

"He made you turn the turtle back and he loves mud-turtle good as any mate I ever saw in my life! He can eat a whole one. Last Sunday didn't he eat half that turtle before the preacher and his folks here for dinner and the way he et he nearly plagued me to death—pull out a leg and say, 'This turtle leg tastes like fish—a cat-fish.' Then he pulled out a piece of the back and says, 'This piece of turtle tastes like possum.' Then he'd pull out another leg and say, 'This piece of turtle tastes like ground hog.' And then he grabbed the neck of the turtle with his fork and said, 'This neck tastes like mutton.' I never saw a man like turtle any better than your Pa."

Symanthia Hare stands under the sassafras at the well with her broad brown hand on the bark of the tree and her long slender fingers wrapped around the body of the tree like the tiny leaf-vines of a pumpkin wrapped around a sourwood sprout on a steep bluff. Her eyes with a steel glint of mountain-river blue, gaze down the path at Emory waddling up the path like a turtle toward the well box. Her face, the color of a turning sassafras leaf in September, shines like a leaf in the autumn sun, her figure unbent by years of childbearing and toil in the fields is straight as a pawpaw sprout, her hair black as a crow's wing is done up in a tobacco twist on the back of her head and her teeth are the color of peeled poplar bark.

"And Mama, he said," says Ella Mae, "that them turtle eggs he et was snake eggs—them turtle eggs I skeered the old turtle off the nest and got. He said they was black-snake eggs and that they was pizen to eat——"

"Shut up," says Symanthia, twitching her fine-curved brown lips in an unpleasant fashion above the white teeth, "I have heard enough already about your Pa—I don't want to hear anythin more. Wait till he comes up here!"

"And he talked about you and Issiah runnin the place and told me to come and tell both of you when I told him I was goin to tell you on him. Oh, but he got mad."

"Shut up! He is right here now," says Symanthia, "and let me do the talkin——"

Sweat drops the size of beads and the color of granulated sugar drip from Emory's eyebrows and the end of his nose in the July sunlight. His shoulders sway beneath the weight of the sack, sway rhythmically to his slow mule gait, sway lazily as the wind in the milkweeds.

"It's time you's a-gettin in here, Emory Hare—blastin this child and threatenin her with a switch when she caught a turtle over there bigger 'n a crock. Well, as you like turtle and then you run her away when she had a turtle hooked bigger 'n you ever caught in your life. What's this place a-comin to anyway? What would it come to if it wasn't for my old packhorse bones?"

"Hold your tater," says Emory, flinging the sack from his shoulder and wiping the granulated sweat from his eyebrows and the tip of his nose—"hold your tater, Symanthia, for mine's hot. I want you to know I don't want no turtle meat for supper and never any more of them turtle eggs——"

"You said I cooked you pizen black-snake eggs, didn't you —that I was tryin to pizen you," says Symanthia, shelling the sassafras bark with her long fingers from the body of the tree.

"I never said you tried to pizen me. I said I didn't want any more of them turtle eggs and I don't. Pennix Eggers told me today that turtles don't set on eggs like a chicken and Ella Mae said she shoved that turtle off the nest and got her eggs. Now who has lied? Ella Mae just picked up them eggs and I'll bet five dollars to a dime they's black-snake eggs. Every time I think about them eggs I et last Sunday I get sick at my stummick. I don't want no more turtle and no more turtle eggs. You get that right now."

Emory wipes more sweat from his brow with the cup of his hand and he flings the tiny white beads down through the sunlight to the ground.

"And more than this," says Emory, "I want you to know I am runnin my own house from now on. I wear the pants and what I say about this place goes or I go, one," says Emory, wiping more sweat and lifting the sack as something starts moving in the sack. He holds it by the sea-grass string.

"What have you got in that sack, Pap?" says Ella Mae, shifting her foot on the grass by the well box so as to miss a pile of chicken manure dropped by a pet leghorn hen that lays every day at three o'clock on the well box in a coil of the well rope.

"They ain't a bunch of snake eggs in that sack. It ain't for you to know just what is in that sack. Ask me no questions, my little pert one, and I'll tell you no lies," says Emory.

"You are drunk again on that blackberry wine. I saw somebody had used the gourd this mornin, for it wasn't hangin on the right apple-tree limb when I went down there to get me a drink after breakfast," says Symanthia.

"Drunk hell—I ain't drunk. When I stand up for rights I'm always drunk. Now you listen to me. When I sell my tobacco again I'm gettin the check cashed. You ain't a-takin any more of my checks. Not another time are you wearin the pants. I can make my cross on the check. God knows I wouldn't know my name if I'd meet it in the big road. But I been a henpecked man. That is what is wrong. Your brother told Mart Wedlock that if he was in my place he wouldn't live with you twenty-four hours. He said it. They ain't no missin it, for he said it."

"Shut up! Shut up! I won't have it. You are crazy drunk as

a lizard. You a-actin like this. I won't have it," shouts Symanthia biting into a piece of sassafras bark.

"Yes—but you will have it," Emory's squinted eyes snap fire, "you will have it. You will have the truth. You have to have it. I ain't drunk. But when I want to get drunk, I'll get drunk and from now on I'll not hide any more whisky in the barn either. I'll carry her on my hip and I'll drink when I please and where I please."

"Go in the kitchen and put a fire in the stove, Ella Mae," says Symanthia.

"Don't you do it, Ella Mae. You carry in that pile of stove wood out there. Go right on out there and carry in that wood. Hear me?" says Emory.

"Yes," says Ella Mae.

"Heed me then!"

Ella Mae walks slowly toward the wood yard. The sun beams down. The chips are thick on the ground as dead leaves in an autumn wood. Ella Mae walks past the wash kettle, walking carefully over the sharp-pointed chips to the wood pile. She takes one hand and rows the stove wood on her arm that is wrapped around the sticks like a barrel hoop around the barrel.

"That is the way I aim for her to mind from now on. That is the way I aim for Issiah, Tinnie and Belle and Tim to mind me. You are goin to listen to me too. You've been puttin these youngins up to spy on me, to watch me get a mornin dram from the barn loft. What if I sent somebody down there to spy on you when you got a drink of wine. Symanthia, it takes us both to have these youngins and I know you are their mother—but you listen to me. I got a hand in helpin to raise them. From now on when they don't raise up just right I aim to take 'em by the hair of the head and jerk 'em up a little ways. Don't the Book say if you 'spare the rod you spile the child.' If you put the child up to do somethin against its Pap, you spile the child."

Symanthia turns to walk away. Her bare feet step lightly on the chips. She walks toward the kitchen.

"Wait a minute. I want to tell you some more. Ever since

I been married to you, your people has henpecked me. Now that is over. I don't want any more of your lazy kinsfolk layin around my place. I'll show 'em the door and tin-can 'em and turpentine 'em like a suck-egg hound if I catch 'em here anymore. Wait a minute, Symanthia. I ain't through here yet. Your people 's talked about me worse than if I was a dog and yet they come snoopin around my table and get their feet under it—then they go away and talk about me. I am tired of it. I am blind. I been livin under a petticoat government too long."

Symanthia walks by the kitchen steps. She holds to the door-facing and gives her body a lift into the kitchen with her hand. She walks into the kitchen where Tinnie and Belle are getting dinner dishes cleaned.

"You got all that wood carried in, Ella Mae?"

"Goin after the last load, Pap."

"All right."

"What's all this fuss about?" says Issiah as he turns around the corner of the kitchen. "I was out there tryin to wean that calf by lettin it suck my fingers in the bottom of a pan of brand and milk and great-scotts-and-fire-bugs I thought the top was comin off 'n the house out here!"

"Now you mind your own business, son," says Emory.

"You talkin to me?" says Issiah.

"I ain't a-talkin now to your brother nor to your mother. I mean you. Your name is Issiah, ain't it?"

"Yes."

"Well—it is Issiah I am talkin to."

"What have I done, Pap?"

"You been tryin to run this place. Now I am going to try my hand runnin it. You are goin to listen to me and be glad to listen. In the first place, I want you to know if I want to sell one of them cows down there it is my own business. I started to sell one the other day to Jasper Lynn and Jasper told me that you said to him that the cows belonged to you and your Ma and you wasn't a-goin to sell a one of them, that I didn't have nothin to do with the cows. Listen to me, young man. Who bought this land you live on today and made this house for you and brought you into this world? Who bought them cows down there when they was calves and who has raised the feed? I'll sell them cows when I get ready. I got a debt comin due on the mules. I want to pay it. The cows can calve again and we can have more cows, but we can't get mules from mules. You know we got to have them mules if we make bread. We got to have them for the new ground. We got to have the cows too to give us milk. Now I'm older than you and your Ma is a good woman and I am your Pap. Now you hull out of here and cut grass for the hogs!"

"In a minute, Pap," says Issiah, tall and lean as a bean pole, freckled-faced as a guinea walking with his eyes to the ground and his fingers stiff and strutted like the feathers on a turkey gobbler's wing.

"No minute with me. You do it right now. No wait a minute," and Emory leaves his sack by the well box and picks up a sassafras club and makes at Issiah. He lashes the stiff limb around his legs. Issiah lets out a whoop and starts running to get the scythe hanging on the fence.

"All right, Pap. All right, Pap."

The wet coffee-sack by the well box moves as if there was life in it. Emory walks back to the well box, lifts the sack onto his shoulder with a swing and a grunt, then he strides around the corner of the kitchen into the front yard. The hot wind, scented by the smell of wilted corn blades and silks, blows from the long corn rows that swerve into the left back of the pig pen. The scent of corn is mingled with the scent of winds from the pines on the cow-pasture hill, the soap-slick poplar leaves flutter in the wind all day and the pussley and careless that grow behind the pig pen.

"Ella Mae, you got the wood in now?"

"Yes, Pap."

"Come here then."

"All right."

"You see them rocks out there beside the road?"

"Yes."

"Go out there and pile them up then."

"What do you want that done for, Pap?"

"Don't ask me a question like that or I'll cut the dress off'n your back. You just do as I tell you. Never ask me why I want this done and that done, but you carry out my orders from now on. Hear me?" says Emory, his steel-blue eyes gazing menacingly from under the lifted side of his slouched hat.

Ella Mae runs out across the front yard, under the low bushy-topped poplar where Emory rests in the evening after the work in the fields is done, where he sits and watches the shade creep up the hill from the poplar tree as the sun lowers over the chestnut tops on town ridge. Ella Mae passes through the gate and down beside the yard palings where the tall sunflowers hold yellow cheeks to the sun for kisses. She begins to pick up rocks on the yellow clayey bank and stack them in a nice heap, small rocks that a girl of eleven can lift.

Tim comes off the hill, ax on his shoulder, grasped with a stubborn hairy hand near the butt of the handle, the other hand swinging at his side to the rhythm of his autumn-leaf tanned face, the bones protruding under the tanned skin like the little stems that run through the canvas-green of the sycamore leaves. His brogan shoes clip-clop on the grass with a hollow sound.

"What's the matter, Pap, that everybody's gone to work around this man's house? I see Issiah cuttin grass, Ella Mae pilin rocks—what in the world is goin to happen?" says Tim.

"Let me tell you, son. You are goin to marry Dolly Pratt some of these days if my thinkin is right. It 'pears to me your mind is already settled on the question. Now when you marry her you wear the pants. Don't let her get 'em on first. If you do, it's hard as the devil to get 'em off 'n her and back on yourself. Now you mind what I am tellin you. Your mother is a good woman. But look what I got into. Look at her own people how they have treated me—et with their damn dirty stinkin feet stickin under my table all the time too! Listen, from now on Emory Hare wears the pants around this house. I mean I am goin to wear them! No petticoat government can keep me blind any longer."

The beads of sweat run from Emory's brow and drip off at the tip of his nose, they run into his eyes. He rakes them off with the cup of his hand and flings them onto the grass. The drops of sweat glisten on his thin briar-stubble beard.

"Tim, you tell that gal right now that you are goin to run your own house and if she don't like it right now is the time for her to squeal. That is where I missed it. I pussy-footed around and let Symanthia start the whole works. I listened to her. You won't make no mistake by givin her your mind to begin with—just as much as you respect yourself is as much as your wife or anybody else will respect you. You know yourself, Tim, that I work like a slave and pay my debts. I am an honest man and a good law-abidin citizen and my family 's got so they won't respect me. Well, from now on they're goin to respect me and be glad to respect me. I am at the head of this house. W'y Issiah and your Ma 's even got me ruled out of all this stock that I work here like a brute to feed o' a winter—all in the world that I got is that bull. The twelve cows belong to the rest of the family and I can't sell one if I want to. Symanthia gets my checks and cashes them because I have to make my cross. From now on I make my cross and carry my money. I ain't a henpecked man no longer."

A stranger, tall and lean with a straw hat on that is going to seed, with a hatchet face and a corncob nose and a pair of searching eyes comes out the path by the barn, under the fringe of oak trees by the barb-wire fence, out under the little pine tree by the sweet-potato bed and through the gate into the yard. Emory and Tim sit silent and watch each time his gangly bean-pole legs move awkwardly like churn dashes up and down.

"Hello," says the man.

"Howdy," says Emory with his eye on the coffee-sack that is moving at his feet, "is there somethin that you want?"

"Yes," said the man, twisting one end of his corkscrew mustache with his forefinger and his thumb, "I am Jake Pinefore and I just moved into the Hollow. I wanted to borrow your shovel plow to plant me a late tater patch. John Stevens told me you had one."

"Open up that coat, Jake Pinefore."

Jake opens the coat and eyes Emory searchingly from his toes to his slouch hat.

"I just wanted to see if there was a badge of the Law of any kind under that coat. Looks a little suspicious to wear a coat in July."

"Well, I ain't no Law," says Jake, "I just moved to the creek."

"It is a damn good thing," says Emory, "I won't stand for no Law to come into my house spyin on me with a badge under his coat. I don't do anythin to hurt my neighbors. I don't steal from them. I don't fuss with them. I don't bother their wives. I make my own bread by the hardest work with a grubbin hoe and a plow. And I don't intend to have the Law on my premises spyin on me. This land belongs to me. The Master made it, but it is mine. That corn is mine and them trees—that barn and this house—the wind above it and the stars and all of it is mine. Get him the plow, Tim!"

"How long can I have it, Mr. Hare?"

"Keep it long as you want it. When you get through with it, bring it back to the barn lot and just lay it over the fence where we'll see it. We'll put it in the tool shed."

"Thank you."

Tim walks lazily with the man down over the bank to the late sugar-corn patch. They walk out past the sassafras by the well box and over the bank by the pasture's edge where iron-purple weeds weave in and between the rusty wires in the fence like slats through the ribs of a basket.

"Pap, I got the rocks piled up," says Ella Mae, "what must I do now?"

"Pick them off that pile and carry them across the road and make a new pile."

"What for, Pap?"

"Don't ask me what I ask you to do anything for. You just go on and do it."

Ella Mae begins to whine, whimper her lips and to carry the rocks across the road and to pile them in a new pile.

"Come out here, Tinnie, right quick!"

Tinnie comes to the door, sweat running from her red face

where she has been working around the hot cook stove in the kitchen. Her blue eyes twinkle, her red lips twitch and her blond hair has fallen across her cheek. With a brush from her hand she shoves it back in place and says: "What do you want, Pap? Does somethin ail you?"

"Plenty ails me around here. Bring that split-bottom chear out that old Feldrix Quillen made—the one that ain't got that wire in the bottom to pinch a feller when he sets down in it," says Emory.

"That's funny for you to ask me to bring you a chear, Pap!"

"Yes, that's very funny. But you do what I say and make your remarks afterwards."

Tinnie goes back through the house to get the chair. Her fine stout body moves swiftly through the room, her long blond hair streaming down over her shoulders.

"Come out here, Belle."

"What do you want, Pap?"

"Don't ever ask me what I want. I'm tired of it—hear! Come and see what I want."

Belle comes to the door. Belle, the image of her mother, eyes blue as mountain water, teeth pretty as bark, and hair black as a crow's wing. Her sinewy body, straight as a young poplar sprout, is prettier than a poplar sprout clothed in blue gingham with white checks in it and trimmed around the collar in a narrow white lace made by her own long fingers of her shapely hands.

"Bring my pipe to me off'n the machine. Fill it with tobacco —a twist you'll find upon the wall plate above my bed. Bring me a match too. Don't waste a minute. Time lost ain't never found again," says Emory.

"Anything else you want?" Belle snaps and turns back through the room.

"If they had a been I would a said so."

"What's the matter with Pap?" says Tinnie as she picks up the chair he always eats in in the kitchen.

"Children, don't ask me," says Symanthia as she raises up from over a skillet with meat sizzling in the popping grease and the heat dazzling over the red-hot crossbar between the caps. "He's actin like he's drunk, but I can't smell a thing on his breath. He's tryin to take the place. They ain't no reason to him and I got away from him quick as I could. I ain't goin back where he is. Talkin about bein henpecked and a petticoat government and my people and me ownin the cows and all that stuff–I never saw him act like this since we been married these twenty-six years. I'd like to know what he's got in that coffee-sack though–keeps a-movin all the time."

"Put the chear under the poplar tree for me, Tinnie."

Tinnie carries the chair out across the yard, across the grass stubble walking barefooted. Emory follows her, his arms swing idly at his side.

"Set it right here for me."

Tinnie puts the chair down and whiffs back into the house, her lips drawn tight, her eyes focused straight ahead, very careful never to glance at her father's slouch hat, thin uncut beard, with the drops of sweat shining on them.

"Here is your old pipe, tobacker in it and matches and all," says Belle, as she runs out to Emory, hands the pipe hurriedly to him, and starts to run back.

"Just a minute," says Emory, as he sits down in the chair facing the pasture field, "light my pipe for me."

Belle strikes a match on a rock. She holds it between her cupped hands to guard against the lazy July wind that will instantly snap out a tiny flame and encourage a larger flame in the dry brush. Emory wheezes on his pipe stem and puffs a blue smoke into the July lazy wind. Belle starts to run back in the house.

"Wait a minute–wait a minute," says Emory, "you take that double-bitted ax out there in the chop block and go up there on the hill and cut a dry dead locust pole for stove wood, Belle."

"Me, Pap!"

"Your name is Belle, ain't it? And I didn't say Tinnie. Now you go on and do as I tell you."

Belle walks slowly through the back-yard gate. She goes through the gate to the chop block, she pulls the ax from where it is sticking in the chop block, she flings it across her shoulder and strides off to the oak-covered bluffs back of the barn where so many of the little black locusts have been blighted, have died and are rooting out on the bluff.

Ella Mae has finished carrying the rocks across the road and re-piling them. She walks up the path under the pine tree and through the gate and out where Emory is sitting under the poplar tree in his easy chair, watching the sun go down over the chestnut tops on the ridge.

"I'm through, Pap. Got anything else you want me to do?"

"Go in the house and help your Ma if she needs you." Emory spoke kind and Ella Mae trotted up the path to the door.

"Just a minute, Ella Mae," says Emory as he blows out a blue wisp of smoke, "tell your Ma I said for her to come out here."

"Well."

Emory blows another wisp of smoke into the blue air. The smoke is bluer than the hazy-blue summer day. The katydids sing down in the cornfield by the pig pen, the whippoorwills begin to holler back on the hill by the old rail fence and the beetles start their seething singing around over the yard in the stubble grass.

"Did you want me, Emory?" says Symanthia, as she comes to the door, leans with one hand on the door-facing and her neck slightly bent outward. She blocks the dying sunlight from going in at the door. It cannot go through her.

"If I hadn't wanted you, I wouldn't a sent for you. You know that. Come on out here. Don't you ever ask me if I have sent for you or if I haven't sent for you——"

"What's the matter with you, Emory? I've never seen you act this strange."

"Well, I am goin to act this way from now on. You can just mark this down right now. I've been a turkey gobbler with his tail feathers pulled out. I am ashamed. I ain't been my own boss at my own house."

"A turkey gobbler with his tail feathers pulled out. Are you in your right mind, Emory, talkin like that?" says Symanthia.

"I ain't in nothin else but my right mind. Come here and get this sack and clean these fish and have them for supper," says Emory, blowing smoke that drifts over in little blue sheets to the rows of corn. "I got a mess of fish here and I want them for supper."

"Emory, supper is purt nigh ready–all but a-settin the table."

"Supper ain't nigh ready yet. These fish has to be cleaned and fried before supper is ready. I'll throw every dish off 'n the table if they ain't. I am runnin this house, my little lady. You give me the britches this very day and I wear them from now on. It ain't you and Issiah that's runnin this place any longer. Get them fish and get them cleaned," Emory says.

"Lordy, but they are heavy!"

"Forty-two pounds."

"Where did you get all these fish, Emory?"

"Don't ask me such a question. A good wife never questions her man."

"I'll bet you caught them in a net and that's against the Law."

"I guess the north side of this farm runs up on the blind side of the Tiger, don't it? Ain't all the coal under this hill mine? Do they tell me how to get it–pick and shovel, blastin powder, dynamite–anyway. It belongs to me. Don't half of that river belong to me? I wanted a mess of fish and I got a mess of fish. Them's good fish too. Nearly all of them catfish –what ain't catfish are carp. I don't want no more of them mud turtles for a while here on Sunday when a preacher is here for dinner and I don't ever want any more turtle eggs, hear me!"

"Yes," says Symanthia.

Symanthia shoulders the wet sack. There is still life in it. The sack barely shakes. She starts toward the house with the sack on her shoulder, her powerful womanly body slightly weaving under the load.

"How would you like to carry them three mile for your family–wantin your family to have fish instead of turtle and then the youngins start poppin up in your face tellin you they was goin to tell their Ma on you? W'y your blood would bile, that's what it would do."

"I can't get all these cleaned for supper."

"Clean them all, too. There is Tinnie in the house and Ella Mae."

"But I got bread baked. And I got buttermilk and butter and tomatoes and potatoes and butter and stringed beans and biled corn. I got supper already."

"No you haven't till you cook them fish."

Symanthia turns the corner of the house to go around by the kitchen. A tall frame is an outline against the sky where the sun has just gone down as Emory looks toward her back. The sack weaves to and from like a dead leaf hanging to a white oak in February rustled by the wind.

"We'll have fish for supper too," says Emory as he blows out a wisp of smoke and it goes toward the ground, "and we're goin to have fallen weather the way that smoke goes to the ground. The fish will be done by the time Belle and the boys gets back and gets ready to help eat 'em."

From where Emory sits under the poplar tree in his easy chair, he can see the milk gap with the old feed boxes and the old iron fish fryer where Symanthia pours out warm sweet milk for the cats that gather night and morning at milking time to get their milk. He can see the cows lying down under the locust shade. Charlie, Emory's bull, comes walking out among them from where he has been standing under the locust shade. He bellows and paws the earth with his feet. The dirt and grass fly back over Charlie's back and he horns at the wind.

"I wish that bull would quit tearin up all the grass in the pasture," says Emory and blows the smoke from red, beardy lips.

Now Charlie takes his horns and hooks each cow a little until she gets up. All get up, but one. She is old Roan, the oldest cow in the pasture, and the boss of all the rest. She will not get up when Charlie gently puts his horns to her neck. Again he hooks her a little harder and a little harder until he braces his hind feet and down on his knees he presses his weight against her with the dirt flying from his cloven feet. Roan leaves the ground. She gets up and with her long tongue kisses Charlie's face moist.

"That's me from now on," says Emory, "when you make 'em know who's who around the house then they respect you. Look at Roan how she respects Charlie. They won't respect you if you don't make them. I am the bull in my pasture from now on."

Beside the pig pen a game rooster "quirt-quirts" to his hens. They come running. Each hen tries to be the first to the rooster. He gives the first hen to him a jar fly he caught tangled in a tuft of grass buzzing and trying to fly. She takes the jar fly, flings it with her bill against the ground, to kill it and the rooster "quirt-quirts" to her again and loves her with his wing stiffened around his leg.

"That's me," says Emory, "I'll bring the fish at this man's house and Symanthia's goin to take them. I'll bring in the grub. She'll never starve and my youngins won't starve long as I can raise my arms to hit a tap with a hoe. But I'm goin to master my youngins."

Emory blows out blue wisps of smoke on the almost-night air. The smoke twists like little clouds in creamy waves, goes up and down for a few seconds; thins and then disappears forever—mixing with the whole wide world of wind.

The turkeys come up from the pasture field, the twenty-one turkey hens and the two gobblers. One gobbler got his tail feathers pulled out one by one when he got back to fight before the corn-crib door every morning when the chickens, geese and turkeys went there to get shelled corn for breakfast.

The turkey gobbler with the tail feathers leads the flock. He is in front with the hens following him. The gobbler without the tail feathers lags to the rear of the line. They come along the yard fence walking towards the barn. The hens walk with their blue heads bobbing up and down in rhythm to their loose swinging bodies. The gobbler in front takes time to strut when the pig grunts and the cow bawls. His wattles turn from buttercup-blue to June-rose red. His snout reddens like a wind-blown ember as he marches in front. The gobbler that walks behind has nothing to say.

"The gobbler that's in front is me from now on," says Emory, "I used to be like that gobbler behind. My tail feathers was all pulled out and I didn't have nothin to say. But from now on I got a-plenty to say. I am goin to rule my roost. Man was made to rule his roost. And when a man rules his roost, a woman likes it. If he don't, then she ain't satisfied, for she tries to rule the roost and don't know how and somebody's got to rule it. From now on I am the man that rules the roost. It is about time for them fish to be done."

The turkeys pass in single file to roost. The blue smoke swirls in little cloudlets–off among the morning-glories that are vined around the stalks of corn. One cloudlet follows another cloudlet like flecks of foam where water pours over a rock, whines, riffles and then flows on. There is a red ember spot in the sky above the chestnut tops. The beetles are booming in the yard grass. The katydids are calling down in the corn by the pig pen. Emory rests in his easy chair under the bushy-topped poplar tree and blows thin blue cloudlets of smoke to a lazy wind-free July world.

THE moon was comin up over that fringe of poplar trees last night when I saw Radburn and Hankas coming through the greenbrier thicket by the pig pen. I knowed jist what had happened when I saw them together. They had been over the hill to Mort Anderson's to get some of that old rotgut licker. I knowed I was goin to have a time for the night. I saw them come through the patch of ragweeds this side of the pig pen. Radburn was holdin to the apple-tree limbs. Hankas was talkin with his hands. I could see them just as plain as day. The moon shined on them and if they had been rabbits I could have shot them both, it was so light. Not even a wind was blowin to make a racket. It was the quietest night a body might nigh ever seed. The pigs thought I was comin to slop them when they passed the pig pen. The pigs grunted a little bit. Then they went back to the old sow.

I heerd Hankas say to Radburn: "We gotta take the medicine back to Lake. He is cut purty bad. I could see the blood. It is all over my hand, see! People will think I cut Lake with a knife. God Almighty knows I didn't cut Lake with anything." Then Radburn said to Hankas: "Be quiet so America can't hear you. If she thinks there's trouble she'll be right into it. She's soon hit me as not. She's soon hit you. I know her. I have lived with her long enough to know her. When we first married and got into a racket she knocked me down the first lick she struck me right above the eye. She didn't have on no knucks neither. She done hit with her plain fist. I've lived with her thirty years now and I know she'll fight. Right when we was first married and my stepma Middie pulled a pistol on Pap, she walked right in and said, 'Give me that gun.' Then she struck her with her plain fist right above the eye—the same place she allus hits 'em and God only knows how long Middie laid there."

"America allus wuz that way at home. When us kids was playin about the place, she whipped all of us but me. I could whip America. I watched and never let her get the first lick. But ever time I whipped her, Pap throwed a fit and jumped all over me. I allus told Pap she'd whip the man she married if she ever got the first lick. She allus plugs a body right above the right eye."

"She is a hard woman to live with, but she is a good woman. Last winter I'd a been a dead man if hit hadn't been for my wife. You know Lefty Penix, don't you, Hankas? Well, he come over here and we got a holt of some bad licker. We must have went crazy. We got right over there by the corn crib and started to fight. I don't remember hit. But they said Lefty had the corn knife that we keep stickin out there in the crib log to cut the cow corn with. He had that knife and was makin for my throat. America saw him. And she come runnin right through the snow shoe-mouth deep and hit Lefty right above the eye. He had long been sobered up before he come to his senses. Both of that man's eyes settled black around them for a week and a big door knob riz under Lefty's right eye. But my wife saved my life. If she hadn't run out there, I'd a been in hell right tonight."

I could see them comin up closer to the house. There was Radburn, my man. He wore the same old dirty overalls that he'd been wearin all week in the 'backer patch. They was all gluey and would stand alone in the green 'backer glue. His shirt was dirty and his beard was out all over his face. Just me here and I was ashamed of him. Beadie went home with the little Jurdan girl to stay all night; Fonse and Gilbert went to the square dance; Libbie and Win went to see Sister Mossy last week and they ain't got back yet. I was right here—well, Pap was here. But he's sick in there in the bed. He can't do nuthin. Pap has one foot in the grave and the other foot ready to slide in. I knowed Hankas and Radburn was drinkin that old rotgut they got over to Mort Anderson's. I knowed trouble was a-brewin. Everytime Radburn gits a drink he thinks he can lick me. He gits to thinkin about me knockin him down and he wants to try hit me over and show me he can lick me. Everytime he gits a drink of that old rotgut in him, hit is a fight here. I knowed what was goin to happen.

Before they got up to the house I went in the back room and looked under Radburn's piller. I found his 32 automatic. The moon shined in at the back-room window and left a white place on the floor. I stepped out where I could take a good look at the 32. Hit looked right purty fer a pistol. I looked into the chamber and saw that hit was loaded. Then I said to myself: "Ready, Hankas. Don't care if you are my brother. Ready, Radburn. I don't care if you are my man. Hit won't be a fist above the eye this time. Hit'll be a bullet." They come up and opened the door. There was Hankas, my brother, and he's a big man. Some over two hundred that man is, and mean as a copper-head. I could see in the moonlight he had one of them old sour drunk man's frowns on his face. He looked like the devil. His arms come down nearly to his knees. They are hairy as a dog. His arms is nearly big as fence posts. He had on his old gluey 'backer clothes too. Hankas has a big blocky body without a pound of fat. He's solid as a rock. But he ain't got much of a head. Hit is a little head for sich a big body. I know how us children used to laugh at him and call him "simlon head." He'd git so mad. He'd want to fight. He could whip everybody. Well, I said if I ever got a house o' my own, I'd whip him or I'd kill him before I'd let him run over me. Pap allus upheld for him at home, because Pap was afraid of him and Mother was too.

They come in the house. They hushed talkin for a minute when they come in. Radburn struck a match and lit the lamp. I could see he was drunk as a biled owl. Hankas staggered over to the mantelpiece and helt onto hit long enough to fill his pipe with my best smokin 'backer. He lit his pipe over the lamp and he looked at Radburn. Then he wiped his hands on his gluey overalls. Pon my word, I wouldn't be caught wearin dirty a clothes as them men had on. Hankas said to Radburn: "Call America. Reckon she's here. We got to git the turpentine and git back to Lake. He's cut purty bad. Look at the blood on your hands and on my hands. People will think we cut him. God knows we didn't. I like old Lake. He's a bully good fellar."

"Yes, and think about him layin out there bleedin in that

ditch." I just stepped from the back room into where they was by the mantelpiece. I had the 32 in my bosom. I had my hand on hit. If they had started anythin, I aim to let 'm have hit right above the eye. I said, "Who got cut?" Radburn said: "W'y America, Lake Burdock got cut. He's out there bleedin in the ditch." And I said, "Where did he git cut and when?" Hankas said: "Don't know how he got cut. He jist got cut 's all we know about hit. He jist fell. He's cut on the hip–place big enough to lay your hand in." And I said: "This don' sound right. Somebody had to cut him. Let me see your knifes. Both of you drunk and you wouldn't know hit if you did cut him." Well, Hankas looked at Radburn and Radburn looked at Hankas. Then Radburn said, "Hankas, we'd better let her look at our knifes." They took their knifes out and they wasn't a drap of blood on 'em. I felt so good. I felt like gittin down on my knees and prayin to God Almighty. I didn't want 'em to have to go to the pen for knifin. "Pon my word, Meck," Radburn said: "We didn't cut Lake. We didn't cut him. No." Then I said, "How in the world did he get cut?" Radburn said, "I don't know." Hankas said, "I don't know." There Hankas hung to the mantelpiece. The very Devil was in his eyes. I knowed I was goin to have trouble that night. The Devil was in his broth a-brewin. I said: "You ain't takin no turpentine out'n here. You go bring that man to this house. Go now before he bleeds to death." And they went out the house. Radburn looked at Hankas and Hankas looked at Radburn. They never said a word to each other ner to me.

I walked the floor. I was so uneasy. I was more uneasy than I was the night Brother Tim and Candy got in that cuttin scrape with the Tinsleys. Tim got his right eye cut out, and Candy got his juggle vein nicked a little and a couple of cuts to the holler. But he lived. One of the Tinsleys bled to death. The other lived but ain't been able to work none since. I was so uneasy that night. But I was just about that uneasy this time. I didn't know what had happened. God knows I didn't. Whippoorwills hollerin up there on the hill and some leaves fell off the trees. I could hear them blowin so lonesome. And I jist paced the floor. The moon shined right up there over the hog pen. I could see the moon then jist like I could see hit last night. I could see the rails on the hog pen jist as plain as I can see my hand before me now. I was so uneasy. The moon kept gittin over further in the sky—out past the hog pen and round to the right near the Hoggens' Graveyard. I could see the tombstones over there on that pint. Hit made me so lonesome—jist like last night. I could see the tombstones and the moon. I could hear the whippoorwills hollerin and the dead leaves a-rattlin in the wind. I guess some tears come down my cheek. I thought I felt tears runnin down my cheeks. I don't know.

Then I looked through the back-room winder and I seed two men comin carryin somethin. Hit looked like a log. They was staggerin up the cow path from that gate right down yander. I heerd Hankas say, "Let's put him down, Radburn, and open the gate." And I saw them throw the log-lookin thing from their shoulders jist like they'd throw down a sack of corn. They opened the gate. Then they shouldered the man. Mercy, how I felt. I thought: "Now what if they bring him here and he dies from that cut. We'll all go to the pen. What if he dies on our hands. People will think we kilt him and the Law will git us all fer killin him. Merciful God, what if he's to die here. A dead man in the house. What would we do? What could we do?" But I saw Radburn and Hankas comin wobblin up the yaller bank down yander on this side of the gate. They wobbled like ducks. The moon shined down on them. It was light as day. And here they come carryin that man. The lamp was lit up in the front room and the moonlight come in at the back-room winder.

They come right to the front door. Hankas was behind, carryin Lake's shoulders. Radburn was in front, carryin Lake's legs. Radburn shoved open the door and brought him in feet foremost. And he was bleedin frum the seat of the pants. The blood jist poured on the floor like water from the raindrip. Hankas said: "Meck, git the turpentine quick. He's bleedin purty bad." And I said: "You're so drunk you don't know what you're talkin about. Turpentine ain't goin to stop that blood. Hit takes chimney sut to stop blood. Stick your head up that fireplace there and git some chimney sut from behind the jam rock. Do hit quick. Put Lake on the bed first." They throwed Lake down on the bed hard enough to break all the slats. Lake was drunk as the Devil wanted him to be. Then I said: "Radburn, you pull his pants down so I can see where this man is cut. We got to do somethin fer him." Radburn says, "You ain't no doctor, air you?" And I said to Radburn: "I may not be no doctor, but tell me nairy nuther woman that's delivered more babies in this country than I have, and I'll eat her blood raw. Who's cured more sick than I have among cattle and men? Who's cured more colic and fever than I have? Who does the people come to when they want help—even for drunken fits and blind billiards? I guess you remember that mule's front legs that had all the skin peeled off'n 'em like hit was bark the time he tried to jump the wire fence—who sewed that up? Never was a scar left. Who sewed up a duck's back that the hound pups tore the skin off in a three-cornered fleek? The duck lived, didn't hit? Take that man's pants down. I aim to look at that cut, and if I can I aim to sew hit up."

Radburn started undressin Lake. I went into the kitchen and put a fire in the stove and put water in the teakettle. Then I started to huntin fer some white thread and a darnin needle. By the time the water het, I had the darnin needle and the thread. Radburn had the clothes from off'n the cut. Hit looked like he had been whacked with a corn knife. And I said, "Radburn, let me look in Lake's overall pockets." I took his overalls—blood-soaked and dirty with green 'backer glue. I heerd somethin rattle in the hip pocket. And my Lord, how hit did stink with that old rotgut whisky. And what did I find in the pocket on the seat of his britches? I found a broken bottle. "Here's what's cut him," I said, "a bottle. He's fell on hit. A rotgut bottle. If hit wasn't fer his wife, I wish hit had cut him in two. He's got as good a woman as ever the sun shined on and out carvortin 'round like this. Drinkin 'round and leavin his family at home. I'll sew him up this time. But never again will I do hit." Radburn looked at Hankas. Hankas looked at Radburn. They never said a word. Hankas looked mean as the Devil out'n his black eyes. "Goin' sew him up, air ye?" he looked at me and said. And I said, "Yes, I'm goin to sew him up if this darnin needle don't break."

By this time the water was warm. I brought hit in from the kitchen. Radburn helt the lamp. I swathed out the deep lash. Lake jist laid there and moaned like a fat hog. Then I put the turpentine on. Hit jist keep bleedin. Hankas give me the chimney sut and you'd a laughed to a seen Hankas atter he went up behind the jam rock. He was black as a piece of wet chestnut burr. I daubed the chimney sut in the lash. I knowed hit would leave a black stripe under the skin when hit healed over. But I didn't care. I wanted to save him on account of his wife, Polly, and his five young 'uns. I used the chimney sut to stop the blood. I poured in the whole bottle of turpentine to keep hit from gittin sore. Then I pulled up the soft sides of the cut and made Hankas hold them while I used the darnin needle. Lake flinched a little when the needle went through his skin. I took thirty-seven stitches on that man. And when I got through, the stitches was jist as even as if I'd been tuckin up a skirt that was too long.

Hankas jist set and looked at me. The Devil was in his black eyes. I had the pistol in my bosom. I jist wanted to git away so he couldn't git the first lick. I kept my eyes on him all the time. I said: "Pull his pants back on him and throw that glass out of this room, Radburn. Put Lake in the bed. And I don't want any more rotgut whisky brought in this house tonight." Hankas said: "Who's runnin this house? You or Radburn?" And I said, "I'm runnin my own house and them that don't like hit can git out." "Us go, Radburn," said Hankas. They staggered out. Hankas said when he left the house, "Poor home, ain't hit, Radburn, when you ain't got a word to say in your own house." Radburn didn't say a word. He turned and looked back at me. Then they went out into the moonlight, around the corner of the house, under the dark night-shade of the hickory tree—down over the hill toward Reek Finney's house.

They left me in the house with Lake. He was drunk. I thought he would sober up before they got back and want to know who cut him and what he was doin sewed up. But I had the pistol. I could shoot him if he started anythin. I went to the kitchen winder. I looked out. The moon was goin down over the cornfield where the boys had cut the early piece of corn. The fodder shocks looked like wigwams between me and the moon. I could hear the lonesome whippoorwill. I could hear the katydids out in the dead grass by the cow lot. I could hear the pigs gruntin. I could hear Lake's breath go up and down and then sizzle like the wind goin through the dead sticker-weeds back of the smoke house on a windy day. And then I heerd the dogs bark over at Reek Finney's house. I went to the back yard. I looked over at Reek Finney's place. The house was dark and the moonlight showed on the winder lights. Then I saw the winders lit up with lamplight. I knowed Hankas and Radburn was over there. Then I heerd them talkin and cussin around. I heerd Hankas ask Reek if he wanted a drink and Reek said yes. Then I heerd them cussin some more and runnin the dogs over at Reek's house fer barkin at them. I heerd Radburn say: "I'll git my knife out and straddle that dog's back and cut hits throat if hit don't shet up that barkin in my ears. I've seed a lot of blood tonight and I wouldn't keer to see a little more."

Well, I didn't want Lake to sober up. I wanted him to stay drunk till mornin. So I hunted fer the whisky jug that Radburn and Hankas brought in the house but didn't take out again. I found a gallon jug behind the door with a sea-grass string run through hits gill. I got the jug and I went to the right, over from where Pap was a-layin and I opened Lake's mouth. I poured rotgut from the jug with the other hand. I guess I poured a pint down him. He guzzled hit down and licked his lips. Then I pulled the pistol from under the bosom of my dress. I looked at the little barrel. I said: "W'y this can't kill a man. I'd ruther trust my fist. The barrel is too little. Look at this little hole. Look at that big man Lake. Look how big Hankas is. Hit would take a bigger pistol than this to kill him. That barrel ain't as big as my middle finger and ain't much longer." So I took the pistol back to the bed and took the shells out'n hit and put hit under Radburn's piller.

I went and looked behind the meal barrel and got the double-barrel shotgun. Hit looked more like a gun to me. Long bright-blue barrels glistened in the lamplight. I brought the shell box from off'n the wall plate. They wan't but two shells in the box. One was loaded with number three shots and one with number fives. I put the shell loaded with number threes in the left-hand barrel for Hankas. I put the shell loaded with number fives in the right-hand barrel for Radburn. Then I pulled the trunk out and put hit slonch-ways across the corner of the room so I'd have more room to shoot from. I blowed out the lamp and I got behind the trunk. I pinted the double-barrel over the trunk and I cocked both triggers and turned the safety off.

The chickens had begin to crow fer midnight. I stayed right behind the trunk with the double-barrel in my hands ready to shoot. I seed the fire in Hankas's eyes. The Devil was in his eyes. I jist waited fer him to come back. I knowed he would want to start somethin. Well, I heerd him comin. I heerd him come up through the cornfield and cuss about the moon goin down. I heerd him say he fell on the sharp edge of a cornstalk where the boys had cut the potato patch of corn. I heerd him cuss about the night gettin so dark. Then they come to the door. Radburn opened the door. He struck a match and lit the lamp. Then he said, "Wonder where America is?" And then he hollered and hollered: "America, come here! America, come here! I want some buttermilk. I want fresh water. I want some clean clothes." I never said a word.

They went over to the bed where Lake was. They pulled them up a couple of chears and set down by the side of the bed. Radburn said, "Wonder if that 'll git all right where America sewed up that place?" Hankas said: "Yes. I'd ruther have her as any doctor that's in Berryville. She's my sister and bad to fight, but I'd ruther have her by my side when I'm sick as anybody I know." "Cut on glass, wasn't he, Hankas?" "That's what America said." "Do you reckon she'd swear that if the Law gits us all before the court." "Yes, I believe she would." "Well, he's drunk, ain't he? Air you drunk? Am I drunk?" "Git that gallon of licker from behind the door, Hankas, and let's have a snip before we take our shoes off."

Hankas staggered over to the door. He got the jug by the sea-grass string. He took hit over to Radburn. There they set. They wuz jist so drunk they didn't know who hit was in the bed. Radburn put his arms around Hankas. Hankas put his arms around Radburn. Then Hankas said: "You have got a decent woman, Radburn, but she don't treat you right. Now she has left you." "Surely she ain't left me. What will I do about somebody to cook fer me?" "Yes, she's left you." "I'll see." Then Radburn called: "America, America, come here! I want a drink of water. My head is killin me, America, come here." Pon my honor, hit was right laughable. Then he got down on his knees and looked under the beds. He looked behind the doors. I leveled the gun right on his head. When he moved, the gun barrels moved. I kept the gun right on him. I kept hit right on his temple. He never did git to the trunk. He went back and set down by Hankas. He said: "You're right, Hankas. She's gone. She's left me." Now I kept the gun pointed right at them.

Hankas said: "You got a good woman and you'll miss her some. But hit's the best thing for you. You can live right here by yourself and do your own cookin. Lake can stay with you part of the time. I'll come to see you often. Jist let her go and the Devil take her. You don't need no woman nohow. You can do without a woman more than you can do with a woman. She runs the house. She's hit you with her fist and deadened you two or three times or more than that. She won't do to fool with. Now you can bring the pig pen out here behind the smoke house and keep the dogs in the back room there at night. You can put your cows in the mule pasture and the mules in the cow pasture. That will make hit closer to milk out there by the sand rocks. You can make hit all right and you'll be a lot safer right here with your childer or without anybody."

Then they became silent. I kept the shotgun leveled about with their temples. The night out behind the winder was blacker than chimney sut. The whippoorwills kept hollerin. The katydids kept hollerin out behind the smoke house. I wasn't skeered a bit. I was jist lonesome. God, but I was lonesome. Three drunk men in the house. One of them a brother fer the Devil. I didn't like hit—all the stuff he was tellin Radburn. I didn't want Radburn to run with him and I told Radburn he would git him in trouble. But Hankas jist come up and got him. He can do hit every time. Radburn 'll jist do anything Hankas says. He'll follow him any place. And when he gits that old rotgut whisky in him he'll do about anything else.

About four o'clock a chicken crowed and Radburn waked from a doze. He said: "Ain't that boy of Reek's a funny boy? Don't he like licker? W'y when I give him that bottle I had to pull hit away from his lips. But poor boy, Hankas. They have to give him pizen to keep him alive. Hit's the God's truth. They feed that boy pizen. He ain't but ten years old and he weighs two hundred and ten pounds. He walks like a string-haltered hoss. Ever notice him? His face is red as a beet. He's marked with a turkey. Before he come to this world a turkey gobbler flogged his Mama out by the corn crib one mornin. That's what the matter with him." "And you say that he has to take pizen medicine so he won't die?" "Yes, hit takes about all the money that old Reek can make to keep that boy alive. He has that boy that eats pizen and eleven more boys stouter than old Reek is. He has seven girls and they ain't much good." "Well, I'll be dogged." "Reek is a clever man as you's ever about the house of." "Reckon that boy got drunk on the licker you give him?" "W'y, yes, he got drunk and even old Reek had to hold to the cornstalks to git up the hill when he left us down there in the holler." "Well, I'll be dogged."

I kept the gun right level with their temples. They dozed off again. Lord, how I did pray for daylight. I never closed my eyes for a wink of sleep. I never put in sich a night in all my life. I watched the clock. I could see the minutes was creepin up. I could hear the sparrows workin in the box. Hankas riz up and said: "Radburn, we forgot somethin. Give me the whisky quick. We have forgot Pap. We ain't offered Pap no whisky."

Radburn got up and walked over to Pap's bed with Hankas. Hankas helt the jug to Pap's lips and said, "Come on, Pap, and drink with us tonight." Pap waked from a doze and said, "I don't want no drink." "Come on and have one," Hankas said. "Ain't you goin to drink with us?" "No, I ain't goin to drink none of that stuff. Hit is a sin. The Lord has saved me and I promised the Lord I wouldn't drink no more licker. I aim to be good as my word." Then Hankas turned and said: "I'll be dogged. Lord has saved him and he promised not to drink any more licker to the Lord. Wonder what the Lord wants fer nuthin. Well, I'll be dogged. My own pap won't drink with me and him so nigh the grave." I kept the double-barrel leveled right on his head. I thought: "If you start anythin here I'll get you with a gun this big. Hit will kill you. This ain't no toy 32. This is a gun that will kill." Hankas sat down. He dozed off to sleep again.

Of all the snorin I ever heerd in my life hit was from them three drunk men. Of all the strange noises—fiddles, shotguns, mauls, hammers, drums, and axes—I could hear all kinds of noises. I prayed for daylight to come. The sparrows begin to chatter in their boxes. The pigs begin to grunt. The whippoorwill shet up. I could hear the quails hollerin down in the crab grass. I knowed daylight wasn't fer away. I took the shells out'n the gun. I slipped out the back winder. I come around and opened the kitchen door and come through to the meal barrel. I put the gun behind the meal barrel. Then I come into the front room. I took Radburn by the shoulder and I said: "What's all this goin on here? Run me out'n my house last night, didn't you?" And he said, "I don't remember if I did or didn't." "Well, you did," I says. "I stayed in the woods all night. The moon went down and hit was so dark I couldn't follow a path out and you was drunk and took the place." Hankas waked up and I said, "Brother Hankas, you tried to pour that old rotgut licker down your dyin father's throat. You are a brute." "I didn't do nothin like that, did I?" And the tears jist streamed down his beardy face and dropped off the ends of his beard. He got up and sneaked out home. He couldn't look me in the face.

Lake waked up. He put his hand on his hip and hollered, "O Lord God, my hip! Whut is the matter with my hip?" I went out of the room. I guess Radburn must to 'a took his pants down and they both looked at his hip. When I come back in, Radburn looked at me and Lake looked at Radburn. Radburn got the express and hauled Lake home. Before Radburn left with Lake he sneaked up to me and he said, "I'm plagued to death over whut happened to Lake."

I never ast whut happened. I knowed whut happened and I wanted to make Radburn tell me, but he did feel too plagued. We both jist hoisted Lake in the spring wagon on a feathered tick and hauled him home to Polly. I felt a little uneasy about maybe a little piece of glass was left in the lash and hit might not heal. But in a few days Lake was walkin around. I heerd my boy say that he was in the crick with Lake, and his body was allus dirty as a pig on the seat. Radburn looked at me. I looked at Radburn. We never said a word.

"YOUR Pop is dyin," says Mom, "you'll have to go after the Doctor. It is a long way to send you, but you are all the one I have to send. You'll have to go to Greensburg tonight. Saddle old Fred and go and bring the Doctor back with you. Your Pop can't die and leave me with all these children. There are four mouths to feed, not much to feed them on and a dark winter here."

Here lies Pop in bed. His face is flushed red, the red color there is in an October red-oak leaf. He kicks the cover, the heavy home-made quilts and he says: "They ain't never been nothin in this country like this influenza. It's a plague and I believe I'm a goner. Has to be somethin to thin us out, I guess. If it ain't one thing it is another. Get me a Doctor, son. We ain't got the money tell him, but if he will come the cow will stand good, or the horse or both of them. Money don't matter when a body wants to live."

Mom comes to the door with me. She takes a piece of pine kindlin and sticks it between the forestick and the firebrands and gets a tiny blaze with a tiny black smoke swirlin up. She lifts the lantern globe and touches the kindlin fire to the wick. She lowers the globe and wipes off a speck of mud with the corner of her checked apron. I can see Mom, tall, sinewy, dark as a pawpaw leaf bitten by frost, her straight black hair, her white teeth there in the dim-lighted room. I can see the tears roll down her cheek without the curve of her lips for cryin. Pop back in the bed, kickin the quilts with his feet and fightin them with his hands.

Our house is far away from all other houses. We cannot see the smoke from another house. We are so far away our chickens cannot meet and mix with our neighbor's chickens. Pop used to say that we always wanted to stay that far away. "When you live so close to a neighbor your chickens mix, take care, you are goin to have a fallin-out." Mom didn't want to move to this place. I remember Mom cried when we moved here. We thought we could do better by payin one-third rent and have some bottom land down between the hills, than we could by payin two-fifths grain rent and farmin all hill land. We give one shock of corn and fodder now and take two ourselves. We used to give two shocks of corn and fodder and keep three out of every five. If you clear the land of briars and sprouts and hoe the corn and know how hard it is to raise, you will know then that there is a difference in share-croppin, if you give one-third grain-rent or if you give two-fifths. That is why we moved to this last house in the Hollow. And Martha Smith told Mom before we moved, "Mrs. Powderjay, that house is hanted. I'll tell you that before you go. No family has lived there more than two years. They was a woman that killed herself in that house. She got tired of livin because she didn't have anybody to talk to. One day when her husband was out in the field she hung herself from the upstairs window with a sheet fastened to the bedpost and to her neck. You'll never be able to live there. Lights are seen all around the house at night. There are two graves under a plum tree in the garden. You will hear all kinds of noises there. They ain't a house in a mile of you and the foxes come right in and get your chickens in broad daylight."

Now, we are here, Pop down in bed with the influenza, our crops failed last year in the craw-dad bottoms and we haven't anythin to go on for the winter. That is why Pop got a job on the railroad section and walks four mile to and from his work, eight miles a day and ten hours work, to keep us goin. And Pop is bed-fast.

The tiny bright flame flickers under the lantern globe. I set the lantern on the floor, put on a slip-over sweater and overall jacket over that to cut the November wind, put on a pair of rabbit-skin mittens and a sock cap that I stretched down over my ears. Mom ties a scarf around my neck. I walk over a white field of snow to the barn. It crunches beneath my brogan shoes. The stars are pretty in the deep blue winter sky. They twinkle coldly up there in the heaven. The wind hits my face keen as a razor blade and it bites the skin on my face like tiny mouse teeth. Fred is prancin in his stall. He has never laid down on the warm bed of cornstalks yet. I go into the stall, lift his bridle from the harness rack, blow my breath on the bridle bits and warm them so they won't take the hide off his tongue. I put the bridle on Fred, knock off a few dirty flakes of mud with the currycomb, put on the saddle blankets and the pads, throw on the saddle and girt it tight for the long rough ride. I lead Fred out of the barn, pat his neck, for he is my friend tonight, and he must take me over a long rugged path. He must be fast and sure-footed, an art hill horses learn sooner or later and an art already perfected by mountain mules.

I am in the saddle. I do not need the lantern. When the moon turns dark I may not be able to follow the path without it. I tie it to the saddle. It is too cold to hold it in my hand. I blow out the tiny flame. I have matches in my pocket to relight it with if the moon goes down before I get back. I rub Fred's neck and say to him: "Now, boy, let's go. A straight piece of road. Slow here, Fred boy. Slow. Slow. Slow. It's a bad place. Take it easy." The stars are in the sky above me. The bull bat screams. I can hear the hoot owl laughin under such cold moon and such cold sky filled with stars. I have to pass a graveyard and I am afraid of a graveyard at night. There are the white tombstones among the briars and brush that loom wiry and black above the snow. There are the broken-top trees at the edge of the graveyard and the old iron fence bare of snow. And I think, "What if Pop has to come here and sleep in this quiet place with only the wind to blow over him and the bull bats to try to wake him with their screams and the hoot owls to sit up there in bare chestnut tree tops and laugh all night over nothin."

Fred gets his breath hard. He is wet around the saddle. I have to hold a tight rein. He is wiry and wants to tear up the mountain path. The snow crunches beneath his feet. His breath is loud as a wisp of wind in a tangled patch of briars. Over the ups-and-downs and around the steep shoulder of the mountain, I am on my way to Greensburg. We'll be there in another hour. I wonder how Mom is making it with Pop and Mary and Barbara and Finn. I left a warm fire burnin and a light from the big fireplace that danced all over the room. It was a light different to the light of the stars. I love to ride beneath the stars on a winter night. My toes are not cold. I wiggle them in the yarn socks Mom made for me. I'll not get cold. I talk to Fred and pat his neck: "Fred, you can take it, boy. Be careful your feet don't slip. Good old boy." The wind whips through the leafless trees and through the dead grass. It is such lonesome wind. I love to hear it, but it makes me think of Pop back there in bed and no Doctor.

And I think: "If Pop dies, Mom and me can get along. I plowed old Fred a few furrows last year. Pop let me try it when we was plowin in the oats and he said I done right well for a boy of ten. I'll stay with Mom and do my best. She said for me to bring a Doctor and I am goin to bring one if I don't get home till noon tomorrow."

I can see the lights from the little town. I am on the mountain ridge over it and soon I'll be goin down the snake path to it. I can see the houses lighted. I'll go down a-past the old Rigley barn, out past the old stave mill and into Doctor Frederick's office. He is the Doctor Mom wants. She says he's the best Doctor in town for she has seen him save so many women's lives. I'll get Doctor Frederick.

Fred pauses, slips, throws his body this way and that to keep from sittin down. He is goin down the steep snake path. The ground is frozen and there is a sheet of snow on the frozen ground. It makes it bad for Fred, for he is slick-shod and his shoes are not corked. Snow balls on his feet. I get out of the saddle, take a stick and knock the frozen balls of snow-ice from his feet. I jump back in the saddle and he walks down the mountain better.

We dash out the street to Doctor Frederick's office. I jump down, throw the bridle rein over the gate post and run in the house. Doctor Frederick is tall, swarthy and lean. He meets me. I say, "Can you go out in the Hollow to Mick Powderjay's house tonight?"

Doctor Frederick says, "Who is sick?"

"Pop's got the influenza," I say to him, "and Mom said tell you to come whatever you done, that she didn't have the money when you come, but we had a horse and cow and you could have either one of them or both of them if it took that much. Pop is awful sick. He's kickin the covers and goin on somethin awful."

"It's a awful late hour to get in that Hollow tonight, Sonnie," says Doctor Frederick.

"I can't help that," I says, "Mom said for you to come and for me to bring you. I'll have to bring you. I won't leave till you go."

"I can't get my car in that Hollow. I'd head into the ditch some place. Roads are as slick as glass and they's so much doctorin to do. That flu is everyplace. Wait till I get a sup of my cough medicine."

I don't say it to the Doctor, but it smells to me like pure old whisky.

"Now you go on," says Doctor Frederick, "and ride your horse to the mouth of the Hollow and I'll be there about the time you get there. I can drive that far. You can get me another horse and I'll ride on in the rest of the way."

He corks the cough medicine and puts it in his overcoat pocket. I run out of the office, leap into the saddle and snatch the rein from the gate. I am off with the wind. I ride with the wind. And I say to myself as I ride, "I got the Doctor, I told Mom I would. Pop won't die. Pop can't die." I hear the car comin. I have just been here about five minutes. I don't have another horse. We are not goin to ride Fred double. The Doctor can ride him and I'll walk. Doctor Frederick is not able to do much walkin. It must be past midnight now. The car chugs up to the old bridge. Doctor Frederick gets out, puts coffeesacks over the engine and gets his pill bag.

"Where is the horse for me to ride?" he says.

"This is the one for you to ride," I say. I untie the lantern from the saddle. The moon is goin down. It must be far past midnight. It is gettin dark. I light the lantern. Doctor Frederick climbs into the saddle. I hand him the pill bag. We are off up the Hollow. I follow the horse.

"This is a devil of a place for a man to live," says Doctor Frederick. "You can't get in and out. It's dangerous for to ride into a place like this and road so slick this time of a winter mornin."

Gray clouds scud the sky. The owls keep laughin. The bull bat screams. The wind whips through the roadside briars like drawin saw teeth across a rock. The road is dark. I get in front of Doctor Frederick and light the way with the lantern. I am warm enough to throw off my sweater and jacket and go in my shirt sleeves. It is hard work walkin through the snow and keepin ahead of the horse. But the Doctor is goin to see Pop. Pop must get well. What will we do if he doesn't? What can we do? I can hear the crunch-crunch of the snow beneath the horse's feet. I can hear the creakin of the saddle. I can hear the horse gettin his breath. I can hear myself gettin my breath. But I cannot hear Doctor Frederick gettin his breath. If I could though, I would carry him in myself to see him get Pop well.

We go past the Powell place. The only way I can tell it is the Powell place is by where they leave the jolt wagon set in the woodyard. The snow is fallin again. It is turnin warmer. Rabbits have eaten the bark sixteen inches high on the sassafras sprouts. That is just how deep the snow is goin to get. The rabbits know more about it than we do.

The house is in sight. I can see the light in the window. Mom has never gone to bed. "Yonder is the house, Doctor Frederick. We are here. We are here! A Doctor for Pop! I told Mom I'd fetch you. She'll believe me now."

Doctor Frederick gets down off the horse. He is stiff, to see him get down out of the saddle. He is tall, pale and stiff with long legs and long bony arms and big joints and veins in his fingers. The snow preeks softly by the saddle bag—big white flakes, one can see in the lantern light.

"Welcome in, Doctor Frederick. I have never been so glad to see you. Mick is rollin and tumblin back there in the bed and just me with him back here. The children are all asleep. It is so lonesome here and Mick so sick."

"A body about pays for all they get out of life," says Doctor Frederick and he uncorks his cough medicine and takes a swallow. "If it wasn't for my cough medicine I couldn't keep going."

He goes back to the bed where Pop is. I sit before the fire

and mend up the brands. I hear him say: "Mick has the flu. It's something like the old-fashioned grippe."

Mom says, "It's killin a lot of people now, ain't it, Doctor?"

"Yes, a few," says the Doctor, "but we all got to die someway and sometime. I'll do my best. You give this medicine every hour and this every two hours and he'll be some better after daylight. It's hard to tell who'll get over a thing and who won't."

"Now about the pay, Doctor," says Mom, "we'll pay you when we can. We have a horse and cow, some chickens and our meat in the smoke house and what little dab of furniture you see here in the house——"

"Stop such talk," says Doctor Frederick, "I've been doctoring in the Powderjay family twenty years and I've never lost a cent yet."

The chickens are crowin. It is four o'clock. I sit by the fire and punch the dyin embers with a hooked-end poker. A tiny flame leaps from the embers. My work is not done yet. I have to take Doctor Frederick back to his car at the mouth of the Hollow.

"Wait a minute, Doctor. You cannot go until I make you a biler of hot coffee," says Mom, "I know you are feelin sort of drowsy after bein up nearly all night." Mom goes to the kitchen and brings the coffee pot in the front room and sets it on the wood embers.

"Won't be long till the coffee will be a-bilin," says Mom. "It is a cold clear frosty mornin out with a lot more snow on the ground and a little coffee won't go bad with you."

"I could stand a cup all right," says Doctor Frederick.

We can see that Jack Frost has carved many beautiful things on our window panes, many more beautiful things than we have in the house. He has carved a castle out of the frost with windows and a sky above and trees around the house. Beyond the Jack Frost carved windows we can see a white world and plenty of frost in the air. The air is thin and cold as ice. It whistles around the eaves of the house. The chickens still sit on the black-oak roost, clutchin the bare branches of the tree with their toes. Their feathers are all ruffled. The barn is white.

The creek is a white sheet of ice, all but the riffles where the water ran too fast to freeze.

Doctor Frederick likes the coffee Mom makes. I like it too. It tastes good. It is warm to the stomach. He drinks one cup. "Another little taste of that coffee and I'll be on my way to the mouth of the Hollow."

Mom puts cream and sugar in the coffee. "That is enough cream, Mrs. Powderjay. That will be enough sugar." Pop is sleepin in the bed in the corner of the room. The firelight is dancin to the far end of the room. It shows the color of the pieces in the quilt that is spread over Pop's bed.

I go to the barn and slip Fred a bundle of cane-fodder blades and eight ears of corn. He rolls the corn in the box and eats. Slobbers roll from his lips. Then he mixes with bites of corn, cane-fodder blades. It does not take Fred long to eat. And when we come back from the trip to the mouth of the Hollow I'll spread out a bundle of corn fodder for old Fred on the snow. He eats a quick meal now so we can get the Doctor back.

The snow crunches beneath our feet. The snow is frozen. The wind bites the fingers and stings the face. I walk behind Doctor Frederick. Fred slips on the snow and ice. He is a big horse. He carries the Doctor with ease. Frost has gathered on the hairs of his chin. They look like little silver spikes. The white breath goes from Fred's nostrils like streams of fog. This is a cold mornin.

"I'll be back once a week," says Doctor Frederick "till your Pa gets better. You meet me here each Wednesday at six o'clock. If he gets worse, come and get me at any time."

He gets in his car. I leap into the saddle and Fred trots back up the Hollow. He is goin toward the barn. Fred goes faster toward the barn than he does away from it. I come back to the house, take the bridle and saddle off Fred, put him in the barn lot. Then I get a bundle of corn fodder and spread it on the clean white snow. Fred nibbles the fodder and the wind blows his tail till the hairs tangle like a bunch of saw briars blown by the wind.

"Winter is here," says Mom, "and we don't have meal to

make us bread. We don't have enough feed to last us for the horse and cow and chickens and hogs. Our feed will play out before March. Mick back there in the bed sick. God knows what will become of us. Doctor Frederick is a mighty fine man. I've knowed him ever since Barbara was born. He'll do all he can for us. He knows he'll get his money."

Mom walks before the fire and stands. She puts tobacco in her pipe, pushes it down with her forefinger and dips it down among the embers. Mom sucks the stem and blows the blue smoke out into the room. When Mom is worried she smokes hard. She sucks the long pipe stem hard and fast.

We have for dinner corn bread and milk and beans. For supper we'll have beans, milk and corn bread. We have our cow Gypsy. We raised our corn and we raised a good pole-bean crop. The bunch beans hit too, those that we planted out of the swampy bottoms. I can see the sun come over the high hill that lines in the Hollow, the hill so high that its shoulder cuts into the sky. There are streaks of sunlight runnin from the sun like streams of blood. I can see the bushy-topped pines silhouetted against these streams of red sky-blood. The world is so big. What lies beyond these hills? Days come and go beyond them. Winds whine over the snow and the dead grass. Pop's face is white as the snow. He never talks much. He takes medicine and stays in bed. Mick Powderjay is gettin to be a pile of skin and bones.

Today we haul wood with old Fred off the hill. Mom puts on a pair of Pop's overall pants. She picks up the double-bitted ax and says: "Come on, son. We got to get wood to-day." We go up the hill, through the briars and sprouts till we come to the timbered top of the hill. Here is where the fire ran through the woods last Spring and killed the trees. See the tall skeletons silhouetted against gum-leaf sky! See them tall and darin in the wind with white coats of sap-rotten on their bodies. See my mother cut one with an ax! She can swing the ax like a man, tall, sinewy, strong as the hills that she has lived her days among. Strong and solid as the hills that have given her birth.

Chip-chop. Chip-chop. Hac-hack. Hac-hack. One, two,

three, four. One, two, three, four. Hic-hack. Hick-hack. One, two, three, four. Hack. Hack. Hack. Hack. One, two, three, four. Hack. Hack. Hack. Hack.

"I'd like to know what is holdin that tree," says Mom. She has a big notch chipped out of one side, a notch pretty as any woodman can make with an ax, pretty as the notch the rabbit makes on the young sassafras sprout, or the muskrat makes on the elder bushes it cuts for a dam. The wind blows against the tall tree skeleton that is lodged up in the winter icy wind. I can see Mom look up at the tree. I had better get Fred back out of length of the tree. It may fall a different way than it is notched to fall. One lick. It goes lumberin to the earth. The snow flies up like dry powder when the skeleton kicks up its heels.

I bring Fred up to the tree. I unhitch the trace chains and loop them to singletree, clevis the single tree to the drag chain and hook the drag chain around the butt of the tree. I get on Fred's back so I can rein him through the brush with the bridle. I say "Get-up." Dirt flies, dirt mingled with snow and leaves from powerful feet as they grip the earth with the weight of his huge sorrel-colored body, his flaxen mane and tail. The brush snaps and the drag begins to move. It bends down the brush and the briars and makes a path to the wood yard. I unhitch the drag chain so that it will slip from under the log, undo one of the trace chains so that there will be length enough for him to snake the single tree and log chain back and they won't hit his heels. We follow the road back that the log of wood made. It is a dry seasoned-out black oak. It will make good stove wood and good firewood. I go back and Mom says: "Two more for you. I'm slayin these trees. I can keep you busy." Mom can cut the trees better than she can drive the horse through the brush. I can drive the horse better than I can cut the trees. I haul all afternoon to the wood yard off the tall hill back of the house. It is the hill we do not go beyond. It is the hill that only the sun goes beyond, the wind and the wild geese.

Wood is in our wood yard piled high. Mom and I fix us a rack by drivin two stakes X-wise across a chunk of wood.

We lift the ends of the light logs into the X and saw them off. Mom can use a saw better than I can. Snow fell on the logs in the wood yard last night and we sweep it off today with a broom-sage broom and saw up the logs. We have a tall pile of stove wood and firewood. "I'll teach you to work, son," says Mom. "If you don't get sick we can make it."

Pop has to lie in bed. His face is not like it was when he followed the plow and burned the brush and was always sayin: "Come along with them sprouts, Shan. I'll soon be up with you." And Pop would be right behind me, plowin. Color would be in his face. Strength would be in his arm.

He would talk to Mom and laugh and say, "This 'll bring the best corn that ever growed out of God's green earth this season." That was Pop. He was like a sprig of wild honeysuckle. Cut him down and he would grow again. But now he lies in bed and takes medicine. He does not talk. There is not the color of sunshine in his face. The dead oak-leaf color is all gone. His face is the color of gray ashes where the brush pile has been burned. Pop cannot tell Mom not to work. He does not know that she works. He cannot care.

"Our table is run down," says Mom. "We must have money. We are out of salt, sugar, coffee, lard. We are plum out of everythin. I used to help Pap make split-bottomed feed baskets. I can do it myself. You go to the hill and cut me the prettiest little white oaks that you can find. Bring them down to the barn. Cut the white oaks that don't have a limb on them. You can't rive splits through knot holes. They just won't rive."

I take a pole ax and go to the woods. I find plenty of white oaks that are the right size without limb on their pretty slender straight bodies. I cut through the frozen wood with my ax, then I drag them down to the barn. We build a fire in front of the barn and we heat the white oak till the sap runs from them. Mom splits them with an ax, then she rives them with a fro and knife. She whittles down the pretty white clean splits. Then she whittles out ribs and handles for the basket skeletons. She weaves the skeletons. Then, around the bones of the skeleton she works with the pretty splits.

We make three sizes of baskets. We make peck-sized feed

baskets, half-bushel split-bottomed feed baskets and bushel split-bottomed feed baskets. "You are to sell the baskets," says Mom, "and get in the timber and I'll make them. Sell the peck baskets for twenty-five cents, the half-bushel baskets for fifty cents and the bushel baskets for one dollar."

I go to Mart Pennix's house and I say, "You want to buy a basket, Mr. Pennix?"

"A basket! Let me see! What kind of baskets do you have?"

"Feed baskets."

"Let me look at them."

He takes a basket and looks it over, feels of its ribs, looks at its weave and he says: "That basket is built for service and not beauty. I'll take a half-bushel basket and one of your bushel baskets. I need the half-bushel basket to carry corn to the fattenin hogs in of a mornin and the bushel basket to nubbin the calves from." He takes the two baskets to the corn crib and I put the dollar and half-dollar in my pocket to take home to Mom. I go from one house to another. I sell the baskets. The farmers buy them. I do not tell who makes them. I just sell them.

I go to the mouth of the Hollow and get the Doctor once a week. I carry up water and split kindlin and feed the stock and help Mom with the baskets. I ride Fred to town and get the things Mom has to have. At night Mom, Barbara, Mary, Finn and I sit before the log fire and listen to the wind howl around the chimney and the eaves. The smoke often comes out onto the floor and Mom will say: "That is a sign of fallen weather. We are goin to have more snow. The rabbits has gnawed twenty-two inches high upon the sassafras sprouts and we are goin to have twenty-two inches of snow."

Mom will say; "There's not anything here I am afraid of but them graves out there under the plum tree. It is not the snow I am afraid of, not the work about the place, but I am afraid to pass them graves at night. Just to think them little children buried out there under that snow in our garden. When spring comes I'm going to fix them graves up. If them was children of mine buried out there and somebody lived in this house, I would want them to fix up them graves and keep them fixed up. Put flowers on them. I can't stand to see a grave go back to nothin but a forgotten place."

Pop doesn't seem to get much better. The flu has gone. The fever has gone. Pop is left weak and white. He lies in bed without any color in his face, a heap of skin and bones, and takes medicine. He never talks. He never laughs anymore like he used to laugh. I hate to see Pop in bed. I hate to think he'll have to rest in a bed of dirt like the two children rest in a bed of dirt under the plum trees in our garden. Doctor Frederick does not come once a week now. He comes once every two weeks. He says Pop's constitution is weak and that it might be spring before he is able to stir again if he is able then.

The snow holds to the earth. November has passed, December, January and it is February now. The snow is twenty-two inches deep in places. I take old Raggs and hunt the rabbits. They cannot run through the snow. I just walk up and pick them up. They are lean to the bone. I hate to kill them when they are so easy to catch. They are a beast of prey. They are good to eat and we need meat. I pick them up in the deep snow. I dig them from the water seaps. I track the possum to his den and dig him out. I catch the skunk and trap the mink. I put their hides on boards and let them cure. It will mean money to us and we need money. We owe the Doctor for comin to see Pop. We have to pay the Doctor. If Pop dies we will have to pay the Doctor and buy a coffin for Pop too. And then, you cannot fool me, there is goin to be another one at our place. I can tell now by lookin at Mom. She is not lean as she was in the early winter, nor does she swing an ax like she did then. We have supplied the country with baskets. We have eighty dollars saved to make a crop in the spring. That is a lot of money for us. We'll come again in the spring though hard luck has hit us now.

A woman comes to our door. She walks over the snow, a heavy woman with a big clean face and a wide laugh, her blue eyes dancin behind heavy glasses. She comes to the door and she says, "Does Mrs. Powderjay live here?"

Mom goes to the door. She says, "I am Mrs. Powderjay."

The woman says: "I'm working with an organization, Mrs.

Powderjay, that can be of some assistance to you if you are interested. I learn that you are in needy circumstances and I observe that you are."

"Well," says Mom, "I thank you for your kindness, Mrs. Hamptin, but we have made it this far and we can make it on. I brought these children into the world and married this man. When I'm not able to work and none of the rest is able to work, then you can take care of them with your organization."

Mrs. Hamptin gets up and leaves the room. I can see her wobble across the foot log, past the well box, turn the curve to the right of the point, past the apple trees that stand bare and black on the snow-clad wind-swept hill.

"We'll sink or we'll swim together. I married Mick Powderjay and I'll stand by him and my children till Death parts us. I'm not goin on the County either. What is a person that will go on the County? I'd work my finger nails off and toe nails off before I'd go on the County. That's what that woman was after. She was goin to put us on the County. She'll do it over my dead body. I'd plant corn till the middle of July before I'd go on the County."

Our chickens freeze to death and fall off the roost. We find one and two under the roost every mornin stiff as a frozen piece of dirt. We find dead birds around the fodder shocks. We find dead quails and dead rabbits. Life is dyin. The winter is so severe and dark. Clouds scud the sky. Big flakes of snow fly through the crispy wind. The sun comes out somedays and it is weak as a copper plate in the top of a chestnut tree. It doesn't have any more power than the copper plate for it doesn't begin to melt the snow. We have not seen the ground unless we dig down through the snow to see it since last November. Barbara says to me, "Shan, wonder how the land will look when the snow goes off the hills again and the trees get green and Pop gets out of bed and walks around like he used to?"

When our chickens and guineas freeze to death we carry them to the wood house and make tiny wooden coffins for them. We put them in the coffins and carry the coffins up on the bank above the kitchen and make graves for them. We shovel away the snow with a corn scoop and then we dig down through the frozen ground with a coal pick. We shovel out the frozen clumps of dirt, bit by bit, then we put the boxes in each little grave and Barbara preaches a sermon about them goin to Heaven and leavin the cruel fields of snow and the cold wind that knows nobody and cares for nobody. We put the frozen lumps of dirt back on the tiny poplar-plank coffins, crumble the dust in on them, then we scoop back the snow and leave the dead chickens and guineas in a world of silence beneath the snowdrifts. Often their craws at death have been flat.

We keep as many as forty rabbits hanging on a joist in the smoke house and let them freeze. The meat is better after they freeze. It will soon be too late for rabbits. It will soon be matin time and the heavy snow is still on the ground. We see the weak sun come up in the icy winter heavens and go down beyond the hills the way the wind blows. We do not go beyond these hills. We do not know if people die beyond like sheep, if the birds freeze to death and the chickens die and the crops fail. We do not know for we have not been beyond the barriers. We see the sun go beyond and we hear the wind.

"Pop is gettin better," Mom says. "I can see some color comin back to his face. When the sap revives in the spring tree, new blood will revive in him. He'll need a good tonic of wild-cherry bark, may apple, slipper-elm, yellow root and sassafras boiled together. That will be good for his constitution. Wait till spring comes back and he'll come out of that bed." Mom is given Pop boneset tea now. She goes down beside the creek and finds the old boneset stems. I dig down and get the roots from the frozen earth. "When new life comes back to the turtles, the terrapins and the snakes, and sap goes through trees anew, then blood will flow through your father's veins and he'll come out of that bed." Pop drinks the tea every day.

February is goin day by day beyond the barriers of hills with the settin sun and the wind that blows that way. Winter has been so long this year. We have not seen the ground. Winter is dark, though the sun comes up durin the day and the moon and stars gleam down on a world of snow at night. The sky reddens at sunset like streaks of ox blood fringin out from a ball of fire where the sun was and each spangle jinglin with the green top of a mountain pine silhouetted against the sky where the high hills shoulder to the sky.

Pop says: "Spring will soon be here. I would love to be out now cuttin wood and puttin it in ricks and clearin ground. This is the time to start clearin ground, now while the snow is still on. It is a good time to work. My ribs and hips are bout to cut through the slats of this old bed. I have been like a cold-blooded black snake waitin for the spring. I have been here the winter long in a dream. I am feelin better now. I want to eat." And Pop asks about this hen and that hen, if they have frozen to death and how we have got along with the wood the winter long.

Mom says, "Wait a minute, Mick Powderjay," and she goes into the kitchen. Where the flue goes up in the kitchen loft, Mom lifts up a board and brings her pocketbook. She comes up to the bed. She takes out of the pocketbook, one by one, eighty one-dollar bills. Pop's eyes get as big as saucers. "Where did you get all that money?" he says.

"Never mind that, Mick," says Mom, "but we made it honest. Me and that boy right in there." And Mom puts it back in the pocketbook and this time she saunters off toward the smoke house like a hen huntin a nest. Mom will keep the money long as she can. She knows what is goin to happen to her. She did not know what was goin to happen to Pop. I can see Mom is not as active as she was and she is not shy before me anymore. She talks often to Mary and Barbara.

Mom goes to the barn with me. While I feed the horse she milks Gypsy. Gypsy won't let a man milk her. She follows Mom all over the barn lot. Fred follows me. I pat his nose. Gypsy is only givin a quart of milk at a milkin. She will be fresh in April, but she is goin dry too soon. We do not have enough feed to feed Gypsy all she wants. Our feed is scarce. We are buyin sixty shocks of fodder from Broughtons for ten cents a shock. I will haul it to the barn over the snow on a fodder sled with old Fred. That will take six of our dollars.

The sun is up today. Water drips from the eaves of the

house. Icicles melt into water and drip-drip from nine in the mornin till three in the evenin. White clouds scud the sky. Winter has started breakin up. Warm thaw winds blow through the bare Kentucky trees. One can feel them, warm soft winds, winds that remind one of rain. There will be rain and freeze and thaw and rain and freeze again. But spring is comin.

"Mom," I say, "are we goin to rent this place again and farm next year like we did last year?"

Mom says: "We are goin to rent this place again if we can rent it and we don't find a place that is better. We failed last year on the bottoms. Craw-dads et up the corn. This year ought to be a dry season and the bottom ground hit and we'd raise a couple of cribs of corn. We'll put in some hill land and not take any chances on a season. I must see Mr. Woodrow before very much longer and have him draw up a artikle. We want it in paper with strangers so they won't be no trouble if me or your Pop would drop off."

Little Finn and Mary went upon the hillside today. It has been Finn's first trip out of the house winter-long. Mary was upon the hill when we buried the chickens and the guineas in the snow. The snow is melted off under the pine tree up above the kitchen. Barbara, Mom and I go up under the pine tree and we put our feet on the ground. Here the pine needles feel soft from the weight of twenty-two inches of snow. The long winter is breakin. There is a smell of dampness under the pine tree. It is a cold dampness. Finn jumps up and down and he says, "Goody, goody, goody, ground–ground–ground."

Today trains of crows have flown back among the bare trees searchin for old corn rows and for places to build. They coupled off and searched among the tall trees on the south hill sides.

The earth looks today like a spotted hound dog's back. There is only clumps of snow here and there and the swollen streams run blue spring water. Spring has broken. Birds have come, the sparrows to the martin boxes and the wrens to the rag sack and tin cans in the smoke house. Robins, lapwings and jays have come back. It is the time to look over the land for next year's plantin. Crows fly over carryin sticks and mud. Pop is out of the bed. He walks across the floor, thin as a sack of bones, white as the petal of a needle-and-thread in June. "I am like a old black snake comin to life," says Pop, "I thought the old Master was goin to call me, but He has left me for another summer, another spring."

Mary comes in today and she carries a sprig of greenbrier leaf. "The first green of spring," says Mary. It is the first green of spring that I have seen.

"Poke green ought to be a-comin out," says Mom. "I'll have to get out and get us a mess of greens around the edges of the rich clearing." I see the windflowers comin out to bloom. It is March. The land smells clean and sweet. The land is good to smell.

Mom sends me to the store. I bring back seed potatoes. I get feed for the cow and the chickens and the horse. I get food for the family. I get what Mom tells me to get. Mom is goin to have a baby. I know it. I don't know what we will do without Mom. I don't think Mary knows about Mom. Barbara knows though about Mom. Barbara is old enough to know. We can see Mom walk out by herself. She will stand and watch a bird buildin a nest. She will listen to the redbird sing from a bare poplar twig.

Weeds are comin back to the south hill slopes. Once again the sheep bells tingle on the high hills. The air is cool. The percoon is in bloom and the blue violets bloom by the old stumps and stacks of rocks in the pasture field. Butterflies flit to the water hole for the cows. Spring is here. I know the spring is here. It is middle of March and I start to clear two acres of hill land to put in corn. I must cut the briars and sprouts and windrow them up the hill so they'll be easy to burn when time comes for spring burnin.

Our chickens pick the green pepper weeds that grow by the barn. Our hound dogs go out and run the foxes by themselves and tree the possums and hole the rabbits. Pop says: "Don't hiss them dogs on a rabbit this time of year. The rabbit might be a old she about to have youngins. Be mighty careful. If it hadn't been for me, old Fleet would a-catched a old she rabbit up there in the old apple orchard yesterday. She holed it in a little piece of log that she could a tore open in a few minutes longer with her mouth. The log saved the rabbit till I got old Fleet away."

Today the grass is green, flutterin in the wind. Mom takes a garden hoe out under the plum tree that is beginnin to put out green buds. I can see her rake the graves with a hoe and fix little pieces of broken dishes and blue vases on the graves. Mom smokes her pipe. I can see the blue smoke in the blue March wind. It goes in a stream upward from her long-stemmed clay pipe. She chop-chops with the hoe and works around the headboards. She pulls away the dead grass. She cleans the stubble from the sprigs of fresh springin flowers. Mom is not supposed to work now.

When I go out to clear ground after the work is done around the barn, I can see Mom comin down the path smokin her pipe. She comes to the clearin and she says: "If I could only be in here with you things would be different. It will be different when your Pop gets well enough to work again. I am makin him drink that bitter yarb medicine. It will do him good. He is feelin better now. He is walkin upon the hill. But his strength ain't come to him yet like it will come to him. You have been a good boy to work this winter and you ain't been no place but to town and right back. I am goin to make you some shirts and some pants and buy you a better pair of shoes and start you and Barbara and Mary to Sunday school next Sunday. You are growin up like heathens back here in this land that God has about forgot."

And Mom will pick up a brush I cut down with an ax and pile it on the windrow. She will pick up another and another and she will say: "I wish I could be out here with you. I love the spring. I love to dig my hands into the dirt, just to think of the days I have worked with your Pop—right by his side all day long and loved it."

It will not be much longer until Mom will have to quit work. She will have to go to the house for a while. I know how she loves the dirt, the wind, the sun. She loves the out-of-doors. She does not care for the house and she cares less to lie in bed. But Mom loves the trees, the briars, the wind, the grass, the wild flowers and the stars. I have seen Mom saunter off to the woods and watch the lizard catch flies from the side of an oak tree. I have seen her find a birds' nest and would not touch the birds with her hands. She said the ants would eat them if you did. I have seen her sit out on the hills among wild roses and watch the white clouds in the June sky drift beyond the barrier of dark green hills that enclosed the Hollow like an iron rim that shouldered to the heavens. I know Mom does not like to lie in bed.

Our chickens cackle under the apple trees and wallow in the dust under the corn crib. We have a pretty flock of hens left after the cold dark winter. They lay eggs and we sell the eggs and buy coffee and sugar. "Did you know our chickens has got the limber neck?" says Mom, and she carries a young hen from the barn whose neck goes first one way and then the other. "These chickens is gettin to somethin, maybe maggots. Somethin them old hounds has carried in." Mom gets some turpentine and puts it in meal dough, spices it with red pepper. She fixes it in a crock.

"Catch all the chickens and put them in the cow shed and let's dope them and save all we can," says Mom. "It's maggots in their craws. That hen died. I cut her open to see what was wrong. Maggots was workin out of her craw. Spring is here and these hens are after worms in the early spring. Dogs has carried somethin in here. I smell it. Maybe it is that instead of the cold damp smell of winter leaves that comes in the early spring when buds begin to swell and life starts all over in the plants again."

I catch the hens and put them in the corn crib. Mom goes to the crib and I hold them while Mom puts dough down their throats. Pop hobbles to the corn crib. "That's bad luck to have to lose all them pretty chickens this time a year when a body needs them most. You can't save them when they once get maggots."

"We can save part of them," says Mom, "and if we had got to them in time we could have saved them all. I tried the turpentine on the maggot I cut out of the hen's craw and the maggot didn't last five seconds. It's gettin the turpentine in their craws in time. Hurry it up and hand me the chickens."

I hand them fast to Mom and I hold their bills open. Mom puts gobs of turpentined and peppered dough down their necks. The hens shake their bills, crane their necks and walk off when I throw them back out the crib door. Mom says: "Here is one it's too late to fool with. She is nearly dead. She is sufferin. She won't last much longer." She puts them in a group on the crib floor. They can't lift their heads. Their necks are limber. They sit there and quak, quak.

"Now," says Mom, "put these sufferin chickens out'n their misery. Put them in a coffee-sack and carry them up there in the Hollow and take a ax and cut their heads off. That is quicker death than to let them die here the way they are. Don't be long about it."

I take the hens, one by one, put them in the coffee-sack. I take my pole ax. It is all I can do to carry the hens at two loads. They are not heavy. They are not fat. I take them upon this hill at this pine tree. I get a block of wood and I take them out one at a time. They cannot get away. I put their limber necks across the block and cut off the heads. I dig a big hole under the pine tree and throw in all their bodies and their heads and then I shovel in the yellow dirt. I pile rocks over the hole.

As I go back to the house I smell somethin that Mom says she has smelled. It is not the sour damp winter leaves throwin off scent to the spring wind. I follow the way the scent comes. I see the green flies swarm from the grass in the yellow spring sun. Here it is. It is an old horse knee one of the hounds has carried in. The maggots are a-workin alive on it. I gather broom sage and pile over writhin yellow-nosed worms. I strike a match and they shrivel up and squirm before the quick thin heat, more than leaves do when they burn in midsummer heat. I will not tell Mom. She will want me to get rid of a good possum hound. Mom has saved over half of the chickens with her remedy of turpentine and red pepper.

I get the potato patch plowed down in the rich dirt by the

barn. This week is the time to plant the potatoes, for it is in the light of the moon. They will grow big and at the top of the ground Pop says, and will be easy to dig. The signs are in the skies. We must plant them to get a good yield of Irish potatoes.

Pop slices the potatoes to drop into the hills. I furrow the ground with long deep straight marks. Barbara covers the potato eyes with a hoe and Mom drops them. It is late March, the sun is yellow in the blue spring sky. It is the time to work. It is the time to plant potatoes. Mom says, "I have to go to the house, Mick."

Pop says, "Son, jump on that horse as quick as you can and get a Doctor. Don't ask no questions, but go. Get Doctor Frederick if you can."

I unhitch Fred from the plow, throw off the harness in the potato patch and without a saddle I stride the mountain trail the way I went after the Doctor for Pop on the cold winter night. Up the Hollow, around the slope, past the graveyard where the saw briars and the sprouts are greenin now and will soon hide the tombstones. I go over the hill, around the ridge and down to the town in full gallop except for the uphills. "Dr. Frederick, get out home soon as you can. Mom is sick. Maybe you know what is the matter with her," I say to him.

He jumps in his car. When I get home he is there. Mom has a little boy. Another brother for me and Finn. He is so small. He was born before the Doctor got there. He does not weigh two pounds. Mom looks at him and laughs and we gather around the bed to look at him. Finn says to Doctor Frederick, "You got any more babies in that pill bag?" Doctor Frederick laughs.

Mom says: "The dresses that I made up there on the hill for him are all too big. He's the least baby I ever saw. I'll have to pin him to a pillow. I'll lose him in the bed." I remember seein Mom sit out in the woods makin little dresses and when I come around she put the work up. Now, I understand. "I hate to hear him cry," says Mary, "he goes like a mouse a-squeakin. Let me carry him, Mom. Let me take him out to our playhouse under the walnut tree. He ain't big as my baby I got Barbara made for me."

"I'll keep him here," says Mom, "he's so tiny. Little ears and little tiny fingers. A little tiny cry. A little tiny mouth. But ain't he pretty?"

We want to play with the baby. "The Doctor didn't bring Mom that baby," says Mary. "I heard him cryin before the Doctor come. Mom got that baby some place else."

Barbara is tall, slender, with two pretty rows of white teeth, eyes blue as the March sky, with hair the color of dyin wheat straws. She cooks for us now. She burns the bread. She gets our dinner today. Mom says, "Shan, you go out in the smoke house and look in the coffee-sack of rags where the wren builds and lift up the rag to the left of the nest and get my pocketbook."

I go out and get the pocketbook. It is just where she says it is. I hand it to her. "How much do I owe you, Doctor?"

"Ten dollars for the trip," he says.

She counts him out ten one-dollar bills. The Doctor put them in his pocket. "We'll get you that other bill soon as we get on our feet a little."

I go to the field and clear the ground. Pop comes 'n helps me a little. I can see that Pop's color is comin back. He eats more now. He feels better. Mom is doctorin him now. He is takin Mom's yarb medicine. I cut a sprout down. Pop throws it on the windrow. I cut a swath of briars with the scythe. Pop forks them on the windrow. The sun is above us. The wind blows by us. We hear the wind. We see the sun. It is spring. We love to work in the fields. But I do miss Mom. She does not come these days and smoke her pipe and say: "I wish I could be out here. We'd do things."

Three days and Mom sits up in the bed and rips up the baby's dresses, cuts them down and makes them to fit. Barbara can't make a dress. She can make a paper doll dress for Mary's rag doll. She can't make a dress for my tiny brother. He is not big as a doll. Mom keeps sayin: "I'm tired of this bed. I'm comin out of here. I can't stand it any longer." In four days Mom is up. She is workin in the house.

"You can't get out of bed," says Pop, "you are out of bed too soon. You should stay in bed ten days and you ain't been in bed but four days."

Mom does not answer Pop. Mom will do the way she pleases. She pleases not to lie in bed. She walks out in the garden now and makes a lettuce bed and plants some early potatoes for summer use. Mom sets the hens. She marks the eggs with bluin. She plants flowers in the yard. She is up and goin while Mitchell sleeps.

April is here. Sun is pretty in the sky. Green is back to the hills. Gypsy picks the tender sprigs in the pasture. Birds sing and the hens' combs are red. They cackle in the woods. The crows fly over. They caw and caw. They carry worms to their young hidden back on the steep slope in the dense cloud of pine fingers that wash the wind on the mountain side. Pop is behind the plow again. His face is gettin red like a rooster's comb. I am clearin the hill land to be sure of good croppin this year.

Mr. Woodrow rides his bony mare up where we are workin and he says: "You sure are gettin along well to have all the trouble you have had. Is there anything I can do for you?"

Pop says, "Not now, Mr. Woodrow."

"Well, we didn't put it in the artikle we drawed up, but I'll give Shan several days work along since he's got big enough to plow. I'll give him twenty-five cents a day and you and your horse a dollar and a quarter. Twenty-five cents for the horse and a dollar for you."

"Funny," says Pop after Mr. Woodrow leaves, "that a horse gets less than a man just because he is a brute and he does so much more than a man."

I get a day now and then when I have time. I work for Mr. Woodrow. We work from sunrise in the mornin to sunset. I take the quarter home to Mom. Pop works the same way and so does poor Fred. He comes in at night a horse of a different color. His sorrel hair is the color of a wet blue cloth, slobbers hang from his lower dropped lip and there is a white thick lather between his hind legs.

"Mitchell don't grow a bit," says Mom; "if he grows I can't tell it. He ain't strong like my other babies. I am afraid. Somehow, I fear. I dreamed last night that Mitchell played with a lot of babies up there on the hill under that oak tree. I couldn't climb the hill to get him. I had to stay at the foot of the hill to watch him."

We plant the corn in the fields Pop has plowed. I'll soon have the two acres of hill land cleared. We'll burn this off and not plow it. We'll just double-furrow the weedless soft new ground after the fire runs over it and plant it. We'll plant beans in with each hill of corn and drop a few pumpkin seeds in the soft loamy places and around the old stumps.

Pop is plantin corn. I am ready to fire the new ground. April the nineteenth here and the new ground not ready to plant. I see Mom comin down the path to the clearin. She is wringin her hands and cryin. I can hear her. Pop stops the horse, "What in the world is the matter?"

"Mitchell is dead. I can't go back into that house. Mitchell is dead."

Pop leaves Fred hitched to the plow. I run off the hill. We go to the house.

"I found him dead," says Mom, "on the sheet. He's never been like my other children when they was babies. He's dead! He's dead! I can never stand to go back in that house. He died in that house."

"You must take it easy," says Pop; "that's got to come some time or the other. And it has come to him before he knows the world like you and me knows it. He is better off than we are."

The Finneys and the Martins come to sit up with us. Our work stops. We go to town and buy a tiny coffin, one so small a person could carry it. "He must be put away nice," says Mom, "not in a home-made coffin, but in one bought with pretty linin. We can pay for it. He must be dressed in a pretty robe."

Mom does not sleep while the coffin is in the house with Mitchell in it. She goes and looks at him and the tears fall. "The dark winter behind," Mom says, "now it is the spring and death in the spring when the world has changed so." Mom drinks coffee, black coffee without cream or sugar. She slips out and saunters beside of the creek that flows swollen and blue from recent spring rains. She will smoke her pipe. She will not smoke in the house in front of the Finneys and the Martins.

"He must be buried on land that Pap owns," says Mom, "he's the only blood kin I got that owns any land. I don't want him to sleep like these little children out here in this garden. Pap's land is same as my land. We'll haul Mitchell there. He'll not be on a stranger's land. He cannot be buried there."

It is tomorrow. Fred hitched to Mr. Woodrow's spring wagon leads the way through the April mud. It is April 21st. I remember. Mom and Pop ride side by side through the drizzlin April rain. They ride in the buggy next to the spring wagon bearin a little box. We go to Grandpa's place five miles away. It is noon and we are there. The grave is ready. It is a little grave with heaped-up yellow dirt under a pine tree. Grandpa shows us the way upon the hill.

There is a little crowd here. Mitchell does not know about the world. He rests in the dirt of the world. We leave him on the hill, a part of us, my father, mother, my brother and my sisters. We leave him a part of the Kentucky earth. It is strange to leave one on a hill to sleep so long, one that you have seen breathe and move tiny fingers and blink an eye and cry like a little squeakin mouse.

The horses race back over the April roads. We are tryin to beat another rain. The skies have been clouded all day. "See the sun," says Mom to Pop as they ride back together, "first time today that I have seen the sun."

UNCLE JEFF

PA AND Finn and me are on our way to see Uncle Jeff. Uncle Jeff is in a railroad hospital at Ferton, West Virginia, and he is likely to kick the bucket. Don't know though, Pa said Uncle Jeff was tough as an old rooster. But there must be somethin wrong. He sent for Pa. And Pa takes us along, he says, to help him get about in the city and to find the hospital. Pa hates the town, for he can't read and he gets mixed up in signs. Pa never knows where he is goin unless he asks someone and he says he hates to be askin everybody he meets where this is and that is. So Pa up-and-takes us boys. And we are glad to go with him.

"I told Brother Jeff," says Pa, "to quit that damn railroad when they offered him the little pension that time. That would have been better'n stickin' it out for a few dollars on the month and endin up in a hospital among strangers where a body don't know narry a soul."

"What is the matter with Uncle Jeff, Pa," I said, "that he is about to die?"

"He is a broke-down man," said Pa with tears in his eyes. "He is like I am. Look at me—I am a broke-down man. If you follow workin on a section long as your Uncle Jeff, then you would have one foot in the grave and the other ready to slide in too. He's been on that Chatworth section for thirty-three years. Could have been a boss if he had had the education. Can't read. Just like I am. Now you boys see that it pays to take education. I couldn't take it for there was none offered here in these Kentucky hills when I was a boy."

"Wasn't Uncle Jeff in a wreck one foggy mornin on a motor car?" asked Brother Finn.

"Yes," said Pa, "Brother Jeff and eighteen more men were hit by a Big Sandy train. The car was in the fog and the train was in it too and they didn't see each other. Your Uncle Jeff leaped like a frog or he would a been where some of the others are today. Part of the motor car and some of the men flew through the air and lit on them like a bird. Brother Jeff was knocked cold as a icicle. When he woke up they had him in the railroad hospital in Ferton where we are goin now. Brother Jeff has not been well since. He is not able to work. He is like a horse too old to plow but has to pull the plow just the same. I am a horse too broke-down to pull the plow, but I have to pull it just the same."

"We are in Ferton now," says Brother Finn, "we are in West Virginia."

And Pa says: "Yes, West Virginia, look how these damn big-headed people hold their heads up above us. It is not like back over there in Kentucky. I went to work in the mines up in Cattle Branch, West Virginia, when I was sixteen years old and the place where I boarded had so many bedbugs I had to leave. I'd like to tell these people about the bedbugs they got in this State—more than any State in the Union."

Pa asks Finn to read the signs. Brother Finn is younger than I am, but he can read. He has been to school and he can cipher some and read pretty well. He is not like Pa.

But here we go. People do look at us and Pa gets hot behind his collar. Pa is not as big as we are. He walks between us with a big gray overcoat on that strikes him around the ankles. I found the overcoat in an old house and gave it to him. I believe he sorty thinks I stole it. Finn is almost a head above the crowd and my old blue overcoat just strikes him about five inches above the knees. But Finn looked right good in it. I have a new overcoat and I look better than Pa or Brother Finn. Pa's hair is out a little long and it rolls up a little at the edge of his thick felt black cap. I don't have on a hat. Finn has on a gray felt hat. And we walk up the street toward the hospital.

Pa says: "Ferton is a big town. Look at these big houses that cover a square."

Pa likes to see flashing signs. He asks Finn to read them for him. Finn reads the signs for Pa since Finn reads better than I do.

Then Pa says: "It took a lot of money to build that house. It took piles of money—a flour barrel of money. I'd like to see all the money it took in one pile. I'd like to be in it with a coal scoop for five minutes and I'd have all I could shovel. I'd never go back out on that section. Boys, look at these houses, won't you. Damned if they ain't a plum sight."

We do not ride a street car to the hospital. We walk to it to save the money. We will need the money gettin back home and Finn and me have planned somethin for Pa. We are goin to surprise Pa. He has never seen a picture show and we intend to take him to one after we leave the hospital. We are now in sight of the hospital.

Pa says: "Here is the place they had Brother Jeff before. Walk right in, boys—I've been here at this place before."

And we walk in behind Pa. He walks up to a desk where a woman in a white dress is writin somethin on a piece of paper.

Pa says, "Jeff Powderjay in this hospital?"

"Jeff Powderjay? Yes, he is here."

"I want to see him," says Pa.

"He is too bad to let anyone see him," says the woman and she looks mean out of a pair of nose-glasses.

"Beats all," says Pa. "A man comes forty miles and can't see his dyin brother."

"Well, you can't see him," says the woman, "and that's that."

"Well, by God I will see him," says Pa, "or they'll be more patients in this hospital than you already got."

I saw Pa was gettin hot behind the collar and so I whispered to Finn: "Get a hold of Pa before he gets us all into it. You can do more with him than I can."

Finn takes Pa by the arm and says, "Come on, Pa, and let's see the hospital doctor. He'll let us see Uncle Jeff."

Down the corridor we take Pa until we come to a sign that says DOCTOR.

"Here," says Finn. "Wait a minute." And Finn finds him.

"You want to see Jeff Powderjay?" says the doctor. "It is good that you have come to see him. None of his kin have come to see him and he will not get back to Kentucky alive, I am afraid."

"Can we see him?" asks Pa.

"Yes," says the doctor and he leads the way with a bunch of keys in his little soft hand.

"Look at that hand, won't you," says Pa. "What if he worked like I have to, tampin ties and laying tee rails. Makin sod lines and makin right-of-way. He wouldn't have hands like that. Look," and Pa shows us his hands–hands that we have seen and felt so many times before.

"Here we are," says the doctor. "You'll find Jeff Powderjay right in that room." He opens the door and walks away.

Pa goes in first. "Hello, Jeff," he says, "do you know me?"

"Know you?" says Uncle Jeff. "Know you? What do you think I am? I'd know you in hell, Mick. You are boy number eleven, and I am number ten. Ain't that right?"

"Yes," says Pa. "And we are supposed to have the same Mama and Pappie–and I believe we have. Pa was a scoundrel, but Mama was a decent woman."

"Yes," says Uncle Jeff. "And you come up to see me kick the bucket."

"I come to see you," says Pa.

"Well, I am goin to kick the damn bucket this time," says Uncle Jeff.

Finn doesn't say a word. Pa and Uncle Jeff are doin all the talkin. But Uncle Jeff spies Finn.

"Come over here, you little son-of-a-gun," he says. "You look for all the world like your Pap. Come over here and say good-by and old-Satan-bless-you-Uncle Jeff. And you," pointin to me, "come over here, you big son-of-a-gun and say good-by and Satan-bless-you to your Uncle Jeff."

I see it is gettin under Pa's skin. Pa is twistin and squirmin in his chair. Pa doesn't do that unless somethin is gougin at his heart.

Pa says, "Take it easy, Jeff."

And Uncle Jeff says: "Take it easy, hell. It is that big-tailed thing they got waitin on me. She is tryin to kill me too soon. She knows I ain't goin to get out of this hole this time. I got out once before–and I prayed to God to get out. Now I am cussin and prayin for the Devil to get me."

"The Devil?" says Pa.

"Yes, the Devil," says Uncle Jeff. "I want to go somewhere and the Lord won't have me. I've been prayin to die ever since I got broke down in that wreck and God won't take me. I guess the Devil will. I want to go some place."

I wish that Uncle Jeff would let loose of my hand. He is holdin to my hand and talkin to Pa. His hand is soft and warm and wrinkled like a thawed-out black snake. His lips have fallen down at the corners, beard is over his face—a white and red-sandy beard. His eyes are the color of faded slate.

"Give me a chew of red-horse," says Uncle Jeff. "A damn liar, Mick. Doctor says no—but give me a chew of red-horse, and I'll give you a cup of water in hell."

Tears come to Pa's eyes and he says to Finn, "I'll give him a chew even if that doctor throws me out of this hospital."

"That is what I want—it tastes sweet," says Uncle Jeff. "You know I am glad that I have chewed tobacco. It has been enjoyment to me all my life. It is that damned big-tailed nurse. She is tryin to kill me. I want to go back over on the Big Sandy and die there. I want to go back home to die, back where Pap and Ma died. I am goin back too."

"Now lay in the bed, Jeff—you can't get up," Pa is coaxing Uncle Jeff. "Lay still and you'll be able to get home by next week."

"Goddamn you, Mick, don't sit up there and lie to me like that. You ain't foolin nobody, not even yourself. You know more than that, surely. The Devil, the Lord and the ground are goin to get me—maybe one, maybe all three. I hate to leave my little children by my second wife—but goddamn her she is a bitch and I know it, a bitch. That bachelor can run her all he damn pleases. He has run her and I know it—the-son-of-a-bitch."

And I say to my brother Finn while Pa and Uncle Jeff are talkin, "I remember Uncle Jeff before he married his second wife. He was a handsome man then. He was a young man in the bloom of life. He married Aunt Tinnie, as pretty a woman as ever the Kentucky sun shone on. They had three children by that marriage, Daisy, Silva and Jewel. Then Aunt Tinnie died and lost her fourth baby with her dead body, you understand. Uncle Jeff worked on the section and raised three girls until they married and had homes of their own. He always said he would never bring a stepmother in over his 'three little dears.' He had a time hirin a girl to take care of them and buyin food for them on a section man's wages, but he did. He raised three fine girls too. Then they left him in the old house alone. So he goes and marries this last wife. An old man and a young woman. Results. You see, you know."

"I remember Uncle Jeff givin me candy and showin me how to fight bitin dogs," says Finn. "That was when he used to come and visit us livin on the Collins' place."

And now Pa and Uncle Jeff are talkin louder than ever.

"We had the measles together, Mick," says Uncle Jeff, "and they had us down in the left-hand corner of that big room instead of the back room, I remember. And you looked through a crack in the wall and saw the only turkey Ma had, and you said, 'How about eatin that turkey, Jeff?' And I said, 'W'y that is a go, all you'll have to do is say the word to Ma.' And you said the word to Ma. She killed that turkey for us. I'll never forget it. You got anything you wanted because you was her baby—you was child number eleven."

"That is right," says Pa. "After Ma died the girls found some cake she had put away for me. I was her baby."

"The nurse is comin," says Finn.

"Keep that goddamn big-tailed thing out of this room," says Uncle Jeff. "Keep her out, Mick."

"Time to take your medicine. Time the visitors should leave, too," says the nurse.

"Time for you to get out of here and stay out of here," says Uncle Jeff.

"He is out of his head," says Pa.

"You are a goddamn liar, Mick, and you know you are," says Uncle Jeff. "I am just not goin to get out of here alive and I want to get out of here alive and die back over on Big Sandy. And I don't like a goddamn gown to sleep in. Look at this—looks like a mother-hubbard on me. And I don't want that damn medicine."

"I'll call the doctor then," says the nurse. "You must take your medicine."

"I've done that all my life," says Uncle Jeff. "I've took my medicine—thirty-three years of it on a section and the last part of it with a crooked woman. I've had all the damn medicine I want. I'd sooner be in hell. It doesn't matter a damn to me. I ain't been such a mean man. I'm not such a good one. I've always had trouble gettin right and wrong straightened out."

"You are goin to take your medicine?" asks the nurse.

"No, by God."

"Die then."

"That's what I am goin to do and you are goin to do."

But the doctor comes in. "My good man, take your medicine," he says.

And Uncle Jeff says, "Don't ever send that damn woman back in here. She don't know what it is all about."

The doctor laughs and says, "No, she doesn't know what it is all about."

"Now, Mick," says Uncle Jeff, "you didn't bring the scissors back you borrowed that time—you promised to bring them back Saturday."

"Out of his head," says Pa—"out of his head sure as God made little green apples."

"But, Mick, you can give me them scissors in hell. I'm not out of my head. You're goin home, I see. We will not meet here again—we'll meet in hell. Bring them scissors."

Pa holds his shriveled snake-like hand and wipes the tears with his other hand.

"Good-by, Uncle Jeff," I say.

"Good-by, Uncle Jeff," says Finn.

"You boys don't work on no goddamn railroad," says Uncle Jeff.

We walk out holdin Pa. He is a little chicken-hearted and he says: "Brother Jeff is a goner. That work has got him. The time he got hurt they offered him five hundred dollars for compromise and if they paid him that he didn't get to keep his job. So he took the job. Look at him now. He is a dead man. He had thirty-three years of it. I have had nineteen. Look at me—a wreck. I never was stout as Jeff. Jeff was the best man among us boys."

We go down the Ferton street holding to Pa. Pa is nervous. I have never seen him this nervous before.

"Is is three hours before we can get a bus out of here, Pa," I say, "what do you say we see a show?"

"I never saw one of them things and I don't want to see one," says Pa.

"We got to spend some time some place."

"Well, just as you say, then," says Pa. "Not as I care, but looks to me like we are goin to be late about gettin back home and doin up the work. Cows to milk, hogs to feed, mules to put in the barn, and your Ma can't do all that work. It is killin her.

"Fine buildin," says Pa, "wish I owned it, but it took money to build a show house like this. Even to velvet rugs for the feet."

Pa sits between us in the theater. He likes the news flashes. "Funny how they do that," he says. "I'll have one on the boys Monday mornin. They won't believe me when I tell them about this."

And the picture shows a man's wife in love with another man. They slip to a hotel. "Just like Jeff's wife exactly," says Pa to Finn. "That woman ought to have her neck wrung off, doin like that."

"Be quiet, Pa," says Finn. "You are in the theater and people will hear what you say."

"I don't care if they do," says Pa. "A woman like that ought to be shot. She is just like Brother Jeff's wife, only she slips to a hotel and Jeff's wife slips to the brush back up there on Big Sandy."

When we start to leave the theater Pa says: "The power of man is mighty to do a thing like that. But the Bible says man will grow weaker and wiser, and damned if I don't believe it. The boys won't believe me when I tell them all of this."

And we go out where the bright lights in Ferton are flickerin. We catch the bus back to Kentucky.

Pa says: "Work not done up or anythin. Here it is dark. We got about thirty more miles to go and walk four miles after we leave the main road."

Over the silent, cold earth and back home. The stars shine in the heavens. But we need a lantern to see how to throw the fodder over to the cows. We feed the cows and the mules, slop the hogs and get in the wood.

"Jeff and me used to do this at home," says Pa, "but we'll never do it anymore together. I'll be the next one—I'll be the next to go. If you boys ever work on a section I'll hant you from the grave. Get the least wages in the world and do the hardest work. The men that set up in the engines and ride get five times much as I get. I've worked like a dog and will come down to the end unless you boys take me and your Ma in—come down to the poorhouse. Goddamn a poorhouse to hell! Our section is not far from the poorhouse and they got bastard babies over there, people crazy as hell and pregnant mothers. Got the damnest mixup over there you ever saw. What if I would have to go there in the end and take your Ma. Wouldn't that be awful? I couldn't stand to take her there the way she has worked and bore my children. This is a hard world after all. Think of it, so much to have and so hard to get. Yet, there is plenty—plenty, but not for me nor my kind. I can't read. I ain't been no place. I never had a chance to go to school. Now I have to take what I can get. Poorhouse may be all I'm able to get."

It is the next afternoon. The rain is fallin and low black clouds, it seems, just scud above the leafless timber. The wind whips through the saw briars. The cows, standin humped up in the barn lot, chew on the ends of old cornstalks. The mules run alongside the fence and bite each other's necks and snicker.

"Sign of fallen weather," says Pa, "when mules play—and sign of a death when two mules ride each other.

"Just as I expected," says Pa, when Finn reads the telegram saying that Brother Jeff is dead.

"Gettin up in the paper to get a telegram," says Finn.

"Because of that telegram," says Pa, "somebody will have to go to the poorhouse or the orphans' home. That fellow that runs Jeff's wife might take her now, but he won't take the children. They'll have to give them away or send them to the orphans' home. Jeff dies a pauper after thirty-three years of hard work. I can't keep his children. I can't take them. I'll do well to raise what I got."

We see Pa gettin ready. He puts on his old blue suit—his Sunday suit he bought from Lark Jenkins second-handed. He puts on one of Finn's shirts and black bow tie. He takes a black hat out of the trunk and brushes it up a little. He wears it. Ma say he looks real nice. Pa walks out into the rain with all his good clothes on. He is goin to catch Number 8.

Pa has a pass and he can ride right up on Big Sandy. That is one thing they do. They haul him free. But he has to ride in one of the poor coaches—one for the poor people. But Pa is poor and he doesn't mind. He wouldn't know how to act with them Big Bugs on that train in a coach where a man is hired to wipe your shoes off as you leave the coach.

We see Pa go. We see him cross the pasture, go between the wires of a barb-wire fence, then to the ridge road. We see him leavin in the rain.

We do not want to go. We understand that Pa is a little nervous. Uncle Jeff's house is a little two-room shack and part of us would have to sleep in a bed made down on the floor unless some of the neighbors would invite us to stay with them. Pa's other brother, Uncle Joe, used to invite us, but Uncle Joe and Uncle Jeff had trouble about their wives fightin and they have not spoken to each other since last June. Uncle Joe's wife called Uncle Jeff's wife a slut. Finn and I don't go. We leave it up to Pa.

Finn and I, we understand. We were up to Uncle Jeff's last Decoration Day. Pa, Uncle Joe, Uncle Jeff, Finn and me all went to hunt Grandma's grave. We went up the hollow back of Uncle Jeff's house and through heavy timber where the squirrels played right before our eyes. There was a white fuzz from the leaves of such dense foliage that it choked us to breathe it.

"Here," said Uncle Joe, "I used to carry Micky—you and Jeff back in 1882. We had this in corn that year and Pap built that rail fence you see there. He split them rails and built that fence back then."

Pa stopped and picked up a rail. "The hands that split them

rails tanned my jacket with a hickory withe a many a time. He worked like a brute and died a pauper," he said.

We gathered the wild flowers—the wild bleeding heart, the wild snowballs, the mountain daisies as we went along. Pa, Uncle Jeff and Uncle Joe helped us. Uncle Joe had to walk with a cane. We walked slowly through the woods, partin our way through the dense undergrowth of greenbriers and ferns and wild snowball bushes that lapped across a once traveled path.

"This is the right road," said Uncle Joe, "though I ain't been to Ma's grave since she was buried. I never wanted to go back. We have to go out here and through where Pap took that last forty-acre lease from Steve Bocook back in '93. It's all growed up till you wouldn't know it."

There was a dim toe-path leadin down through woods that looked as if they were the trees that Adam roamed among.

"And Grandpa cleared this up once?" I asked.

"Yes," said Uncle Joe. "We farmed this, cleared it up and got it in the first year. Put a rail fence around it to boot."

We followed the dim path through the ferns and under the tall trees. Uncle Joe carried the basket and parted brush with his cane. Soon we came to a point out in a grass field that sloped gently down to a little valley stream of water.

"Over there is where Ma is laid," said Uncle Joe.

When we got there no one could definitely locate her grave. Pa said: "Call old Joe Blevins over here. He knows. He still owns this farm, don't he?"

"Yes," said Uncle Joe.

"Boys," said Joe Blevins, "there are eleven of youn'ns buried here and your Ma is in the middle. She is number six. There are five before her and five after. Right here is the place at this sunken sankfield mound."

Uncle Joe spilled his basket of flowers there.

Uncle Jeff said: "We three brothers are all that's left. I'll be the next to come here. I can't stand work any more and when a once good horse gets so he can't stand work then he is through. You know that. Now right here is where I'll be put. You see to it, Mick."

It was by a little peach tree. Finn stood under it in the bright spring sun and I pulled off a few of its green leaves and one of its old but not shedded blossoms and crumbled them in my hand.

As the rain keeps fallin here and Pa has just gone out of sight now, I understand. They will haul Uncle Jeff on a wagon around the skirts of that hill we walked over. It will be a long haul, but they will haul him to that point and dig his grave by that peach tree. The rain will be fallin perhaps. It will be white rain and will soak down where I crumbled the peach tree leaves and the faded blossoms last year. Dirt will be piled high there. Pa will be there.

"Wonder if Uncle Jeff's wife will be there?" I think.

It is best to let Pa go, for this is bad weather to sleep on a floor. We don't want to do it. We know where Uncle Jeff will be planted for he told Pa and Pa will see to that. It will be where the green peach tree leaves and the pink peach tree blossoms were crumbled down last year. There will not be the sound of a train whistle back there.

ANSE MADDOX has heard how pretty the preacher is. He will go to church this Sunday night and see her, though he does not attend the Unknown Tongue revivals, for he chooses to cling to the Faith of his people, the Forty-Gallon Baptis. They are people who see no harm in drinking licker. The Unknown Tongues have come into their Holler neighborhood and have preached against licker. Anse will not go to hear them—but he lashes them with his tongue like preacher John Madden did when the members of the Baptis church met in the beech grove and prayed to God to drive out these invaders of the Faith.

But Anse hears Fliam McCleanahan say: "You ought to see that Unknown Tongue preacher. Boys, she's a beauty. She is one of the prettiest little tricks I ever laid my two peepers on. I am goin to get saved shore as the world if she keeps on preachin. I am goin to quit my weaked ways of doin and be a better man."

Charlie Blaine comes up to the chip yard where Anse is feeding his snakes. "Say, Anse Maddox, you want to come to church tonight over there at the pine grove. That Unknown Tongue preacher is pretty as a picture. Young men are gettin saved right and left. Boys from our church too. Think I'll get saved. She's goin to show her Faith in the Word tonight by lettin a rattlesnake bite her. Might be you'd like to see this since you fool around with copperheads, black snakes and blowin vipers all the time."

And Anse says to Fliam: "Soon as I feed my snakes and shave my face and put on clean clothes, I'll be over. Might be a little late, but I'll be there. You go on. Don't let me hold you back. I'll be about a hour late."

Fliam and Charlie hurry down the cow path and cross the drawbars. They are soon hidden among the tall corn on their way to church. Anse feeds his snakes milk and eggs and meat. This is time to feed them. One meal a week and it is time to feed the snakes. After he has thrown in a couple dozens of eggs, three or four pounds of beef that he has brought from the smoke house and poured a gallon of warm sweet milk in a wooden trough, he reaches down with his hand and pats the old daddy rusty-mouthed copperhead on the back of the head. Daddy copperhead never moves his body. "Perfectly tame now," says Anse.

He runs into the house and pours hot water from the teakettle into the wash pan. He takes down the mug from the top of the safe. He makes lather from the soap in the mug. He spreads the white soapy foam on his face. He takes out a long black-handled razor from a case on top of the safe. He rakes it a few times across his pants' leg. Then he begins to take swaths down his face like he is cutting grass with a scythe. "I'll soon be ready. I'll see that preacher tonight. I want to see her handle the rattlesnake."

When Anse shaves the part beard and part milkweed furze from his eighteen-year-old face, he runs to the hickory-pole clothesline upstairs and grabs his best pair overalls and a blue store-bought shirt. The overalls are pretty and clean and the starch in the shirt smells sweet and clean after smelling all day in the cornfield the old sweaty sour-smelling work shirt and the weed-stained overalls. He gets the black slippers he picked blackberries and bought last week over in Riverview. Anse runs to the mirror now. There he sees himself, a tall bean-pole boy with hair the color of rye straw and eyes almost mullein-leaf gray—a slender face that has been tanned by the cornfield sun to autumn oak-leaf brown. And the blue overalls and the blue store shirt and the black slippers—how they match. Anse turns before the mirror and twists to get a view of his back, his shoulders, and his face.

"W'y I look good as them boys over in Riverview that dress up all the time and don't have nothin to do," says Anse.

Anse Maddox, the long-legged bean-pole boy, runs down the path past the snake box, past the barn—he leaps the drawbars—takes across the buckwheat field—then through the corn patch. Dew has fallen on the corn blades and that reminds him he must not get his clothes wet with dew. He must not run anymore or he will get wet with sweat. He slows down to a fast pace. He wants to get to the meeting. He can hear them singing, over across the creek now. He can hear them muttering words to God no human beings but members of their church can understand. He has often wondered if they can understand. He wants to get across the creek and up the cliff to the pine grove where the young woman is preaching and showing the Faith in the Word by letting the rattlesnake bite her.

Anse sees the creek is swollen from recent rains, but he knows where a tree has fallen across the creek and serves as a foot log in time of highwaters. So he runs to this tree and like a gray squirrel running through the limbs of a beech tree, Anse runs across the body of this log, like a squirrel—and then through the dead branches of the top. He is now across the creek. He knows an easy way to get upon the cliff without having to go all the way around the circling wagon road. There is a footpath with a cedar tree which serves as a ladder, for its branches have been cut off and little steps are left of branch stubs. He climbs this tree and is right up near where the meeting is. Anse can hear the singing and the shouting amid the sweet strains of the guitars. He cannot wait. He takes no path around, but he plows through the patch of green persimmon and pawpaw brush and finds himself before a congregation of Holler people.

Lanterns are swinging to the pine boughs and the dim lantern lights light up the green boughs of the pines. The white and gray moths flutter around the lanterns seeking the light. They beat their thin wings against the pine-tree needles. Above the pine trees, there is the white light from the stars in the robin-egg-blue colored sky. And there is a big harvest moon among the stars that seems to be gliding through robin-egg-blue waters like a golden sail and spreading a golden light down on a green world. The whole overhead Anse thinks is pretty. It is one of the prettiest roofs he has ever seen—far prettier than a new red-oak board roof just nailed on a new log house with all of its sweet red-oak wood smell.

Alas for the roof! Alas for all—the young preacher rises

from prayer. She has been kneeling down by a pine stump. It is the mourners' bench. Perhaps this stump was once part of the split pine log seat Anse is sitting on. There are split pine logs the people sit on. The ends of these logs rest on piles of stones and stumps. Pine needles and pine burrs are scattered over the ground floor. Anse can feel them through the new black slippers on his feet. If he had been barefooted they would have stuck his thick-skinned feet that trail behind the cutter plow without shoes—that follow the cattle with only one shoe and that one near the oxen.

But that pretty preacher! Never was there a mountain girl as pretty—there she stands upright now. She is from Ohio—that far-away Ohio. Anse heard she was from there, but that does not matter. Here she stands unafraid before his people—going to let a rattlesnake bite her. To Anse her black hair was prettier than the love-vines after the frosts have curled them black. And there are black combs with white sets in her long black free-to-the-wind hair. The white sets sparkle from the dim lights of the lanterns where the wing-beating insects hum-hum in the night air. There is a white bracelet on her arm—Anse can see it loosely slide up and down her arm as she lifts her arm toward Heaven. The sleeves on her arm are loose like a robe that Anse thinks God used to wear when he was on this earth. Her dress is white and flowing like a robe—her teeth are white. Her face is white as the petals of a white morning-glory and just as fresh as a white morning-glory petal in the June morning dew. Her lips are soft-looking and curved enough in her smiles to show her two rows of straight white teeth. "She must be an angel from Heaven, God has sent here to the Holler to save us mortals from the gates of Hell," Anse thought silently. "She's pretty as a angel in Heaven."

Anse noticed on the very front log sit Fliam and Charlie. They are drinking in every word the young preacher says. Anse watches Charlie look at Fliam and Fliam look at Charlie. Anse watched both of them though they could not see Anse watching them. "They are in love with Sister Combs," Anse says to himself, "but she don't want lazy boys like neither one of them. They ain't no count to work. They ain't no count for nothin. They are weaked—cuss and drink licker and chew tobacco. She must not look at neither one of them. If she does I'll tell her about them. Onery things tryin to go with a angel like she is. God sent her here. How can she get up and preach the Word like that when she ain't a day over eighteen years old if she don't have the Spirit of God in her!"

"If you have the right kind of Faith in the Word, folks, you will let a rattlesnake bite you. Don't the Lord say in Luke 16, 'Thou shalt take up Serpents'? People, you cannot have the Faith in the Word and drink whisky and use filthy terbacker. What will you do in Heaven for whisky and terbacker? There will be no saloons there. There will be no spittoons there. You will not want to dirty the streets of gold with old black amber spit. You will not want to get drunk in Heaven. People, why do you do it? I will show you my Faith in the Word." And she takes a little box from beside the stump with a heavy screen wire over the top of it. She holds it before the congregation. They can see the huge rattler writhe in the box under the dim lantern light. They can see him lick his tongue out and his forked tongue quiver as the pine needles quiver in the wind overhead.

"Sing a song, folks—" And the guitars begin to strum over in the corner. They are played by three pretty girls. And these words thunder loud as the people in the congregation sing.

I've been redeemed,
I've been redeemed,
By the blood of the lamb,
BY THE BLOOD OF THE LAMB
Saved and sanctified I am—
I've been redeemed—
I've been redeemed—

You can't go to Heaven on roller skates,
You'll roll on through Heaven's pearly gates—
I've been redeemed—
I've been redeemed—

You can't go to Heaven, girls, and wear a rat,
You can't go to Heaven, men, and carry a gat,
I've been redeemed–
I've been redeemed–

I went down in the valley, went down there to pray,
Well I got so happy, folks, stayed down there all day–
I've been redeemed–
Yes, I've been redeemed–
By the blood of the lamb,
BY THE BLOOD OF THE LAMB
And saved and sanctified I am,
I've been redeemed–
Oh, I've been redeemed–

People now are standing and holding hands and uttering words no one but the Unknown Tongues can understand. It is the language by which they commune with God. Can you understand the wind? Does the wind say words? Do they say words? If you could only hear. They moan like the wind overhead in the pine needles and they sisish-sh-sh like the wind going through the persimmon and the pawpaw sprouts on the cliff top. And now the music is growing swifter. People are falling on the pine needles between the log seats. People are saying words not understandable and they are groaning and looking toward the stars. Amid the din of groans and the swift, almost dance music, one can hear, "That is Tim James's wife, Lulu James over there. She got saved last week. Them babies Nettie Shuttleworth is holdin up there is her babies. See her down there rollin in the weeds."

"That is Bob Harriman over there rollin and talkin in Unknown Tongue to God. He used to be a Forty-Gallon Baptis. He got saved here the other night and he got up and told the people if they only knowed what he knowed they'd all get out of that Forty-Gallon Baptis Church. He said the Devil had 'em good as he wanted 'em drinkin licker and playin cards and chewin that old filthy tobacco."

"That is Abel Pratt over there. He come clean the other night and confessed to shootin Bill Abrahams at the square dance that night. Don't know what the Law will do with him now. He got that smart lawyer over in Riverview, Silas Stump, and he beat the court and proved himself innocent. Now he has come clean with the whole story."

And there sits Anse watching Fliam and Charlie. He sees them start for the mourners' bench, crying and shouting as they go: "I'm a lost man." "I'm a lost man, I'm deep drownin in the rivers of sin."

Sister Combs says: "Bless your sweet young hearts. You fine-lookin young men comin up here tonight. God needs every one of you."

Chills run over Anse's back when she said this. He wanted her to say something like this to him. He didn't like Charlie and Fliam. A horror struck him all at once. He hated these boys now. Last Sunday they were friends and fished together in Goat Creek. But now he hated them. He turns his eyes toward Tim James. There he sits looking at his wife. He looks like a gorilla. There is horror beaming from his narrow bean-slit bullet eyes. The blue beard on his face is three days old and his hair is down on his neck. His lower lip sags and there is amber spit gathered in the corners of his mouth. His faded blue shirt sticks close to his broad bent shoulders and one suspender is fastened over his shoulder while the other falls limp and dangles down on the leg of his jeans pants, patched and dirty.

He says over and over to himself: "Nothin to these Unknown Tongues. I thought I told her about comin over here. Rattlesnake. Bet it's got its teeth pulled."

He looks at his wife and then at Sister Combs. "Forty-Gallon Baptis is the only church on God's side. Ain't nothin to these Tongues. Rattlesnake. Bet it's got its teeth pulled."

"Now if you don't believe that the Unknown Tongues have Faith in the Word, let me show you God will not let the poison from this rattlesnake hurt me. He says, 'Thou shalt take up serpents.' " And from the little box with the wire top, she takes the huge rattler that shakes a warning with his tail and writhes through her hands. He squirms up in her hand till he has good biting action with his huge rusty neck. She holds her arm up. She works her arm toward the snake's head. The snake bites her. Again, she moves and the snake bites her. The people hug close to each other, shudder and say, "OOOO –OO–OO–OO, my goodness. That snake."

Tim James rises from his split-log seat and he walks up toward Sister Combs. People think he is going to the mourners' bench. When he gets up to the preacher, he says: "Give me that snake. Give me that snake, I said."

Sister Combs gives the snake to Tim James. He catches it by the neck and it bites him and someone says, "It will kill you, Tim James, a Forty-Gallon Baptis with no Faith."

"It won't kill me neither. This snake ain't got no teeth and I'll bet you a dollar it ain't."

Tim gets his big butter-paddle hand over the rattler's throat and he chokes its mouth open: "Come up here, Lulu! Get up out of them pine needles and come here. It ain't got a tooth in its head."

"You just can't see them. It's got 'em."

"If it ain't got no teeth, I've got a rusty-mouthed copperhead over home in the pen I'll go and fetch and show you who's got Faith in the Word and who ain't," says Anse as he rose from his split-log seat and carried a couple of splinters in the seat of his overalls with him. "Sister Combs has got Faith in the Word and I know she has, Tim James. It's you–you old bull you, that ain't got no Faith in nothin but the Forty-Gallon Baptis. I'll go fetch the copperhead." Anse runs from the congregation–through the bushes he goes like a wildcat.

"Maybe that snake ain't cut its teeth yet," Mart Findley says to Tim as he still chokes the snake's mouth open and looks into the place where the forked tongue was still moving.

"It ought to be old enough to have tushes," says Tim, "–got seventeen rattles on it and two buttons."

Sister Combs stands amazed in the pulpit by the stump. There stands Tim James pranking with the snake as if there were no church but a snake show. And over to the left of him is Lulu James down on the pine needles talking to God in Unknown Tongue, unconscious of all going on–at least in this world. Drops of sweat cling to her forehead like white icicles cling to the drips of the smoke house in winter. There she lies with her hair tousled and her two babies crying and screaming at their mother down on the earth, moaning words they do not understand. Fliam and Charlie have caught the spirit of the thing and now they lie down among the pine needles with many others. There is Jake Thomas down with them and Seed Lenix and Fonse Perkins, and Sylvia Moore and Daisy Redfern and Lester Oaktree. They are all Forty-Gallon Baptis too. They are seeking this new Faith in the Word. Here stands Tim still playing with the rattlesnake and he says: "No wonder you let this snake bite all the Unknown Tongue people the other night to show people in my church that the Faith in the Word in your church was better. No wonder they all lined up around the mourners' bench and you first let the snake bite you and then you went along and nudged its head to their arms and it bit all of their arms. No wonder. This snake has only got gums. It can only gum a body."

"Let us pray for Brother James," says Sister Combs. "He needs our prayer."

And she kneels by the stump with her white face hidden down on the stump and she prays unknowable words among the other unknowable words to the God in the clouds above the pine tops. It is all a clatter of unknowable words. The babies are scared, but they pray for Tim James while he still fondles the rattler's mouth and strokes its head and looks for its teeth. The insects buzz around the lanterns, seeking the light in their little night and the white and gray moths beat their thin wings still against the pine needles—while above the white clouds race across the blue heaven and the white stars and the golden moon give light. The wind plays among the pine needles and whispers in the sprouts.

Anse runs every step of the way home and gets the snake; and like a ghost, tall and thin, and dressed in blue with a pair of black slippers on his feet, he runs like a light tall ghost back through the buckwheat, through the dewy corn—cross the log that lay across the swollen Creek—then he scales up the cliffs like a ground hog, and up the cedar tree ladder like a squirrel. He holds the copperhead close to his bosom and when he reaches the top of the rock shelves, he plunges through the green persimmon and the pawpaw sprouts like a bull. There he was with the copperhead and they are all down in prayer.

"I've got the snake," Anse cries, "I've got the copperhead, Sister Combs."

She gets up off her prayer bones with tear-swollen eyes. Maybe it is the copperhead she was praying about. Maybe it is the bite it is to give her she has fear of. And all eyes turn toward her but the eyes of Fliam and Charlie and Tim James's wife. They lie stretched on carpet of pine needles and half-conscious they lie there and slobber and groan to God.

The pretty young preacher takes the copperhead and holds it to her arm. It bites her. She flinches. She holds it to her bosom. It bites her. She flinches. She holds it to her face. It bites her. She flinches. "Bite me all over, copperhead," Sister Combs says, "I'll show 'em my church does have the Faith in the Word. Now if the Forty-Gallon Baptis have it, come up here, Tim James, and let this snake bite you."

Tim stands still with his face looking down and his feet stirring among the pine needles on the ground. He makes no answer.

"Come on," says Sister Combs, "don't you have the Faith in the Word?"

"No," says Tim.

"Get in my church and get the Faith in the Word," she says.

"Bite me, copperhead. Bite. Bite me again and again," says Sister Combs.

And the copperhead bites her till its neck is tired. It charges at her face, breast, arm and throat till it can charge no longer. She goes back to preaching from the pulpit stump. She preaches loud among the din of the sinners crying already for repentance of their wickedness, such as shooting with intent to kill, chewing tobacco, drinking whisky and playing poker. And there is one repentance of a chicken thief and of a young girl who has given birth to a baby out of wedlock. She confesses trying to kill it before it was born by taking hot baths in water flavored with spicewood.

After thirty minutes pass Sister Combs says: "Where is the copperhead venom? Where is it? I cannot feel it. I have Faith in the Word. Come all of you before tomorrow comes and join the happy throng."

"Maybe my wife is right," says Tim James as he flings the rattlesnake over the heads of everybody into the green persimmon sprouts. And he runs up and throws himself down by his wife. People now come from every side, children and all. They gather close as they can to the pine stump, praying to God to give them mercy at this mourners' bench.

All go to the mourners' bench but Anse. Only the pine needles on the floor and the empty half-log seats are left. They hold their faces to the earth and beat their fists against the ground. "God give us mercy. God give us sinners mercy. We ain't never knowed the light before."

Anse walks from the middle seat up to the front. "Come with me, sweet angel," says Anse. "You're sent here from Heaven to us in the Holler. Come with me–" and he takes Sister Combs by the hand. She follows him. And they pass Charlie sitting on top of Fliam with his suspenders down from his shoulders and the white flesh at his waist line showing where his shirt has worked up on his back. Drops of sweat are on his face. Charlie is saying to Fliam, "Now say your words to God, Fliam," as Charlie takes his fingers and shapes Fliam's lips this way and that–"now say your words to God, Fliam."

Anse has the most beautiful earthly creature by the hand he had ever seen in all of his life. "Come with me," he says again to her.

"I am comin," she says. "I am comin with you––"

And they go into the sprouts the way Anse brought the snake, under the green leaves, away from the light of lanterns, moon, and stars. They go into the dark under the leaves. He holds her soft warm hand in his. They leave a whole stack of human beings gathered around the stump praying for forgiveness of their sins. And as they walk down the narrow fox path to the shelves of rocks, they can hear the cries of the people up under the pines. They can hear the winds in the sprouts near them. Here is a bright place by their feet and here is another bright place. The spots look like gold.

"What is this?" says Sister Combs, "this bright stuff under our feet."

"That is fox-fire," says Anse, "ever see any before?"

"What is that stuff I smell that is so sweet?" says Sister Combs.

"That is snakeroot blossoms," says Anse.

Down the path, over the shelves of rocks, they went their way till they come to a green little bottom. "What is the yap-yap like a barkin rat I hear up on the hill?" she says.

"That is the barkin fox you hear," says Anse.

They walk down the little dew-covered grassy bottom, hand in hand.

"Where are we goin?" she says.

"To my home," says Anse. "You will go with me, won't you?"

"Yes," says Sister Combs.

Back upon the shelves of rocks they can hear shouting and praying as the wind blows toward them. "I loved you, Sister Combs, before I ever saw you," says Anse, "when I saw you I was jealous of you. I didn't want Fliam and Charlie to speak to you."

Above them the bull bat screams, and Sister Combs flinches some and comes nearer to Anse. Anse would gladly pull her close to him and kiss her, but he is afraid. Each time he slightly pulls at her loose sleeve she timidly pulls away. They start to climb the next hill that leads up through the cornfield. Under the green hickory trees they go, Anse holding her hand and leading the way. The wind rustles through the leaves.

Anse says: "Plenty of poison snakes in these woods. The fire drove them in these woods when we burnt the clearin last spring. You know poison snakes like to stay in woods where the fire has never burnt over the ground——"

"Yes, I've heard that," she says.

They pass over more fox-fire. Anse reaches over and takes

hold of her long braid of loose flowing black hair, blacker than the night under the leaves on the trees. He fumbles at her long black hair and he holds her hand more tightly.

"What are you doin?" she says.

"I am tying you to me forever," he says. And the sets in the combs in her hair sparkle in the dark. "I love you," Anse says to her. "I love you more than any girl I ever saw. I want you for my own. I want you to marry me and let us live here. I can raise bread for us. Let me tell you what I done tonight. I went to get the copperhead. I wanted to show them somethin. I wanted to show Tim James. I pulled that copperhead's teeth with a pair of shoe brad pullers a long time ago. I didn't want to see no copperhead with a good set of teeth bite a girl pretty as you."

"That copperhead didn't have no teeth?" she says.

"No," said Anse.

She tears loose from Anse and runs into the green night woods. She leaps like a deer. Anse stands still. He can't move. He can see her white dress zigzagging down through the dark green wood. Anse cries to her: "Sister Combs. Sister Combs. Stop. Stop. Stop." She goes on breaking the brush and running. Anse takes after her. He runs over the hill the way she has gone. He runs like a rabbit. There is no trace of her. Anse stands in a briar patch now, under the moonlight, and the angel that has come to the Holler had slipped from him, perhaps, forever.

"If that copperhead had only had some teeth," Anse says, looking at the wind quivering in the moonlight.

MOUNTAIN POORHOUSE

IT IS Sunday. Kirby and I haven't a place to go. We could go fishin, but Sunday bathin beauties are splashin the water, so the fish won't bite. We could go to the "singin" down on the creek, but the boys won't be the least bit friendly down there today after the little row we had last night in the dark. Kirby snaps his finger and says, "I have it." "Have what?" "W'y let's crank the flivver and cross the hill to a Tennessee poorhouse." And I say, "It's okay with me."

The flivver chug-chugs like a mowin machine, for we have it in high gear runnin like a potato bug across a pretty Tennessee meadow. Now we go down in the creek-bed road and the gravels fly—up through a wood yard and barely miss a nice flock of fryin-size pullets. We breeze down the bank, coast a little to save gas, and then we strain up the next hill and through a pair of drawbars and out where a pretty hard road squirms like a house snake around the Tennessee hills. "Won't be long about gettin there now," says Kirby.

We pull up to a barb-wire fence and Kirby steps on the brake. The Ford is hot and it blows like a hot horse. We get out and Kirby says, "There she is right over there in the field." And I say to Kirby, "What's over there in the field?" "The poorhouse," he says. "See that lean-to built out of rough oak planks that looks like a coal shed? Boy, that's her. That's the poorhouse." "The hell it is."

This poorhouse is a lean-to. However, it leans to nothin. It is built like a cow shed. It has five stalls in it. Each stall has one bed, a little stand, a little heatin stove with a belly the size of a nail keg. Across the road the poorhouse keeper lives in a big fine two-story weather-boarded house. He sees us talkin to the inmates over across the wire fence on his premises. He comes over. "Hello, Kirby," he says. "Hello, Radner," Kirby says. "Meet my friend Stuart here." We shake hands. His big hand has grown fairly soft for a farmer's hand. It feels like a butter paddle. "You boys lookin here, air you, Kirby?" "Yes, Mr. Radner, we're just out spongin around." "Well look around here and make yourselves at home. See what you can see." Kirby takes a package of Stud from his pocket and nervously rolls a cigarette. "Tax got so high here on ready-mades I've gone to smokin my own. Ain't near so much tax here on Stud in Tennessee as there is on ready-mades." Kirby puts the cigarette to his mouth and Radner lights it with a match for Kirby. The cigarette is curved like a chicken's bill. Kirby and Radner talk and I go down where the row of rooms begins.

The first has an old woman in it. She must be seventy-seven. Her knee cap is out of place and is around on the other side of her leg. She grumbles and says her knee is nearly killin her. It and her leg below the knee are swollen twice the normal size. She says, "Oh, if I could only get out of this place!" Out on a bench just below her stall sits "Uncle Peg." He is the life and noise of the fifteen inmates of the poorhouse. "How did you lose that leg?" "Lost it in the mines. Ain't been much good since I lost it."

While I am here talkin to Uncle Peg a couple of small boys come out. One is a baby wearin a dress. I ask the boy his name. He says, "Bill." "What is your last name?" Uncle Peg says: "He don't know his name. He is a half-brother to this little boy with the dress on. His mamma is here. She is in that room down on yon end of the house. She is the only one that knows who their daddy is. She ain't never been married. She didn't have no place to go with them two little boys so she come here. Them is right pert boys and if it wasn't fer them here the place would be a lot lonesomer." And I ask the older boy, "How old are you?" "I don't know." Uncle Peg says, "That boy is eleven years old and he ain't been to school a day in his life. Them boys is shore to God fine boys though."

Kirby is still smokin on the Stud cigarette. He is talkin to Radner too. They talk and Radner talks with his hands. He points to the corn patch and the potato patch and then he points to the house across the road where he lives. I look along in the stalls. There is only one door to each room. That makes five doors along the front. I go on down where I hear a noise in a stall. Uncle Peg hobbles along on his wooden leg with me.

We go into one stall where a skinny man is lyin on a smelly mattress. "What is the matter with him?" I say to Uncle Peg. "W'y he was sent to the pen in Nashville and they made a girl out'n him over there them fellars did and he ain't been right since. He takes spells and he comes right out'n that bed and falls all over the floor. He bruises hisself up awful when he falls. See them little pipe-stem legs. He can't hardly walk on legs like them. I'd ruther have my one good leg and my one wooden leg as to have both of his'n. Radner keeps them old overalls on him and no underwear because he's so bad about wettin the bed. That mattress is nearly rotten." There he is on the mattress a heap of skin and bones. His face is pale blue and his lips are a deeper shade of blue.

Uncle Peg and I go on down the front of the poorhouse. In next to the last stall we find an old man of about eighty workin on a chair. And Uncle Peg says after we get past where the old man can't hear: "He's been a bad'n. He's kilt two men before he come here. He's been in the pen. He won't do to fool with, but he's good when people mind their own business. He used to work in the mines too. He's busy all the time doin somethin. He likes to work. He can't quit work. He'd go crazy if he didn't have a chear to fix 'r somethin."

In this last stall is a woman under heavy quilts on this hot June day. Uncle Peg says: "Don't talk to her. She's lost her mind. She'll be right out'n that bed if you talk to her. Jist let her do the talkin and you listen and she'll stay in the bed." "How do you do, Buddy. What time is it? Half-past the corner. Half-past the corner. Half-past the corner." I do not answer. She pulls the quilts over her and lies back down in bed.

There is a woman here that can't talk. There is a young girl here that helps Radner's wife over at the big house across the road. There are two more elderly women here and two women I judge to be in their late forties. They sit on a little bench Radner had built for them in front of the shack. They watch the people pass down the road. There is not much for them to do around the shack. There is not much furniture in it. There is no yard to keep clean. Cookin is done over at Radner's house and carried across the road to them. Uncle Peg says to me as I start walkin to where Radner and Kirby are: "Son, ain't you workin fer the Government? If you are working fer the Government can't you help get us that old-age pension of $25 a month? That would be a lot of money and we could live better than we are livin here on that much money—$25 a month!"

Kirby is rollin another cigarette as he talks on to Radner. Radner says: "W'y they ain't nothin here in this poorhouse but a bunch of whores, outlaws and killers. That's all they air. They ain't got nothin comin to 'em. Why didn't they work and save somethin like the good people's done?" "How long have you had the poorhouse?" I say to Radner. "Since early last spring. I underbid a fellar round there in the bend. I bid under him a nickel a person per week. My bid was $2.30 for each one a week. Now I got fifteen, you see."

"I don't see how you can make anythin out of that, Radner. How can you feed them fer that?"

"Now I don't mind to tell you, boys. Just don't say nothin about it. But I plan to feed them on $150 for the first six months. You see I got peas and beans in the garden, roastin' ears and 'taters are comin' in a plenty in the garden purty soon and I ain't goin' to be out much. I aim to feed them rough grub jist sich as beans, 'taters, peas, corn, middin-meat and greens. I'll make about $678 in clear money. I ain't tellin this every place and to everybody. But I'll come out all right. And I get some help from here among these women. They help my wife. I can make it all right with what little gin-whackin I do about the place here."

"We had better be goin," Kirby says and he takes the last draw off his home-made Stud. "Well, come back again, you fellars. Come back some time and gas around with me when you ain't got nuthin' to do." "Thank you a lot," says Kirby, "come up and gas around with me some time."

We crank the flivver. We get inside and Kirby says, "I tell you I never want to go to no poorhouse and be treated like that when I get old."

ACCIDENTAL DEATH

IT IS summer now of 1930. Hundreds of hobos, red, yellow, black, white, coal-dust black, are ridin the freight trains. No one can tell just the color anyone is for the coal soot. The hobos are coal-dust black a-sittin on heaped-up cars of Kentucky mountain coal. One can see them ridin the short blunt-tailed coal train, ridin on tops of the cars—under the sawed-off edges of the coal cars, on the couplin pins under the cars on mattresses fixed on bed springs. They sit upon the heaped-up coal in the July sunlight like crows perched on pine-tree branches to roost. When the dew begins to fall they go down under the car and sleep on the bed springs.

The train comes down the Ohio River Valley, screakin, weavin in-and-out, out-and-in—puffin, blowin for the July sun and the burnin coal in the engine's belly makes the train hot—cinders are flyin—coal-dust, coal smoke. It comes like all-out-of-doors, only the train is black like all-out-of-doors is not black. But anybody walkin alongside the track will stop to watch the antics of this short train loaded with Kentucky mountain coal after it comes down Big Sandy and gets out on the main road line. It is like a man goin down the highway to the city for his first time.

The sky is filled with July hotness. No one gives a damn whether he works weather like this or not. The section men don't like the smell of the cross-ties they are diggin under the rails. They stand amid ragweeds wilted to the cinder bed—sweat streamin from their sun-cooked faces. They stand with picks in hand, and scythes in hand. They like to see the train pass so they can rest their backs. It is a hot day. It is hot as hell. They stand and thank God they have a job of $2.70 a day in this Depression. They talk about the easy life of the hobo a-sittin upon coal cars and ridin all day in the sun with long wire hooks trained to grab their dinner buckets off the hand cars. They wonder when the Depression will end. If they are goin to get another ten per-cent cut on their wages.

They wonder if this is the cut that will bring an end to the Depression.

The train chugs smart-alecky by like a Jersey bull. Boss Man Oliver Pigg spys what he thinks is a "Shine" a-sittin upon a heaped-up car of mountain coal. "That black ain't no coal black. That is real black skin," says Boss Man Oliver Pigg. "I can pick out his eye with this turnip of a cinder."

"A five-spot you can't," says Mule-face Hunt. Away goes the cinder and catches the man on the temple. He tumbles from his roost—not like a shot crow—but like a stuck hog. He doubles up before he hits the ground.

"Good work, Cap Pigg," says Cackleberry Spriggs.

"Good work, Boss Man Oliver," says Rough-house Evans.

The black man, coal-black or nature-black, rolls in the hail-gray ballast. "God Almighty," is all he says. His temple is caved in like an old cellar. The blood, color of rotted red-oak leaves, oozes like sap from the end of a burnin fore stick.

"Accidental Death," says Mule-face Hunt.

"Accidental Death," says Cackleberry.

"Yeah—Accidental Death—" says Boss Man. "Better have Corner Stone though, boys—better to have it done in accordance with the Law. You know what Whale Isom got into over buryin that man like a cut-up dog that time. Have this done with the Law. You needn't pay me the five-spot, Mule-face. Keep that and buy you some cigars."

Corner Stone comes twistin like a wilted weed in the soft July wind. He comes up the bank. "Hot as hell, ain't hit, boys. How can you stand hit out here nigh this rusty steel that draws like a open fireplace all the blasted hot-as-hell sun out'n the Heaven. Dead man, huh——"

"Yeh—dead Shine, Corner Stone. Tumbled off'n that car like a bird hit by one of them juicy wires."

"Country is too full of men goin yonder and yon with nothin to do. Gettin dangerous for a nice woman to walk down the railroad track anymore. Scum o' th' earth rides these freighters anymore—yeh—rotten scum o' th' earth."

Corner Stone carefully examines the dead man. Spits on his finger. He wipes spit on the man's hot face. "Black don't come off. He's a Shine. Dead as a mackerel too. I wish I had his pretty white teeth—turned up here in the July sun. Shame them teeth has to go with the man and me have this damn old pinchy false set."

"Shoo away them green flies," says Cackleberry Spriggs to Corner Stone. "I can't stand to see green flies around a dead cow in the summer time, let alone around a man."

"Okay, Cackleberry," says Corner Stone. He shoos them with his sweat-wet handkerchief.

"Hot day—a damned hot day to examine a stinkin black corpse. Pity the train didn't grind him into sand-ground sausage meat for the black cross-tie ants. Hot day, too, for a body to smell a body.—Smell of my shirt, Mule-face. Smells like a dead stinkin body."

Corner Stone takes a stick. He punches in the caved-in hole in the skull. He twists the end-twisted stick around like tryin to twist a rabbit out of a beech log. "Feel it," he says. "No, not a rabbit bones, but that cinder he drubbed up when he fell off. It's a accidental death. Fell offen a train makin sixty a hour. A dead Shine—boys—that's all. Give me some smartweeds to wipe off my hands with and kill the scent so I can fill out the pad." He rinses his hands in the smelly smartweeds. He fills out the questionnaire of the accidental death.

"A County casket, boys. Notify in the paper for his relationship. Ain't nothin in his pockets to identify him by. Nothin but a piece of bread a mule couldn't chaw. Craw is empty as a settin' hen's craw is empty in July when the worms all go in the ground."

"Must we take him to the morgue, Corner Stone?" says Cackleberry.

"Morgue won't have him when they ain't no money for the undertaker, you know damn well. Buy a County coffin and then pam him off on the Undertaker Snikes! No. Not that, Cackleberry Spriggs. Take him to Wheatley James' barn and leave him. Wheatley will let you have his barn since they ain't no Shines around here to take him to. I know old Wheatley. Tell him I sent you with him."

The truck ambled in with the County casket of thin uncovered knotty pine wood, and a little thin black suit wadded up like a sleeping black cat in the bottom of the casket. There was only the bosom of a white shirt and a little black-ribbon tie all gathered up like the tuckers in a petticoat Cackleberry Spriggs' wife wore. The truck driver said: "You section men have to load him and dress him. The train killed him. You have to bury all the train-hit stock, don't you, and the cut-up dogs. You have to dress this man, put him on the truck–unload him at the barn. I ain't gettin no scent on me."

"Okay, big boy truck driver. Wait till someone pulls your chain. Ain't you got no sense? Don't you know we ain't been out here all these years to not learn what we haf to do and what we don't haf to do? Keep your pants on. We'll do the dressin and the undressin. Crank up and haul this man down there by the crick under them beech trees. You can do that, can't you?"

They undressed him. They threw water on him from their hats–washed off the temple blood. They put the County suit on him and the half-shirt and the tie. Only Mule-face could tie a necktie among the lot.

"Yank him in, boys," said Boss Man Oliver Pigg. Cackleberry at one foot, Mule-face at the other. Boss Man and Roughhouse with a shoulder a piece and into the pine box they throw him. The blue flutter of gasoline-smoke and wind comes from tail of the whirrin, dronin July-hot engine. The truck with men hangin to its sides like wood ticks to a cur dog's back, ambled up the yellow sun-dried bank to Wheatley's barn.

The clover has been cut–sweet-smellin July-cut clover–fresh–and piled high in the barn loft. There is no place for the coffin there. There is a place in the cow shed between the manger and the feed box. There is where they put the coffin between the feed box and the manger.

This night Boss Man Pigg is afraid of the darkness. He will not go to the tool shed to play stud poker. He is afraid to pass Wheatley's barn. The next day passes. A day like the day before, dust, heat, wilted leaves, hobos of 1930–drouth–July sun with parched lips and parched land and empty bellies–another day. Time is goin. Children with ribbons on their hair —Wheatley's two little girls come to the barn lot and pluck the wilted daisies thirstin to death for water and for food. They pluck the daisies and they say: "We smell that old dead man. Pop said he was swelled like a rat."

Another night: dogs lurk—hungry dogs with 1930 stomachs and carpet-wooled hair. They sneak through the dew-revived daisies and whiff at the cow-shed poplar planks. They nose for a wide crack. Then they snoop through the sticker weeds by the manure pile.

Another day: the buzzards circle the barn. The white-clean washed clothes includin Wheatley's white Sunday shirt flip buoyantly on the clothesline. It is a hot wind stranglin the wilted guts in the barn-yard sticker weeds and the tight-laced daisy stems. No one calls for the dead body. Looks like it belongs to Wheatley. It has been in his possession two nights and two days. Ready for another night—another day?

"God, I'd like to meet the boys for a game of stud, but damned if I pass that barn tonight. A black spirit may meet me and hant me. I jist ain't goin. I don't care what the boys says about me. Got to git that body out and bury it tomorrow. Got to get this mess all cleaned up. Smells like a rottin lizard. My wife, Lizzie, can't hardly slop the hogs or milk the cows."

On the third day after they had got "their day in" on the section, Boss Man Oliver Pigg, Cackleberry Spriggs, Muleface Hunt, Rough-house Evans, Corner Stone, Preacher Bag McMeans and Wheatley James, owner of the corpse now, go into the barn and get a couple of coal picks, a double-bitted ax and a shovel. They carry the pine-box coffin out across the railroad. Up through the wilted poison vine they go. They go upon the mountain side for burial.

"Damned if I don't get a dose of poison here in these vines. Poison takes to my skin like water takes to low ground," says Cackleberry. On and on up through the mountain-side smothery brush—where July soft wind can't seep through the green leaves like water through a sieve. Water streams off the leather-tan faces. Preacher Bag nearly faints. He braces to a few weeds. He manages to climb. He carries a pick and the Bible. He is lucky. The section men bear the box on their shoulders. It is their duty to bury the cut-up dogs on the track and the uncalled-for dead.

Here is the place they will bury the unknown man. On this side of the rusty fence. Within the rusty fence are the graves of white men and white women. Sunken graves where wilted saw briars trail over like cucumber vines. Here are broken pieces of dishes and little rusted tin-cups with dead flower stems. One grave is adorned with a wild rose. But they can't bury the black man over there. That is more sacred earth. They bury him on the outside of the fence. Cackleberry starts diggin the hole. Sweat streamin into his eyes. It is the wilted bushes that smother out the wind. It is the tall thin grass. Grass now dyin for bread from the earth and water to drink. The bread the grass has to eat is hard as the piece found in the black man's pocket. It is just as hard and dry too. The hole goes down through the dry dirt–down, down, for five feet. The ground is still dry.

"Good enough hole," says Boss Man Oliver. "Good enough, boys," as he looks down their sweaty collars like he does on the section. They put two plow-line ropes under the box and four men let it down into the hole–the hair strings flyin from the ropes.

"Dust to dust," says Preacher Bag, "dust to dust. His sperit color of the night goes back. Maybe it goes back to the night. But his sperit is some'ers about us maybe in this wilted grass. Hidin with beamin eyes right on us like a tiger's eyes."

He sprinkles dry dust into the hole. He says: "This body will come out of this hole when the mighty trumpet blows and shakes the earth. Maybe all of us standin at the grave will see each other again."

"Shovel in the dirt, boys," says Boss Man Oliver Pigg. The boys eat up the dirt by shovel spoons. Soon the dry dust is eaten down to the wilted grass. They gather the ropes, picks, double-bitted ax and Bible and walk down the trampled mountain path—down to the railroad tracks across by Wheatley's barn.

"We'll be down to play stud with you tonight, boys," says Boss Man. "We'll be at the tool house soon as I git washed up and these sweaty clothes changed."

"Okay," says Cackleberry.

GROAN leads the way along the cow path; his Disciples follow. The cow path is narrow, the pawpaw bushes are clustered on both sides of the path and they are wet with dew. Brother Sluss pulls a pawpaw leaf and licks off the sweet dew with his tongue. Brother Sluss is like a honeybee. The moon floats in the sky like a yellow pumpkin, dark yellowish like the insides of a pumpkin.

Groan and his Disciples, Brothers Sluss, Frazier, Shinliver, Littlejohn, Redfern and Pigg, are headed for the Kale Nelson Graveyard. It is approximately one mile away, across Phil Hogan's cow pasture, Ben Lowden's pig lot, Cy Penix's corn patch, thence through the Veil Abraham's peach orchard to a flat where the ribs of an old house (the old Abraham's house) are bleached by the autumn sun and cooled by the autumn night wind. The robe Groan wears is similar to the robe Sunday-school cards picture Christ wearin when He walked and talked with His Disciples. It has a low neck, loose flowin sleeves. It is long and tied with a sash at the waist line. The loose sleeves catch on the pawpaw twigs along the path.

"Tell me more about the ten virgins, Brother Groan."

"I don't know about the ten virgins and I ain't discussin the ten virgins. You know there was ten of them, don't you? And you know one of them was Virgin Mary, don't you?"

"Yes I know that, Brother Groan. But tell me more about them."

"Brother Sluss, we have other things to talk about. Leave me be won't you. I want to talk with God. I want to feel the sperit. I want to show you what Faith will do tonight. Leave me alone. I am talkin to God now. I am in God's presence. Leave me be, will you?" Brother Groan carries a bundle under one arm. He carries a walkin staff in one hand. His loose sleeves are hard to get between the pawpaw twigs alongside the path.

There is silence. Brother Groan talks to God. They keep movin. They come to the drawbars. One by one they slip between the drawbars, all but Brother Frazier. He is too thick to slip between the rails. He crawls under the bottom rail. Now they are goin through Ben Lowden's pig lot. The moon above them is pretty in the sky. It is still a yellow pumpkin moon—that darkish-yellow, the color of the insides of a ripe sun-cooked cornfield pumpkin. The dew on the crab grass in the pig lot sparkles in the yellow moonlight. The September wind slightly rustles the halfway dead pawpaw bushes. The crickets sing, the katydids sing, the whippoorwills quirt-quirt and the owl who-whoos. Brother Groan mutters Unknown Tongue whispers to God.

"Brother Groan is goin to show us the Faith tonight."

"Brother Groan is talkin to God."

"No. That is the wind over there in Cy Penix's ripe corn. That is the wind in the corn blades talkin. That is not Sweet Jesus talkin."

"Be quiet, won't you. Brother Groan is tryin to talk to God."

"I ain't said nothin."

"No."

"It is the wind in the fodder blades, I tell you."

"The wind!"

"Didn't I say the wind?"

"Yes, you said the wind."

"Then why did you ask?"

"Because I thought that you said that Brother Sluss said that God whispered."

Brother Groan is first to mount the rail fence. His sleeve catches on one of the stakes-and-riders, but he gets over into Cy Penix's cornfield first. One by one his Disciples climb over the fence. Here is the ripe uncut corn in the yellowish wine-colored moonlight. The dead blades are whisperin somethin. Maybe it is: "The dead lie buried here, the dead of-ever-so-long-ago. But they lie buried here under the dead roots of this ripe corn."

The corn blades whisper to the wind. There is a sweet dew on these corn blades for Brother Sluss to lick off with his tongue, for Brother Sluss is like a honeybee. This dead fodder is buff-colored in the yellowish pumpkin-colored moonlight. Brother Sluss leads his Disciples through the field of dead corn. There is a ghostly chill of night piercin the thin robe of Brother Groan's; and the overalls and the unbuttoned shirts of his Disciples.

There is a loneliness in the night, in the moonlight that covers the land and in the wind among the trees. There is somethin lonely about dead leaves rakin against one's clothes at night, for they too seem to say: "The dead lie buried here, the dead of-ever-so-long-ago. But they lie buried here under the livin roots of these autumn trees."

Lonely is the quirt-quirt of the whippoorwill, the song of the grasshopper and the katydid. And there is somethin lonely about dead fodder blades the way they rake against the wind at night.

"Does God talk, Brother Littlejohn?"

"W'y yes, God talks. Ain't you got no Faith?"

"How do you know?"

"Because it is in the Word."

"Be quiet, please."

"It is the wind in the dead fodder."

"Are you sure that is all?"

"Yes."

"No."

"Why, no?"

"It is Brother Groan feelin the sperit."

"How do you know?"

"I saw him jump up and down right out there before me."

"I saw him too jump up and down out there in the path. I saw his sleeve catch on the brush. I saw him in the moonlight."

"He is feelin the sperit then."

The peach orchard is not a new set of teeth. Too many of the teeth are gone if each tree is a tooth. Many of them are snaggled teeth too. Brother Groan walks under the peach trees too, and the good teeth and the bad teeth chew at his robe. Brother Groan gets along. The dead leaves hangin to the peach trees are purple. One cannot tell tonight. But come tomorrow afternoon when the sun is shinin and look. There are half-dead leaves on the trees and whole-dead leaves on the trees. The wind fingers with the leaves. Brother Groan's sleeve has caught on the tooth of a peach tree. Brother Sluss hurries to free him. The sleeve is free now. The Disciples move on. Brother Groan is silent.

"Where are we goin, Brother Shinliver?"

"To the Kale Nelson Graveyard."

"What for?"

"Brother Groan is goin to show us the Faith in the Word."

"How?"

"I don't know."

"By the Word?"

"No!"

"How?"

"I told you once I didn't know."

"Is that you talkin, Brother Redfern?"

"No."

"I thought I heard somebody."

"That was the wind you heard."

"Yes—that was the wind."

"Yes, that was the wind in the peach-tree leaves."

"Ain't we about there?"

"About where?"

"Kale Nelson Graveyard?"

"Right up there!"

"Right up where?"

"Right up there—see them white tombstones! That is the Kale Nelson Graveyard."

The moon is high above the Kale Nelson Graveyard and the wind is down close to the earth on this high flat. The dead weeds rattle. The dead grass is whisperin somethin. Maybe it is: "The dead lie buried here. The dead of-ever-so-long-ago. They lie buried here under our roots. We know the dead lie buried here." The loose leaves rustle in the wind. The moon is still big as a pumpkin floatin in the pretty night sky. The moon is still the color of the insides of a pumpkin.

Across the bones of the old house, Groan and his Disciples

go. The myrtle is vined around the old logs. There is a pile of stones here, a pile of stones over there. Here is the butt of an old field-stone chimney. There is a gatepost half-rotted. Ramble rose vines climb halfway the rotted post. Here is a bushy-top yard tree with hitchin rings stapled in the sides. Here is a patch of blackberry briars. The wind blows through the blackberry briars and the blackberry briars scratch the wind. You ought to hear this wind whistle when it is scratched by the briars. If the wind dies, it cannot be buried here where the dead weeds whisper: "The dead lie under our roots, here in the Kale Nelson Graveyard." If Brother Groan dies, he can be buried here. Brother Groan is the kind of dead, when he does die, a grave can hold. Listen: Brother Groan is goin to speak now: "Gather around me, ye men of the Faith. Gather around me, ye men of God. Gather around me here. I want to show you there is power in The Word. Gather around me and let your voices speak in the Unknown Tongue to God."

Here on the myrtle-mantled logs of the old Abraham's house men are groanin–men are cryin to God. They are pleadin to God. They are mutterin quarter-words, half-words and whole words to God. It is in the Unknown Tongue. Brother Sluss is on the ground now. He rolls out into the graveyard. He breaks down the dead weeds that just awhile ago whispered to the wind that the dead lay under their roots. Brother Sluss smashes weeds half-dead like a barrel of salt rollin over them. Brother Sluss is a barrel-bellied man. He rolls like a barrel. Brother Littlejohn's pants have slipped below his buttocks. Brother Shinliver is holdin to a tombstone and jerkin. Brother Groan is cryin to God. He faces the yellow moon and he cries to God. Brother Frazier is pattin the ground with his shovel hands and cryin to God. "Come around me, men, come around me, you men of Faith, and listen to the Word. I aim to show you what the Faith in the Word will do. It will lift mountains. It will put life back into the dead bodies on this hill here tonight. Here are the dead beneath these weeds and the dead leaves. And one of these dead shall breathe the breath of life before mornin. Brother Sluss, get up off the ground and go right out there to that chimney butt, look under the jam rock where the pot-hooks used to swing and bring me that coal pick, that corn scoop and that long-handled shovel."

"Where did you say to go, Brother Groan?"

"Out there and look in the butt of that chimney."

"Out there by the blackberry briars, Brother Groan? I'm worked up with the sperit."

"What are you goin to do, Brother Groan?"

"Through me, Brother Redfern, God is goin to give new life to a dead woman this very night."

"Who, Brother Groan?"

"My dead wife."

"Your wife!"

"Yes, my dead wife. What do you think I brought this bundle of clothes along for? They are the old clothes she left in the shack when she died. She is goin to walk off this hill tonight with me. She is goin to live again through the Faith in the Word. It will put new life into the dead. It will lift mountains. You see, Brother Sluss come here with me a year ago today when my wife was buried here on this hill. You remember my wife, don't you, Brother Sluss?"

"Yes, I remember your wife. I was by her bedside prayin when she died. I heard her last breath sizzle. I heard her say, 'I see the blessed Saviour.' Then she was gone. I followed Joe Mangle's mules that pulled her here that muddy September day last year. When your wife died, I thought I'd have to die too. I just couldn't hardly stand it. You had a good woman."

"That cold rainy day was the day I waited till they had all gone off'n the hill but the grave-diggers and when they was throwin over her some of the last dirt I watched them from behind the butt of that old chimney there in the blackberry vines—I was scrounched down there in that hole where the pot-hooks used to swing. And when one of the grave diggers said: 'Boys, since we're so nearly done and the weather's so rainy and cold, what's you fellars say let's slip down yander behind the bank and take a drink of licker? Looks purty bad to drink here over this woman's dead body and her a woman of God's, but a little licker won't go a bit bad now.' And they all throwed their shovels and picks down and took off over the bank. While they was down over the bank I slipped out beside the grave and took a long-handled shovel, a corn scoop and a coal pick–I had this in mind when I hid if they ever left their tools. I wanted to see them throw the dirt in and I didn't want them to see me. I hid the tools in the butt of the chimney where I was hidin. And I said to myself, 'I'll come back here a year from today and I'll put new breath in her through the Faith in the Word.' So, I got the tools. I hid them right here. I stayed with them. The boys couldn't find their tools and they argued how funny it was their tools disappeared so suddenly, said it was such a strange thing. Some men accused the other men of not bringin their tools. They throwed in the rest of the dirt on my dead wife, then they swaggered full of licker off'n the hill. A red leaf stuck to the long-handle shovel handle. I think it was a leaf blowed off'n that sweet-gum tree right over there. There was death in that leaf same as there was death in my wife. Dead leaves are on the ground tonight, not red with death so much as they was red with death last September in the rain when my wife was buried here."

"Brother Groan, I knowed your wife. She was a fine woman, wasn't she?"

"Yes. My wife was a very fine woman."

"Brother Groan, I knowed your wife since you spoke about her. Your wife had a harelip, didn't she? She was marked with a rabbit, wasn't she?"

"Yes, Brother Redfern, my wife had a harelip. But she wasn't marked with no rabbit. God put it there for the sins of her people. And my wife wouldn't let no Doctor sew it up. My wife would say in church, 'God put this harelip on me for the sins of my people and I shall wear it for God.' My wife was a good woman."

"Brother Groan, I remember the woman with the harelip. And she was your wife! Well, I saw her five summers ago, a tall woman slim as a bean pole with a harelip. I saw her in Puddle, West Virginia. She was in God's house and she said the words you said that she always said about her lip. And one thing she said has always stuck with me. It was somethin like this: 'A man swimmed out in the river with his two sons. He was a good swimmer and they tried to follow him. He led the way for them. One went under the water and never come up again. The father started back with his other son toward the river bank and under he went too to never come up again. 'My God Almighty,' the father cried out, 'my sons are lost. They went the wrong way too far and I led them. I led them into this danger.' And your wife fairly preached there that night. And the sperit of God was there in that house."

"Brother Groan, I was in Venom, Kentucky, two summers ago and I saw your wife. She was in God's house there. She had a harelip I remember and all her teeth nearly showed in front. They looked like awful long teeth. I remember when she was talkin to God she had a awful hard time sayin her words to God. She got up and said the words you said she said about her lip to the people, then she pulled her sleeve up and showed where she was marked on the arm by the belly of a sow. There was a patch of black sow-belly skin on her arm and thin sow-belly hairs scattered all over it. And there was three small sows' teats about the size of a gilt sow's teats. And your wife said: 'People, God has marked me because my people have sinned against God and I am to carry the marks of my sinnin people. I aim to carry the marks too. No Doctor can cut the one off'n my arm or sew the one up on my lip.' Brother Groan, your wife was a good woman."

"Yes, Brother Littlejohn, my wife was a good woman."

"Brother Groan, I remember your wife. I saw her in God's house. It has been three years ago this September. I saw her at a tent meetin at Beaverleg, Ohio. And I'll die rememberin one good thing I heard your wife get up and say. She said: 'Women, if I had a man mean as the very Devil which I ain't got, I would get up and cook for him at the blackest midnight. I would get a good warm meal for him if I had the grub to cook for him. Why? Because where he is goin after he leaves this world there he won't have no sweet wife to cook for him.' Yes, I remember your wife sayin these words. She had a hard time speakin her testimony to God, for her words was not plain. I remember your wife and the half words she said. It was September in a hayfield near Beaverleg, Ohio, where the tent of God was. Your wife was a good woman, wasn't she?"

"Yes, my wife was a good woman, Brother Pigg. She was a good woman. You are goin to see my wife again. She is goin to walk off this hill with me. You bring the corn scoop here and shovel down through the loose dirt on top of the grave far down as you can shovel and lift out with the short-handle corn scoop. Here is the place. Start right here. Here is the place my wife was buried a year ago today. Yes, my wife was a good woman."

"Did you say to begin here, Brother Groan?"

"Yes, begin right there."

"Right at her feet?"

"I don't like to do this–mess with the dead."

"Ain't you got no Faith?"

"Faith in what?"

"Faith in the Word?"

"Yes, I got Faith in the Word."

"Dig then!"

"Well."

The moist September grave dirt is scooped out like loose corn out of a wagon bed. When the scoops of dirt hit the dirt pile, they are like so many dish rags hittin the kitchen floor. Dirt hits the dead weeds and the dead leaves on the ground in little thuds. The big moon is yellow above the dead dirty grass and the white tombstones and the rain-cloud gray tombstones. The Disciples are silent now except for the wet dirt piece-meal in the ground. Brother Fain Groan is whisperin to God.

"I need the long-handle shovel!"

"Here is the shovel, Brother Pigg. Leave me dig a little while, Brother Pigg. Ain't you about fagged out?"

"Brother Littlejohn, I believe I will let you spell me a little."

"You have sure scooped this down some, Brother Pigg."

"I raised enough sweat. Closed in down here and the wind don't hit you right."

"Wind can't hit a body down in this hole, can it?"

"No."

"Boys, I'll know my wife by her lip. Thank God, I ain't ashamed of it neither. She told the people she wasn't ashamed of it. And I ain't ashamed of it neither, thank God. God don't heal this old clay temple of ours only through the Faith in the Word. I'll put breath back in my dead wife's body and she'll become my livin wife again. My wife–you have seen my wife and you'll know my wife when she is risen from the grave, Brother Sluss, and breathes the breath of life again."

Brother Groan walks out among the graves. His face is turned toward the stars. He whispers unknown syllables to the wind. The wind whispers unknown syllables to the weeds and to the dead leaves.

"I thought I heard a voice."

"A voice!"

"Yes."

"Ah!"

"The voice of God."

"No."

"It was the voice of the wind."

"Yes."

"The wind."

"The wind in the dead grass."

"Well then, did you hear the voice?"

"No."

"What did you hear?"

"I heard the wind in the grass."

"The wind!"

"Yes. The wind. The wind."

"You are gettin way down there, Brother Littlejohn. Let me spell you a little while with that shovel."

"All right, Brother Redfern. The ground is gettin hard here. Bring the coal pick down with you."

"Did you know there is a slip on one side of this grave?

There is a hole down in this grave like a water seep. That is what made the shovelin easy. That is why we are gettin along fast."

"Is it?"

"Yes."

"Throw me down the pick, Brother Pigg. I have found some white tangled roots down here. Wait! I may be able to pull them out with my hand. A root this big down this far in the ground. I don't see any close trees. It must have come from that wild-cherry standin over there on this side of the blackberry patch."

"Can you yank them roots out with your hands or do you want the coal pick? The ax end of the coal pick will cut them."

"Wait! I'm stung. The root flew up and hit my arm. Wait! Stung again. Wait! Here it comes. May be a snake! My God Almighty, but I'm stung. It can't be a snake though—a snake this deep down!"

"I'll see if it is a root. If it is a wild-cherry root it is a chubby wild-cherry root nearly big as a two-year-old baby's thigh. My God, but it has stung me. It jumped and stung me. I am bit by a snake and you are bit by a snake. Yes. It is a snake. Strike a match! Watch—it is goin to strike again. Watch out. There! See it strike. It is a rusty-mouth grave copperhead. My God!"

"Come out of the grave, Brother Redfern. You have been bit by a rusty-mouth grave copperhead."

"Let us have Faith in the Word."

"Give me your pocketknife, Brother Littlejohn."

"What for?"

"To cut out the bite and suck the blood."

"Ain't you got no Faith in the Word?"

"Yes, but I know what to do for a copperhead bite. We ain't no business here messin with the dead nohow. It is against the Word to prank with the dead. Don't the Word say, 'Let the dead rest. Bury the dead and let them rest'? Give me that knife."

"Brother Redfern, I'll cut your arm on the copperhead bite

and suck your blood and you cut my arm on the copperhead bites and suck my blood."

"All right."

"God, ain't this awful out here this night."

"Brother Pigg is bit. Brother Redfern is bit."

"Go down in the grave, Brother Shinliver."

"Are you afraid to go? We're bit and we can't go back. We're goin to get sick in a few minutes."

"I thought I heard a voice."

"You did."

"Yes. Is it God's voice?"

"No. It is the voice of Brother Groan."

"See him! He has opened the bundle of clothes he brought. He is holdin up a woman's dress he brought in the bundle of clothes he carried up here on the hill tonight. He brought them clothes to dress his wife in when we get her dug out'n the grave."

"New clothes?"

"I'll ask and see."

"No—the clothes she used to wear. The dress Brother Groan liked to see her wear. The dress she looked so pretty in. Here is the hat she wore. It is a high-crowned black hat with a goose plume on the side. And here are the shoes she wore last. They are peaked-toe, patent-leather, low-heeled, button shoes. The clothes are right here for the woman soon as she comes out of the grave and the breath of life goes into her lungs."

"I have hit the wood, men. It is the box. I'll have to shovel the dirt from around the box so we can lift it out. I need hand holts. Wait till I clear some of the dirt away with my hands. I'm stung—stung like a red wasper stings right in the calf of the leg. Its teeth are hung in my pant's leg. Get me out, men —get me out quick—It is another copperhead."

"Leave him out of the grave, men. See it. It is a copperhead. Its fangs are hung in his pant's leg. Hit it with a shovel handle. Cut it with a knife. Kill it!"

"Cut the calf of my leg, Brother Littlejohn, with your pocketknife and suck the blood, for I can't get to my leg to suck the blood out and the blood won't come out fast enough unless it is sucked out."

"All right."

"Strike a match. It is a she copperhead. Its head ain't as copper as the he-copperhead's. I thought it must be a she, for the old rusty-mouthed one was the he-copperhead."

"Ain't you got no Faith in the Word, Brother Shinliver?"

"Yes, but Brother Littlejohn, we ain't got no business messin with the dead. The Word says, 'We must bury the dead and bury them so deep and leave them alone.' Don't the Word say that? I don't want my leg rottin off. Cut my leg and suck the blood."

"All right."

"I got that copperhead."

"Strike a match."

"See how gray the belly is turned up. It looks like a poplar root."

"Are you afraid of that grave, Brother Littlejohn?"

"No, I ain't afraid of that grave."

"Get down and shovel awhile then."

"You want the coal pick?"

"Yes, the coal pick."

"God–God I'm stung. The first pop out'n the box and I'm stung right on the soft part of the jaw. The sting was like the sting of a red wasper."

"You stung, Brother Littlejohn!"

"Stung! Yes! My God! Take it off! Take it off! Its fangs are fastened in my flesh. Take it off, men. Take it off!"

"Yank him out'n the hole, men. All right. Come, Brother Frazier."

"Cut that snake off with your pocketknife. Cut it through the middle and it'll let loose. I've heard they wouldn't let loose till it thundered, but cut its guts out with a knife and it'll let loose, I'll bet you a dollar."

"Wait, I'll get it. Got it. Feel its fangs leavin your jaw?"

"No. My jaw is numb."

"Cut his jaw, Brother Frazier, and suck the blood."

"All right."

"You're hit awful close the eye."

"Makes no difference. Cut the bite and suck the blood."

"Let me down in that grave. I'll take that coffin out by myself. I ain't afraid of no copperhead—no grave copperhead can faze me."

And Brother Frazier, short and stocky two-hundred-and-fifty-pounder goes down into the grave. He is a mountain of a man. He lifts one end of the box, coffin and dead woman—he lifts it from the gluey earth. He lifts one end out and puts it upon the grave. The other end of the box rests down in the hole.

Brother Pigg and Brother Redfern are gettin mighty sick. They were bitten by the first copperhead, the rusty-mouthed grave he-copperhead. Brother Redfern and Brother Pigg are down under the hill by the wire fence. They are wallowin on the weeds. They are sick enough to die. They have a very high fever, the arm of each man is swollen and numb. They do not know they are wallowin on the weeds in the graveyard, they know no more than the dead beneath them.

Brother Groan comes up with the button shoes, the dress with the white dot, the black high-crowned hat with the white goose plume. Brother Fain Groan does not have a screw driver to take the coffin out of the box and the woman out of the coffin that the mountain of a man Brother Frazier lifted out of the grave hole alone. Brother Fain Groan grabs the coal pick. The box boards fly off one by one—these water-soaked coffin box boards. They are all off. Here is the color of an autumn-seasoned beech-stump coffin, rather slim and long the coffin is—but Sister Groan was tall and slender as a bean pole, remember—Brother Groan doesn't have a screw driver and he puts the sharp end of the coal pick under the coffin lid and he heaves once—only a screak like the tearin off of old clapboards pinned down with rusty square-wire nails. Another heave and another heave, still another and another—off comes the lid.

"My God Almighty. My wife. My God! My wife! Oh my God, but it is my wife. Perfectly natural too! My God! Oh my God Almighty! My wife!" Brother Groan just wilts over like a tobacco leaf in the sun. He wilts beside his dead wife. She wilted one year ago. The whole night and the copperheads is nothin to him now. The night is neither dark nor light to him. He knows no more than the dead woman beside him.

"That's Groan's wife all right. See that lip, Brother Sluss."

"Yes, that is Brother Groan's wife all right. Strike a match. See that arm where it is crossed on her breast. That is Brother Groan's wife all right, Brother Frazier."

"She looks like a rotten black-oak stump since the wind hit her on the face, don't she?"

"She looked like a seasoned autumn-beech stump before the wind hit her face, didn't she?"

"Yes, she did."

"But she looks like a black-oak stump now."

"No. She looks like a wet piece of chestnut bark."

"Ain't it funny the things the wind can do. Change the looks of a person. Talk with God. Whisper around in the corn like Brother Groan whispers to God."

"What is it that smells like wild onions in a cow pasture?"

"No, that smell to me is like the sour insides of a dead persimmon tree."

"Let's get away from here. Shake Brother Groan. Get him up and let's go."

"Brother Groan won't wake. See how hard I pull his coat collar. He don't breathe. His heart has quit beatin. Feel! Brother Groan, get up and let's leave here! He's dead sure as the world. Brother Groan is dead! His breath is gone! Let's get out of here!"

"I tell you it don't pay to tamper with the dead."

"The Word says the dead shall be at rest. They shall be buried deep enough not to be bothered by men plowin and jolt wagons goin over the tops of them and the cows pickin the grass from over them. The Word says the dead shall rest."

"I think I ruptured a kidney liftin that box out awhile ago by myself. No, it don't pay to tamper with the dead."

Brother Frazier and Brother Sluss walk away from the grave. Brother Frazier walks like a bear. He is a short, broad man.

He has to squeeze between some of the tall tombstones. Brother Sluss does not have any trouble. Here is Brother Littlejohn wallowin in the graveyard. He tries to get up and he falls back. He acts like a chicken that has lost its head, but Brother Littlejohn has not lost his head, his head is big and swollen. He does not know anymore than the dead beneath him. Here is Brother Shinliver. He lies with his swollen leg propped upon the grave. He, too, is dead, dead as the dead under the ground—dead as Brother Groan; dead as Brother Groan's wife. Brother Pigg and Brother Redfern are lyin lifeless now; lyin down beside the wire fence where one first comes into the graveyard. They were tryin to get home. They couldn't get through four strands of barb wire stretched across the wind. They know no more than the grass beneath them; the dead beneath them. There is vomit all around them on the grass and the dead and the half-dead weeds and the dead leaves. Brother Sluss and Brother Frazier leave the graveyard. They are afraid. They leave the dead there and the sick there with the dead. They go down through the peach orchard, the corn patch, the pig lot and the cow pasture. They are crossin the cow pasture now—down the path where the pawpaw bushes trim each side of the path. Brother Frazier says: "Brother Groan died beside of his dead wife. Or was that put-on do you suppose? Was he in a trance or was he dead?"

"No, Brother Groan is dead. His heart stopped beatin and I suppose he is dead. I guess that kills the old clay temple when the heart stops beatin."

"I don't believe Brother Groan had the right kind of Faith in the Word."

"Let your wife die—be dead a year. Go at midnight and dig her up and look at her and let the moon be shinin down on them lip-uncovered front teeth of hers and see what it does to you. See if your heart beats. See the pure natural bloom on her face at first. Strike a match and see the wind turn it black right before your eyes while the match is still burnin and you'd forget all about the Faith in the Word."

"Yes, I saw that. I got sick too. I tell you it don't pay to dig up the dead. The Word says the dead shall have their rest. The Word says the dead die to rest, that they shall be buried deep enough to get their rest without bein bothered by cattle pickin grass from over them, wagons makin tracks over them, men walkin over them. Then we go out and dig up Brother Groan's wife. It is the Word that filled that grave with copperheads. The copperheads was put in there for a purpose when Brother Groan hid in that chimney butt and hid them tools in there that he stole from the grave diggers. We have worked against the Word."

"I got awful sick there at the grave when the coffin was opened and I saw Groan's wife. Lord, I got sick when I saw that mark on her arm—looked plain-blank like the belly of a young sow. I saw the lip too—a three-cornered lip and it black as a last year's corn shuck. It had long white teeth beneath it and one could see the roots of her front teeth. And then her face was the color of a rotten stump. I saw the face turn black as the match stem burned up in the wind. Lord, I had to leave."

"It wasn't the looks that made me sick. It was that awful scent when the coffin was opened. I smelled somethin like mushrooms growin on an old log—a old sour log where the white-bellied water dogs sleep beneath the bark."

"Smelled like wild onions to me."

"I don't believe that Brother Groan had the right kind of Faith. I have never thought it since we was all supposed to meet down there at the Manse Wiffard Gap at that sycamore tree. We was to crucify Brother Groan that night. We was to tie him with a rope to a sycamore limb. And he said his sperit would ride to Heaven right before us on a big white cloud. We went down there and waited around nearly all the night and he never did come. I don't believe he had the right kind of Faith in the Word."

The sun is up. The bright rays of sun, semi-golden fall on the peach tree leaves semi-golden. The oak leaves swirl like clusters of blackbirds in the wind; oak leaves, red, golden, scarlet—semi-golden oak leaves the color of one that stuck to the shovel handle last September. There is fire in the new

September day. The wind is crisp to breathe. The tombstones gleam in the sun; the wind has dried the dew off the weeds; the wind has dried and half-dried the vomit on the leaves and the grass and the vomit that still sticks to the lips of the four senseless yet livin men that lie in the graveyard with the dead.

The neighborhood is astir. They hunt for Fain Groan, Wilkes Redfern, Roch Shinliver, Cy Pigg, Lucas Littlejohn; David Sluss and Elijah Frazier could tell where they are but they are ashamed. They slipped in at their back doors. They are in bed now sleepin soundly as the dead.

People know here in the neighborhood that Fain Groan has a band of Disciples; that they meet out two and three times each week in the woods and in old houses; but they have always come in before daylight. The neighborhood is astir.

But Constable Ricks sees somethin from his house. He sees somethin goin on up at the graveyard. He has seen plenty of buzzards and crows workin on the carcasses of dead horses, but he has never seen such swarm in all his life as he now sees upon the hill at the graveyard. He sees crows sittin up in the wild-cherry tree; enough of them sittin upon the limbs to break them off. There are the guard crows even. The ground is black with crows. He hears the crows caw-cawin to each other and to the buzzards tryin to fight them back. But they are turkey buzzards and they won't be whipped by cornfield crows. They bluff their wing feathers and their neck feathers right out and like fightin game roosters take right after the crows. The crows give back when they see the turkey buzzards comin. They don't give back until then. Crows fly from the ground up in the wild-cherry tree and then back to the ground. They change about crow habit, some guard while others eat.

Constable Ricks starts for the Kale Nelson Graveyard. He is ridin a mule. He leaps the mule up the hill. He sees a pile of fresh dirt before he gets there, he sees somethin like a box on top of the ground, somethin like a man, somethin like a pile of clothes. Up to the graveyard and he sees. The crows fly up in a black cloud. The buzzards are very slow about it.

but they fly up too. He ties the mule to a fence post. One buzzard alights on the back of the mule and scares him. Constable Ricks rides the mule back fast as the mule can gallop to Coroner Stone's house. He calls Coroner Stone from the corn patch. He jumps on the mule behind Constable Ricks. They gallop the mule back to the graveyard. Here are all the crows and buzzards back and more are comin.

When they scare the crows and the buzzards off Brother Groan and Brother Groan's wife, they fly down at the lower end of the graveyard, they fly down to somethin on the ground. Many as can find a place alight on the fence posts. Constable Ricks runs down there and shoos them away and strikes the air at them as they fly with the long-handle shovel he picks up back at the grave. He finds four men on the ground and he finds plenty of sun-dried vomit on the leaves and on the dead weeds. Wilkes Redfern, Roch Shinliver, Cy Pigg, Lucas Littlejohn are lyin senseless on the ground. Constable Ricks thinks they are dead the way the crows are tryin to get to them and the way the buzzards are fightin back the crows from them. He goes up and feels over each heart to see if it is beatin. All hearts are beatin. The flesh of each man is cold. The warm September sun has not thoroughly thawed them after the cool night. "Found four men senseless but yet alive, Fred. Come down here. Let's take care of the livin first." Constable Ricks picks up a clod of dirt and he throws it at the crows with intent to kill. The clod goes through the whole flock of crows and does not touch a feather.

Coroner Fred Stone stays with the dead and livin at the graveyard while Constable Ricks jumps on the mule and gallops over the neighborhood to tell that he has found the missin men. Coroner Stone finds the rusty-mouthed copperhead, the she-copperhead and the young copperhead. The snakes are dead, wilted and limber like a dead horse-weed in the sun. He knows the four men have been bitten by copperheads down under the hill by the wire fence where one first comes in the graveyard when walkin up the path and not ridin a mule or bringin a team. He looks at the face of Brother Groan—it is black—black as a wilted pawpaw leaf. It has been picked on by the crows. But picked on is all. His face is old and tough. It is tough as crow meat. Brother Groan's wife's face is the color of a young blackberry sprout hit by a heavy October frost—wilted and soggy black. Her face has been picked on by the crows. Most of it is gone. Coroner Stone looks carefully at the dress with the white dot, the patent leather low-heeled button shoes, the black high-crowned hat with the white goose plume in the side. They are in Brother Groan's left arm, his arm is wound around them like the short stubby body of a copperhead and his dead fingers clutch them like the copperhead's fangs. Before the neighborhood gets back upon the hill and Constable Ricks comes with the spring wagon to haul the four senseless men home, Coroner Stone holds his inquest: "Fain Groan committed suicide when he dug his wife up and looked at her." He said, "I know he planned to dig her up because here are the old clothes I used to see her wear." That was Coroner Stone's duty.

When Constable Ricks comes upon the hill he arrests the dead man. He thinks that is his duty, for he doesn't know much about the Law. He arrests him on the charge of "Public Indecency." Then he says, "My duties have been faithfully performed within the 'sharp eyes' of the Law."

The neighborhood men put Fain Groan's wife back in the coffin and give her a second burial. They hang the copperheads on the fence wires, for they say it is a sign of rain to hang a dead snake on the fence. They throw the four men in the wagon, senseless but livin men, throw them in like four barrels of salt, throw in Brother Groan with his loose flowing robe like he was a shock of fodder with loose stalks danglin around the edges and they hurry them off the hill in the spring wagon.

Quinn Snodgrass claims the body of Fain Groan. Fidas Campbell claims him too. Quinn Snodgrass is the brother of Fain Groan's second wife, Fidas Campbell is the brother of Fain Groan's first wife. His third wife didn't have a brother to claim him as it is the custom to be buried by the first wife and that is in keepin in accordance with the Word. But Quinn Snodgrass got the body of Fain Groan.

It was the first house beside the wagon road and the team pulled up and they carried his body in the house, though his dead body was still under arrest for Public Indecency. That day Quinn shaved the long beard from his face and cut his hair. He pulled the Christlike robe from his body and bathed his body in water heated in the wash kettle, put the moth-eaten minister's suit on him and prepared him for a nice clean burial. Out in the cow shed hammers and handsaws were kept busy all the time makin his coffin. The next mornin he was hauled in a jolt wagon with four boys a-sittin on his coffin to Pine Hill Graveyard and buried beside of his second wife, Symanthia Snodgrass. He was still under arrest for Public Indecency for diggin up his wife so the crows and the buzzards could expose her parts.

There was a quarrel between Beadie Redfern and Sibbie Frazier over Fain Groan's wife's clothes that were picked up at the grave upon the hill. Sibbie got the hat and shoes and Beadie got the dress. Men came and claimed the tools and thanked whoever found them. Tim Holmes claimed the long-handle shovel. Carlos Shelton claimed the corn scoop. Bridge Sombers claimed the coal pick. All testified they had been missin since the day they buried Fain Groan's wife the first time, a year ago the day before.

It is tough now to see Cy Pigg and Wilkes Redfern tryin to plow with one arm. Looks like they both would make a good plowin team. Wilkes lost his left arm. Cy lost his right arm. It is horrible to watch Lucas Littlejohn tryin to eat with just one jaw. One can see his teeth grind the food and watch some of it squirm out through the hole in his jaw if one wants to watch it. The Doctors couldn't keep the flesh from rottin and fallin out though pokeberry roots and sweet milk did heal them. And there is Roch Shinliver, fat as mud, hobblin around on a wooden leg. People knows his tracks by a big shoe track and a peg hole in the ground. His leg is all there–the bone is there–it has never been taken off where the flesh rotted from the copperhead bite and the muscles rotted and left the white bone.

I

FRONNIE goes to the door. She stops suddenly, turns her head and begins to cry. "Pap is dyin. My God, Pap is dyin." There is old Battle Keaton. See him lying there on the bed. See him lying there—his face cold and white—white as a frost-bitten beech leaf is white when the sun comes out in September. His white face upturned to the low plank loft where spider webs hang filled with the skeletons of dead flies. Battle's eye sockets are like little muddy pools and the eyeballs in these sockets are like dead chunks of black-oak wood floating on the muddy water in these pools. There he lies—see him! Old Battle Keaton! The frizzly long slim beard on his chin and the flat slabs on his jaws is like the pine needles, like the bull grass too in the walls of a crow's nest. It is frizzled up, this long white beard of old Battle Keaton's, and a mouse could hide in it. Mice could make a nest in it. The wind comes through the window on the northeast side of the bed and it plays with Battle's white crow-nest beard. It bends down a slim beard and then it lifts it up again. The wind does this. And it nibbles like a mouse at the upturned corner of a sheet. One can't see the wind, but one knows it is the wind. And the oak-chunk eyes of old Battle Keaton's, now frozen in the muddy pool eye sockets, are fixed on the spider webs hanging to the planks in the loft and to the pine-pole rafters of the house.

"Come here, Fronnie! Come here, Fronnie. I said, come here Fronnie! Fotch me a snip of water so I can wet my parchin tongue. It is dry and hot as a pile of sand in July. I can't get the words off my tongue. They hang to my dry tongue, God knows how they hang to my dry tongue." Fronnie gets the gourd dipper of water from the zinc bucket, she takes down the long-handled gourd dipper with the double-black stripe running around the big end of the gourd. There are two gourd dippers at the water bucket and Fronnie gets the long-handled dipper. She dips the gourd into the zinc bucket and lifts the water in the dipper to Battle's decayed potato-hole mouth and holds the dipper so he can drink. Battle Keaton sip-sips and he sip-sips and sip-sips the water from the gourd. And more water than old Battle drinks from the gourd is now falling, warm water, though, it is and not fit to drink—water though, is falling from the eyes of Fronnie Bradberry. "Feel any better now, Pap?" "Yes, I feel better. I mean I feel some better. I feel some better, but I don't feel nigh right yet. I don't feel at myself—not nigh at myself. I feel like a baby with little pink hands—with fingers you can move around just like fishin worms. That water didn't get all the way down. That water lodged like a lot of green apples in my windpipe and I can feel every lump of that water. I wish you'd take a stick and punch it on down so I could get some wind down my windpipe. Give me another swaller of that water and I want to tell you somethin." Fronnie dips the gourd into the zinc bucket—she carries the water to Battle. And this is water from the well that Battle found the vein of, water far underground, with his magic peach-tree forked branch—and for twenty years his daughter Fronnie has drunk water from this well. Battle sip-sips the water—sip-sips and gurgles the water down like water falling over tiny rocks where the ferns have their drooping heads stuck into the water.

Battle has sip-sipped the water now. Water for thirst. Water to make words. "That water shoved that other water on down and now I have some room to get wind down my windpipe. Wind gives me wind to make words for you to speak to you and tell you, Fronnie, my baby girl, what I want to tell to you. Water clears up my windpipe and water wets my tongue so the words won't stick to the end of my tongue. Words pile up on the end of my tongue like dry chunks when I'm cuttin off the sweet-tater ground and pilin up dry chunks in the spring o' the year. But I can talk. My tongue is slick as a meat skin."

"Pap, don't you feel any better? Can you see the loft right above your eyes? Wait. Can you see my hand?" Fronnie waves her hand above the dark eyes set in the dark pools. She waves her hand above the dark-chunk eyes and under the loft. And Battle says: "Yes, I can see your hand. What do you think my eyes are anyway, things to see out'n of, and can't see with? What do you think my eyes are for, to eat with? Askin me if I can see your hand and it's as plain to me as daylight is plain to me! Then you ask me. My God Almighty, Fronnie–and you ask me! Do you think I am half-way dead, or whole-way dead, or what?"

"No, Pap. I just didn't know about your eyes."

"Well, I know about my own eyes. I can see the planks in the loft with my eyes good as I could see them when I was a young man. See. There is a pine plank by a chestnut plank and a poplar plank on tother side of the pine plank. I laid that floor forty-six years ago, before I ever went to Flint County. I never was, and will never be satisfied with that piece of work I done. Every day after I walk to the wood yard and hobble on that old sour-wood cane–I come back in here and take my rest on this bed and I lay here and look up there at that loft and wonder just why I put down a pine plank between a chestnut plank and a poplar plank."

"Can you see them planks like that?"

"W'y, Fronnie, I lay here and I watch that old striped-backed spider up there on the loft–she has stripes down her back just like the stripes on the big end of the water gourd. I watch that old spider day in and day out. I watch her when I come in after I walk to the chipyard every day. That old spider is allus out there next to that chestnut knot hole. I watch her spin her web and trap her grub. And then she goes over and drinks all the fly's blood if she catches a fly and if she catches a hornet she don't suck his blood right then but she just holds him there and starves him down first. But that old spider catches the flies. Look up there at the bones of the dead flies. After she drinks the blood of the fly the body of the fly gets dry as powder. I guess after it gets dry it crumbles up in dust and the dust of the dead flies fall down here on my bed and I wallow in the dead dust of so many flies. That's what I been thinkin about here lately. Well, I lay here and I think I can reach up there and get that old she-striped-back spider sometimes. I want to cut its guts out with a knife. I want to crush that spider between my thumb and my index finger so bad I can taste it. God knows I ain't got no use for no damn fly, but I can't stand to see them lay up there in them webs and have to die by degrees. I have to lay here on this bed and I can't lift my arm sometimes to reach for that spider. My arm is too heavy for me to lift to the loft. And I think of old Tid Coons who used to run a sawmill and work his men eleven hours for a dollar and ten cents a day. He was a striped-backed spider like that one up there on the wall."

"Pap, don't you want some more water?"

"Not now. I'm tellin you, Fronnie, about old Tid Coons. And old Tid took the blood out'n twelve men instead of twelve flies. Old Tid is dead and gone now and he didn't take his money with him. His children is runnin through with his money—runnin through with the blood he sucked out'n us. But he was a spider spinnin webs from one hilltop to another hilltop—just so that they had timber on them. The words are hangin to my tongue and I got a lot of things I want to tell you. Words on my tongue are like dry straws in a haystack and there is just as many words there as there is straws in a haystack. Bring me some water, Fronnie—words hangin to my tongue and I can't get them off without water. I feel like a little baby with pink fingers and little mouse-paw hands."

Fronnie holds the long-handled gourd to Battle's lips—lips parched, dark like a hole black and chipped around the edges in a sound Irish potato. Battle sips and he tastes his tongue and he tastes his lips. And he tastes again and he sips-in water into his potato-hole mouth, water the color of thin air, water sweet to taste—sweet as the thin petal of a blackberry blossom. Battle tastes again and he tastes his lips and his tongue—his tongue, blue-looking and thick like the tongue of a calf, comes out of his mouth and feels for water and slips back like a mouse going into a little dark hole. He tastes again and again he tastes and he swallows. And he hunts for more water with his tongue like a mouse comes out of a hole afraid of a cat and looks around for water the color of thin air.

"Ain't you goin to take me out on the porch, Fronnie, since the day has got up and you got the dinner dishes cleaned and put away? Take me out there, and put me out there on that bed on the porch. I can't stand to look at them planks up there in that loft and that spider any longer. I want to feel the sun again and let it shine on my face. I want to feel the wind on my face. I want my eyes turned to the cornfield where Snider is plowin. I want to watch the corn grow. I want to take a stalk of corn in my hand and squeeze the growin green juice out'n it. I like to watch Snider plow the mule and Vicey cut the high weeds behind the plow."

"Pap, I can't take you out there by myself. Wait till I call Snider and Vicey."

Fronnie goes to the door. And she calls, "Snider! O Snider! Come here, Snider." And Snider says, "Yeh–whoa! Yeh–whoa! What do you want, Ma?" "You and Vicey come 'ere and help me move Pap. He ain't a-restin well." "All right, Ma. But when a body's workin that's the way you do. Stop him. Call him right in out'n the field, to milk a cow, cut some wood and move Grandpa."

Snider ties the mule to a splintered stump. Vicey goes ahead –she is running, her brown, moving legs cut through the wind. She goes through the four-stand rusted barb-wire fence –into the pasture and down a bank–steep, daisy-covered–up the hill then under the blooming locust trees–and then to the house. Snider walks slowly under the stalks of green corn, head-high, and over the head slightly, and corn twice head-high. Snider walks slowly, his big bare feet sweaty and dirt covered, spread over the plowed ground like a soft wind-bloated bullfrog mashed down, pressed flatly on the ground. When Snider turned this ground for corn, his father Sweet-bird walked between the plow handles. Snider drove the mules –and he wore a shoe on the foot near the mules. Snider's feet are scaly–a heavy skin to protect his blood from the cold of March and April.

"Come in here, Snider, you and Vicey, and help me carry Pap to the porch and put him on that half-bed out there. Pap ain't feelin nigh right. He wants to talk all the time. And he's been drinkin water and talkin all mornin."

"I know Grandpa. He wants to get out here on this porch where he can look over there and count the rows of corn I plow. Then when Pa comes in he'll tell Pa and you know Pa will cuss the top of the house off if I ain't done a big day's work. Grandpa's got eyes like a buzzard. I don't care if he is eighty-four years old. He can see that hill over there and almost count the cornstalks. He can if the sun don't get in his eyes. He ain't sick as he lets on. He wants to tell Pa I am lazy and have Pa jumpin all over me when Pa comes in from grubbin. Now Ma, that's what Grandpa wants. Everytime I help put him on that porch I have to fuss with Pa that night over how much plowin I done that day. You know how he beat me up that night Bud Timberlake drunk that pizen licker and come home and driv that little lamb off'n the hill and cut its throat with a butcher knife. You remember that night, don't you?"

"Your Grandpa is childish. He is gettin so much like a baby. Your Grandpa is old. He is very sick. You must pet him like he was a baby with little pink toes and little pink hands. He has been a hard-workin man. He used to do as much work as two men. Now he can't work and he likes to watch people work."

"But I don't want to work like Grandpa. Look at his hands in there, won't you? They look like a bear's claws–Look at them. If I'd take my shirt off and drag it across Grandpa's hands it would hang up on his rough hands and the shirt would tear. I don't want hands like Grandpa's."

"Your Grandpa is awful sick. He says words hang on his tongue. He asts me to give him water so he can moisten his tongue and talk to me. Your Grandpa is awful sick."

"Awful sick."

"Yes. Said he felt like a baby with pink hands. Come to the door. Look through there at Pap. See how pale Pap is. His face is white as the burnt-out dirt around the wash kettle. All the blood in it has been burnt out. All the color in it has been burnt out. And Pap has worked hisself to death. He has worked hisself to death on the hills of Flint County. He has cut so much timber there and he has cut timber all over these hills too. He has helped to build nearly all the roads in this County and in Flint County and he has helped to build the railroad bed for the Big Sandy Railroad. He has worked like a brute since he was a little boy. His life has about burnt out'n his temple of clay—nearly stone deef too. Be of mind and don't say nothin loud enough for him to hear you—it will hurt his feelins. He's like a baby with pink hands."

"Mama, is Grandpa bad-off?"

"Yes, Vicey. Your Grandpa is sick enough to die. He ain't likely to get over it. He is likely to die, your Grandpa is."

"Poor Grandpa."

"Come on, Snider. Let's make a saddle pocket with our arms and slip it right under Pap's head and shoulders and, Vicey, you can get between Pap's legs and put one under each arm and we can carry him out here on the porch. You can tail him to the bed that way, can't you, Vicey?"

"Yes, Mama."

"Just pull the covers down. He's got on his shirt and his long drawers. He's dressed all right——"

"How do you make a saddle pocket with your arms, Ma?"

"Don't you know how to make a saddle pocket, much as you've carried the little girls around?"

"No."

"Hold your right arm out straight. Catch your right arm with your left at the wrist. Grip it tight. I'll do the same. Like this, see. Yes, you have done it right. Now catch my left arm with your right hand and grip it tight and I'll catch your left arm with my right hand and grip it tight. Now let's put our arms right under Pap's head and slip them down under his shoulders. That's good. Jump in the bed, Vicey, and pull the cover down and get between Pap's legs. Put a leg under each arm and follow us. Vicey, shove us just a little. Pap is heavy. Pap will weigh two-hundred pounds."

Under the door they go from the front room, through the dining-room, thence the partition door to the kitchen, then out on the back porch. Now they lay Battle carefully on the bed. And now they fix his eyes toward the cornfield and the sun. There is a little valley between, a fence, a daisy field, four barb-wires and some wind.

"Yes, I know how Pa is and how Grandpa is."

Snider and Vicey cross the valley and up through the daisies on the pasture hill, through the four strands of barb wire stapled tightly and stretched loosely to knotty black-locust posts—through the wind into the cornfield. Snider unhitches the mule from the splintered stump, he puts the rope lines around his shoulders, he steps between the handles of the double-shovel plow and the mule gets-up. The moist dirt begins to crumble around the green stalks of corn—moist dirt, cool, soft to the big mushroom feet of Snider Bradberry. Vicey picks up the goose-neck hoe. And she lifts it higher than her shoulder and she cuts the sour-wood sprouts. She watches for a snake—a copperhead—Vicey is afraid of the copperhead.

Stumps are low black things in the cornfields. They are sawed-off blocks of dead men—dead-men trees. Once they were living things. They were living things drinking wind into their leaves—drinking rain and ground water into their bodies. But now they are dead. Green corn is pretty, sprung from the roots—green corn in the thin blue air—air thin and pretty as running mountain water. Roots that ran deep into the loamy earth are now a rotted bit of wood—color of tobacco-stain under the earth where the dirt is moist and cool. Battle Keaton is an almost dead oak root lost in the loam of the earth.

Battle looks toward the cornfield. Now see him. There he is on the half-bed on the porch. His darker black-chunk eyes are frozen glass in the muddy pool of eye sockets—frozen and glued on the field of green waving corn—corn so pretty just before tasseling time—just before the last plowing. He counts the time in minutes it takes Snider to drive the mule around to the drain at the west end of the field and turn and come back in a row of corn. He counts the furrows Snider makes. And he thinks, "Ah, well, young men today don't work like they did when I was a boy. Men today ain't what they used to be." Battle sees little Vicey's hoe gleaming in the sun when she lifts it above her shoulder to cut a black-locust sprout. Battle Keaton says, "The sunlight is so good to feel. The sunlight is good to me. I love the sunlight. I always loved the sunlight. I love the wind. The wind is cool on my windpipe. The wind is good to breathe. I can taste the wind, I wish I could get up and go over there and plow a round around out there to that drain. I wish I had some new parts and I'd be all right. I need a new set of legs and then I could beat that boy over there a-plowin. I could walk to the wood yard without a cane. If I couldn't beat that boy over there a-plowin I'd quit. I'd do more in one day than he does in three. I aim to tell his Pa this very night that he ain't doin all the work he can or all the work he orta do. But he is like his Pa and his Pa's people. He ain't like his Ma Fronnie and my people."

Shadows shift in the cornfield—shadows shift and sunlight dances on the green cornblades like little mice playing hide-and-go-seek in dead fodder blades. Shadows shift—those just a little broader than a blade of corn. They swerve as the wind bends the stalks of green corn. Battle can see the cornstalks bend over and the shadows shift as the wind blows, but Battle can't smell the green corn in the wind flavored with the scent of pussley and he can't breathe again that sweet hot scent of wind from the cornfield and feel the dry-hot, soft-plowed dirt beneath his feet, the rope lines around his broad shoulders and his hands on the hickory handles of the plow with a whoa-whoa and gee-haw in his mouth. Battle is now a living mass of pale dirt—a temple of clay, the color of clay, where the fire has burned it around the edges of the wash kettle. Color has been sucked from, blood has been sucked from, his temple of clay—Time has sucked his blood and his color—Time is a spider catching flies in a little thin web on the low sky roof of earth house. Time is going to leave Battle a skeleton—his clay, burned dry is going to crumble and leave his bones—a naked tree so the wind can pass between his ribs and sizzle like his last breath will sizzle in his passing.

Battle watches the mule come and go and the mule go and come. He sees the mule and he loves to watch the mule step over the stumps and the rocks. He sees the sun, the bright, living sun—he sees the sun with glassy-fixed eyes—he sees the sun pretty and golden in the sky, shine down through the air clear as water in a mountain stream. He sees the pretty, green, living, growing corn and the moist dirt thrown up at its roots —he can see it—he has eyes like a buzzard. Age has brought his eyes to seeing distant. He sees the slender weeds growing and dancing in the sun and throwing up wind-bent arms to the sun. And Battle says: "Oh, if I had only two good legs. It is my legs. They ain't got no power no more than broom straws. They're what's holdin me back—my legs. If I was just young again and had life to live over I'd make it different. I'd love to do it all over again. I didn't do it right this time. Next time I'd know more about how to handle life. Life. Life. Life. Life. Life. Life. How good it is to live Life. I hate to leave it, and I ain't goin to leave it if I can help it—Life. Life. Life. Life. Life. Life." Green corn growing and pretty wind blowing and cows feeding on the green grass—feeding green grass over by the side of creek waters under the locust shades. Bees sucking on the bean blossoms in the cornfield beans and sucking on the summer cedar tops and the sweet-gum berries. Why not love life? Life in this summer season—so feather light, so full, so energetic—roots going down into the earth and blossoms waving on long stems from the earth—up, up, skyward in the pretty wind. White clouds floating over. Why not love life, Battle? You, Battle, with only hours to live. But you are like a baby, Battle. You are like a baby with little toes and pink fishing-worm fingers. We know you, Battle—we see your pale temple of clay. We know what the spider has done for you. Where is your blood? Your blood has been drunk back by the earth and all the color and heat there was in your body has been drunk back by the earth.

"Here is more water, Pap. Here, Pap. Here, just another little sip."

Slowly he sip-sips the color of wind water. Slowly. Slowly. Now he sip-sips. He cannot raise his hand to the gourd. His hand is heavy, but words will be light now. They will come better from his tongue. His tongue won't try to hold his words. He sips-sips slowly the color-of-wind well water.

"There is a sheet of darkness before me. You take your hand, Fronnie, and pick up this black sheet and take it upstairs and put it on the quilt stack. Don't put a black sheet over my face to blind me to the sun and the cornfield. No. No. No. I want to see the corn grow. I want to watch lazy Snider plow the mule. I can't see the mule go and come and go and come with this black sheet before my eyes. I can't see the tall corn in the pretty rows—the pretty, tall, green corn. Come here, I want to tell you somethin, Fronnie. A spider has got me in a web and got my blood. My blood is gone, I knowed my blood was gone last night when I went back—I went back last night, Fronnie."

"Went back where, Pap—where did you go?"

"I went back over there on the Runyan Hill where Daid is buried. I went over there by her grave and I set down there and stayed a long time. And I thought of the day when Pete Lennix hauled her up there in the express with that old pair of grays he used to drive. After I set by the side of her grave I got up and I went all over that hill. I was back out there on the ridge where we used to work that piece of corn together—out there at Pine Flat cornfield. You remember, Fronnie—you's a little girl when me and Daid tended that piece of corn. Well, I went back there last night and looked at the old furrow ridges under the briars and sprouts. The briars has just about took that hill—the saw-briars and the greenbriers. The pines are as big as a body's thigh—and the oaks are short and dumpy—the way old, poor, worn-out land makes them—short, dumpy and tough as leather. I want to tell you, Fronnie, that is the place I want to be buried—right over there by Daid. I want to have the briars cut out and the sprouts—a place big enough to dig a grave to put me in. That place is growed up an awful lot but I want to be buried there."

Words Fronnie cannot say: "Pap's dyin shore enough. My God, Pap is dyin. His hands are turnin purple above his wrists like frost-bitten pawpaw leaves turn purple. His hands have shriveled like the branches of a tough-butted white oak cut and left to bleed. His hands are purple. The tough skin has begun to shrivel and turn purple. He was not back over there at that old graveyard last night unless it was his sperit that went back over there. Pap was right here in bed. That old pasture hill where the graveyard is ain't growed up neither. Too many cows in there to let it grow up and it ain't good enough ground to grow sassafras sprouts, let alone grow up. It might grow lonesome pine sprouts–graveyard hills around here always does grow lonesome pines. My God, Pap is dyin."

"More water, Fronnie."

"Here, Pap."

Sip-sip. Sip-sip. Sip-sip. Sip-sip.

"I don't want to be hauled back yander to Flint County and be buried by Pansy. Too fur to haul me, Fronnie, to be buried by your mother. I was back there, too, last night. I walked back there and went over all them old hills I used to farm in corn. Your Ma's grave is flat as a board. I took a stick and put it up at her head. Nothin there. I wanted the place marked. The ground is flat where Pansy is buried–flat as that hard yard out there. You know I don't want to be buried there. I want to be buried by my second wife. I know people will talk about that but thirty-eight miles is too fur a-piece to haul a corpse. It would take two days to haul me there on a wagon. I don't want to be on the road that long when I am a dead man. I want to be put right in the ground soon as you can get me there."

"Pap. Pap. Pap."

"None of that, Fronnie. It ain't goin to be so bad atter all. It's just like goin to bed. Your Ma was the woman I loved, but I just don't want to be hauled thirty-eight miles when I'm a corpse. Your Ma was a pretty woman and a pure woman. I loved your Ma more than any of my wives. But I don't want to go back there and be buried in that flat ground and be hauled thirty-eight miles back in Flint County."

"Don't, Pap, don't–don't talk like that. I can't stand to hear you."

"I want you to quit actin like you are actin. Don't you know this is goin to come to you like it is comin to me and it is goin to come to everybody else that's born in this world. Now I want you to see I'm buried by Daid. I want you to see that I'm buried in the Runyan Hill Graveyard. It ain't no fur piece to haul me–about three miles here from Sweetbird's. And you see they won't be two men buried there by Daid. They hauled her first man back some'ers out in Ohio and buried him. Daid is sleepin up there on the hill by herself."

Sip-sip. Sip-sip. Sip-sip.

"See that my coffin is made of black oakplanks and that the planks are not worm-eaten and that they don't have no knot holes in them. See that I have a good stout box that will keep the clods from gettin into my eyes. See that it has a lid made of wild-cherry boards and that they ain't no brass handles on it—no brass any place about it. See that old Half-pint McAlister makes it and old Ugly Bird Skeans digs my grave. Now I want you to see that I ain't hauled back to Flint County and I want you to see I ain't hauled down yander and buried on Peddler Pint where my third wife is buried—buried down there among her people and them a lot of strangers and people I didn't know. Her people cussed me like a brute and I heerd all I wanted to know about it. They cussed me because I was her fifth husband and she was my third wife. They said she'd wore out four men and I'd be the fifth she'd wear out. And when she died they said I'd wore out two wimmen and she was the third woman for me to wear out. That's her people and I don't want to be buried down there among them—strangers to me. Water."

Sip-sip. Sip-sip.

"Pap."

"See that I'm put in my coffin just like I go to bed—that I have my shirt on and no necktie—my shirt and my long underwear. I don't want any shoes 'r socks on my feet neither. I want to lay down in my coffin just like I lay down in my bed—to bed is where this old clay temple is goin, Fronnie. To bed. Yes. I don't want no hat on my head neither, for no one ever goes to bed with a hat on. I want a blue work-shirt on and my long heavy drawers—I want my clothes clean and no smell of sweat in them or smell of brush smoke. I want to be laid over there on the Runyan Hill by Daid near them old cornfields where we used to work together, from sunrise till sunset together."

"Pap, don't talk like that."

"Now I'm goin, I got to go. I can't put it off no longer. I would put it off if I could, but they ain't no use to talk about it. Fronnie, it ain't so bad atter all—this thing called Death that all men fear. We all got to feel the sting of death, don't the Word say so? The sting of death. Yes. Ain't I lived a good long life? I ain't been cheated out o' much time in fourscore and four years. What more can I ask out'n the Master? Eighty-four years of time to live. Lift up the veil you got over my eyes, Fronnie—lift up the dark veil betwixt me and the sun. Lift it off. I want to see the sun. I want to see the sky. I want to see the rows of tall corn and the fresh moist dirt where Snider plowed today. I want to see the corn once more. I've plowed so much corn and when you was a little girl you carried water out on the hill to me in a red lard bucket. And once I remember you turned the water bucket over and spilt the water on the sand and again you played along so long the water got so hot I couldn't drink it. I want to see the corn once more. I've plowed so much corn and I love to raise corn —just think of the good old days back in Flint County—I want to be buried, Fronnie, over there on the Runyan Hill Graveyard next to my old cornfields."

Fronnie says: "I ain't got no black sheet over his face. It is the shadow of death over Pap's face. Death has put a black curtain betwixt Pap and the sun. And Death is hold of the curtain. Death is goin to draw the curtain. The shadow of Death defies the sunlight—the hands of Death over poor old Pap's eyes. My God. Oh, my God—merciful God. Pap is goin. Pap is goin. My God! Pap is dyin."

Fronnie runs to the smoke house. The tears are running down her cheeks. They run like crystal beads down her leaf-colored cheeks (autumn leaf-colored from working in the sunlight in the cornfields) and the beads drip to the dusty ground where the crystal is lost, lost in the dust. Fronnie wipes her eyes with her apron and she calls: "Snider, you and Vicey come here. Come here, Snider, you and Vicey. Pap is dyin. Pap is shore dyin." Snider brings the mule and Vicey brings her hoe. Snider rides on the mule's back and puts his big bare feet upon the trace chains and he holds to the hames with his hands. Vicey follows the mule–through the gate and down through the pasture daisies they come. Vicey keeps up with the mule. Now they are in the chip yard, now they are at the porch where Battle is struggling for his breath.

"Your Grandpa is dyin, Snider–dyin. Slowly he is dyin. See him. He is dyin by degrees."

"Yes, Grandpa is dyin. He is dyin by degrees like the cat did when it swallowed the mattock." Snider jumps on the back of the mule. He clutches the hames with his big hands and he puts his big bare feet on the rusty trace chains–puts them right where the back band goes over the mule's back and the belly-band goes under the mule's belly. Snider starts the mule in a mule lope.

"Where are you goin, Snider?"

"Goin over to the flat after Pa. He's grubbin over there yet. Be back in just a few minutes."

"Water, Fronnie."

"Yes, Pap."

Sip-sip. Sip-sip.

"Fronnie. That veil. Can't you take it off? Fronnie, that veil. I must be goin, Fronnie. Where is the blood of me? Where is my color? My blood is covered over the cornfield among these hills. My blood, Fronnie, I'm goin. Blood and sweat of mine is on the bare hills where they ain't no timber –where there is old corn rows. That's where my blood is and my color is. I helped to cut the timber and build the railroads and the turnpikes. I done the blastin of hills for roads and blasted mountains down. Can't no more, Fronnie–I'm a baby –I'm going some'ers, Fronnie–I ain't old, though–if I had a pair of new legs I'd be all right. All I need is new legs and I could go on about my business good as I ever did. But somethin's got me. I need wind. My words. Words, Fronnie. Water."

Sip-sip.

Here comes the mule in a full lope. The mule is carrying double. Sweetbird Bradberry is on the mule in front and Snider is riding behind. Snider is holding to his Pa's overall suspenders–here they come round past the pig lot–full speed, mule speed, they come. Under the poplar trees where green leaves flutter and the wind oozes through the green smooth leaves with the slick-soap sides. The wind oozes and the mule lopes–the pigs grunt and run to the trough for slop–through the barn lot the mule lopes. It is getting its breath hard. The mule's sides work in and out like a bee smoker. But it goes full speed into the yard–Sweetbird and Snider roll off and run into the house and then to the back porch where Battle is silent–silent as death.

"Good-by, Fronnie. Good-by, Sweetbird, I'm gone. Shadow around me. See, Fronnie, that when I'm buried I'm put away just like I was goin to bed. Good-by."

Hear the sharp sizzle of wind–wind that sizzles like wind coming out of the mule's nostrils. It is the last breath of wind that Battle draws. It is a sharp sizzle of wind and it goes like wind pressed in a vise, if wind could be pressed in a vise. It is wind come out where the walls fall in. It is wind that if it could speak would say, "Wind has come in here and gone out for the last eighty-four years–but now the wind time is over and past." Battle has died on his back, too–Fronnie turned him over when his breath came hard and the veil came between his eyes and the sun. Battle turned over on his back to die like a copperhead fighting a forest fire turns on its back to die. The thin white beard on his face bends down when the wind blows, but when the wind stops the beard rises again. The wind blows over the pale face and then it blows on to the cornfield where there is life in the green corn. And it kisses the green blades of living corn–kisses the green blood and the life in the growing July corn. It blows off the soft, downy beard of Battle's then onto the green weeds dancing with joy under the setting sun–weeds so full of life–green weeds without form dancing under the July sun–dancing for the wind.

Fronnie is crying. More water comes from her eyes than the last sip-sips Battle took. Fronnie is afraid. She puts her arms around Sweetbird. Now she takes her arms from around Sweetbird's shoulders and she goes to the wall and leans against the wall to cry. "The last water Pap drunk as a mortal man. The last water. Poor Pap. Gone. A hard-workin man for us children. He slaved like a dog to raise us. Went through thick and thin. And now. I can't stand it, Sweetbird. I can't never go through with it——"

"But you must, Fronnie. We got our children to raise. You got to help me. You can't act like this. We all got to die, Fronnie——"

"Yes, but see him suffer so. He hated to die so. He wasn't afraid. Not even afraid of the stain of death. No, Pap wasn't afraid."

"I've liked old Dad better than if he was my own Dad, and you know it. Nothin on this earth I wouldn't do for Dad. You know that, Fronnie. Been on many a spree with Dad before the Lord took him on His side of the fence. Had many a good hunt with him. Poor old Dad. God knows I hate to see Dad go."

"I remember when Mother died how he used to cut timber for twenty-five cents a day and how us children farmed at home. How we worked and God knows we didn't have enough to eat in the house. We'd go get apples off a little tree beside the road–didn't belong to nobody–we'd get apples there enough to fry for breakfast–we had a cow and she made butter enough to go with our fried apples and we et corn bread. We didn't know what biscuits was. Corn bread for three meals a day. Pap raised us all without a blemish on our characters. Now death has to take him."

And here he lies. Two hundred pounds of man once–now two hundred pounds of clay from a burned-out temple that men called his body before death. He was a man of brute strength. He worked all of his life like a brute. And what about the future? Did he save for the future? Why did he die with Fronnie and her man Sweetbird? "How can you put corn in a crib and keep it twenty years? You pintly can't do it. The mice will heart it. The mice will eat the hearts first, then they'll go to eatin the meal of the corn. How can you put away molasses in barrels and keep it twenty years? It turns to sugar like sweet grains of sand–coarse to eat and not molasses and not sugar. That's what I made. I made it from the hill slopes. I can't keep it forever and I'll get old atter a while.

Twenty years is a long time to keep corn against the mice and the wind—twenty years of a man's life is a long time."

Fronnie says: "I'll see that Pap is not buried by my mother or his third wife—that old woman where strangers are buried by her side and then to bury Pap there amongst strangers. I'll see he's buried by Daid, my stepmother, on the Runyan Hill. Daid was so good to Pap and they got along so well."

"Fronnie, you know the only two things I ever had agin your Pap?"

"No, Sweetbird."

"Well, Dad was such a strong Democrat he stunk. And before the Lord got him on His side of the fence, he could just put more good licker down him than I could. It laid in his stummick so good. He could just pintly put 'er all over me when it come to drinkin."

"Pap said just a few days ago you's the only Republican he ever voted fer in his life—said he voted fer you when you run fer trustee. I'll see that Pap is give a nice burial. I'll see he ain't laid to rest by that third woman. A woman afraid to cross the river. Said she was afraid of a bridge. I'll see that Pap is buried in his shirt and drawers without a necktie just as he wanted to be buried on the Runyan Hill. I'll see his coffin is made of black-oak planks with a wild-cherry lid."

The sun is red behind the mountain. The wind stirs the green July corn. The wind sings a song in the July corn—and on the low-loft the spider spins a web—the fly goes in. The spider jumps on the fly and the spider drinks the blood. The fly works its legs slower and slower. Tomorrow, fly-dust will fall down on the bed where Battle used to sleep and dream of the web of life he had been caught in—how he kicked like a dying fly, but time took back his blood and gave it to the cornfields and his hills—his hills—and now time would slowly disintegrate his burned-out clay to mix forever with the elements. Fronnie goes into the back room, the room used by visitors only, and she puts a clean sheet on the big wooden bed—the bed Battle and Pansy slept on their bridal night sixty-four years ago. Fronnie carries the dirty sheets upstairs, and the quilts, and she puts them on the stack by the chimney—the chimney that runs like a big white weed stem through the middle of the house.

"Ready now to bring him in," says Fronnie. "Ready now to bring Pap in and put him on the wooden bed in the back room. Come and help, Sweetbird."

Sweetbird and Fronnie make a saddle pocket and they slip their knots of arms down under Battle's shoulders—no use to put their arms under his head too, for his neck is stiff as a poker. They drag Battle from the bed on the porch, thence through the partition door, thence through the dining-room, front room, and then the back room. His heels dragging on the floor turn up the corners of the rag rugs. They put half of him on the big wooden bed. Then they lift his dead legs onto the bed. Now his whole body lies on the clean sheet. Fronnie goes and gets another sheet and spreads it over Battle—puts two pennies on his eyes to make them close.

Now Battle lies. You cannot see him for the four corners of a room. It is hard to see through logs. But a spider on the low loft above sees Battle—a mouse comes through the newspaper-papered wall, preens his nose—he too sees Battle. Fronnie and Sweetbird see Battle. The sun sees through the windowpanes and a glimmer of dying sunlight falls on the white-apple-blossom sheets. Battle's beard, tall, slim, white-as-it-is beard, not white as the sheets though, gleams flashy in the golden dying sunlight that falls through the windowpanes and one hole where a windowpane used to be. Battle's beard is white as a leaf-stained hen egg. Battle's beard would be white, but it has tobacco stain down near the roots of it and fresh tobacco stain on the ends of some of it, and the sun makes the tobacco-stained beard gleam reddening gleams in the sunrays. But there Battle lies—on a bed big enough to hold him, in a house he built with his own hands big enough to hold him in life and to hold him in death. There he lies on a big wooden bed. He has only gone to bed for a last long sleep. Only, Battle Keaton is a silent man and no one knows if he dreams of the ax and the saw and the cornfields where the brush grow now, where the crows fly over and where the old furrows of twenty years ago are like little potato ridges in a sandy bottom. Battle Keaton is silent. Silent. He does not heave up and down at the chest like a bee smoker getting its wind. When the wind sizzled from his nostrils after his chest last heaved, then it grew forever still and the walls of the earth-house were ready to cave in. The setting sun gives its last rays for the day to Battle for his last time to feel the sun—sun on his cold, silent, burned-out clay. Life. Life.

"Get on the mule, Snider, and go tell the neighbors Pap is dead. Go up Turkey Creek and down Hog Branch and over on Buzzard Roost. Let 'em all know Pap is dead but the Turners. You know how vile the Turners is and how Pap hates them all since they killed Pap's cousin that foul way that time. Pap wouldn't have a Turner here when he was livin and we ain't goin to have them when Pap is dead—come snoopin around then tryin to make up with us to get to kill another one of us. Don't tell them nary word about Pap's death. But tell the neighbors to come that we aim to have a settin-up here tonight with Pap's corpse. You stay here with me, Sweetbird. You stay right here with me. You ain't goin to get no whisky in a time like this. It won't help you—Everytime you have trouble, you drink down your trouble. You ain't goin to drink licker over Pap's dead body. Pap dead and the sun gone. Me here with Pap. Sweetbird, you ain't goin to leave the place."

"Dad dead. The only fault I had to old Dad he was a Democrat and it is still a fault with me. A dead Democrat is still a fault with me. A better man never walked than Dad. And the only fault Dad had with me was me a-bein a Republican. But I was born a Republican—my Pap fit back yander in that war. And I'm a Republican long by God as I live. I'm one of them old rusty kind."

"Forget about bein a Republican and Pap bein a Democrat. Stay with me and it a-gettin dark and them lonesome whippoorwills a-callin out yander in the apple trees. One lit here on the porch the other night and that was a sign some one in this family was goin to be called home."

"Fronnie, be back just in the minute. I got to tell Snider before he gets away not to ride the mule he plowed all day over there in the cornfield. I want him to ride the mule he left stand in the barn lot all day—that mule that is well rested. You know how a boy is. Don't know how much a brute can stand."

"All right, better hurry. Snider gets in a hurry when they ain't no work, nothin but jantin round all over the country. You'd better hurry if you want Snider."

"Oh, Snider! Son, don't ride that mule you plowed today. Ride the rested mule."

"All right, Pap. I got you."

Snider rides the mule from the barn in a gallop. There is Snider, tall skinny as wild onion sitting on a little saddle that his end covers till nothing is seen but the spur of the saddle running up his backbone. His big bare feet dangle as the mule gallops away from the barn—the bridle reins are flung loosely in the wind—the mule and the rider are free-free—free down among the stumps, the corn now. Up the toe-path through the corn, across the hill and onto the ridge that leads to Turkey Creek. There he goes. See Snider between you and the sun and how he covers the saddle—his long legs dangle nearly to the ground. The mule still gallops.

"Uncle Eif, come over tonight to the settin-up. Grandpa's dead."

"Old Battle Keaton dead! What! Old Battle Keaton dead. Well I'll be dogged. When did he die?"

"Died this evenin at two o'clock."

"Old Battle Keaton's dead, Till. Did you hear what Sweet-bird Bradberry's boy just then said—said his Grandpa was dead and wanted me and you to come over to the settin-up tonight. I'll be dogged. Don't Death slip up on a man."

"Silas, Pa said tell you and Esther to come over tonight to the settin-up. Said for you to bring some hymn books too. Grandpa is dead."

"You don't mean Battle Keaton is dead, do you?"

"Yes, I mean Grandpa is dead 'er I wouldn't a been comin round over the country on this mule tellin the people. I mean just what I say."

"When did he die?"

"He died this evenin at two o'clock."

"Well, ain't that a funny thing. I was just talkin to old Battle two weeks ago. I went over there and bought them two stunted pigs off'n your Pa. He was well and hearty it 'peared. He seemed to be gettin on pretty well for a man of his years. He was tellin me about his third wife bein afraid to cross the river before she died—afraid of a bridge and a boat. I'll be doggone. Old Battle Keaton is dead. Hear what Sweetbird Bradberry's boy just then told me! Death will finally slip up on a body 'specially atter they get old as Battle Keaton. I spect old Battle's up nigh a hundred years old."

"Drew, Pap said for me to tell you Grandpa was dead and he wanted you to come to the settin-up tonight and bring your guitar and some hymn books. He said for you to bring Ellis Thombs along to second on the banjer—said for you to be sure and come."

"You mean to say old Battle Keaton 's dead."

"Yes, I mean to say Grandpa is dead 'er I wouldn't be goin all round over the country on this mule tellin everybody but the low-lifed people about it."

"When did he die?"

"Died this evenin at two o'clock or right about two."

"What was the matter with Battle Keaton—strong as a brute I allus thought."

"Don't know just what was the matter with Grandpa. I was in the cornfield and Ma called me in and said he was dyin and when I got over there and went and got Pa, Grandpa kicked the bucket. Old age kilt Grandpa. That's what Ma said that done it. Old age. Grandpa kept complainin around and said all he needed was new legs."

"But legs don't help a man when the Lord calls him. The Lord needed Battle Keaton 'er he wouldn't be a dead man this minute. The Lord took him, son. The hairs on your head is numbered. Your days are numbered and when you live that number out, all the Doctor's medicine and the Doctors and new legs in this world ain't goin to save you, son. Are you a Christian? Are you a saved man?"

"Hell no. I ain't no saved man."

Snider rides the mule away at full gallop. The mule was once brown. Now the mule is black. Sweat has made the hair wet and stick to the mule's skin. Snider's pants are sweaty at the seat. They stick to the little brown-butter-colored saddle—bright leather, old, but well taken-care-of leather. Snider goes through the Turkey Creek country and tells the neighbors. He tells everybody but the Turners: "Grandpa is dead. Pa said tell you to come over to the settin-up tonight."

Snider crosses the Pine Hill and over onto Hog Branch. The moon is out now. The moon is pretty, shining down through the pines on Pine Hill. The moon hangs like a smattering of bright-colored apple butter in the water-colored sky—a washed-in moon it was—washed in the color of bright-colored apple butter.

See the moon hanging above hills in the blue soft velvetiness in northeast Kentucky. See! the moon is very pretty in this softness. It is under this moon Snider rides—right out in the pretty life that Battle loved—the life Battle fought for, fought Death for like a copperhead—Such night this barge of man Battle, full of life and living would love. Here is where Battle has lived all of his eighty-four years. It was here where Battle chose to live, and where Battle chose to die. It was here where the oaks grow stubborn and not so tall—where the land is thin and where the brush grows stubbornly on the rocky tall hills. These hills gave Battle nourishment for his tough flesh. Such pretty night and Snider rides to tell about the death of one clay temple, charred white by living—by the fire of living.

Up the toe-paths, across creeks and through the paling gates where yard apple trees loom ghostly shadows in front of unlocked doors—doors to log houses where men and women sit resting in front of them on the stone doorsteps and in chairs. They sit resting from a hard day in the cornfields. Sweaty and tired they sit and listen to the whippoorwill calling far over across the green cornfield to his mate sitting on their front-yard gate. Snider walks up each path and peers into the gloomy darkness on both sides for biting dogs. He says Grandpa died this evening at two o'clock and Ma and Pa wants you to come over to the setting-up tonight if it ain't too late for you to stir. Bring some hymn books if you've got any.

Under the muddle of smiling autumn dead-leaf moon, from under the tangles of green yard trees, Snider creeps back to his mule—silent, stealthy and on the watch he creeps. Then he leaps to the butter-colored saddle and away to another house.

And here where looms a path of high oak trees, poplars, pines, here where logs were stacked together forty-six years ago to build a house—Here where all is silent save the throbs from Fronnie and the grunting of hungry pigs and the moo-moos of unmilked cows—here are voices. Here comes a long line of people following the toe-path up the hill. The leader has a lantern in the moonlight. The lantern guides his brogan footsteps between high rims of ragweeds alongside the toe-path. Under the bright July stars where the corn is whispering to the wind and the wind is whispering to the corn—they come. Up the hill, up the hill—slowly, along—they come. Women follow their husbands up the hill—follow the men in overalls and blue shirts covered with overall jumpers to keep back the July night wind from the sweaty shirts—made wet by following the plow. Women wearing their threadbare shawls and smoking their clay-stone pipes.

"Come in you folks and get you some chears. Just set any place you can find a seat and any place it's handier to you. How are you, Della, you and Sweeter and Linda?"

"I'm purty good, Fronnie. A little bit tired though—worked like a dog today. Got that swamp piece of bottom ground worked out and it nearly worked us all to death to do it—took all hands and the cook too."

"I'm tired too. Been workin in new ground all day."

"I stuck pole beans today till my back aches like I had the belly ache."

"I'm tired enough to stretch right down there on that hard floor and go to sleep."

"Fronnie, we are awful hurt about your Pap dyin. We just couldn't believe it was the Lord's will—good a man as Battle Keaton ought to be spared a few more years here on this old earth of trouble and sorrow. But guess that's why the Lord's kept him all these eighty-four years. Kept him till he did see the light."

"Yes. It must have been the Lord's will to keep him till he got on the side the light was on."

"Yes. My Pap was a good man if there ever was a good man on this earth. You know Pap quit his drinkin two years ago. He jined the church and got right with God. He used to stay with me and Sweetbird after Daid died and Pap was sorty weaked. He'd drink licker with Sweetbird and they'd work hard all day—drink at night like young men. But when Pap's hair begin to turn, Pap saw he was goin down yon side of the hill toward the settin sun. It was the time Finn Fultz from Flint County helt that protracted meetin over on Hog Branch in the schoolhouse that Pap come across with the Lord and got on the right side. Sick as he got before he died, suffered the way he did, when Sweetbird offered him licker a week ago this very night Pap said, 'I'll see Death starin me in the face before I'll drink that weaked water.'

"And Pap died with that kind of faith. I ain't a bit uneasy tonight that Pap is a angel in Heaven and right in this room lookin at us mortals in this world of trials, tribulations and sorrows. Pap's with my mother this very night and maybe with his second wife Daid. He'll see my little sister that's dead. Pap is a angel in Heaven tonight though his old temple of clay is right over there wrapped up in them sheets."

"I was over there on Hog Branch when Battle got saved. I went up in the same altar call and was saved at the same time Battle Keaton was. I remember how Brother Finn Fultz prayed with us till after midnight and how Brother Battle come through and he'd jist come through and I saw the light—Yes, I remember well as if it had been yisterday."

"I knowed Battle Keaton when he was a young man and out in sin. We growed up together. He was the best ball player and tree climber I ever did see when he was a boy. When he jumped the broomstick with Pansy McClintlock I was right there. I slipped in where he was to sleep that night and helped to tie the cow bells to the bed slats. Been a long time ago, folks, but I remember well as if it had been yisterday. Fronnie, I remember when you was born—you first saw light on that big wooden bed where Battle lays a corpse. Your mother and your father first slept together on that bed. I have seen Battle go through life. I am a old man now. My hair is white. I am goin down the side of the hill Battle has just went down.

"I saw him go through life—full of life when he was a young man, powerful and big all his days. A big man. A good man. I remember him—yes. Yes. I remember him. Now I see him over there in death. Birth. Life. Life. Life. Slowin down. Then Death. Ain't it all a funny thing. We are just as 'the Word' says. We are put here for God's purposes. He wants us to obey. I know God cries when one of us goes wrong. It is all the will of the Lord."

"Yes, Alec, God hates to see us go wrong. We have our seasons just like a flower. That leetle baby over there with the pink hands and the pink tender lips is a leetle flower bud. Now what does she know about life? All she knows now is to suck milk from her mother's breast. She'll soon blossom into her youth and be a flower and know about life. There [pointing to Snider] is the young man—carefree. Doesn't care if it snows oats. He is in the very blossom of his youth. It is the spring of his season.

"Here is Fronnie in the summer of her life—here is Fronnie giving birth to a brood and workin for her brood. This is the summer for Fronnie. Here am I—a tree with leaves turnin and blowin off when the wind blows—I am in the autumn of life. Yes, the autumn of life. I'm startin down the hill—goin to the winter of life.

"There is Battle over there just passed to the big Beyond, beyond this winter of life. We are like a flower growin by the waters, Half-Pint. We are like a flower growin by the waters, Ugly Bird—here to bloom today and die tomorrow. In spring we come forth from the roots of old stumps. And we grow and put forth leaves and we blossom. And we bring forth fruit, good fruit and bad fruit in our season just as 'the Word' says, Fronnie—in the autumn our fruit is garnered and our leaves shrivel—our lives are beautiful sometimes in our old brown leaves, but not very often, Ellis. We just go down to decay.

"Then what? Don't you know? Winter. Decay. Death."

"You are right, Ell Dollarhide. You are right."

"Yes, Half-Pint. I think he's right too."

"Yes, Fronnie. Life is a funny thing. But we are all here for a purpose. We all have a mission. And when that mission is done the Lord takes us home. The Lord will love and care for us all. He has the hairs on our heads numbered."

"Strike up a tune there on your guitar, Drew Thompson. Bring over here the banjer, Ellis, and set nigh him so you both can get together. Let's sing, 'I am comin, Lord.' Battle loved that song."

"All right. Let's read a line and sing a line."

"All right."

The stars shine over the clapboard roof. The stars shine down on a lonely log house, big enough though to be unafraid if houses are afraid at night. The light of the stars is pretty, shining down on the clapboards—down on the green yard grass wet with drops of dew already. The stars listen, but the wind won't listen. The cool night wind keeps whispering to the soapy leaves on the poplar trees. Inside the house there is music. Hush! Listen! Music comes out where a windowpane is out. Music comes out and wind goes in. Maybe the wind chases the music out. Sunlight went in at this hole in the window this afternoon. Sunlight went in at this window and it shone beautifully on Battle's beard—made the tips of it a glint of amberish red. Wind went in at this hole and played with the corner of the sheet where Battle was dead and lay covered with a sheet—with a sheet under him. But hear the wail coming on the wind!

> Tho' coming weak and vile
> Thou dost my strength assure;
> Thou dost my vileness fully cleanse
> So spotless all and pure.
>
> 'Tis Jesus call me on,
> To perfect faith and love,
> To perfect hope, and peace, and trust
> For earth and Heaven above.

And He assurance gives
To loyal hearts and true,
That every promise is fulfilled
To those who bear and do.

More words through the hole in the window float out to the wind at night. Words follow the wind out at the hole and float on the night wind under the bright stars. Under the night sky with white clouds floating in the sky. Under the soapy poplar leaves and the words rub their soft sides on the soapy sides of the leaves and against the tender green ribs of the leaves. Don't you hear the words and the wail of guitar music on the night wind? Wonder if Battle hears?

Wonder if Battle is the wind and in the wind he rubs against the slick bellies of the poplar leaves and kicks his toes against the green ribs of the leaves—Wonder if he is wind in a pair of clean long drawers and a blue shirt—a work shirt washed clean and without the smell of wood smoke and sweat. The wail of words and music again:

There is a land of wondrous beauty
Where the "Living Waters" flow,
The word of God to all has said it
And it surely must be so.

No tears are there, no blighting sorrow
From the cruel hand of Death;
No flowers fade, no summers perish
By the winter's chilling breath.

I've loved ones there who passed before me,
They'll rejoice to see me come,
But best of all, I'll see my Saviour,
Who will bid me welcome home.

And now the words of songs do not come from the window to the night winds. The words of song are silent. And Holy-Joe Madden is there and he prays words to the winds. The words are loud and they are jumbled words—filled with Thee's and Thou's and Thy's. They come out the window and slip along the belly of the wind. The pretty night wind—the words of Holy-Joe Madden ride out like the words of the songs—out among the poplar leaves and over at the pig pen through the leaves on the sweet-gum trees. Hear them! Words! And then:

"Poor Pap. Dead. Dead. Dead as a beef. Over there—See!"

"Fronnie, no ust to take on like that! We all got to die."

"Yes, but Sweetbird. You don't understand. He is my father. He is dear to me. I know more than you do what he has went through with for us and it makes him nearer to me."

"Yes, Fronnie Bradberry, you'll worry yourself sick."

"And the way he wanted to be buried like he was just layin down to take a nap of sleep——"

"How was that, Fronnie?"

"Half-Pint, he told me he wanted to be buried with his blue work shirt on, open at the collar without a necktie—wanted to be buried in his long white heavy winter drawers. See, Pap never would wear a necktie—not even on the day he got married. And he didn't want to be buried in one. He wanted Ugly Bird Skeans to dig his grave and you, Half-Pint McAlister, to make his coffin——"

"He did——"

"Yes."

"And you said, Fronnie, he wanted me to dig his grave, didn't you?"

"Yes, Ugly Bird, that was Pap's dyin request."

"I'll shore dig it then."

"I'll shore make that coffin too. I don't want no dead man back here hantin me."

"You know people request some of the funniest things before they die. You know old Bennie Wellkid before he died ast that they bury him in a hollow black-gum log—just poke him down in it feet-first and nail some boards over the end of the log and bury him standin up back yander at the roots of a big pine tree—the biggest back yander on the Wellkid hill."

"Did they bury him that way, Ell?"

"No. They was ashamed to bury him like that. Ashamed

that their neighbors would talk. But since they buried him they've been sorry ever since. They talk about diggin him up and buryin him that way yet. They wish all time they had put Bennie away the way he requested."

"Why?"

"W'y he's hanted them. They think he has. A man has been seen run across the road several times nigh the place where they buried Bennie. He's been seen there by Wellkid's kinsfolks. He runs across the road and sometimes keeps ahead of them for a little while and then he just jumps over in a ditch among the high weeds. Tom Wellkid has packed a pistol ever since he seed it there one night. Said he'd fill it full of holes—a ghost back here where it don't belong hantin people who had nothin to do with buryin its body."

"Let's sing another song and some of us can stay and some of us can go and come tomorrow night—You aim to have the buryin day atter tomorrow at ten o'clock, don't you, Fronnie——"

"Yes if we can keep him that long."

"Drew, can you play 'Where will you spend Eternity'?"

"Yes."

"Strike up the tune then."

The knife blade nimbly shifts on the strings. And there is a wail of music and of words. They float as the other words out onto the night wind—to the poplar leaves and to the cow pasture and maybe to the ears of Battle, the wind ears of Battle—and maybe Battle hears and Battle laughs like the violin of wind at the words:

Where will you spend eternity?
The question comes to you and me!
Tell me, what shall your answer be?
Where will you spend eternity?

Leaving the straight and narrow way,
Going the downward road today,
Sad will their final ending be,
—Lost through a long eternity!

Refrain
ETERNITY! ETERNITY!
Lost through a long eternity!

Repent, believe this very hour,
Trust in the Saviour's grace and power,
Then will your joyous answer be
SAVED THROUGH A LONG ETERNITY!

The wind leaking in at the window holes and between the undaubed cracks and through the newspapered walls cannot sizzle like the last breath of wind that Battle breathed. No. Damned if the wind can. Damned if the wind can whisper through the green leaves on the hickory beside the corn crib like the wailing of the cornfield voices so used to "Old Black Joe" and "Nellie Was a Lady." No. No. There is the wind however and there were the voices just a few wooden minutes ago. There is the moon above the house—a red oak chip of moon—floating like a red oak chip on a clear pond of water. This moon is shining down on the clapboards—moss-covered, shining down on life, down on Death—death between the two white sheets. There is the color of burned clay between the sheets, a pile of clay burned out like a candle in the past eighty-four years of living. But it will burn no more—not even for the saw swish-swish music of the cool silver wind in the green hickory leaves and among the slick-bellied green poplar leaves. But the clay is quiet, not as the sheets are white, but it is quite white, and it is silent as the sheets are silent—quiet as the sheets, all but the corner of one where the wind blows through where a windowpane used to be and shakes the corner of the sheet with unseen hands.

Hear the cornfield voices. Hear them! Some are soft like the spirit of wind—maybe the spirit of Battle Keaton that is a piece of wind in the wind—maybe the spirit slipped out like the wind through the place where the windowpane used to be and rubbed its belly on the icicle-colored jaggers of sun-dried putty—maybe, maybe so. Maybe his spirit is a pretty piece of wind out now under this red-oak chip moon so red-wasp-floating-like in the pond-colored sky—maybe, maybe so. Hear the voices as the figures go down the toe-path under the pretty moon—hear them? Maybe the spirit of Battle Keaton hears as it slides among the soapy poplar leaves, fresh in the moonlight and the wind and jewel cover with sparkling beads of dew—may be the spirit of Battle Keaton as it goes wind-like through wind and counts the rows of plowed corn and talks to the corn whispering in the night wind and goes back to the hill where Daid is buried, where Pansy is buried in Flint County—goes back to the old cornfields at night where bushes have grown above the prints of corn rows left. And maybe the thumb and the index finger have crushed the guts out of the striped-back she-spider—no one knows about this spirit of Battle Keaton, except no one exactly knows about it.

Now the dog howls by the window where the wind goes through the place where the windowpane used to be, where the words and the music came through and the sunlight and wind went in. The voices get faint and fainter. The moon is getting red and the moon is sailing potato ridges of clouds like a red apple floating in a blue stream of mountain water. The dog barks and the people talk. Figures are walking the toe-path, figures of living clay the hills have made tough, for they belong to the hills—tough like the roots of the oak that sinks into the hard Kentucky clay.

And now the voices die—voices of figures in the dark worming along the toe-path through the field of green corn. The dog does not bark at the window. The wind is all that's singing now—the wind in the green corn, in the poplar leaves and around the hole in the window. And let the wind sing tonight. No one pays heed to the wind and the moon. Tomorrow many may give heed to the wind and the sky, for this is a season for growing.

Leaf Shelton, Purvy Winston, Rosa Winston, Jack Tarr, Amos Tarr, Lena Feathers, Ina Sneed, Leona Warm, Roy Chitwood sit up with the corpse tonight—sit up in the back room beside the dead silent clay. The rest have gone home. They were tired out, worked hard in the cornfield today. Part of them will not work tomorrow. They'll drop out of crops long enough to pay the last respect to the burned-out clay of Battle

Keaton's–Battle has been one of them so long and they have known Battle so well, that when he died a tree fell–a tall tree fell in their little forest.

II

"Sweetbird, I brought my handsaw and hammer over this mornin. I brought all my tools. I'm ready to begin that coffin –where is the lumber? Down at the barn?"

"Yes, Half-Pint. It is down at the barn. I got a lot of good straight seasoned oak planks down there and they ain't got no knot holes in them neither. You'll find the wild-cherry planks up over the cow shed on the rafters. Chickens been roostin on them, but the manure is dried now–just brush it off and go ahead. It won't matter much."

"Have you got any of them square-bellied tens and eight-penny nails, Sweetbird?"

"Yes. You'll find them in the tool box. The tool box is in the corn crib locked up. Here is the key. That damn boy of mine, Snider, steals out all my wrenches and loses them. I had to lock the tools up."

"All right."

"Half-Pint, I'll have to go over and see Ugly Bird about diggin the grave–I guess he's about ready to start work now."

"Where do you aim to bury him, Sweetbird–with his first wife or his second wife or his third wife?"

"He requested Fronnie to have him buried by his second wife and that is just what Fronnie means to have done. People will talk, I told her, but she don't care. You know how a woman is to have her way–people will talk about Battle bein laid over there on the Runyan Hill by his second wife–there is where Fronnie is goin to have him buried."

And Fronnie says: "I aim to have Pap buried on the Runyan Hill. That was his last request before he died. And that's what I aim to have done. He wants to be buried by Daid. I know people will talk about me having Pap buried by his second wife, but let them talk. What do I care what people says. This is the last thing I can do for Pap and I aim to do it."

Half-Pint says: "Heaven has always been a funny thing to me and this makin the right connections from this world in Heaven. Now I wonder how Battle Keaton will act when he gets in Heaven among all three of his wimmen. Wonder which one he'll run around with in Heaven and which one of the five husbands his third wife will choose. I wonder about such stuff as this and if they'll be any marriages in Heaven, and if men and wimmen has all the lust took out'n 'em."

Winky Blair comes up and he says: "Nice coffin you're makin, Half-Pint, if you'll get some that chicken manure off'n the lid—Smells this hot July weather—nice coffin you're makin though."

Fidas Keen comes down the path and he says: "Sweetbird, I come over to shave Battle and wash his body and lay him out in the coffin—to cut his hair if it needs to be cut and put the clothes on him you want put on him."

Sweetbird says: "All right, Fidas. The razor, the one Dad give me after he quit shavin and he told me his Pap used the same razor—the razor and the shavin brush and mug—you'll find them there on the little shelf above the water bucket in the kitchen—hot water a-plenty in the teakettle. Go right out there and shave Dad and get him ready for the coffin. We'll soon have the coffin made—coffin ready to put Dad in."

Ugly Bird Skeans tells his wife Georgia: "I'll have to leave the crop long enough if the weeds does take the crop to dig that grave for Battle Keaton. I'll have to take my grave tools, my broadax, my coal pick, my mattock and my poleax and double-bitted ax. I have to help pay the last respect to a dead man. It is the last time I have a chance to help Battle. So just mark me out'n the cornfield today. You ought to go over to Sweetbird Bradberry's and stay with Fronnie. She's nigh grieved to death. No use stayin here and workin today. Take a day off when a body's dead. Corn won't spile. If it spiles, let it go."

"Ugly Bird, when will the buryin be?"

"Tomorrow at ten o'clock Fidas told me last night comin back."

"Reckon he'll keep that long and the weather so hot?"

"Yes, hell yes. He'll keep that long if they'll fix that hole in the winder there by his bed so the flies can't come in at that hole. Yes, hell yes, he'll keep that long. It ain't hard to keep a body in July under two days, but over two days it is hard to keep a body in hot weather. That will just be the rest of this day, tonight and a piece of tomorrow. Then Holy-Joe Madden will preach the funeral."

"Are you goin now, Ugly Bird?"

"Yes. I am goin now, Georgia. I am goin to the Runyan Hill Graveyard and dig a grave for Battle."

Morning. The sun up pretty and getting fairly high in the sky. White clouds move out across the sky and shadows trail on the earth below—follow like shadows, follow the crows flying over the July earth. And at the big log house birds carry worms to the young birds in nests in the eave vines. Spiders are catching flies in webs on the low-loft Battle helped to build.

Down at the barn. Hear the pigs grunting for their slop. It is late this morning. The feeding has not been done. It is late and pig grunts are loud as the hammer's head hitting the planks in Battle's coffin—and the moo-oo's of the cows are loud as the oo-zoo's of the handsaw running through the wild-cherry planks to build a coffin lid for Battle's coffin. But men are working. Five men are working at the barn now. If you could only see them. There goes one with a wild-cherry plank. There goes one with a hammer and a handful of square-bellied nails. There is another with a handsaw. They are making a coffin.

And here is the Runyan Hill Graveyard—a hilltop overlooking a little world of streams and valleys—a long narrow patch of potato ridges where seeds are buried that will never sprout. They are called the clay-temple seeds. And here are men this morning—working in the sunlight amid the old trumpet vines, honeysuckle and sand briars—near the mass of green pines where wind keeps talking like it talks to the corn. Here is Ugly Bird already. He is showing the men what to do. He is showing them how to dig the grave. Down in the earth now one is working, working—throwing out long-handle shovels of dirt—

over his shoulder on the bare ground and on the saw briars. There a shovel full is coming up, see it! It is fresh moist-looking clay. There is a big yellow heap of clay thrown up now and when a shovel is emptied on the egg-end top, sprangles of yellow clay roll off into the sand briars and down among the honey-suckle vines. And here is where the pale burned-out temple of Battle's clay will mix with fresher clay—fresh yellow clay will mingle with the burned-out wash-kettle clay in the clay temple called Battle Keaton.

The coffin is done now. Pert and Ellis and Half-Pint carry it toward the back room. They carry it from the cow shed. Pert and Ellis run a stick under the front end of it and carry on each side of the coffin and Half-Pint tails the back end of the coffin and follows toward the back room. It is a heavy box because oak wood is heavy wood and wild-cherry wood is a heavy wood. It is made of oak and wild-cherry—made with square-bellied nails and plenty of them too. They have gone under the yard pine trees now where the path leads on the northeast side of the house—down across the burdock by the side of the house and a-past the hollyhocks then.

"Heavy damn thing, ain't it, Pert?"

"Yes, it's a heavy damn thing, Half-Pint."

Into the door they go—into the hole in the house. Fronnie opens the door and holds it open. The door has a spring to draw it closed. Now the coffin is in the back room. Fronnie lets the door fly closed. She hurriedly places two chairs down with backs toward the window—two rest pieces for the ends of the coffin to rest on. Pert has lifted hard at carrying the coffin into the house. His face is red as a Roman Beauty apple. Ellis is wiping sweat with the corner of his colored shirt he pulls from under the draw string under his pants. The tail of his blue shirt is wet and he sticks it back under his pants—rolls and lights a cigarette—cigarette rolled in brown-sugar sack paper. Now they stand—Half-Pint looks at Battle—Battle now getting white and whiter like the color of the tip-end of his beard when the sun is not shining on the tip-end of his beard.

"Ain't no hot water in that teakettle," Fidas Keen comes in and says—"Ain't no water a-tall in that teakettle. It's dry as a chip—been dry a long time. Fronnie, I want hot water to make lather to put on Battle's face so I can scrape off them beard. I want to get Battle dressed. It is nigh two o'clock and people will be comin in here tonight to set up with the corpse."

"I'll heat you some water, Fidas—just a minute."

Silence is in the room now. Silence, and a smattering of wind that comes in the room from the hollyhocks and the green-hickory leaves. Silence is in the room and Battle is in the room—Battle white and dead, dead as a beef. His white beard tips are toying with the smattering of wind that comes through the place where the windowpane used to be and where the windowpane ought to be now to keep out the wind and the flies. If Battle could only see the sunlight close to him; if he could only see the room and Half-Pint, Ellis, and Pert standing silently in the room. Yes, if Battle could only see—see the coffin resting on the chairs made of the rough lumber and lined with old worn-out quilts and a pretty white muslin sheet spread over the quilts—a feather pillow for Battle's head—a pillow made of goose down and goose feathers—ah, if Battle could only see. There is the green grass in the yard. There is the silver wind in the poplar leaves and there is a green field of pretty waving corn. Battle is blind to it all. If Battle could only see as he did when he watched the Spider on the low-loft trap the flies for grub. And there is the razor now, the mug, the lather and the shaving brush. And there is the wash tub with plenty of hot water in the back room now. Fidas is in the back room—no women, not even Fronnie, are in the back room now. If Battle could only feel the big razor going through his long beard and cutting it with little scrape-scrapes like mowing machine blades cut cane stalks pencil-sized. If Battle could only see again, could only know again, could only see again——

"Here are the clothes for Pap. There are the drawers—they are spotless, for I washed them last night and dried them by the kitchen fire. They are clean and white—spotless white just like Pap wanted them. There is the blue shirt—faded some though it is. But they are clean and don't smell sweaty and don't smell of brush smoke. Take them when you need them. Here they are by the door. Just come here and get them."

"All right, Fronnie. Keep that door closed, for we are about ready to wash his body now and get him ready for the coffin and get him in the coffin."

"Is that all the clothes you aim to have put on your father—just a pair of drawers and a shirt? What is the matter, Fronnie, with that black suit I saw Battle wearin over on Hog Branch to the Protracted Meetin?"

"I aim to have Pap buried just like that, for that is the way Pap wanted to be buried and that is the way I intend for Pap to be buried."

"Just with a pair drawers on and a shirt!"

"Yes."

"Why?"

"It was Pap's dyin request. That's why! He said he was a-layin down just like he was goin to sleep and get out'n the bed on Judgment Day at the sound of the trumpet."

"Ain't you goin to put a necktie on him neither?"

"No."

"Why?"

"Because he never wore one of them strings around his neck in his life. I aim to see he is buried in his shirt and drawers just as he requested."

"Then the coffin will have to be worked over. We have made a long straight lid and when we lift the lid to let people look at Battle they'll see him a-layin there just in his shirt and drawers and they'll think we forgot to dress him—And people never will get over talkin about it. You know how the Turners will talk if they ever get a hold of it."

"Damn the Turners. I can lick every damn one of them. All dishonest as hell. All mule faces fur as Sweetbird Bradberry is concerned. I can lick 'em all. I don't want a damn one of 'em snoopin round at the funeral either. If there is you'll see another funeral and see it pretty damn quick. I double-dare any one of them to say anythin about old Dad there and let me get the straight of it. I'll show you a cockeyed Turner less."

"Half-Pint, we can just saw that lid into down about where Battle's heart is and nail the lower part down and raise the rest of the lid—that'll only show Battle's face and his hands crossed over his heart."

"Let's carry it out, boys, and get this done."

"All right."

And here comes Lula Riggs. Lula Riggs comes with an arm load of flowers and she says: "Miss Bradberry, here's some flowers I picked and brought up here for the corpse. Here is some ironweed blossoms, some honeysuckle, violets, corn flowers and buttercups."

And Fronnie says: "Thank you, Lula. Thank you a big lot for all these pretty flowers."

Fronnie takes the flowers and puts them in the back room. She places them inside the door. Fidas meets her there and takes the flowers—Fidas inside the back room getting Battle ready for burial.

And here comes Violet Egbert. She comes across the cow pasture with a load of flowers. One can see her from the window—here she comes—"Miss Bradberry, here is some flowers Mama sent over for the corpse. Here is some wild snowballs, some susans, some white clover blossoms, some buttercups, pinks, white daisies and some sunflowers."

And Fronnie says: "Thank you, Violet. Thank you a big lot for the pretty flowers." And Fronnie carries them to the door and hands them to Fidas. Fidas carries the flowers on back through the room.

And here comes Jack Chitwood. "Miss Fronnie, here is some flowers I brought over to go with the corpse. Here is some sheep-shower blooms and some goldenrod partly green and some Scottish thistle and pea-vine blossoms and some sunflowers and mornin glories."

"Thank you, Jack, for the flowers. Thank you a big lot, Jack, for all the pretty flowers."

And here comes Pert, Ellis and Half-Pint with the coffin now. They come under the yard pines and through the front door and through the partition door with the spring to it. They go in the back room with the coffin and put it on the same two chairs. And Ellis says: "Got it right this time. It's a good piece of work. It will hold any dead man and hold him for a long time—hold him against time, dirt and worms. That is a good coffin—good as I ever seed a coffin made. But Battle needs a good coffin if ever a man needs a good coffin."

"I got the dressin done and while you fellars was a-gettin the coffin finished, I shaved Battle's beard off and washed his body all by myself. Look at that water there in that tub, won't you. That will show you what I been doin. Been cleanin a dirty dead man by-hell—a man plum dirty. Look at that water, won't you! But he is a clean man for burial now. He's good and clean too—ready to be in that coffin. And if he was a dad o' mine I would put a pair pants and a necktie on him. Can't tell where the spirit of a man goes when he is dead and it must go in the same dress that the body went to the grave in, surely it must. Them old long winter drawers and that old blue work shirt without a necktie—hell's fire!"

"But when a man requests a thing done, I say do it as he wants it done and not as you want to do it. That body is his body and he's the right to say what must be done with it instead of you sayin. That body was alive just a short time ago. It breathed wind into the lungs in it and et grub. It was a livin body. But now it is a dead body—dead as a beef. I'm just like Fronnie. If it was my father I'd put him away as she wants him put away—the way he requested."

Half-Pint and Fidas catch the wash tub under the ears and carry the water to the back porch to pour it over the bank. There they go with the water and Fidas says, "Ain't that water awful black?"

And Half-Pint says: "Yes, that water is damn black. That water is damn black." And when they pour it off the porch there are long wisps of dirty whiskers settled in the bottom of the washing tub—whiskers, long and silky—like twisted dirty silk ropes—And that is the beard that Battle wore—the beard that the wind played with—And now they carry the empty wash tub out to hang it on a nail in the smoke-house wall.

Fidas says: "Funny thing about that corpse I never had to happen when I was shavin any dead man I ever shaved. He had been dead ever since yesterday and when I cut a little place on his neck with the razor when I was goin down on his neck after some long scattered neckhairs and you ought to have watched the red blood spill out of that place—come out'n there like he was a live man. You wouldn't a thought that, would you, white as Battle Keaton is?"

"No."

"Well, I've shaved many a corpse and I never had that to happen before." Now Battle Keaton is in his coffin. Ellis and Pert put him in. Fronnie came in and bossed. Fronnie is in the room now. She is crying. Her eyes are swollen and puffed like red-pepper pods left in the rain. She saw that Battle was placed well onto his soft old-quilt bed—she saw he was firmly tucked away before the lid was nailed down on him.

And the light of another day is gone. The light has gone somewhere—has fallen on the green hills in northeast Kentucky. The sun has gone down beyond the green mountains of leaves on Peavine Ridge. There are red banks of clouds where the sun used to be. But the day has gone and the night comes on—night with her stars and her golden moon—moon the color of a red-oak chip.

And here is Battle.

And here is Battle. See him! Look at Battle in his coffin and the scent of wild flowers fills the room—wild flowers cover the homemade coffin. There is Battle silent and pretty in his coffin. He is clean and white and there is the scent of wild flowers in the room. The lid of the coffin down to his heart is thrown back so people can go and look at Battle's face if they want to see his face—It is night now and the people are comin in to the setting-up with the corpse. His death has spread out among the hills and people have come from far and near to see Battle in his last appearance—the last before he rests in the bosom of his native Kentucky shoemake clay. And some tonight have brought arm loads of wild flowers and yard flowers—There is an armload of wild roses and there are many wild yuccas, buttercups, touch-me-nots and four-o'clocks.

Flowers crown the head of the casket. Flowers are everywhere over the room. There is the sweet scent of wild flowers.

There is the pretty glow of wild flowers under the yellow light of the lamps—under the golden glow of the moonlight that hits the windowpanes and streaks across the back-room floor. The people are coming in now. See them as they come up the toe-path through the cornfield and walk under the cherry trees by the garden. See them as the moonlight falls on the moth-eaten black shawls and the overalls—See them. They come up the toe-path—up from the cornfield. They come to see Battle for the last time—the last time unless it is to-morrow when they open him for the last sight of his face as he resigns himself to the earth forever.

"Come on in, you folks. Make yourselves at home.

"Come on in, folks—just set any place you can find a seat.

"Anybody is welcome in my house but a person that has the last name of Turner. No Turner is welcome in my house. If a Turner is here now I want that Turner to get out before I put him out. I mean business, too. If a Turner goes to Heaven I don't want to go there. If one goes to Hell I know I don't want to go there. I hate a Turner and Dad didn't allow none here when he was livin and by-hell Sweetbird Bradberry ain't goin to allow none here this night when poor old Dad Keaton lays a corpse. No. Dad is too near and too dear to me. Dad got on the Lord's side of the fence, but he could never forget the Turners."

And now the wail of the guitar and the wail of the words and the power of words float out upon the night wind.

Could my tears forever flow,
Could my zeal no languor know,
These for sin could not atone
Thou must save and Thou alone;
In my hand no price I bring,
Simply to Thy cross I cling.

While I draw this fleeting breath,
When mine eyelids close in death,
When I rise to worlds unknown,
And behold Thee on Thy throne,
Rock of ages cleft for me,
Let me hide myself in Thee.

Hear the words on the night wind. Hear them! Hear the dog howl by the window! Hear the wail of the guitar! Smell the scent of fresh wild flowers. See the people in the back room—see them! See Battle white as chalk in his coffin! See it all—this is the night of stars and wind and death—this is the night. Hear the winds whisper—something about tomorrow it seems—this is the night of silence, stars and leaves and death.

Out on the wind there are words floating among the leaves —floating on the wind. There are stars in the sky. There is wind in the corn. There is a red oak chip-colored moon riding in a pretty color-of-pond sky. See it all—see Battle too. He is in his coffin—even if Battle could only see this night!

I THOUGHT somethin funny the way Finn took the gun and stayed off rabbit huntin every day in the week rain or shine. Sometimes he brought back one little puny rabbit. Sometimes he didn't bring back airy one. He allus went the same way over that yaller bank below the house and down by the hog lot. I can see him yet a-goin over the bank with a double-barrel gun throwed over his shoulder—a-shinin in the sun—both barrels just shinin blue as a pair of black-snakes on a sand-bank in the spring. He would allus say to me, "Ma, I'll bring back the bacon."

Maybe you ain't seen my boy Finn. In the last year he's growed up like a hickory sprout. He can't wear his Pa's shoes any more. We had to cut the doors out a little for him. He's got so tall. And when he bumped his fard on the door facin he just cussed a blue streak. I couldn't stand it no longer hear'n him cuss so weaked around before the little youngins. I had Mick to cut the doors out for him. He's got so tall that he had to sleep slonch-ways on the bed. He got to cussin about his feet stickin over the end of the bed and gettin from under the kiver. I jist sold cream, chickens, butter and eggs and bought that boy a bed long enough to keep his feet warm and I made the quilts long enough to go down over his feet so he could sleep in comfort. He quit cussin then around the house.

He never was much of a hand with the girls to my knowins. He was allus so thin and had big blue eyes with a off-look in them. His face was freckled as a guinea. He 'peared to be bashful around wimmen. He just stayed in the woods with a gun after the croppin was done. His Pa grumbled about buyin him shells—said he'd break a man up buyin him shells. And I said, "Well you'd better buy him shells to shoot a few rabbits and birds with than to have him doin like a lot of boys around here—a-gettin the good girls in trouble, tellin them they'd do this and do that—marry them and a lot of stuff." I says, "You look at Frank Kimsey's girl had to marry that snotty-nosed thing of Alec Tremble's that gadded all about over the country and sold licker. Look at that girl of Fidas Blevins' that had that sixteen-pound baby—a little bit of a stringy-headed thing not out of school yet. Didn't weigh a hundred pounds. Like to never got him to marry her. When he did marry her they just went on havin big babies and he never did treat her right." Mick just set there. He never said a word.

And I says to Mick: "He never looks at a girl around the place. He's good to help me. I call him in out of the fields to help me cook a meal's vittals and he'll come right in and put on a apron and help me. I can call him in when somethin gets wrong with my sewin machine and he'll come right in and fix it."

And Mick says: "You ain't give him time to do his kavortin yet. He's too young. Your brothers warn't no angels. I ain't been no angel, but the part of my life before I married you belongs to me. It was the best. You can have the rest. That boy will come out'n it like a bull one of these days. You know the time the Law come over here lookin for him when he's just eleven years old, don't you, over that Seymore girl they sent to the perform school for goin to the woods. You remember he run out there, the little shaver did, and climbed right in the top of that oak tree to get away from the Law—scared like a rabbit and shakin all over."

A good woman don't want to remember stuff like that. They want to forget it about their men and their boys. I just never thought of it. Mick remembered it. In the spring Finn would take the gun when the trees was a-puttin out and go over the hill and say he's goin to get a ground hog. Trees were kindly leafed out. No time to hunt. I'd tell him the old ground hogs had youngins. In the summertime it was squirrels. In the fall it was birds and rabbits. In the winter it was polecats and foxes.

It was Reece Fiddler's girl that come around Finn all the time. I could tell. She went to callin me Mother. Well, I got plagued at her sayin Mother to me for this and Mother to me for that. Then she come to me one day and wanted my little

Effie to go down on the creek by that big hole of water and go in a-swimmin with her where everybody could see them a-showin their legs and I just wouldn't stand for it. When my mother was a-washin clothes behind the smoke house and a stranger come behind the smoke house and spoke to her she made it her business to roll her sleeves down right there and not show her arms above her elbows.

Symanthia Fiddler wanted to work for me. She wanted to make her home with me. She was a pretty girl if she'd a had any clothes to her back and a girl good to work as I ever saw. She wanted to leave that shanty in the timber woods they lived in and I don't blame her for that. It was put up with slabs from the mill and roofed with third ply rubber-roy roofin. Rain just poured in and they slept on the dirt floor. Reece wasn't able to work much. Just ginned here and there where he could get the ginnin to do for fifty or seventy-five cents a day. Symanthia helped him sprout pastures off for twenty-five cents a day. She could use a scythe like a man and then go to a dance and dance all night.

I told her to come on over. We was in the crop then and it took all hands and the cook too—strawberries to pick and corn to plow and terbacker to hoe. It just kept us goin from daylight to dark. Symanthia said she'd made enough money to buy her a few dresses sweepin out the timber cutters' shanties. That was when they's a-cuttin out the Harkreader tract. The mill had to make eleven sets to get that big tract of timber.

Symanthia brought six right pretty dresses in a pace-board suit case. She came to stay with us. A prettier girl, I believed, I never saw. Her eyes was pretty as a sleepy-eyed doll—one of them old kind us youngins used to play with when we was girls. Her hair looked like brown sealin wax you put around fruit jars and she was big and neat as a limb and strong as a ox. She just put on overalls and worked like a man right about the place and just whistled and sung all the time. Her cheeks red as the comb of a layin hen.

I wonder how she bought all them dresses pretty as they was, silks and satins of about all kinds and colors. I give her the room off to herself up on the edge of the kitchen. We cut that room off from the kitchen when Aunt Minnie come to stay with us so she'd have a room by herself when she took one of them drowsy spells. I give this room to Symanthia and told her to make herself at home and she said she would for me not to worry about her.

I'd pon my soul to God I never saw a thing crooked out of that girl. She made herself at home with us and better help you never saw in your life. Her Ma come after her one day and told her she had to go home and she said she wouldn't go back to that shanty. I felt sorry for poor old Tillie Fiddler comin after her own born blood and she wouldn't pay no attention to her. She said right there to her own mother, "You know, Mom, I'd go some place if I could change my name from Fiddler. I hate the name. I don't look like the Fiddlers. I ain't got their red hair and their simelon heads. I ain't got their old snaggled teeth and their little pipestem legs. I don't believe I'm a Fiddler."

Poor old Tillie just stood there. She was so took over the way Symanthia was actin and the tears just streamed down her cheeks. She just has a few old snags in her mouth sharp as a cat's eye-teeth and they kindly stuck out in front and her little bony legs did look like pipestems. I felt so sorry for her. If Symanthia had been a girl of mine I'd a took her home or we'd a fit all over one of these hills. I'd a whopped her or I'd a killed her right there. Raise a devilish youngin and let one stand up and talk to you like that after you go through the pain of birth for them. That's too much!

Well, I said to Tillie: "I don't want you to think I'm harborin Symanthia here. She wanted to just come and make her home here and she begged me too. I let her come. If she didn't come she'd go someplace else and the Lord knows where a good girl can get these days. If they go to town, they ain't good long. You know that. Them factories spiled many a good girl right out'n these hills. Used to be when a good girl went away in respectable duds on her back she come back with her jaws all smeared with red paint and one of them hobble skirts on till she couldn't move her legs when she walked. It's better for Symanthia to stay right here in a good Baptis home."

Tillie Fiddler just turned and walked off and cried like her heart would break: "And my own girl has turned me down after me raisin her the best way I could–with a lazy no-count fox-huntin and fiddlin man to keep and a pack of lazy triflin boys that I have to whop like mules for not workin in the fields after I bend over somebody's washtub five days out'n the week. It will all come home to you, my little lady."

I noticed Finn never took the gun anymore and went a-huntin. He stayed at home and worked better than he ever worked. I noticed at breakfast time Symanthia would give Finn the best plate, a blue plate that's got a hunter in the bottom of it with his gun up and cocked at some birds flyin over a oat patch. She would give him one of my big thick teacups to drink his coffee from and a big white saucer that didn't have a chip in it any place. Mick used to throw my plates when he got on one of his tears and come home spreein till I pasted his head over once with a milk crock. That kept him from breakin up all my dishes. She always give him the newest spoon and the fork with the straightest prongs and the straightest knife.

Symanthia stayed with us all summer. Mick never said much. He just watched once 'n a while like a man will do. She was good to help me with the milkin and the work around the house. She canned the strawberries and helped to cut weeds from the corn. She was full of life like a boy and she got a good color in her face and was pretty as a doll. One day I told her stayin with us and workin and eatin regular meals agreed with her and she said that it did.

She was so good to help and we had so much work to do that Mick said he'd fix up the house a little bit over on the fur place and move Symanthia's Pa and Ma and family over there. He roofed the house with new boards and chinked and daubed the open cracks and fixed the doors and winders and moved them in with just one wagon load of house plunder for our little rabbit mules. Now you know how much they had.

They was just about on starvation. We let them have taters we's a-feedin to our cows. We went their note at the store and helped them get grub. Symanthia went back home to live with her people after they moved into the house on our fur place.

Finn worked the cornfields near Fiddler's. That piece of ground that runs down in the cove in front of their house—it always took Finn so long to plow it. I begin to think Finn might be in love with Symanthia Fiddler. She was so good to his stummick and that's what a lot of men want. A woman that 'll keep their stummicks filled with better grub than any of the rest gets. I didn't want Finn to marry and get tied down with a woman and a house of youngins. I wanted to send Finn to school and make a big lawyer 'r a doctor out'n him or a school teacher so he could walk with a pencil behind his ear and not have to cut the same sprouts on the same hill every year. I even saw Symanthia come up through the bushes once when I was back in the orchard gettin green apples for breakfast. I saw her come out like a rabbit and meet Finn and they went out on the ridge together. Symanthia and Finn was both barefooted and he put his arms around her and she put her arms around him. W'y they both walked side by side in a path nar enough for a rabbit. I took notice right there. I never said a word. I thinks to myself. "I'll just wait and catch on."

Well, them Fiddlers just cleaned up our place. They sprouted off the hills and used our mules and plowed up big fields for corn. They's the best workers a body might nigh ever seed. They set terbacker out on the hills and they knowed how to raise it. They knowed how to get the ground rid of roots and fixed up for a shovel plow the first year. They knowed how to take good keer of the ground. Never saw a hill a-washin off where a Fiddler farmed it. We furnished them seeds of all kinds and the mules and give them half.

They had a old cow they tied to the end of the wagon and brought and she was nothing but skin and bones and give bad milk out'n one teat, that was the reason they got her for a song and sung it themselves. I couldn't a drunk a drap of that cow's milk if I'd a been a-dyin from starvation. I give Fiddlers the skimmed milk after we took the cream and sold it. Took it away from the hogs, taters away from the cows, and keep them from starvin. God knows it was me that done it, for Mick won't stint a hog from milk.

One day Finn come in to me and said: "They's goin to be a boy come up here to see Symanthia. I used to go to the High School with him. He's a nice boy—got somethin a-matter with his eyes. They're a little crossed and girls don't take to him, but he'll make Symanthia a nice man to tie to. He's a man, Ma, that buries the dead and he gets much as three hundred dollars for buryin one man. He is a undertaker. He wants to come here and see her, for he is somebody and it won't do to take him to her house. It won't do to let him see how Fiddlers live. W'y he can't stand that corn bread and skimmed milk and runty Irish taters. Would you keer for him to come over here this Saturday and stay till Monday mornin? Symanthia might want to marry him. It will be the thing for her to do. I got everythin fixed up between them. She can get her a man."

I was the best pleased woman in the world to know Finn wasn't in love with Symanthia. I said: "Yes, bring her right on. She can come to my house and see him if she wants to. The poor hard-workin girl. Let her get her a man that has a little money."

"Then I'll tell Symanthia and she can write and tell Rodney Pennix to come on up and see her," Finn said. His eyes just a-dancin around in his head.

Symanthia come over to help me clean the house for this young fellar. We washed the house from top to bottom and put clean kivers on the beds, dressers and mantelpieces. We washed and scrubbed till I was vidaciously wore out. And Symanthia would say to me every once in a while: "Wait till I marry this rich undertaker and I'll invite you to see me. I'll have a fine house—big and painted white and a automobile. I'll be somebody and you'll be proud that you knowed me."

And I told her I used to have dreams like that before I married too and about all I'd got from livin was my youngins and my boys give me more worry 'n my girls. Never knowed the minute Finn was goin to get knifed or knife somebody. Get shot in the head. Get addled for life. Maybe get plugged about the heart. I told her it was bad anyway you looked at it. Bad to be a old man and shrivel up like a pawpaw. Bad to have a nest of little youngins and have to work like all-get-out to feed 'em on these old hills. Then in the end never know what would become of your youngins if you die and leave 'em to the mercies of the people. It's awful sweet to dream. When you dance you got to pay the fiddler.

Rodney Pennix come a half day ahead of time. He got lost comin from town. He was four hours late. He was showed the big road and it looked like a body couldn't miss it. It looked like a stray mule could a-followed that road. A man with one eye could a followed it. But Rodney Pennix went nine miles out 'n the way. He turned down the fox-hunters' pint and went down to Ulings. Then he got on another path. He circled into Eif Leadingham's barn like a rabbit. He ast them where he was from Powderjay's and they told him right up over the hill by a big rock and a sweet-apple tree. Dogged if he didn't get turned off that road and come around by Tin Hoggin's house. He ast Ester Hoggins where Powderjays lived. She told him just stay in the road between the persimmon trees all the way around the hill. He couldn't miss it. That's the way that fellar got here.

Effie was out in the yard and she come runnin in the house and said, "Ma, they's the funniest-lookin man out 'n his eyes out here." Well, I run out to see. I knowed it was that undertaker. He was dressed fit to kill with one of them high collars and his curly hair fell off his head all the way around like gold fall-time blades fall from a broom-sage stool. His eyes just went around and around in the sockets like a addled rooster's head when he's spurred. He was dressed in good store clothes, but he was carryin a old guitar.

I said, "Are you Mister Pennix that's come here to see Symanthia Fiddler?"

And he said: "I'm Mr. Pennix, the undertaker. I've come to see Symanthia. I've had a lot of trouble about gettin here.

County roads are hard for me to follow, for I live in town. It's been a long time since I've had my feet on the dirt 'cept the graveyard dirt where we bury the dead."

"Symanthia's in the back room in the house waitin for you. She's a good-lookin girl, a good girl to my knowins and you can just lift the latch and walk in and make yourself acquainted. Finn is out plowin. He'll be in soon," I says to him.

I went on out to feed the hogs and when I come back I heard them in the back room laughin and talkin. Then I heard him pickin that old lonesome guitar and singin, "Those Brown Eyes." Mick allus said a fellar that would gallivant all over the neighborhood with a fiddle, guitar or a old friend's harp with a drinkin-cup over it, wasn't no good. Pap allus said he didn't like the name of Pennix in the mountains. He said the name wasn't no good and to mark his word on that, for he hadn't lived ninety years for nothin.

They had a roastin big fire in the back room in that fireplace, so big that the fireplace on our side wouldn't draw. Finn come in from turnin fall ground. He was wet to his knees and devilish nigh froze to death. When we called them to supper, Symanthia was the proudest girl I nearly ever saw. Her face was lit up bright as the lamp. She said to me in a whisper: "We're goin to get married. He's done ast me to marry him. Said he had plenty of money. He's let me have his sweater with a big S on it for Simpsonville High School where he played ball and they give him the sweater. It's the engagement token."

Well, that boy had to nearly get down in his plate to shovel up the beans with a fork. He looked right well all but his eyes. His pretty curly hair fell down over his stiff collar like a girl's curly locks. He et like he was empty as a holler stump. Mick just passed him the grub and kindly grinned. He couldn't see Mick grinnin at him. Symanthia et by the side of him. Finn et on 'tother side of the table. He would pass the beans and jam and say: "Rodney, have this. Rodney, have that."

Tillie happened to pass by from milkin her cow that was in our pasture. I was out hangin up my milk buckets. I said, "Tillie, come up here and have a look at your new son-in-law."

And she come up and opened the door about big enough for a cat to get through.

She said, "W'y is she going to marry that cross-eyed son-of-a-bitch? I wouldn't have him for all his money and if all his head was strung in gold. What does Symanthia think about nohow? I'll get me a ax and split his goddamned brains out. I could come up behind him and he couldn't see me."

"You can't do that," I said to Tillie. "You had your chance to get your man. You took him. Let Symanthia have her chance."

"It's hard to raise a girl up for a thing like that," she said, "and I would druther have my man with two good eyes and a no-count fox hunter and fiddler than to have that thing. I've done a lot better than she's a-goin to do if she takes him."

Her voice trembled like the wick blaze in the wind. Her catlike teeth just popped when her jaws come together. I was afraid they would be trouble right there. She picked up her milk bucket. She kicked the cat clean off'n the porch. It was tryin to get in the milk. She went out under the sassafras. She went home fast as a pullet wantin to lay an egg.

That night we heard a gruntin in the back room. Finn peeped through a knot hole in the door and crooked his finger for me to come. I don't like to slip like a cat on people. I looked through the knot hole. There Symanthia was on his lap. She's a heavy girl. He was a-gruntin and a-holdin her like she was a baby. He would kiss her and she would kiss him. They would whet their noses together like doves a-cooin. I said to Finn: "I've seen a lot in my time, but this gets me. I can't stand to watch 'em no longer." I quit lookin through the knot hole.

I heard that "Those Brown Eyes I Love So Well," till I was so sick of it. I nearly vomited at my stummick when I heard them words and that old guitar. They just et and run to the back room and fastened the doors. They acted like love-sick kittens. They burnt two cords of the dryest wood we had in two days. Symanthia didn't turn her hand to help me clean the dishes after they et. Rodney slept with Finn that night upstairs. He got Finn loved up and Finn liked to a never broke loose from him. He called Finn his "little dove Symanthia" in his sleep and Finn just had to get out'n the bed and sleep on the floor on a quilt. He said his arms was so tight around him when he waked up that he had his wind cut off. Said he nearly had him choked down. Said he was weak as a cat.

On Sunday, Rodney ast poor old Pap about old Uncle Jim Seymore. He had his name on a piece of paper. Ast how long did Pap reckon it would take him to kick the bucket so he would get him to bury. He ast about Aunt Subrinia Fields. How long it would be before she would die. Said he was promised her body to bury. He had a whole list of the old people's names down to bury. Tellin my poor old Pap this and him ninety years old. You know Pap felt kindly funny. He felt like he might be after him. Then he talked about buryin people in coffins with brass knobs where people had the money and puttin 'em in steel coffins. And I just stood it long as I could stand it and I told him people in our neighborhood made their coffins for their dead and they'd never heard tell of a undertaker before.

I went out to milk on Monday mornin. When I come back to the house Effie told me that Symanthia had left with that undertaker. I was plagued to death afraid Tillie would think I agged the whole works up. Finn said she took her clothes and said she was going to Simpsonville to stay with a married second cousin. She said to tell her Ma not to be uneasy about her. Finn told me they'd been gone about twenty minutes when I come back to the house.

Finn went to town to get the mules shod. Tillie come over to the milk gap. She ast me where Symanthia was. I told her she left with that undertaker, Rodney Pennix. I told her they had nearly time to get to town. And she said: "Oh, My God Almighty! Has she run away with that thing?"

She lammed her milk bucket against the ground and took off toward the house barefooted. She had a old gingham dress on and a old slat bonnet. She went to town like that.

Rodney paid Symanthia's way across the Ohio River, Finn said. He said he got to town in time to see them get on the ferryboat. He heard Rodney tell Symanthia, "Honey, when you want the old coon cack, just call on old Rodney. He's allus got it ready in his pocket to spend." Then Finn said he went up town and was just took to death by Tillie standin on the corner by the drug store. She was barefooted. She had on that old gingham dress and slat bonnet. Finn said she said to him: "Finn Powderjay, was it you that got that thing up here to see Symanthia? [Finn told her it wasn't him.] If it wasn't for havin to wash it out for fifty cents a day over the tub I'd get me a lawyer to send that cross-eyed son-of-a-bitch to the penitentiary for ninety-nine years for white slavery. He paid my girl's way over into another State and she ain't but seventeen years old. If he ever comes back to this side of the river I'll split his goddam brains out with a double-bitted ax."

Finn come on back home and was a-tellin me about it. It was just seven days till Symanthia come back home. She told Tillie she went to Rodney's home and that he didn't play no football. He made the sweater for carryin water to the players on the team. She said his Pap had a little money, that he worked out on a section and a $1,000 he got from his Grandma when she died. She said Rodney didn't have no money a-tall. Said all he got was what his Pap give him. Symanthia said that she had come back home to stay if her Ma would let her. She said she was a fool to leave her home with a stranger nearly blind. A undertaker all time talkin about buryin dead people.

Finn picked up the gun and started huntin again. There was no more land to turn close to Fiddler's house. It was all turned waitin for the winter freeze. He started rabbit huntin. He'd be gone all day and come in without a rabbit. He'd say the game was all killed out by the niggers from town. He couldn't have no luck anymore. He hunted for the next two weeks day in and day out.

Mick just told him one day before he went to work on the State highway that he was tired of feedin a boy that wouldn't do nothin but rabbit hunt. He said he had to haul fodder in and stack it in the barn lot. Finn said he would. Mick says:

"My job is liable to play out after the next County election, then what am I to do? Catch me in a trap. No corn in the ground–no fodder in for the cows. No job!"

I knowed they was somethin the matter with Finn. He went out to work. He harnessed the mules–hitched them to the sled. He went after fodder. He come in without a load of fodder. He said he was sick and had to go to the doctor quick, "I got to go to the Doctor, Ma, and don't ast me nothin about it a-tall. I got to go. You unharness the mules and turn them in the woods pasture."

He took out through the pasture runnin stiff-legged and I hollered and says, "It ain't your heart that ails you, is it, Finn?"

And he says: "Hell no it ain't my heart. Don't ast me no more questions." I saw him top the pint goin fast as he could go out the ridge, past the pines and out of sight.

He come in about three o'clock. Mick don't get in till five. And I says, "What did the Doctor say was the matter with you, Finn?" Finn was down wallerin in the grass. He got up and went to the barn. I could see him fall. I could see him waller in the grass. The dead grass on the barn lot. I took out to the barn and I says, "Finn, you got to tell your Ma what is wrong with you. Have you got a bad disease?"

"That's what I got," said Finn, "I got a bad disease."

"Where did you get it?" I says to Finn. "Did you get it from Symanthia after she's come back from Simpsonville?"

"Yes," says Finn.

"After that low-down hussy's come over here and lived in my house and et my grub," I says, "and then to think she'd come back here with a disease and give it to my boy."

I was so mad I could a bit the iron poker in two. I just shook all over. I knowed what it was. Brother Jake had it twice. Brother Melvin had it seven times. My own boy a layin on the ground full of pain as a water barrel full of wiggle tails. Brother Jake was in Twolick, Kentucky, and a old strollop pecked on the winder above his head. She crooked her finger for him to come in. Jake was just a boy. She hooked him. He come nigh as a pea dyin. The doctor back in the mountains told him to eat apples for it. Drink apple juice. Jake et all the green apples in one orchard. It didn't cure him. Old Lum Beaver's yarb remedy was all that done him any good. It took four months. The second time he got it he used the yarb remedy. It didn't last him but two months. Brother Melvin had it a year and was cured by a Faith doctor on Apple Creek. Then he quit laughin about the sperit's doins.

Mick come in and he said: "What's the matter that fodder ain't in the barn lot? Has Finn got the dropsy?"

And I says to Mick: "Don't be too hard on the boy, Mick. He's bad off. He sprained his back liftin over there this mornin. He was liftin a log in the way of the sled."

The next day I took the team and hauled the fodder and put it in the lot. I saw that little hussy of a Symanthia out gettin wood and I says: "Little hussy, don't you put a foot on that fifty acres of land we live on. You got fifty-two rented over there of ours and you stay on that. Don't you even come nigh me. You ain't fit for a decent woman to touch." She took me at my word and stayed away. She knowed I was mad enough to glom her eyes out with the pints of my fingers.

I told Finn not to tell his Pap. He would go over to Fiddler's with a knife. There would be trouble. He'd run all Fiddlers off'n the place. Maybe knife somebody over it. He was so fractious over anything. I told Finn for God's sake not to tell anybody. If it got out in the neighborhood he'd be a outcast. People would run back to the woods when they saw him a-comin. People was afraid that if they touched him they'd get what he got. When God knows the only way for a man to get it is from a old strollop. Just what Symanthia has got to be—a vidaciously, gallivantin, gadabout, Simpsonville strollop.

Finn kept his medicine in the tool box. He doctored hisself in the cowshed. He'd come out of a mornin and waller on the dead grass and holler like he was a-dyin. I don't know how it got out. It was whispered around that Finn Powderjay had "a bad disease." When he got so he could go to Sunday school, people wouldn't set close to him. The girls wouldn't have a thing to do with him. I thought that it might be as hard for him to get a wife if he ever wanted to get married as it was for Brother Melvin. He liked to a-never got married. Girls was afraid of him. They thought once he had a bad disease he allus had it. He couldn't get shed of it.

I told Mick we ought to get Finn back in school in the middle of the year. I said he needed more education. We sold a couple of the cows and sent him to Wormwood University. I told Mick that was all we could give our youngins was a little education. This was the time to make a doctor out of Finn.

Tillie come to the barn to milk now. I never said a word to her about Finn and Symanthia. She told me that Symanthia had never felt well since she had come from Simpsonville. I never said a word. I thought a whole lot. It come on the end of my tongue. I come nigh as a green pea spittin it out right there. But I didn't. It's kindly toucheous to tell a mother about her daughter when your boy's been into it and all messed up. I thought it best to keep my mouth shut.

One day when Finn was gettin all right and felt better 'n he ever did he said to me, "Get your pipe and go over to Tillie Fiddler's with me." So I lit my pipe and we went over the little hill that is between our house. Finn give me some of his terbacker. We smoked and talked goin over. He said since he had a bad disease, he hated the looks of a woman. Said now he was gettin over it a little. He said he wanted to see that Symanthia got a doctor.

We went in the house and Tillie was took to death to see any of us over to her place. We hadn't been there in so long. She was just fit to eat us up. She couldn't be nice enough to us. I give her some of my terbacker for her pipe. Me and her and Finn sat there and smoked about a hour I guess. Symanthia was there in the bed asleep.

Before we started home Finn said, "Tillie, I want you to take Symanthia to a doctor. Take her to Doc Allbright. She's got a bad disease. She give it to me so damn bad I had to drag around like a broke-down hog for five or six days."

"A bad disease," Tillie screamed, "my God, what is this world a-comin to. It was that crossed-eyed son-of-a-bitch. The low-down curly-headed son-of-a-bitch. I wish he was in hell goddam him. I ain't got no money to pay no doctor with. I wash for fifty cents a day all the washin I can get over among the town people. I get all I can to wash at night to feed these little youngins and clothe them."

"Take her away," said Finn, "the doctor can wait for his money. Save her. I know she's sufferin like a son-of-a-bitch. I know I suffered nightmares and lizards and striped snakes. Don't let her eat no apples for it neither."

I hated to, but I had to tell her that she'd have to move off the place. When Mick found it out, hell would be to pay. She'd better get off while times was good. Get off right now. Soon as she could. Move to town where her washins would be handier and she wouldn't have to carry them across the hill home.

Finn give me and Tillie a pipe full of terbacker apiece and we all lit our pipes with a piece of rich pine kindlin. Finn and me went back across the hill home.

Tillie told me that the doctor said that Symanthia didn't have no bad disease. She said Symanthia had strained herself with the ax cuttin wood the next mornin. She said that was the way lies got started. Finn had come over there and told it. She didn't want to hear no more of it.

I said right there at the milk gap, "I'll go with you to another doctor and pay the doctor myself and let you see she's got a bad disease and she give it to Finn. W'y he wallered over everythin in this barn lot when he was doctorin it. It took his breath, medicine Doc Allbright give him did. That's why he fell off here so. He looked so pale. He walked stiff-legged like a rabbit."

Tillie never said a word. Next day Reece come and ast for our mules to move with. I said: "They're right out there in the barn lot. Go put the harness on 'em and right up there is the wagon. Hitch to it." He went on and got the mules. He took two loads to town that day. He took the last load the next mornin. He moved his corn and fodder later on.

Yesterday we got Finn off to Wormwood University to make a doctor out'n him. I looked in his pocketbook to see if he had the sixty-seven dollars we got out'n the cows. He didn't have but forty-nine. I paid the doctor for him with cream money. I skinted my table. I skinted my little children's back to get that bill paid so his Pa wouldn't know it till he got away. I didn't want Mick to go over there and cause a lot more trouble. Have a lot more sickness and trouble in the world. There's enough of it already for a mother with eleven children like I've raised and a set of boys wild as a bunch of quails. I never told Mick about it after Finn left. What a man don't know won't hurt him.

SNOW covers the earth like a thick heavy blanket. The bare trees stand like silent wooden pegs stuck in the snow. They bend creakingly when the wind whistles through their leafless tops. Icicles hang to the eaves like white silver spears. There is one icicle bigger than the rest at the end of the wooden drain pipe.

"It's a bad night for a bellin," says Finn, "I don't see what makes people want to get married in weather cold as this weather is. Zero weather and T. J. Lester and Daisy Bee Redfern jumped-the-broom and have to stay in a house you could pitch a dog between the unchinked logs."

Finn throws down a fork of clover hay to the mules from the barn loft and blows his knuckles warm with his breath. His lips are blue. His face is red. He is so tall he bends down to miss the barn-loft rafters.

"It's time they're gettin married, don't you think, after courtin each other eight months," I says to Finn, "no use to court their lives away and then not marry. We'd better hurry up and get the mules ready if we're goin to the bellin. Got to curry them and harness them. There's a good moon tonight and we'll not miss the road."

We feed the mules clover hay in the manger. We put yellow ears of corn in the feed boxes. We walk up the path cut through the snow to the house. We have to clean out the guns and get the shells and get all set for the bellin.

Pa is settin before the wood fire. His red face in his hands. He is lookin into the tiny blue flames at the end of the fore stick. His eyes are half closed. He seems to be dreamin. We walk quietly so we won't wake Pa. We tiptoe across the room.

"Where you boys a-goin," says Pa, comin out of a drowsy sleep, "tiptoin across the house like this? I know you boys are up to somethin. No dances, remember that. Steve Bocook's boy got cut to the holler twice over on Long Branch last night and you boys ain't goin to no more dances."

"Pa, don't get so rosy all at once. We ain't goin to no dance. Didn't you know T. J. Lester and Daisy Bee Redfern got married today and we're goin to bell them tonight," says Finn.

"I didn't know it," says Pa, "another poorhouse started. Old Bill-Ike Lester will have to keep that lazy good-for-nothin boy of hisn and his wife too. That's the kind that wants a woman. Them no-count kind. He wouldn't work if you put him at a 'lassie mill where he could sop the pan all day. I had him to work for me and I screamed like a panter and run him home to get rid of him. Now he marries Daisy Bee Redfern, pretty a girl as she is. Children anymore marry on instead of off."

"You got married once, didn't you, Pa?" says Finn, "and what did Grandpa say about it? He said you wasn't worth powder and lead to shoot you. Now he says you're the best in-law he's got and he wouldn't give you for any of his own boys. He used to call you Tom Slackwater's bull before you married Mom. He said you gallivanted over this neighborhood it was a Lord's sight to see—playin a old fiddle and pickin a guitar and dancin. He said you didn't care nothin for the field and the plow and didn't have a head on you for to make a good girl a livin."

"I got belled," says Pa, "now if you boys are goin to a bellin, go on, but be damn sure you don't go to no more of them square dances till the Carpers and the Filsons quit cuttin at them dances. Somebody's goin to get killed and everybody's into it before the fight is over. You know that. You don't know how hard it is to raise a boy and get him cut all to pieces or get him killed until you boys get old as I am."

We go upstairs to dress. Finn leads the way. Before we get to the head of the stairs Finn says to me, "Quinn, did you know Pa's gettin cranky as all get out? Pa's gettin old. He used to drink and fight and carry on somethin awful. He does yet when he gets lit up just right. When he ain't lit up, he just sets around and fusses."

We put on our boots, our heavy sheep-skin coats, our wool caps and our scarfs. We put on our mittens. We are ready.

The moon filters through the window like a white water. It covers everything. We could see to shoot a rabbit on the snow. Clouds are blue as ice on mountain water. Moon is bright as a new silver dollar in the ice-blue sky.

"It's goin to be as cold as blue blazes," says Finn, "better take some of them heavy quilts along to put over our laps. It's goin to be mighty cold a-ridin in that sled. Ten degrees below zero and it's a damp cold along that river. It's a mighty damp cold. The girls will get mighty cold if we don't take quilts along to cover them up good from feet to ears."

We carry four good heavy wool-padded quilts downstairs and out to the sled. We lay them down on the snow. The moon shines down through the bare apple-tree twigs. Chickens roostin on the icy limbs nudge each other and grumble somethin we cannot understand. They look as big as black and white stumps between us and the moon.

"You fix up the sled and get the guns in it," says Finn, "and I'll go harness the mules. I can do it quicker. Barnie ain't used to you and you don't know how to hold his lip when you put the bits in his mouth. I can do that quicker and you fix up the sled."

"All right with me," I says to brother Finn as he runs down the path to the barn, crunchin the snow beneath each step.

I carry corn shucks from the corn crib and put in the bottom of the sled and I brush the snow off the quilts and put them in the sled. I go into the house and carry out Finn's automatic shotgun and my pump gun. The blue barrels gleam blue in the moonlight. They glisten like a blacksnake when it sheds its tough skin in the springtime and the bright spring sun first shines on its new coat of skin. I go back and get the Columbia single-barrel shotgun that has worn out three plungers through three generations of use. Barrel is thin as tissue paper and it is sightless. It is almost dangerous to shoot, but we shoot it anyway. It has been to many many bellins and we feel like it is entitled to fire the salutes to comin generations long as there is a piece of it left to knock off a shell. We take two Smith & Wessons with long barrels that gleam in the moonlight.

I can hear the harness jinglin. It rattles in the icy air like tiny bells. It is Finn comin up the path with the mules. He has them harnessed ready to hitch to the sled. In a minute we will be racin over the snow. Finn backs the mules into their places–Barnie on the off side and Jack on the near side. He hooks the trace chains to the single trees and I fasten the breast yoke to the collars and fasten the sled tongue to the breast yoke. It will be slick tonight and the mules will have to hold back the sled on the downhill runs, for we've no time to rough lock.

"Stand still, Barnie," says Finn, "my but this mule is wantin to go. He's cold. He's feelin his oats. He wants to go. A cold mule always wants to go."

"We are ready," I say to Finn.

"Wait a minute," says Finn, "till I hang a couple of cowbells to the corners of the sled and all the people that don't know about the bellin will know about it and will be out followin us or findin out where the bellin is."

Finn runs into the smoke house and gets two cowbells. He fastens them to the back corners of the sled. We jump into the sled, sit on the coffee-sack padded board seat and put a quilt apiece over our laps. Finn takes the check lines. We are off–over the snow for a seven-mile ride to the bellin.

The bells jingle till Pa comes to the door. We can see him standin between the firelight and us. He says somethin–we cannot understand, but it sounded like he said, "Be careful with the mules and all the shootin." I can hear bells behind us –louder than the church bells on Sunday mornin. The blue sky above us and a big moon in the sky. Dark woods scattered over the white mounds of mountains like the black blotches on a white bird-dog's back. The mules are on their toes–goin at full pace. The wheezin of the frozen sled around the curves down the Hollow and the rattlin of the harness and the ringin of the bells over the crusted snow!

"All right, Barnie," says Finn, and he touches his harness tailpiece slightly with a slap of the reins, "no shirkin here tonight. Not so fast, Jack–not so fast, boy, over this slippery road."

I can see the mules' breath like two huge streams of smoke blown out upon the blue icy air in December. I can see Finn's breath. It goes out in two little curls of blue smoke—one curl from each nostril and one goes to one side of his face and the other goes to the other side of his face.

"Do you reckon Sadie and Dot will be ready when we get to Callihan's?" says Finn.

"Dot's awfully slow. I told her this evenin to be ready by seven tonight. I guess she'll be ready."

"You know Pa's gettin old, sure as the world," says Finn, "W'y he said to me the other day, 'You boys ain't got big paths built to the hog pen and to the barn and milk shed and wood shed like you have traipsin paths over the hills to the square dances. You're always on the gad. You want to run with your chins up and barrels of work around this place to do.' I thought that was so funny. Pa's gettin old. He ain't young no more like he used to be."

We pass the peddler well and turn the corner on one sled runner. Then we shoot up a straight piece of road. I can see the snow like powdered dust fly up from the mules' hoofs. Callihan's house is in sight. The lamp is burnin by the window. We pull up to the house.

"Go in and get the girls," says Finn, "while I knock the balls of snow and ice from the mules' hoofs. They need to be toed and corked for weather like this."

I go in and get Dot and Sadie. They are ready for once when we want to go some place. "All bloomed out, ain't you, Dot," I say as I help her turn up her fur collar and tie her scarf around her neck.

"A winter blossom," says Dot, "and we've been waitin on you slow pokes for a hour. Where have you been all this time?——"

"Had to finish feedin and milkin and get away from Pa. He thought we's headin for another dance. Let's hurry. We want to be there when the first gun is fired."

Dot and me takes the back seat. Sadie climbs in beside of Finn. He has trimmed the snow off the mules' feet and is back in the sled ready to go. It don't take Finn all the time to do nothin when he wants to get some place. We put the heavy quilts over our laps and we set kindly close, you know.

"All set," says Finn.

"Ready," says Dot, "let's dash 'em over the snow."

"We heard them bells a mile away," says Sadie, "and I told Dot you slow pokes was on your way."

"You're wakin up everybody in the Hollow on a still night like this with them big bells," says Dot.

"That's what we want to do," says Finn. "Let 'em know Daisy Bee Redfern and T. J. Lester kicked-the-broomstick."

"Jumped-the-broomstick, you mean," says Sadie.

"Set close and shut up the gab," I say to Dot.

"That Barnie mule," says Finn, "is fleet as any horse in this country when you make it seven miles instead of one or two. I wish old Jack could match him. Mules are the things for slick snowy roads. A mule never falls. He's as sure-footed as a possum."

We breathe the icy air into our lungs. We are feelin warm close to each other under a double of thick wool-padded quilts. The moon is above us in the blue sky. The fields up on the mountain slopes where there isn't timber is light as day.

"Whoa, boys," says Finn, "give me that gun, Quinn, and hold the mules."

I hold the mules and Finn stands up in the sled bed and takes careful aim at something on the bank.

"Pow!"

The mules stand on their hind legs and snort against the checklines. I hold them. There is the smell of powder. There is a cloud of black smoke from the throat of the gun that followed the belchin blaze.

"I got him," says Finn, "see him kickin by that stump up there. I wanted to see what I could do in the moonlight to a rabbit with this old hulda. Wait till I jump out and get it."

Finn runs across the blanket of granulated sugar grains of snow. He goes through the sheep fence up through a cluster of pipe-stem shoemake sprouts by a stump and brings back a kickin rabbit. He throws it in the back of the sled on the straw. He takes the reins. We are off again.

The mules throw their heads into the air and snort. They don't like the smell of gunpowder. We are ridin along the Sandy River now. It is a cold wind that stings our faces from the water. The mules are in full gallop on the road. We'll soon be at Lester's house.

The bells are ringin and the snow is flyin. I don't have much time for the noise, for I am busy holdin Dot in the sled as we swing around the curves. She holds me when we swing to her side and the sled tries to throw me out. I hold her when the swing is to my side and tries to throw her out. I can see the blue-snake barrels of the guns gleam in the moonlight. They are standin in the corner of the sled. The bells are ringin, the harness is jinglin, the wind is blowin little clouds of the white flakes into our faces. Snow follows the sled in a blowin swirl like dust behind a rubber-tired hack.

"Here at last," says Finn, as we turn in the lane past the barn and up to a double-log cabin. Horses stand hitched to the white fence posts. Sleds without teams and drivers are left all over the barn lot and the wood yard. The windows of the double-log cabin gleam yellow in the moonlight. There is noise enough in the house to explode the log walls.

"Take your mules out, Sonny," says Bill-Ike Lester playin with his white chin whiskers and comin closer to the sled. "Wished to my God if it ain't old Mick Powderjay's boys and Effie Callihan's girls. Come right on in, children—come right on in and jine the party. I'll put the mules in and give them hay in good warm stalls."

"What must we do with the quilts?"

"Leave them right in the sled, children. Nobody will harm a quilt here tonight. All you got to watch here is your licker. You know men has a hankerin for licker and they'll steal licker. But they won't bother quilts, you know. What would men want with quilts?"

Dot and Sadie jump from the sled and limber up their bodies by trampin quickly about the sled and crunchin the snow beneath their feet. I rub my mittened hands and then help unhook the trace chains and do up the checklines. Uncle Bill-Ike Lester unfastens the breast yoke and Finn leads the mules from the sled and gives them to Uncle Bill-Ike to put in stalls.

We get the guns and the pistols and Dot takes the cowbells loose from the sled. We walk through the gate toward the noise. "They're gone," says Freddie Hix. "Can't find them nowhere. We've looked every place for them."

"Who's gone?" I say to Freddie.

"Daisy Bee and T. J. ain't been heard tell of around here tonight," says Freddie, "and we've looked all over the place for them. We've looked behind the meal barrels and the flour barrels, in the barn, the corn crib—upstairs under the beds, behind the quilt stacks, behind the dressers, the doors, the curtains over the presses—We've looked in the cellar, the smoke house in the 'backer barn, the sheep shed, the cattle barn—We've looked every place there is to look. We can't find them nowheres."

"Do you reckon they got away," says Finn, "when they just got married this evenin and they ain't but one road leadin out of here? Somebody would a-seen them leavin surely. You know they didn't walk. Do you reckon they're hidin out over at Short's or Leadingham's?"

"No, we just sent searchers over there and they've looked the places clean. They can't find hide nor hair of them any place."

"Don't reckon they went to roost with the chickens?" says Mart Hensley.

"Look what a crowd here and no bellin."

We go into the house. All the neighborhood is here. Here is Kate with Tom Longsmith. Here is Eif Shelton with Martha Sowards. Here is Chicken Gullett with Symanthia Skidmore when he ought to be with Lizzie Porter. Don Hix is here, Sammie Banks, Luke Endsor, Viddie Pembroke. The house is filled like a beehive. They are all movin around like bees without a queen.

"I know exactly where them two is," says Alexander Pitts. "I was at this very place fifty years ago to a bellin and I know right where they hid. It's a good warm place. I remember that night fifty years ago was a night just as cold as this night. They got a better roost than the chickens. They ain't away from this place and if you'll elect me captain of the bellin crowd I'll get them for you."

"You're elected captain right now," says Herman Moore.

"You're elected captain right now," cries go up from all over the house.

"Take us to them," says Eif Shelton.

Alexander Pitts runs his big hand through his bird's-nest beard.

"Follow me," Alexander says. The beard and whiskers around his mouth muffle the sounds of his words.

We go out behind the house. The big chimney is built onto the bigger lower half where the fireplace is, and it leans away from the house big enough for two to hide behind.

"A dollar to a dime, boys, right up there behind that chimney 's where they're at," says Captain Alexander Pitts combin his beard with his big sticks-of-stove-wood fingers. "Get me a clothesline prop and watch me twist 'em out'n there like they's a he and she rabbit."

"Come out'n there," says Captain Alexander Pitts, "before I twist you'se out'n there like a couple of rabbits in a holler tree!"

There is frozen silence like the ice in the creeks. Not a breath stirs. Not a sound.

"Come out'n there and we won't twist you. If you don't come we'll twist every dud off'n your backs and ride you T. J. on a rail till you holler for mercy. Now you answer me. This is Captain Alexander Pitts tellin you to come out and give yourselves up to the crowd while times is good."

There is silence behind the chimney and among the breathless starin crowd.

"They ain't in that place, Captain Alexander Pitts," says Bill-Ike Lester as he comes around the corner of the house from the barn.

"They are in that place, Bill-Ike. I come to this place to a bellin fifty years ago. They hid on us. A big snow was on the ground like this one tonight. We looked every place for them. We couldn't find them. We got ready to go home and old Lem Sperry come out and says, 'Boys, there's one place we ain't looked.' He tried to see behind the place and he couldn't. He ast me to fotch him a willer pole and I got a fishin pole that was layin up in that big oak tree over there. He stuck it behind there and he begin to twist the pole. And he says: 'Boys, I've got 'em. They're here.' And he twisted 'em right out up there on them rocks. Fetch me that clothesline prop and I'll show you who ain't in behind that chimney and who is."

Jerry Pratt brings the long clothesline pole. It creaks frozen like in the icy wind. The crowd shuffles their feet on the crunchin snow. All eyes starin up the chimney and the big moon in the sky above the chimney. The icicles hangin to the eaves glisten like silver roofin nails in the moonlight.

Captain Alexander Pitts takes the pole in his big hands. He lifts it up straight in the wind, then twists it behind the chimney rocks into the dark hole.

"I feel 'em," says Captain Alexander, "I feel 'em shore as God made little green apples. There they are. They are a-holdin my pole. The fish has got the bait. What did I tell you? Now, what did I say—a dollar to a dime. Want a bet, any of you? Wait till I twist 'em a little. They'll have to come or holler."

Alexander twists the pole with his big hands, his beard is bent by the passin wind like the twigs on the oak tree. His head is lifted—face up and his blue eyes glued onto the hole between the big chimney and the house.

"There they are," the cry went up from the crowd with thin puffs of white air streamin from each mouth toward the moon as T. J. come up to the moonlit edge of the hole with the end of the pole twisted into the tail of his coat.

"Come down from there or we'll ride you on a rail like we did old Abraham Howard's boy Ezekiel fifty years ago. Come out'n there right now—you two pretty redbirds and we won't do nothin to you to amount to anything."

"Get that ladder from under the house there and set it up against these rocks so Daisy Bee can get down and we'll come without being twisted any more with that pole. It catched me right in the back and it hurt a little bit–" says T. J., his lips curvin to a broad laugh and his teeth showin in the half dark and half moonlight, his eyes shinin like a tomcat's eyes in the dark.

Millard Pierce gets the ladder from under the floor they used to get up behind the chimney. Daisy Bee went up the ladder, T. J. climbed the logs and held to the chimney rocks after he'd scooted the ladder back under the floor. Millard puts the ladder upon the chimney, Daisy Bee bashfully comes from her dark warm den between the chimney and the big log house and sets her tiny feet on the ladder steps and starts down, her face always turned from the laughin crowd. T. J. follows her down the ladder, holdin to one of her hands.

"Here we are," says T. J. as they step on the snow. "We've heard every word you said about us and it's been hard to keep Daisy Bee from laughin at you. I had to pinch her and make her mad at me to keep her from bustin out and laughin––"

"Yes, bustin out and laughin," says Captain Alexander Pitts, "I know how a young man pinched his bride the first night to keep her from laughin. You ain't no more pinched that gal of Bill-Ike Lester's than I pinched her. I's married one time, my boy, and I know how it goes. I'm married yet to the same pigeon. Her wings ain't a-droopin one bit. She flies the same now that she flew when she was a young bird–right back there she is smokin her pipe. Ast her if I pinched her to make her quit laughin when we's a hidin out behind the smoke house to keep from bein belled."

Everybody laughs and Daisy Bee turns her head and runs into the house. T. J. follows Daisy Bee into the house.

"Gets your guns, everybody, and plow pints and cowbells, wash pans, water buckets, wash tubs–everybody–hear–let's start the racket right now. This is the orders from your Captain Alexander Pitts."

"How about the automatics, pump guns, and Winchesters, Captain–don't you want us in front?" says Finn, "and the wash-tub and wash-pan thumpers behind us so no one will get shot––"

"Yes," says the Captain, "and I want all horses and mules

cleared from that fence before this shootin starts. I want them in the barn, Bill-Ike. We'll have a lot of people here that'll have to stay all night with you—can't pull their own sleds home, you know, and some can't walk home seven and eight miles this cold night."

"I'll have room for all them the horses and mules leaves. I can hang 'em up on a nail," says Bill-Ike goin to the fence to unhitch the remainin horses and mules and lead them into the stalls in the big cattle barn.

Finn's automatic goes to crackin in my ears before I get started and then I turn my pump gun loose at the moon in the sky. Of all flames in the world them guns belch them from their long slim bellies. I didn't know shotguns could make so much noise. "Shoot right at that little boy in the moon," says Captain Alexander, "dime to a dollar you can't hit him."

Behind us was the beatin of tin pans and wash tubs and water buckets and cowbells enough to make a person go deef. The most noise I ever heard in one place in my life. I shot till my gun got so hot I couldn't shoot it. It got hot as a poker after you punch the brands down with it. Finn was right beside of me and he says, "My hands! My hands they're burnin off a-hold of this gun."

We walk around the house once and unload our guns and have Tim Nipp's boy Sneed to reload our guns while we empty our pistols. Then we let the guns cool while we use the pistols. We come back around the house and pick up the pump gun and the automatic and empty them. We use seventeen boxes of shells there before we know it. Guns right beside of us blazin. The smell of old black powder nearly makes me puke. But we stay in ranks right with 'em, me and Finn do, and we do our part of the shootin. We didn't come to let anybody make more noise than we make.

Them cowbells went like all the milk cows, for seventeen miles square is on a belled stampede right through the yard. The wash pans beatin sounds like people settlin a thousand stands of bees. The whole air above our heads is black with gun-powder smoke. Above our heads is red as ox blood from the gun flames. We can feel the snow and the empty shells beneath our feet. We couldn't hear the snow beneath our feet, like we did when we come into the house. The empty shells felt like corncobs beneath our feet like corncobs around a hog pen.

Captain Alexander runs in front of the guns in front and holds up a pine torch and waves it. He says: "Stay your guns, boys. No more shootin. The mules and the horses is about to tear the barn down and the dogs has all left the place scared to death barkin, and the cats all left the place a-squallin —Now put your guns away and come inside for treat."

We bring our guns down out 'n the air and empty them right there. We take them inside and stack them in the corner. Here is old Fannie Spry settin in the corner in a split-bottom chair and she covers its bottom like a Plymouth Rock settin hen covers her eggs. She is smokin her pipe and tellin about when her and John got married how they belled them louder than we belled Daisy Bee and T. J.

"Right this way, boys," says Bill-Ike Lester, "right this way." We follow him into the pantry. The keg is there. It is uncovered. Dippers hang all over the sixteen-gallon keg. "It's the best licker you ever put your tongue to. Watch it, though, it will turn your heels up. I made it. I know what it is. T. J. won't get married but once I hope—I never have—and I want you all to have a good time. I knowed they's behind that chimney. I helped put them up there. I shoved the ladder back under the floor. It's all a little fun, you know, boys. Boys, for you fellars that don't like licker, right over here is a sixteen-gallon keg of cherry wine, one of strawberry wine, one of blackberry wine and right over here is a sixty-gallon barrel of hard apple cider. Watch your licker and cider. They don't mix any better than Democrats and Republicans."

Bill-Ike Lester walks out and leaves us in the pantry. Gourd dippers are hangin on the rims of the kegs and the barrel. There's plenty of dippers and wine, licker, cider before us. It is like leadin the bulls to the river and tellin them to drink.

In the front room Liddie Lester is passin around a washtub filled with twists of tobacco for the women to smoke. "Help yourself, Aunt Fannie, you and Aunt Liddie—this terbacker won't bite your tongue. It's burley terbacker. Raised it right back yander on the Sam Jones pint in that new ground piece of land. It's sweet as sugar. Take you a few twists with you. Stick them in your pockets for tomorrow and next day."

"All right, girls and children—" says Cora McGinnis, "all you who wants candy come right this way and get it. Lassie candy and candy from the store." She carries a heaped-up dish pan of candy through the room and sets it on the table. There are chocolate drops, gum candy, sugar candy, peppermint stick candy and 'lassie candy that the candy party made two nights before the weddin. The girls and the children walk over and help themselves.

"Cigars a-plenty for the men. Cigars a-plenty rolled from burley terbacker and taste-bud terbacker. We made 'em for this bellin. Help yourselves. Right here they are," says Eif Hammonds, as he carries a split-bottom feed basket with a flour poke torn open and spread over the basket and the cigars heaped up on it.

"Here's popcorn and lassie balls right this way," says Mary Lester, "for anybody that wants them. Help yourself to them." The old and the young help themselves. The old women sit on chairs and on the edges of the beds and smoke their pipes and watch the merriment of the young. Smoke goes out in tiny swirls until the yellow glow of the lamplight is nearly dimmed.

There is the sparklin of the fore stick on the wood fire, the tiny blazes cracklin and the big blazes leapin up between the filler wood and the back stick. The moon hangs over the house like a galvanized wash pan gleamin in the sun. The snow is white in the moonlight. The chickens "queer-queer" from their branches on the trees at the noise in the house below, a house at this time of night that is supposed to be silent as a mouse save the barkin of the hound dogs at the boards that the wind creaks on the barn.

"Everybody help yourself," says Bill-Ike Lester, "there is a time for everything, the Good Book says, and this is the time to enjoy yourselves. There is a time to dance and a time to sing and a time to marry—and a time to bell 'em."

"A time to bell 'em is right," says Millard as he staggers from the pantry door—"It's the best time I ever had in my life. I'm drunk shore as T. J.'s married—I'm drunk. My best old Pal's married."

"When he gets past goin," says Bill-Ike, "put him in that feather bed in the back room. Give a drunk man a feather bed tonight long as the feather beds last. T. J.'s married and he's my last of eleven to marry. Want you people to have a good time. Drink and be merry. Tomorrow you know—you might not be here. Me and the old lady had a big time at our bellin and we've give all our children a big bellin and a heifer and a feather-bed tick to start housekeepin on. That's what we got when we went to housekeepin. We got the bed tick yet and seed from that heifer is right out there at the barn in them cows. I hope T. J. lives with his turtledove like I have lived with mine through all the ups and downs of forty-nine years. I don't believe in puttin asunder what God has jined together."

"Everybody had plenty," says Captain Alexander Pitts, "to eat and to drink and to smoke. If you ain't, let us know right now. If you have, let us know and we're ready to start a little shindig here before mornin. We got Tim Snoddy with his talkin fiddle to give us a few steps and Jim Runyan with his banjer and a couple of guitars. They're lit a little and rarin to go."

"Let's start the dance," says Toby Spry.

"On with the dance," says Liddie Lester.

"All right. Make yourselves useful well as good-lookin and carry out the house plunder into the back room. All right, everybody, help a little and make the work light."

We carry the furniture into the back room. Tim tunes his fiddle and resins his bow. Jim Runyan threads a new string onto his banjo head and tightens the strings. He plucks this string and that string and loosens this one and tightens that.

"We are ready," says Tim, "ready to go. Get two sets out here and let's fill up the floor." And he starts "Birdie," one of Kentucky's best dance tunes. I get Dot. Finn comes in with

Sadie. He is staggerin a wee bit. He has a taste-bud cigar in his mouth, puffin the smoke like a dinky mine engine into little swirls of blue that thin when they reach the high ceilin.

"Who's callin?" says Finn.

"Don't know," says Tim.

"Let Finn Powderjay call," says T. J. "He's a good enough caller to call any man's dance."

"Just as you say," says Finn, "I'm not carin right now."

"Call the dance then and let's get to movin here before midnight. From now on until the chickens begins to crow ain't long to dance."

"Get your partners," says Finn, "let's fill up the floor. All right, we want two more couples. Grab your girls and get out here."

"Here they come."

"All right, turn that fiddle loose. Let 'er go, let cry, let talk. We're ready and a-rarin to go––"

Tim puts the fiddle to his shoulder and he looks straight to the wall on the other side of the room. He lifts the bow, starts whippin it across the strings. The banjo follows, talkin right up to the fiddle and then the guitars.

"That Birdie's plain enough, boys, till you can see the bird," I says. Captain Alexander Pitts is standin beside of Tim with his ear down to the fiddle. "This man is a fiddler. I used to saw around a fiddle a little bit myself."

"Grab your partner," says Finn.

"I take my licker
And I take it straight,
Grab your Honey
And pat her down eight."

Heels click on the floor. Bodies swing to the rhythm of the music. The whole house seems to jar from its foundations. Dust flies up from the floor to the ceilin. There is the fiddle sounds and the banjo that are nearly drowned by the merry voices.

"Ground-hog leather
Snead without a blade,
All hands together
And let's promenade."

The old sit back and laugh and pat their feet and clap their hands to the time of the music. They laugh and smoke their pipes and the cigars and watch the dance go on. "When I was a young man," says Captain Alexander Pitts, "I never missed a dance. We danced a lot harder than the young folks dance today. We had a big time. That was nearly fifty years ago and we had two dances a week. People could dance in them days."

"When I was a boy," says Bill-Ike Lester, "people enjoyed themselves more than they do today. W'y you can't have a dance here but what somethin happens. Lights shot out. Somebody gets plugged before daylight. Somebody gets knifed. Something happens everytime we have a dance. I think they need us old folks out to tame the young bucks. We could be a lot 'f help to them."

"Daisy Bee and T. J. lead out. The Ocean Wave."

The fiddle speaks to the crowd. The dance is growin livelier. "Put the jug up there by Tim's nose. Then he can fiddle," says Jerry Pratt as he wipes the sweat from his face with his coat sleeve.

"He's fiddlin fit for a King," says Captain Alexander Pitts. "I'd like to know who'd want better fiddlin but a hiram-skirm."

"Can't you take a joke, Captain?" says Jerry. The old women laugh. Aunt Fannie Spry laughed. She shook all over and blew smoke from her long-stemmed clay pipe in tiny swirls.

"Hickory log and a poplar stump,
Hole in the floor and everybody jump,
Sash-a-way to the right and don't get wrong,
Meet your Honey and promenade around."

The dance goes on. Finn calls the dance to the beautiful rhythm of "Birdie." Feet hit on the puncheon floor. The slipper heels touch lightly. The tall men and the slender women sway swiftly to the fast music.

"First couple out and circle four.
Right hands crossed and circle four—
Left hands crossed and circle four
And step right through the old side door.
Opposite partners swing and waltz around
Now swing your partner and waltz again—
Swing 'em right and don't get wrong
And meet your Honey and waltz her around.

"Swing Little Susie and Mary Ann
Hurry up Daisy Bee. Don't leave your man."

"I feel like gettin right in there," says Bill-Ike Lester, "I feel like me and my woman is young again. She's a lot purtier than she used to be, I know that. I believe we could get our bones limbered up and do about as good as them young folks 's doin. What do you say, Captain Alexander?"

"Believe to my soul I could," says Captain Alexander, strokin his long white beard and blowin smoke from his beard-covered lips. "Believe to my soul I could dance all night when I hear that music I used to dance when I was a boy——"

"All right," says Finn, "let's have the old folks to dance this set. Let's set back and watch them go through the old steps like they did forty years ago. Fill up the floor."

"We'll limber up our old bones sure enough," says Captain Alexander.

"I'll swing my pigeon," says Bill-Ike Lester, "not a feather dirty and she can fly like she used to. Come out here, Honey. Let's show 'em how we used to dance before we ever knowed we'd have the eleventh boy to marry and us to be dancin at his weddin. Come right here. You look spryer than you ever did in your life and a lot purtier."

"You been to that jug again, Bill-Ike," says Effie, "that's why I'm so purty to you."

"All right—let 'er go, Tim," says Lumber Hix out on the floor with fat Fannie Spry. "We used to dance the night long together, didn't we, Fannie? We ain't changed but a little bit. Got a little fatter and our hair's changed its color a little bit, but we are about as young as we've ever been. We're just sixteen tonight."

Tim takes a drink from the jug. He braces his foot against the floor and starts pattin with one foot and to whip the fiddle strings over the same tune, "Birdie," again. There is laughter and clappin of hands from the young as the old start the dance. "Watch old Uncle Bill-Ike Lester," says Dot. "Watch him swing Aunt Effie. A good-lookin old couple–hair is white as cotton–havin a good time to the end of their days. Wonder if you and me will be dancin like that fifty years from today!"

"I don't know," I says to Dot, "when did we become engaged anyway?"

"There they go," says Millard, "Daisy Bee and T. J. slippin out."

"Let 'em go," says Jerry Pratt. "Don't you know they want to be together some tonight. Let 'em go back to the chimney hole."

"They're gettin in a sled."

"Let 'em get. They can't be together with this crowd. It's two o'clock in the mornin now. Did you know that?"

"Not so fast," says Aunt Kate Fields, "can't take it like I used to. Must be terbacker that cuts my wind. A little fat too, you know. Weight kindly comes upon a body when she gets older."

Uncle Bill-Ike is dancin all around Aunt Effie. He is showin his age.

"Eleven children and he can still dance as good as the young. Watch that old man dance, won't you!"

They follow through the steps of the dance. Time has slowed them down. The white hair tossin in the dimly lighted room. The air full of tobacco smoke. The young bucks comin and goin from the pantry. The music a little slower for the old than it was for the young. But they move through the steps and the dust flies to the ceilin.

"Havin a good time, ain't they," says Millard, "beatin the young. Watch them old Pap's and Ma's of yours and mine cut the pigeon wing and 'Waltz the Hall,' won't you! They know their stuff. Got the old Kentucky 'Waltz the Hall' in their blood and they'll never get it out. They'll dance when they get to Heaven shore as the world. They'll dance right through the pearly gates and up to God on His throne."

"All right. Young people fill up the floor for the last dance," says Finn. "Fill up the floor fast. I see we got one couple, the Bride and the Groom, missin. It's time they's hidin out–Another couple to take their place."

The old couples come back to their chairs puffin and blowin. They come back wipin sweat from their wet foreheads. "Hot out there a-dancin, ain't it?" says Effie Lester, "a lot hotter than a body would think for a night like this."

"Well, let's watch the young take another set. This time the grapevine twist. That is a hard dance. We have to give up everything to the young," says Captain Alexander Pitts, "we have to give up our farms, the dance, the right to make our laws. They have to carry on for us after a while and we have to look back on the past and talk about the things we've done and ain't done. The young women have to bear the children. Our women can't bear any more. We turn that over to the young too. My wife's just borne us nine."

There is the rapid swirl of the swift mountain music, Leather Breetches. Partners swing and promenade. The floor creaks and the dust flies. There is swift life in the mountain young. The dance will soon be ended. It is time now–the last set is comin to a close. The bellin is over.

"Stay all night with us, everybody. Ain't got two good hours to sleep now. You'd just as well put in the rest of the night with me. Ain't got beds enough, but I can hang you up on a nail I guess when the beds run out," says Uncle Bill-Ike Lester.

"We just got to be movin," says Finn, "we got a good seven miles ahead of us yet this mornin over the frosted frozen snow."

"You'd better get a little toddy to warm up, my boy, before you go. Take a little along with you to keep you het-up after gettin hot at this dance and goin out into the cold air along that river."

"All right," says Finn, "we'll take a little snort along with us."

Finn goes back to get us a mornin dram and I go out with a load of our guns. They are cold now, the long blue barrels glimmer in the moonlight. The girls are puttin on their wraps. Uncle Bill-Ike helps us to get our mules and horses out of the barn. They are cold and want to go. A mule always wants to go toward home. There is the laughter of the crowd goin home and the hand shakes, the words, "Come over and see us." "Thank you, we will, you come over and see us." And "Good-by" and the girls leapin into the saddles, and behind the saddles. Plenty of the mules are carryin double over the slick roads. There are teams of mules the boys are leadin out to the sleds and hitchin them to the sleds.

The moon is low above the snow-clad hills. It is bright as day and the sugar-coated earth is silent save for the partin voices, the neighin of the horses and the hee-hawin of the mules to one another at partin. When horses and mules part from one another, they seem to part like people with a sort of friendships with good-bys to one another as they often part not to see each other again.

We are ready to go, guns in the back of the sled on the straw, quilts dusted of snow and straw neatly spread in the bottom of the sled bed. Finn, Dot and Sadie come from the house mittened and wrapped against the icy mornin winter wind.

"Ready," says Finn.

"Ready," I say.

"You take 'em back," says Finn.

"Suits me," I say, "I'd like to have a little of Uncle Bill-Ike's mornin reviver to put a little life in me after the dance."

Finn reaches the glass fruit jar to me. It slushes in the jar. I can see it bead in the moonlight. The jar is warm.

"It is good licker," says Finn, "and a little will help you over this slick road while a lot might hinder you."

"A body don't have to hold these mules in the road or rein

them anyway goin back. They'll go themselves. Just turn them loose and tie the lines to the seat board," I says, "and they'll take us there."

Dot sits close to me. I hold the reins in my mittened hands. The moon hangs in the sky. The wind is cold. Ten million stars are in the sky. It is so clear and cold. The mules go at a full gallop, the creakin of the sled around the curves and the jinglin of the harness and the night wind in the trees are about all one can hear. The black barren trees are studded against the hill slopes like bright stars are studded in the high blue sky. The snow glistens in the creamy light. We see a rabbit run across the road, rabbits afraid of the hunters' guns make use of the night to gnaw the frozen bark from the sassafras sprouts at night.

"We forgot the cowbells," says Dot.

"You're right, we did," says Finn.

The mules keep up a swift gallop around the curves and the sled swerves this way and that. I'm close to Dot. She's close to me. I don't know about Finn and Sadie. They are under the quilts. The chickens are crowin at Barry Underwood's for daylight. The night is over.

PARSIE lives right across the road from me. She moved there last Spring. Her man, Peg-Leg Jake Mullins, rented the place from old Bill Sizemore. I think Bill is wrong in the head to rent to Peg-Leg Jake. He's the laziest man in the world. When he was burnin brush last March he went to sleep close to a brush pile on fire. The fire burnt the leaves out around the brush pile. The fire slipped up like a mouse in the kitchen safe and caught Peg-Leg's wooden leg on fire. It popped and burned like dry shoemake. It was locust wood. It burned right off his body before he could get the strap unbuckled. Peg-Leg hobbled in on a stick to the house. He went to plow one day. He went to sleep when the day got up. The peckerwoods drilled in his wooden leg for worms. That's the God's truth. Old Bill Sizemore must be wrong in the head to rent a farm to him. He'll run old Bill in debt instead of makin money to pay the taxes on the place.

I could tell Parsie was goin to have a baby. I knowed it all the time. I remember last Spring how my man Blue used to hunt with Peg-Leg and Timothy. Say, that Timothy Muscovite was a man I never did like. I never did like that name. Timothy is a big hairy man, with big hands and a face like a monkey. He looks funny beside of my man, Blue. My man looks more like somebody. I've got the only decent-lookin man in this neighborhood. I'd like to see a woman who could love Peg-Leg or Timothy. Peg-Leg's got a fine fuzz on his face where he never shaves. I always say his face is poor as some old land that we got that won't bring weeds and sprouts. His face won't grow whiskers. He's not got a tooth in his head that I've ever seen. His thin jaws just blab-blab and blubber when he talks like the wind goin in and out of a bee smoker. Then he's just got one good leg and it's not any bigger than a hoe handle. I don't see how Parsie can stand him. Parsie's a right good-lookin woman to have six brats.

I could see last May Parsie was goin to have a baby. She went out and worked in the fields a little. That didn't matter.

She couldn't hide it from a woman. She's as pretty a woman as there is in these parts of the country. Ain't but three families here. Just two women. Parsie and me. Timothy Muscovite is too ugly to ever get a woman. He lives by hisself over there in the old Hinton house on the ridge. Ain't nobody in this country knows where he come from. He's got money. We don't know where he got it. He's too ugly to ever get a woman. He don't look like a man. He looks like a brute that walks on its hind legs a-standin up. Great big devil. Big hands and feet and hairy as a dog with a face like a monkey. We heard there use to be a big gamblin man that strolled these parts when they built them tunnels on the E-K railroad. He won money from the workin men every pay day. He rode a big black horse. We heard Timothy Muscovite waylaid him on the other side of the Barney tunnel and knocked him off his horse with a club and robbed him. The horse went to old Sweeter Hensley's place. I've heard Pap talk about it. I don't like for Blue to run with him, but he does. They fox-hunt together.

Parsie, Timothy and Peg-Leg calls Blue, "Duck-Foot" Blue. I never did like that name. There's not anythin I can do about it unless it would be take a pair of scissors or a butcher knife and cut Blue's toes apart. He's web-footed like a duck. His toes, the two next to his big toe on his right foot, are growed together; and the two next to his little toe on his left foot are growed together just about half way up. The two on his right foot are growed together plum out to the end. And people call Blue, "Duck-Foot" Blue Scout. They call me Mrs. Duck-Foot Blue Scout. Law, how I hate that name. If I'd cut Blue's toes apart now it wouldn't matter. He's already got that name. Then it might set up blood pizen. A body just can't tell about them things. Better to leave them as God made them. God marked the Scout family for a sin a way back yonder in the Scout line. A old man by the name of Jim Frailey got two of his toes mashed flat in the log woods. Blue's great-grandmother laughed at his toes. That was right before Blue's grandfather was born. When he was born, he come with two toes on each foot growed together. When he married and had children the seventh child had toes growed together on both feet. That was Blue's father. When Blue's father married, his seventh child was Blue. He's got toes just like his Pap and his Grandpap. It runs in the Scout family.

I never was to say jealous of Parsie. I know she's a better-lookin woman than I am. I'm not a good-lookin woman. I used to be when I was young. When I walked down the church aisle, men riz to their feet and watched me pass. But they don't anymore. Hoein corn and bearin babies for the man I love 's took all that out of me long ago. So much housework to do. So many cows to milk and hogs to slop. So many chickens to feed. A big house to keep clean. It's a pine-log house and for God's sakes, women, don't ever let your man make you a pine-log house or move you into one. They're too bad for bedbugs. They've nearly et us up since we've been here. If I didn't scald twice a week all the beds, the slats and the cracks they'd eat us up. Then I keep my bed casters a-settin in a tin can of coal oil. So it's work around here besides havin a baby every couple of years. That takes some time out.

Parsie's had to work out. She don't go ahead like I do. She ain't worked like I have. I live right here across the road from her and know. She's never done it since she's lived over there in old Bill's house. She's never done the work I have. That's the reason she's held her shape. If she'd a worked like I have! But she ain't. I don't see for my life how she lives with that thin-lipped ugly Peg-Leg man of hers. Pon my word, if I was choosin between the two men I'd ruther have old Monkey-faced Timothy Muscovite. He would provide for a woman and treat her halfway decent if he'd a been good-lookin enough to a-got hisself a woman. He wouldn't a worked her like a horse nohow.

I used to stand up there by the drawbars and watch Parsie goin out there to the sand bottom to hoe corn. She would be barefooted walkin along the path dodgin the saw briars. Peg-Leg would be in front with a mule hitched to a plow. He'd let the mule drag the plow along and scive up the grass and the saw briars. He was too lazy to lift the plow by the handles.

He just let it drag. Parsie would walk behind with her hoe on her shoulder and her lap done up down to her petty-coat with pumpkin seed and bean seed that Parsie would stick in a hill of corn in the rich spots of ground around the old rotted stumps and rock piles. I used to just watch her pass. I would say to myself, "If my hair was just black and pretty as hers I wouldn't begrudge everything I got includin the old cow Gypsy. She's got the prettiest blue eyes. Just like two blue bird eggs. She has got the whitest skin and the longest fingers. Her teeth 's white as chalk. She's pretty as a doll." Then I would say to myself, "I am a liar. Parsie is not pretty. She is not pretty as I am. My hair is light. My eyes are blue. My teeth are fairly good. I am prettier than Parsie. I have four children. I don't want to have the seventh if I can dodge it. But I can't. I am just twenty-six years old. I don't want a duck-footed youngin. I don't want a marked baby just over Blue's great-grandmother laughin at a man's mashed toes. That's too much punishment for God to put on any person. It's not fair. I can't help what she done. Why should I suffer for her sin? I am not a ugly woman. I am a prettier woman than Parsie. I am not a liar."

But I was a liar. Parsie is the prettiest woman I ever saw. I used to watch Blue when Parsie and Peg-Leg come over on Sundays to eat dinner with us. I used to watch Blue to see if I could catch him lookin like a man looks at a woman he likes. I never could see a thing myself. I would fry the meat on the stove. Parsie would be in the kitchen helpin me. We would talk and the meat would sizzle in the pan. I would keep my eye on Parsie. I would glance around to see if Blue was lookin through the front-room door into the kitchen at Parsie. I never could catch him lookin at her. I would be nice to Parsie because she was so good-lookin. I was nice to her because I couldn't be as good-lookin as she was. She didn't know she was good-lookin. And just think her married to that thin-lipped toothless, peg-legged, no-count, good-for-nothing man of hers. She ought to a married Timothy. Just us three families in our neighborhood. Two women and three men. And somethin ugly about all the men but mine and he had his toes growed together. I watched him around the other woman. We would cook dinner for the men layin in the front room on the floor smokin their pipes and talkin about the crops. I could see the smoke goin up toward the ceilin in little blue clouds. And under my breath I hoped and prayed to God old Peg-Leg would get his hair filled full of bedbugs from the pine-wood floor. It's bad to do that, but I did. I don't deny it. I never liked that no-count man. I don't see how any woman could. I am a woman. I know about a woman. She wants a man all the other women like. She wants to walk right in and take him by the arm and say, "Look, woman. I got him. He's my man." And after she gets him, if some woman doesn't want him, then she wants to dump him and get her a man they all want. That's the way it is here. I knowed sure as God made the grass that Parsie would like to have a man like Blue. That made me want Blue more than ever. I had him, but I wanted more of him since I felt like Parsie wanted him. I couldn't help it.

Well, we used to eat Sunday dinners together. We borrowed meal and sugar and coffee from one another. We was the best neighbors you ever saw. But I always watched. I always thought if you had a man worth anythin he was worth watchin and worth havin. So many men these days are no-account. Not worth powder and lead it takes to blow out their brains. I used to watch Parsie more than I do now. She is ready to bring a baby now. I've been listenin for a call from Peg-Leg every night. I've been listenin to hear him come out in the yard and stand under that bare walnut tree in their yard and say, "Oh, Amanda Scout, come over here quick to Parsie." And I've just been lookin to see all six of their children come stealin in over here carryin them infernal bedbugs on their clothes to stay all night any time. I just think every night I'll see them comin. Fall-time here. Leaves dead on the ground and a body so sad this time of year. All this trouble and all this weary. It worries me just to think about it. Parsie is soon to have her baby.

Last summer durin crop-time when we's a workin so hard in the fields and would come in dog-tired and do up the work

–I'd go to bed and I couldn't go to sleep for thinkin somethin. I didn't think it. I felt it. A woman feels like a dog that raises its bristles when it smells where another dog has been. That's just the way I felt. I just raised my bristles when I thought about Parsie. God knows I liked her in a way. God knows I hated her in a way. If it just hadn't been for Blue. I felt like she felt the same way toward Blue that I felt. My bristles would raise. I could just feel a feelin comin in all over my body that Parsie liked Blue same as I did. I just couldn't stand to think about it. God, I cried. God, I rolled and tumbled in the bed. I done everythin. I couldn't forget.

Last summer Peg-Leg, Blue and Timothy would take the hounds. They would leave me and Parsie here together and go fox-huntin. Parsie would sleep in one bed with her little youngins and I would sleep in another with mine. I was filled with the very devil. I could see myself pullin out Parsie's coal-black hair and throwin it to the ground in handfuls like sheep wool. I could feel my fingers goin into her eyes. Law, how I wanted to put my hands on her. But I was afraid. She's a stout woman with her hands. I thought about gettin a scythe blade and whackin her across the face. Then I thought that was not the way to do it. I could get a sickle and sickle her neck like I would a bunch of plantin in the yard. But a better way still to do it was to get a garden hoe off the palings and just light in on her with a hoe and chop her good like choppin weeds. I can fight with a hoe better anyhow. But here was all them little babies around her asleep. Pon my word, I just didn't have the heart to do it. I could just see my man Blue in her. I knowed it was Blue. I just felt it. God knows I did. God knows it's the truth. A woman just feels, that's all. She can't help it. Men never understand like a woman.

Parsie would lay in the bed and snore. Her babies would cry and wake her. When she would rouse up I'd snore just like I was dead asleep. But I couldn't sleep in the room with her knowin she's goin to have a baby. When she would go back to sleep I'd set up in the bed and look out at the winder. I'd see the summer moonlight in the green corn. I'd hear the whippoorwills so lonesome–my God, how lonesome the night would be. Then I'd hear the hounds bringin the fox around the piney pint. I could hear old Skeeter, Blue's blue-tick hound, leadin the pack. He's got a bark like beatin in a rain barrel with a plow pint when he's leadin the pack and when he's behind he squeals like a pig. I'd lay in the bed and listen and think. I couldn't help it. Why was I like I was? Maybe I just thought things. Then I'd think that I was crazy and I'd have to be sent to the asylum. I'd seen one man go there. They used to put him in the corn crib and feed him bread and water every day. A County man come out and found him. They hauled him off handcuffed in a spring wagon. The last words he said to me: "Put my shoes down by the fireplace. I'll not get any more shoes." I didn't have his shoes. I'd never seen his shoes. He was just ridin past in the wagon. What a terrible thing it is to be crazy. It's not anything to laugh about. "Am I crazy as the man I saw in the wagon, barefooted with the hair as long on his face as it was on his head? What a terrible thing."

Then I would think: "No, I am not crazy. I just feel like somethin is goin to happen that I don't want to happen. The wind told me. God told me. I feel it." When we'd come in from work I'd pitch and tear in the bed till twelve o'clock many a night. Blue would be beside me snorin. I'd think to myself: "Wonder if Parsie loves him. Wonder if she has ever told him that she loved him and them lips that trembles in snores—wonder if words come from between them to Parsie: 'Yes, I love you too.' That silent body of a man. It is like a child. It cries to get things. It gets them, then it is through. It is quiet like a child. A woman is not like a man. A woman feels things. A woman understands."

The days passed by last summer. We planted the corn. We plowed it the first time and chopped the weeds out of it. We plowed it the second time and the third time. It was soon over the mule's back. When it got that high we quit plowin it. I'd lay in my bed at night and look at it. I'd look at the moonlight on the cornfield bright as day. I would think: "The night is pretty. The night was made for man and the fox. The night was made for silence. The stars in the sky. The silver-like dew-drops on the corn. The night is pretty, whoever made it and whatever it was made for. I like the night. I love the night."

I watched the moonlight flicker on the corn blades as the night wind blowed them this way and that way. And I thought: "The night is so pretty. The God that made the night made me. I am not pretty. I am such a fool. If I was ugly as a hill, I would be pretty. Quiet, ugly people are pretty. But I can't be quiet, as trustworthy as the earth. I am such a fool. Some women are such fools. I am one. But the reason I am a fool, I can't trust. If I could make myself believe that I trusted like a lot of women. But I can't. I just can't lie about it when I feel a thing. You can trust the earth, but not its seasons of drouth, rain, snow and sleet. You can trust a huntin dog, but not when she comes in her season. Women are a lot like a dog. They have their seasons." I could smell the wet weeds that bordered the corn—the ragweeds and the pussley. The wind from them smelled awfully sour. God, I thought of women and their seasons.

And as the moon rolled along in the flyin fleece clouds I thought about man and woman. If I could only have Blue just so I could hold him in my hand like he was a piece of money. If I only owned him like he was a quarter or a half of a dollar, I wouldn't mind. But no woman can own a man like that. No man can quite own a woman like she was a pound of salt or a dime's worth of soda. There's somethin else to a man or a woman besides that. And there's nothin in the world—not even marriage vows, lovers' vows, God, churches or anythin above the sun or under the sun that would keep man and woman from lovin one another. (Just to show you what I am talkin about, old Felix Harkreader fell in love with his sister. He may not a fell in love with her. He lived with her just the same. They had two children. Young Felix Harkreader lived with his sister and they had four children. That would make the children only havin one Grandpa and one Grandma. They had a little money and they kept it in the family. They didn't marry off to bring any more into the family. The old Grandpa kept a little notebook with the names of women in it he'd met and lived with. If he found one and didn't like her he marked her name off the list. He carried one thousand dollars in a red handkerchief and five hundred dollars in a blue handkerchief. He used the white handkerchief for his nose. Two women heard about the thousand dollars he kept in a handkerchief. They thought it was the blue handkerchief. They had a date with him. One had him upstairs and stole the handkerchief. She thought she got a thousand. She got five hundred. He come home and laughed and said: "They thought they's gettin my thousand, but they just got my five hundred. She's not any good anyway." So he marked both names from his notebook. You just can't trust people. You can't own them. I try to own Blue. I want him for my own.

Just as I expected. It was cold as blue blazes. I'd sent my children to school—all but my little ones. Parsie sent her children to school all but her two little ones. The cold November wind was blowin across the cornfield where we worked last summer. It was a awful day. Wind blowed the rags out of the winders where the lights had been busted out by the hail last summer. I trembled when I saw Peg-Leg comin across the road runnin on that wooden leg. I knowed somethin must be wrong or he wouldn't a got such a move on him. Wooden leg was sinkin in the soft ground where it had got sharp on the end. He'd pull it out and run and it would sink up again. He said, "Oh, Amanda—come quick—It is Parsie. She is sick—come quick!" He took back toward the house. I let my work go and took out toward the house. I knowed what was up. I left my little children in the house. I was afraid they might get burnt up. I hollered to Blue. He was out at the barn. I told him to stay with my little youngins till I went over to Peg-Leg's and Parsie's a minute. Blue understood. He took to the house a-runnin and left the mules' harness on the ground that he was punchin holes in to brad up a little.

I was nearly out of breath when I got in the house. I put water in the teakettle and het it. God knows just how much there is to be done when a woman is havin a baby and they ain't no doctor. But I've delivered a many a baby. I knowed just what to do. I done it. It was a lot of pain for Parsie. No woman wants the pain of bringin a baby into the world. She has to go through a lot for the sake of a child that just grows up and spits in his mother's face and flies off like a wild quail. But they bring them just the same. Woman has her season. She was made to bear children. She is happier lots of times with her children and never happy unless she has them. But I'm tellin you it's a lot of trouble and a lot of pain. Woman pays for her pleasure. I never saw a woman suffer like Parsie. I done the best I could. I hated to see her suffer so. Cattle suffer the pain of birth and dogs and horses suffer. But not any livin bein suffers like a woman. Men don't understand. Women soon forget and are ready to bring another baby into the world. They soon forget all about childbirth pain. I couldn't think for hearin Parsie suffer.

When the baby come a wee thing of cry and a bundle of nerves, I didn't want to see it. But I had to see it. The water was hot. I poured in some cold water and made it lukewarm. I washed the baby. I just couldn't believe before I saw it that it would look like Peg-Leg Jake. I wanted to think that it would look like old Timothy Muscovite. Then I'd hate to see a little baby brought into the world and have to go through the world ugly as old Timothy—so ugly he looked like pictures of the Devil. I just didn't want to look at the baby at all. But I had to look at it. Before I washed it, I thought about Blue over at the house with my two little children. I thought that Blue was just a child. I was his mother and his wife. He was one of my children.

The baby cried. Parsie went off into a doze. She closed her eyes. Her lips were blue. She was bad off. I could tell. She had been too long bringin the baby into the world. I had to wash the baby. I had to care for it. Peg-Leg ran out of the room. I looked at the baby's ears to see if it had little lettuce-leaf ears like Blue. I looked at its lips. I thought I could see cut in the upper lip beneath the nose what we call the "trough" just like it was on Blue's lips. I could see Blue's eyes in its head. Surely, I was dreamin, but I could see the image of Blue in the baby more than in any child I bore for him. It was a boy. It was Parsie's seventh child. And I thought: "Could it be Blue's baby? It looks like him. No. It does not look like him. I am dreamin. This is a world full of trouble and dreams. It has some joys. Not many. I cried over this before. I felt it. Is it a lie? Is it the truth? It doesn't matter. Parsie is dyin. She says: 'It ain't my baby. I never saw it before. Take it away. I won't have it. Who give me that baby anyway—take it away or I'll scream. Timothy brought it here. Timothy Muscovite, the ugly son of Satan. Take it away.' And I saw Parsie. She wilted like a rose throwed in the fire. Her eyes set in her head. She had never remembered. I was sorry that I had hated her and wanted to hook her white neck with a sickle and glomb her eyes with my fingers and fight her with a hoe. I was sorry. But I have to wash the baby. It feels like it is mine."

And then its toes! I thought. I'll look at its toes. I looked—My God—Oh—God. The two little pink toes on the right foot next to the big toe was growed together plum to the end. The two toes next to the little toe on the left foot was growed together halfway up to the end. It is Blue's baby! Oh my God! It was Blue Scout's baby. It is a Scout! I tore my hair. I screamed. Parsie was quiet. She didn't hear me. She didn't bat a eye. I thought she was playin possum on me. I thought she understood. I dropped the baby down on the cloth. It moved its little pink hands and wiggled its little toes like toes and hands of young mice a body finds in the corn shocks in the spring. The baby cries like a little pup. I couldn't help it. I ran out of the house. I wanted to kill Parsie. Blue couldn't help it. It was not his fault. I ran to get the hoe off the palings. I saw Peg-Leg Jake talkin to Timothy Muscovite—two of the ugliest-lookin men I ever saw. I hated them both. Just to think of woman and her child. Think of the mother dog when pups are born how ill she is with the dogs. She makes up with them before her season starts again. God made them that way. God made us all that way. I cannot understand. I took the hoe and run into the house. I thought I would kill Parsie. There she was in the bed. Her face was white as snow. Her eyes was set. She wasn't gettin her breath right. I just couldn't kill her. She was down. I couldn't kill a person down not able to help herself. I don't care what she's done. Here was blood in the room. I thought of that sour smell of weeds last summer when the wind blowed in across the fields into the open winder where I was sleepin. That sour smell. I held to the hoe handle. I thought once I'd chop her head off right where her neck was the least to chop through. That was Blue's baby. Then I thought I wouldn't kill her, for she was goin to die anyway. Her down there sufferin so and me standin up with a hoe to kill her like I'd kill a snake. That was not fair. I couldn't do that. So I walked over and raised the winder. I pitched the hoe out the winder. The dead leaves blowed in when I raised the winder. November winds and them as cold as all get-out.

I got the wash rag and I finished washin the baby. I hated them toes. Just to think! The baby belonged to Blue. You are not foolin me. God don't prank with people for the sins of their people. They carry the mark. Now if I lived to have my seventh child it would have duck-foot toes. It is a mark of Blue's people.

The children come in from school. Peg-Leg sent them all over to the house for Blue to keep. Blue never come about. He acted like a whipped dog. That is a man for you. He doesn't pay for his pleasure like a woman. If he could have only seen Parsie suffer like I saw her. Now her eyes set. Surely she was dyin from childbirth. What a awful death. Only a woman can understand. Only a woman knows. I couldn't kill her with a hoe or a sickle. Poor woman was dyin. I could hear breath come and go and sorty sizzle. She just looked up at the brown-ringed paper on the ceilin where the rain had leaked through. Her eyes were about half open. She said: "I know it ain't mine. It ain't mine. It is Amanda's baby. It belongs to her. She will have it. I won't need it." And when she said that, I said: "Sure, the little thing is mine." I pulled it up and kissed it. The baby was Blue's. The baby was mine. I'd take it. It was Blue's child. I love Blue. All that is him is me. We are together. We are one. His child was mine. I held the baby in my arms. I couldn't love Parsie. I just felt for her. Her there on the couch a-dyin.

The winds played around the house as night come on and the sun sunk down on the other side of the pasture. The bare limbs of the trees looked like they was growed into the white patches of the sky. I could see them betwixt me and the moon. The baby cried. I nursed it with peppermint tea that Peg-Leg found by the old Daugherty gate. I told him right where to find it. Women have got it there before for their babies. All the men in the country has come there to get it for their wives. I never told Peg-Leg about the baby's toes. I told him I wanted the baby if Parsie died. He told me I could have him. I told him I would raise him right and under the eyes of the Lord. Peg-Leg shed some tears. So did old Timothy. I felt sorry for him—him so ugly a-cryin when he walked up with Peg-Leg Jake and saw Parsie on the couch.

I remember the moon that come up. It looked to me like it had a spot of blood on it. I saw blood maybe. It was on the bed. It was on the floor. It was on the moon. Blue was in the house with all the children. He didn't know Parsie was dyin. Her breath got shorter and shorter. It kindly sizzled and she crossed her hands on her breast and she went out of the world. I had the baby in my arms. I saw her go. I can't forget. I called Peg-Leg. He come runnin in. Timothy come in with him. I took the baby and walked out. I took it to the house. I started making clothes for it before its mother was laid out to bury. I was glad she died. I had to be glad. I didn't want to kill her with a hoe. The baby is mine. He is dear to me as my own. I call him Blue. He looks more like Blue than airy one of the children I have by him.

They buried Parsie back by the edge of the sand cornfield where she used to hoe corn before the baby was born. She is buried under that hickory at the fence corner. Timothy Muscovite has moved in the house with Peg-Leg. He loved little children so. They ain't afraid of him any more. I ain't said a word to Blue about the baby bein hisn. I think he understands. I take care of the baby. It belongs to me. Man doesn't understand. It takes a woman to feel and understand. Man is fickle as the wind. The wind will blow the ragweed seeds over the earth. They will grow here and there. Man is not particular. He will leave his seed to grow here, or there, and in awfully poor soil, sometimes.

I

THERE is a belief that gold and silver is buried in the Leadingham Branch—just white sheets of silver running through bright panels of gold. "Just like the streets of Heaven," says Peter Leadingham, "and I will be the man to find all this money in an old clay bank. Clarence Webb told me the needles won't work under any circumstance but one. He says when loadstone is hid under the ground it will draw the needle in another direction. And I got the idea, I'll go bury loadstone on the farms after I've rushed over everybody's farm but my own first." (Each man firmly believed the gold was hidden on his farm. It may have been. If it was it still remains hidden in an old pantry, under a floor, under some leaves, in a cave or an abandoned coal mine.)

A party of men held Red Jacket up and one said, "If you don't tell us where the gold is you'll die."

"Red Jacket lead you to no gold. Red Jacket keep gold to shoe Indian's horse and buy firewater. Red Jacket don't tell. Red Jacket know gold is here. Red Jacket don't tell."

Red Jacket didn't tell. He was hit over the head with a mattock handle and left in Widow Skaggs' hog lot, in the leaves of a tree top that had been cut when the tree was green. The killing took place in September. It was well known on the Leadingham Branch, Red Jacket had lost his life at the hands of a fanatic group of money-crazed men. It was the talk that Peter Leadingham's hogs in widow Skaggs' hog lot, had rooted him from under the leaves and the crows got a little and Alf Sinnett's fox hounds finished him. The hungry hounds packed away the bones. Jim Kearns found thigh bones and a man's skull near the head of Leadingham Branch. Jim says: "It is a Indian's bones. I can tell they are Indian bones by the thickness of the skull. There was a caved-in place too, right across the top where he had been hit with the mattock handle."

Following the murder, revivals were started over Garter County. This was the first time the Free Willers and Forty-Gallon Baptis had gotten together in ten years. Free Willers didn't believe in drinking firewater and Forty-Gallon Baptis did. Before they had defied each other in the pulpit and doomed each other to roast in hell's fire, red pepper and brimstone. They preached the same doctrine: whoever murdered Red Jacket would get more of the hell's fire than Judas got. "Red Jacket is human and he has a soul if he was a Indian," says Brother Peter, "but Red Jacket should have told where the gold was so it could do somebody some good. Poor little children in Garter County that had to spend ten hours hoein corn for twenty-five cents a day could a used some of that gold. Killin him didn't get the money. They didn't do it right. Why didn't they put a fire under him and make him say it?"

Each man accused his neighbor or his neighbor's son of killing the Indian Chief, Red Jacket. No one knew exactly who did it. It was just talk. Who had seen this Red Jacket anyway? A Medicine Man had been in Jimpson Burr for a week selling patent medicines and herb hair tonics that he guaranteed would grow hair on fish. The patent medicine was for the liver. It was told that one man died after taking one of his liver remedies and they had to take a stick and beat his liver to death. He pulled old men's and women's snaggle teeth with his bare fingers. He wore a braid of long black hair and feathers in his crown. Everybody flocked into Jimpson Burr to see him.

Isser Pennington used his tonic trying to grow hair on his glassy head. The hair tonic showed he wasn't a fish. It was guaranteed to grow hair on fish.

Old Peter Leadingham, the first, was considered the Solomon of Leadingham Branch. The young ministers, Owl Webb, Rodner Perkins and London Elam, took the case to old Peter and asked him to pray over this wonder and give verdict on the following Monday morning. Old Peter was the only one that had received the Secon' Blessing. He got Sanctification and it was impossible for him to sin. During the week days he cut timber for Ben Sexton. He made good money. He made sixty cents per thousand. That was fine. All the young men got fifty cents a thousand. That was all right. Peter was getting old. "I go to God for all the bargains I get," says Peter, "and I'll go to God about Red Jacket too. I'll find that money. I'm the only man that has ever seen God, met Him out in the woods and talked to Him in person. I'll meet God out again and find out where the gold is. That will save me from cuttin timber at sixty cents a thousand, even if I do make ten cents more on the thousand than the other boys. I'll keep that under my hat. Buck Sexton told me to because the other men will get sore if they find out Buck is favorin Brother Peter Leadingham a little."

II

During this week-end in September, old Peter Leadingham goes out into a beech grove around the south pasture slope from his house. He gets away from Matilda, his wife. Matilda says: "Peter, where are you goin poddlin out across the yard under the white oak trees on this fine day? Mind that old hen with the young chickens tied to that peg. Don't mash one with your foot."

"Matilda, you ain't got no business askin me where I'm goin and messin up a man that is goin to talk with God. Matilda, you are a old meddlesome. Why don't you attend to your own affairs; dig the taters, wean the two suckin calves; save the milk; cut pussley for the fattenin hogs and patch my pants. That's a woman's work. You certainly ain't no business botherin a man that had been selected by my Brothers in the Forty-Gallon Baptis church to talk with the Lord. Why did they select me? Because they know I'm on the square with God or they wouldn't send me to pray the matter over. I'll fool 'em when I meet God face to face and tell him everythin. God will tell me where old Red Jacket's gold is."

Old Peter heard the winds of September rustle through the dying corn on the steep crab-grass slope. The wind sizzles through his long beard like through the buff-colored corn. He runs his fingers through his beard and plays with them as a child would play with the silks of growing corn. He hears the leaves fall softly to the ground. He sees the wild ducks in the formation of letter L above his head. He hears their honking cries that make him lonesome. "Lord, what a Sunday mornin this is to meet God and have a talk with Him," says Peter. "I am free from the cross-cut saw, the ax and sledge hammer. I am free from Matilda too. She is always fussin at me. She'll be sorry when I find all the hidden gold and every girl on Leadingham Branch will want to play with my beard and ride in the buggy beside me down to Jimpson Burr. She will be sorry then."

Here is a little stream of water emerging from the roots of a beech tree. Old Peter stops to drink. He falls flat on his belly. He puts down one hand for a body brace. He moves the other hand down to hold his gray whiskers and keep them out of the water. He sups the cool clear autumn water into his wrinkled mouth and swallows with gurgles. He gets up, bones creaking, and smacks his lips and wipes the water from his wet beard with his rough scrawny hand. "Good water," says Peter.

He walks twenty yards and kneels to pray. He is alone under the copper autumn leaves and the rustling of a sheen of golden and scarlet beech leaves. He begins to pray the way he used to pray at the Leadingham Church House where so many feel under conviction and were saved. "I am God's mighty trumpet," he says. "God's voice goes through me.

"O God, if you love me as I love you, Almighty, listen to me, give me some of your time, please. Old Peter's never done anythin to you. Here's the whole thing. I'm a poor old man. Eyes are gettin bad. Can't hear well as I used to hear. I'm hard-workin old man and I'm a poor man myself. If you'll just let me know somethin. Tell me where Old Red Jacket's gold is. I'd use it in convertin the Free Willers of Garter County. Them people don't have the Sperets, Lord. O God that money! Why not now? Let 'em call us Forty-Gallon Baptis! Let 'em call us that and they'll get the brimstone, hell's fire and damnation and punched with a three-pronged pitchfork!"

Old Peter stays in the beech grove all day. He prays and claps his hands and preaches and looks up to his glass-domed heaven. Heaven is right above his head. Just a mile or two. It is right up in the air. He could see through it, but he couldn't see heaven until he died. The wind lifted his locks of hair and played with his gray beard. Old Peter is a strong mountaineer. He can eat one side of a hog's ribs at one meal, besides drink a quart of buttermilk and eat a half pone of corn bread baked two inches deep in a ten-by-eighteen-inch pan. He can saw the fiddle and whistle in the jug. He is six-four, has high cheek bones, large hands, protruding mouth, shaggy eyebrows, dull meaningless eyes, thick through the hips with a slightly bent frame. He has scarcely any teeth, a few tobacco teeth, that's all, Doc Blevins couldn't get with the horse forceps when he pulled his teeth that time.

Night comes and Peter fasts like the men of old. He preaches and he prays. He hears the sound of the wind in the dying corn. He feels it in his long gray beard. It whistles through the lonesome autumn beech tops mournfully. The low moon comes up and goes down over the low dark hills dragging a cloud behind it.

Midnight comes with a flight of stars and the sinking moon. Old Peter is growing tired. He is about to give up the ghost. He is so tired. Strange things begin to brew. Sticks begin to pop. Chains begin to rattle. Drunk men begin to call for more "Rock and Rye." "My goodness," says Peter, "I see the old Devil pass me like a fallin star. He must have been scared the way he runs. He goes right up the Leadingham Branch with a pitchfork in his hand. I see him. He has the horns of a two-year-old bull and he looks somethin like a black cow walkin on her hind feet. God will be on next. Here comes the two archangels flyin through the woods carryin torches. They're lightin up the way." Peter shudders. "O my God! Here comes God ridin on a cloud. Two thieves crucified with him are ridin by His side with pointed spears in one hand and torches in the other. God is smoking a pipe like the one I used to smoke.

"O Lord," cries Peter, "what are you bringin them men with spears for–to spear me, Lord? What have I done?"

The Lord speaks like the rumble of thunder: "Be quiet, my good faithful servant, for I am your Master."

Peter is spellbound. He cannot speak. He looks at God in the beech grove beneath the starlight. God and the stars and himself all right out here together at night. "My Baptis Brothers won't believe me when I tell them the straight of things. Neither will Matilda, Old Matilda. I need a young woman. God is just a common man. Sure he is. Everybody has been goin on about his mighty size. He's a little man with the power to remove mountains, stop rivers. God is just about the size of Judd Sluss.

"Now God, you've come," says Old Peter. "Now let's get down to brass tacks and fix up everythin. The first thing I want to know is where is old Red Jacket's gold he told the white men around Jimpson Burr about?"

God says, "I'll not tell you about the gold. No such thing. No. It will cause much confusion here on earth and much killin of men and women who have not been converted into your church but belong to that old boy I run up the holler with that pitchfork. Did you see him?"

"Yes I did, Lord. He was a big hunk of beef, too. I was skeered for he looked right at me."

"That's all right, Peter. I can't tell you where the gold is."

"That's all right, Lord. That's perfectly all right. Do tell me this. Who killed the old Indian?"

"I thought I told you once that would cause a great rebellion in your church around Jimpson Burr."

"Beg your pardon, Lord, I'm so deef I can't hear good."

"I thought I told you once who killed Red Jacket."

"No Lord, you said that you wouldn't tell me where the gold was. That's what I ast you first."

"That's all right then," says the Lord.

"Well, is Red Jacket in heaven?"

"Yes," says the Lord, "Red Jacket is with me. Even if the dogs and hogs did eat his meat he'll arise from that tree top in Widow Skaggs' hog lot on the mornin of the Resurrection when Gabriel blows that old fox horn of his."

"O God," shouts Peter.

"Don't O God me," shouts the Lord, "I hear enough from you Forty-Gallon Baptis in Jimpson Burr."

The Lord pulls His tobacco pouch out of His vest and begins to reload His pipe with tobacco that smells to Peter like his home-grown taste-bud leaf. He fills the pipe and swats fire with His mighty hands. Old Peter shudders. He shrinks slowly to the ground.

"Have some," says the Lord.

"Don't smoke," says Peter.

"Now don't tell that to me," says the Lord. "Didn't I see you go out behind the barn at home and smoke. I know about all the things you have done. Didn't you kiss Ben Sexton's wife? I'm not sayin what old Ben done to Matilda."

Peter can't speak. "Wonder what Ben has done to Matilda. She's always been a nice woman the fifty-five years I've lived with her. Could she be gettin spry and reckless in her old days? W'y hell's fire! What about God smokin like that! My church don't approve of it even if I have been slippin out and doin it. Matilda noses in and tells a few of the members about it. I fixed that up all right, for people knows she is nosey anyway."

"Listen here, Peter, before I go," says the Lord, "I want to leave one thing with you. The Indian has a speret. Red Jacket is a knockin speret. When men are not doin right he'll knock on their hatbands, pant legs, shoes, bedclothes, door-sills, dresser or just any place. He's even knocked on red flannel drawers and night shirts. His knocks will be heard too. When you want to talk to him just do somethin out of the way. If you happen to be the seventh child of the seventh generation you can raise this speret and talk to him. Otherwise, when he knocks, somethin is wrong with your heart. Now go back to Jimpson Burr on Leadingham Branch and preach the Gospel."

Under the white cloud goes the Lord. There is a lot of popping and cracking of sticks. "Can I believe that was God?" says Peter. "Sure it was God. You're damn right. Who else could it have been? He smoked a pipe though! That is sure God Hisself and He is just as common as the men who bring butter and eggs to Jimpson Burr on Saturday mornin."

It is past midnight. Hungry Peter Leadingham goes down the creek under the beech trees for home. The children have searched the woods for him. Little Peter says, "Grandpa gone and Grandma is about to go crazy." She'd been praying because she ain't kept his clothes patched. The whole countryside had heard her screams and went to hunt Grandpa, but no one thought to go right up the holler from the house. They've been over to "Pint" Bishop's saloon and down to old Widow Skaggs and over to the meeting house. "Just think," says Matilda, "he has been my husband fifty-five years and we have quarreled all of that time but the first six weeks. He has been a true husband. He was fifteen when I married him."

They have quarreled, it is true. But they love each other. Neither one had kissed another boy or girl, for it had not been the Lord's will. Peter kissed old Ben's wife, Hanner, out behind the smoke house one night. But that didn't count. Matilda slipped a few nice kisses to Ben Sexton. Peter didn't know it. It is better to kiss a man who doesn't have beard all over his face. It's better to kiss a man with pretty teeth than one that hasn't any.

Old Peter walks down the path and into his log house. "It is great to be back," he says. He pulls the latch string at the front door and slips in. He goes to his bed. He pulls off his pants and shoes and crawls in bed beside Matilda. He touches her with his cold feet, roots her out of her warm place, rolls over in it. He falls into a dead sleep.

Monday morning and the sun begins to peep over the scarlet autumn leaves. Ben Sexton, Toe-Head Gillum, Young Peter Leadingham, Big Eiff Leadingham and Owl Webb walk silently down the cow path that leads to old Peter Leadingham's log shack. The sun yellows the hollyhocks that grow where Matilda throws the dish water from the kitchen window. The sunflowers wave a nod in the tall ragweeds in the garden and sorty droop their heavy heads as if they were young girls ashamed of their mountain shack. A wisp of black smoke curls from the rusty stove pipe setting like a lazy boy on the lean-to kitchen. It has an odor mixed of burnt rabbit and brown gravy stuck to the skillet.

"Lawzy, I can taste that steak Matilda is fryin," says Ben Sexton.

"You said a mouthful, Ben," says Owl Webb, "I'll bet she tastes right where you hold her."

"Matilda is a damn good cook," says Big Eiff.

"Sure thing," says Toe-Head.

"Looks like it's goin to be a purty day, Toe-Head," says Big Eiff grinning toward the sun.

"Yep, right purty."

"Say, wonder if old Peter talked to God last night!" says Ben Sexton as he takes a whiff from his red corncob pipe made from one of the old soggy cobs picked up at Widow Skaggs' hog pen.

"Yep, I spect he did," says Toe-Head, "you know he's good at them there tricks."

"Keep quiet, for we are near the house and Matilda will hear you," whispered Owl Webb.

"Old Matilda is one hell of a meddler they say, boys," says Big Eiff as he takes his forefinger and clears away the perspiration from his bald forehead and throws it off his finger into a wet dotted circle on the dry sand of the cow path.

The five men are going through the goose lot to the kitchen —Old Peter is lying on the chicken-feather bed. He is asleep. His two hound dogs are snoring by the hickory-wood fire with their noses in the ashes. Peter's long squirrel rifle is hanging on pegs on the low sagging loft. His snuffbox is on the dresser. It belonged to his mother. He has kept it for a keepsake. A pot of green fall beans are sizzling over the hickory-wood fire. Matilda has gone and picked them very early this morning before she did the feeding and milking. She came into the house this morning with sticky-bean leaves, red-brown, golden and drab all over her thin calico dress, and her well-worn black shawl. She sold eggs for the dress at twelve cents a dozen to the Webb store. Ben Sexton got her the shawl twenty-five years ago for a Christmas present. She's not worn it much, but kept it in the trunk until the moths started eating it.

Five men go dragging in at the low front door. Owl Webb

is too tall for the door. His forehead strikes the door-facing.

"Damn it, my head," he says.

"Good mornin, Matilda," says Ben.

"Good mornin, Bucky Boy," says Matilda.

The other men shriek four different-toned laughs.

"Where's that husband of yours?" says Ben.

"He ain't got up yet, Bucky. You men make yerselfs right at home. Have some chears." She slaps Ben on the back and they all laugh. Matilda hands Buck out a chair with wire woven in the hickory-bark to make the seat stout enough to keep Peter from breaking through. Ben sits down and jumps up with a scream. "My God. My God. What's that? My God!" He has a steel trap hanging to the seat of his pants.

"My God—O Lord," he yells. "What the——"

"Never mind, Buck, it's a trap, I set it there for the cat. Peter found her in the churn once and it's sorty turned his stummick on buttermilk. I thought I'd catch her at her old trick."

"But Matilda, you got the wrong cat," says Peter looking all the time at the hollow poplar log with a board nailed on for a bottom, used for a churn. Matilda slips up and mashes the spring down with her strong hands and frees Buck from the jaws of the trap. He sighs with relief. But then, Lead and Raggs spring from their sleep by the wood fire just in time! Raggs grabs Owl Webb before he sits down.

"O Lordy—my Lord! Help, Buck! Toe-Head, take 'em off! Take 'em off, you damn fools—Don't stand there. My God! Take 'em off! O Lord!" Owl is fighting Lead to keep him off his face and Raggs has him with a full mouth in the seat of the pants. Old Ben is smiling after the steel trap has caught him in the same place.

"Here Lead, here Raggs," shouted Old Peter who has been awakened by the screams, "what do dogs mean grabbin a man in broad daylight."

"Mean, hell!" shouted Ben. "Pretty damn nice way to live right with dogs in the house and cats in the churn."

"Oh, don't mention that cat, oh don't." Peter holds his head over the bedside and gags. "Listen here, Buck," says Peter, "you've had your way long enough. Now God and me are goin to have our way a little while. Get me. I saw God last night and talked to Him. And listen here, I'm the only skunk livin that has seen his Saviour face to face and talked to Him. I never went blind either when I looked on His face."

"You don't mean you saw God," says young Peter. "What did He tell you? What did He say about me?"

"Never mind what He said about you. It was bad enough. One thing He said: if you didn't let other men's wives alone you would go straight to hell and there wasn't goin to be any sanctification for you either."

"What did God tell you shore enough, Uncle Peter?" asks Toe-Head.

"Well boys, here's my story. God is a man the shape of Judd Sluss. He's mighty friendly. If you went to His place and He had only beans for dinner He'd ask for you to set down and have beans with Him. Oh, God is jist like one of us fellars. He has quare ways. That's all. Now last night I give Him some of my tobaccer smoke."

"You don't mean that God smokes," says Owl.

"Yes I mean God smokes," says Old Peter, "and God smokes a pipe just like I do and the same brand of tobacco. Now let me tell you about God. He means business. I saw the old Devil too. God drove him in front up the holler like He drove the swine out'en that old bad woman back yander. He just looked like an old cow walkin on her hind feet. He carried a red-handled pitchfork too."

"How you tell atter night?" Owl inquired.

"Now you jist keep quiet until I'm through here and then there'll be plenty of time left fer you to bark, Mister Webb," says Old Peter running his hands through his beard. "Now con-surn his hide! Then I looked and here come God with the two thieves that were crucified with him."

"What did he tell you, Pap?" says young Peter.

"Now wait a minute. I'm jist gettin to that. Bear a little with me here. God said Red Jacket was killed all right. He wouldn't tell who done it. He said Red Jacket was in heaven. You see, men, I always told you the Indians has sperets, didn't

I? Well, I was right. Now Red Jacket is a speret—a great knockin speret."

"A great knockin speret!" Big Eiff repeats again. "A big knockin speret."

"Now it's like this, boys," says Peter, "because Red Jacket was killed God gives him the power to knock on hatbands, shoes, nightshirts, doors, windows or planks or just anythin around or about them fellows that plotted to get his gold for their children. A dirty shame that anybody would do a poor Medicine Man like that."

"How do you know when to get him to knock, Pap?" says young Peter.

"Well God told me the seventh child of the seventh generation could say, 'Good speret, Red Jacket, knock two times on the door for me,' and the speret would knock. Sometimes it will have to be petted a little before it will work. All the sinners in the community will be pestered with it."

"There ain't no such thing as a knockin speret," cries Ben.

"I don't know about that for somethin knocked ten times straight on the toe of my shoe this mornin when I started to put it on."

"Toe-Head, we'll just give that thing a test. We'll go down to Lonnie Johnson's. His daughter Belle is the seventh child of the seventh generation, for she has been blowin her breath in young babies' mouths to cure the 'thrash.' Now let's let her know and we'll all gather in. The people in Jimpson Burr will come."

"That's a go," shouts Ben Sexton, "but we must just let certain people know about it for we don't want a whole yard full. We don't want to let Rev. William P. Hankas in on this. He'll claim that he talked to God and found this out. You know him."

"Yes, I know him," says Toe-Head.

"It's purt nigh time we're a-goin," says Owl Webb.

Old Ben gets up, rubs his hand over where the steel trap had caught him and leads the way out.

"Don't be in a hurry, boys. Stay and we'll have some dinner atter while. Then we'll open up a keg o' nails."

The boys all laugh and Old Ben says, "No thank you, we'll be gettin over the hill to our beans."

The three men plod slowly up the cow path the way they came. It is sheathed in a brilliant autumn sunlight. Persimmon leaves are strewn across the cow path. The cow pasture looks lazy in the sunlight as a lizard sleeping on a log in July. The five men enter the cornfield and cross the field to the beech grove. Big Eiff carries his hat in his hand. He says, "Damn it, Owl, keep off my heels."

They looked back to see a little stream of smoke swirl from the cabin chimney on old Peter Leadingham's shack. The wind rustles through the corn and carries the dry thin persimmon leaves and the beech leaves into little rifts like wild birds flying in autumn. The heat looks intense on the dry September pasture fields. The dying corn and the wind harmonize on a lonesome song without words. Soon the men are out of sight.

III

After they've gone Old Peter says, "Matilda, carry the rockin chair out in the front yard for me and wash my feet while I think the situation over."

"Belle is practicin with the sperets," says Matilda. "Windy Meadows told me and Lefty Hern told Windy. He said Belle was raisin 'em right along, but it caused her neck veins to swell an awful lot. She takes fits too, after that Red Jacket works on her a little."

"It is that Brother Melvin P. Hankas," says Peter. "He used to preach with me until he tried to steal the jewelry we got from some railroad men we saved at Peach Grove. We got three watches from three men and he tried to take the third watch."

Men cut down their green tobacco crops when they got saved under Brother Melvin P. Hankas. They set fire to their barns of cured tobacco. "Burn the damn dirty stuff because no one is seen in heaven with a chew of tobaccer or a pipe," says Brother Melvin P. Hankas.

Peter always keeps a "Scandal Board" that he hangs on the

wall in his church. On this he puts the men's tobacco that they throw down when they are under conviction. He puts the old-time rats the women wear in their hair on this scandal board; and the jewelry, tobacco, pistols, knives, rats, black-jacks and ten dollar bills. He takes with him a tent during the summer. They have a net of ropes for the shouting women to climb.

Peter remembers these nights with Brother Melvin P. Hankas. "He'll be right in to get his part of the Red Jacket money with me. That old man just won't be uptripped. He'll be right there. I can't do nothin for Brother Melvin P."

Matilda has pretty well got her Old Peter's feet washed except there are little streaks of dirt between the toes that is hard to get off. It is dried and has to be soaked a little. Peter is asking Matilda to get the side-saddle on the mule and go around to invite his friends to the Johnsons' house for Wednesday evening. Belle Johnson is ready to perform.

Matilda gets the saddle on old Murt. She takes orders from Old Peter to invite Young Peter Leadingham, Windy Meadows, Dad Dysard, Owl Webb, Big Eiff Leadingham, Rick Johnson, Sister Fultz, Lu Nelson, "Pint" Bishop and Widow Skaggs. He warns her not to bother about going out of the way to invite Ben Sexton. He warned her to leave Brother Melvin P. alone.

Matilda rides off down the rocky Leadingham Branch. Lead and Raggs follow her and smell of the fence posts along the road with their tails curled over their backs. They look like men wanting trouble. Peter is alone at home barefooted under the apple tree. He is thinking over the situation and watching the young chickens play hide-and-seek in the tall ragweeds catching June beetles.

Up on the left fork of Leadingham Branch, Judd Sluss is laughing about Old Peter talking to God. His wife is knitting the holes in her new homespun blankets and cussing Judd for burning up the candles she used when company came. Now she will have to use pine torches. The thought in Peter's brain, "left hand knoweth not what the right hand doeth."

Wednesday night. The little line of dusky lanterns can be

seen swinging through the dark up the plum tree bank to the Johnsons' house. They are to be there at eight o'clock tonight. All that are invited come and two who are not invited heard about it and come anyway. They are Ben Sexton and Brother Melvin P.

Peter leads the way into the Johnson home.

"Hello everybody," shouts Peter.

"Hello, Brother Peter."

"Yes hello, Brother Peter," and out from behind the door steps Brother Melvin P. and pats him on the back. "I thought I'd give you a little surprise by gettin behind the door."

"Well you did surprise me shore enough. I didn't know you was goin to be here until I heard that old voice of yours."

"Well, I'm right here, Brother Peter."

"Yes, I know you are here," says Peter.

Peter walks away. There is much handshaking among the members of the reunion. Matilda and Buck are still shaking hands over on one side of the room after everybody has finished. Peter noticed them through the corner of his dull meaningless eye, remembering what God had told him.

"Well we'd better get ready fer action here, boys, or we won't git around to all of you tonight. Peter, you make the announcement and tell them all what this is about."

"All right, Brother Lonnie."

Peter walks out in the middle of the floor.

"All right, now brothers and sisters, listen to the sound of my voice. Tonight is going to be a big night with us. I saw the Lord last Sunday night and talked with Him and I'm not ashamed to tell it; I smoked with Him."

"Smoked with Him!"

"Now be quiet while I talk. Yes I smoked with Him. We got the straight about Brother Red Jacket. He is going to be in your souls tonight. God gives him that power. You know that poor old Indian that was murdered in Widow Skaggs' hog lot—"

"In my hog lot–my God, I didn't do it." Widow Skaggs says this and is trying to faint—

"Now, be quiet, bear with me, people. God is going to show you what He can do."

Peter walks over in the crowd. Belle Johnson steps out with two fox horns. They are shaking every way in her hands. She has a terrible time of holding them.

"Now men and women," says Belle, "you will have to pay Ada Bee Sizemore fifty cents apiece before you talk to Red Jacket."

People hold their breath. "Who is this Ada Bee Sizemore anyway?" says Young Peter. "She is a new one they are springin on us." Here she comes out of a little room. She carries a little Testament in one hand and a torch in the other. She wears a white flowing robe and she has sandals on her feet. "Lord, but she looks like a angel," say Old Peter Leadingham.

"Ada Bee Sizemore is my name," says the strange woman. "I am here to help Little Belle Johnson. She is a youngin at this work. I am ready to take your money and let the knockin speret talk with you. You can ask about all of your dead relatives. And they will talk to you."

"Who's ready now?" says Belle.

"I'll try 'em a whack," says Dad Dysard. "I'll give one day's work just to learn 'em."

Ada Bee goes over and gets the fifty cents and his arm. She leads him in a little room and pulls out a deck of cards. All the time she keeps running her fingers through the cards and keeps asking Dad questions.

"Dad," says Ada Bee, "you go out and sit down in that willow rockin chair in the front room. I have to handle the good Speret and I must be away. I have to be in a trance and never move a muscle."

"All right," says Dad Dysard. He goes to the willow chair and sits down. Ada Bee goes in behind some starched white curtains.

Belle walks in and puts the quivering fox horns on the table before Dad. They still quiver. Dad wants to get up and run out. He is scared. Belle tells him to sit still and get the light on the other world. The women see Dad in such misery they shed tears. The men all hold their heads but Old Ben. He laughs.

"Not a damn thing to it," he laughs louder and louder and shows his yellow teeth. A little white thing slim as a poker, and white as snow on a granite roof, comes up by the side of Dad's chair.

"Hello, Dad," said the voice.

"Hello, Vilet," says Dad. "It's my wife." Tears stream from his eyes. "You been dead for thirty years."

"Yes I was once your wife, but you are married again now."

"Yes, married," and that is all Dad can say. He just sits silently and stares at the figure.

"Though you are married I love you just the same and I am with you a lot."

"If you are my wife how old was you when you died?"

"Thirty-nine."

"Right. How many children did we have?"

"Six."

"How many girls and how many boys?"

"Three boys and three girls."

"How many are livin and how many are dead?"

"Five livin and one dead."

"Where is the one dead?"

"She is with me. She has grown until you wouldn't know her."

Dad melts down. He picks up courage to speak again although his voice is shaky as a reed in the wind.

"Are all my children at home?"

"No, young Hankas is in Missouri. I am with him a lot too."

"Well, what kind of a woman did I get for my second wife?"

"No good."

"Who was she before I married her?"

"Melvina Peavine."

"How do you know my wife is not a good woman?"

"Well, don't ask me. Ask Ben Sexton."

"My God," says Dad. "This Ben Sexton has give Peter Leadingham trouble for the last twenty-five years. Is he after my wife now?"

"You know, Dad, when you married me I was a virtuous woman."

"Yes you were, Vilet."

"You used to sell the cows and buy whisky and go see women, didn't you?"

"Yes."

"If you sow the wind you'll reap the wind. If you don't change your way you'll never be where I am."

Dad grabs his hat and takes out the front door. He comes back. He is afraid in the dark. The men and women see how he is crying. No one else will try it. Peter and Brother Melvin P. punch each other and Melvin P. says, "We'd better not try it on account of them watches." Ben Sexton has become a little suspicious on account of the women. Matilda is right here. Dad says: "She told me the truth about my first wife. About me not goin to heaven is what hurt me most. I'll not be a Free Willer any longer. I was saved under Moses Stricklin. It ain't the right kind of religion."

Dad calls Brother Melvin P. and Brother Peter outside and says: "Boys, I'm lost. Pray for me. I want to join your church. Pray for me."

"Yes, Brother Dysard, we'll give you real religion," says Brother Melvin P.

"You ain't half as bad as I wuz. No church but the Forty-Gallon Baptis could save me. I was so mean when I wuz a young man. I even drove a nail in a horse's foot to make him lame so I could buy him cheap as dirt. I bought him and then I pulled the nail out and he got all right. I was mean. But I took in one of Brother Peter's revivals and got under conviction. Then the next day I was on a mowin machine and I fell like I had a sunstroke. Right there me and my Lord got right and He put his hand on my head and said, 'Preach.' I went to preachin in three days from that time. Dad, you can get right."

Dad Dysard, Brother Melvin P. Hankas and Brother Peter

Leadingham are out in the night. The night is black as your pocket behind the house. They are praying loud as the wind is crying through the plum trees.

In the house it is quite different. Belle Johnson is in the kitchen. All the people are gathered around her but Ada Bee Sizemore. She has the table standing on one leg, two legs, three legs and dancing all around the room. The crowd watches. Julia Shelton is a little girl with ribbons on her long braid of coarse black hair. She is a friend of Belle Johnson's that is the reason she was invited. Yesterday she went to the pasture with Belle to help her find some pawpaws. Belle took a fit and her neck veins swelled. Julia was scared. Belle came to and asked for water and says: "Good Speret, go away. Stay away. I'll leave you alone."

Belle lets anybody examine her hands. She will let anybody sit on her lap but Ben Sexton to see if she is moving the table in any way. They do it. No one can tell it if she is.

"I can hold that table down," says Owl Webb.

"Get on," says Belle.

Owl jumps on the table and says, "Let 'er go."

The table begins to shift from one side of the room and do all kinds of capers. "God, what is all this about?" screams Owl.

"Ride her, cowboy," shouts Ben.

"You ride 'er," shouts Owl half stunned as he hits flat of his belly on the rough puncheon floor.

"Well I can ride 'er, don't you weary," says Ben. "And my belly won't hit no floor neither."

"Let 'em on that air table, Belle," says Toe-Head.

"Yes let old Ben on," says Big Eiff standing over in the corner wiping sweat from his bald head.

"Get on, Ben," says Belle.

"No, Ben ain't goin to get on that table," says Matilda.

"What have you got to do with it? I'll get on if I want to," says Ben. "No petticoat can't keep me from doin nothin."

Matilda shrugs her shoulders and gives two steps backward. Old Ben is rolling back the sleeves of his new store-bought shirt. It shows the muscles in his arms. He unbuttons his shirt at the neck and shows his hairy chest. He looks mean.

His hair is black and coarse as ragweeds and falls across his eyes.

"Show me somethin I can't do," he yells as he leaps on the quivering table. "Hell, I am a man. I'm not a soft boy like Owl Webb."

He firmly clenches both sides with his big rough hands. He sticks his teeth in the rim of the last end board. On the other end of the table he fastens the toes of his ten-and-one-half shoes under the end board.

"Let 'er go, Belle," shouts Buck, "I'm rarin to ride 'er."

"Belle, be careful," says Matilda.

Belle gives the table all of Red Jacket's powers. It quivers and shakes and stands on one leg. Ben holds on. It stands straight in the air with Ben's head downward. Ben holds on. It stands on one end awhile to try to make Ben dizzy, so Owl Webb said.

"By hell, ain't I holdin on, Owl?" Ben looks up with a mean grin on his face. At this minute Ben has to drop.

"I told you you'd come off there, Ben Sexton," laughs Owl.

"Off hell," shouts Ben. He jumps up and catches the table with his hand toward the top. "I'll eat this thing before any Red Jacket can handle me."

Ben is looking more serious than ever. He clenches the top again with his teeth. Over flops the table pinning Ben to the floor.

"O Lord," he moans. "O Lord. Take the table off, take it off."

Everybody is afraid to touch it.

"Take it off, Red Jacket," says Belle Johnson. Off comes the table. It set in its upright position. Ben is stunned. He gets up with all his front teeth knocked out. "Lord, he looks awful," says Matilda, "his new shirt is tore and he's so bloody."

Flem Johnson crawls up in the loft to see if he can see Red Jacket. He comes down in a hurry. He says: "The chains up there are rattlin and the whole loft is shakin. It is too hot for me to stand. The knockin speret Red Jacket is every place. It is a housewarmin. Got old Red Jacket riled up," says Owl Webb.

"One more thing, good Red Jacket, before we go," says Owl Webb. "Does Ben Sexton kiss Matilda Leadingham? Knock three times if he does."

Thump! Thump! Thump! Each time it's loud as a nail hammer hitting the oak boards in the table.

Ben sneaks out of the room. Matilda follows. The crowd begins to slip out afraid of the dark. They hold together. Belle falls on the floor with another fit.

Outside is Dad Dysard shouting all over the yard. Brother Melvin P. and Brother Peter have got him on the safe side.

Outside are Brother Melvin P. and Peter Leadingham with a jug of Kentucky's Melancholy Dew. One takes a drink and then the other. "It is the greatest knockin speret of them all," says Peter. They are locked together and about to twist down together under the plum trees.

The moon comes up and is going down over the low dark hills at Jimpson Burr dragging a patch of clouds behind it. The wind sings a song without words in the plum trees and in the dying corn.

MICK POWDERJAY is nailing boards on the smoke-house roof. It is the last course of oak clapboards. The autumn air is crisp. The dead oak leaves fly from the brushy-topped scrub black-oaks on the yellow bank beside of the house. The leaves drift from the black-oaks—down across the path that the children walk from school. Mick drives a nail into the oak board, blows his warm breath on his red knuckles and looks down the path the dead leaves trail over. "It's time Shan was in from school. Wonder what is keepin him. He's nearly dark a-gettin in tonight—wood is not in and water is not up."

Mick Powderjay climbs down off the smoke house. He takes step by step down the short ladder, carefully placing each step like a chicken when it walks up the ladder in the oak tree to roost.

You can see Mick Powderjay as he walks down the dusty autumn road and shuffles the dead leaves with his brogan shoes. He is a little man going through the autumn shadows toward the Collins' Hill. He is looking for Shan. Dusk is coming fast. The tingling sheep bells on the high hills are silenced. The wind blows through the dead leaves and it is a lonesome wind to hear. The wind stirs the dead grass along the path—grass frost-bitten white and dry-sizzling when the October wind blows chilly from the high hills where the sheep are sleeping under the pines. "It's time for Shan. Fightin again. Fightin I'll bet."

They have come around the turn in the road beside of the apple tree. There comes Shan. "Shan Powderjay, you stinkin Republican, I dare you out into your own corn patch."

"A Democrat Sexton never dared me to do nothin. West Sexton, you and Jim Sexton and no other Sexton can keep me from goin out into my own cornfield."

Shan walks out through the dead white frost-bitten crab grass—out beside a shock of corn. Mick Powderjay watches from the turn of the road. "Didn't I tell you, Shan, not to go out there?" West says, "You know what I'll do to you–you stinkin Republican."

West throws a rock that hits Shan in the ribs. "That's cut my wind–my–my breath–" says Shan–"damn you to hell, West Sexton." He comes out of the cornfield crying. He comes toward West.

"I'll tell the teacher on you for cussin, Shan Powderjay," says Jim Sexton. "I'll tell him and he'll tan your hide."

"Tan and be damned. He's a Democrat like the rest of you."

Shan strikes West in the face. "One, two! Left, right–damn you." West is down on the dead grass.

"My Mommie allus said for me to pertect little West. Damn you to hell, Shan Powderjay. You stinkin, flat-nosed Republican you!"

"One, two, three, four–left right–right–left–left––"

"Enough?"

"No," yelled Shan.

"Enough?"

"No–You can't make me say it."

"Take this coat hanger then over your eye."

Shan is staggered down on the dead grass. He is crying mad. He wipes the tears from his eyes with his bloody hand. "There'll come the time when I'll clean ever Sexton o' the name. I hate them. I hate both of you."

"Shan–oh, Shan–come on up this road before I come down there and limb the rest of the shirt off'n you. Get on to this house fightin around agin–" Shan walks ahead of West and Jim. Shan is crying. His eye is closed. He can barely see.

"What are you into it again over?"

"Because I am a Republican, Pop."

"Why are you a Republican?"

"Because you allus told me to be, Pop."

"That's right, son. I did allus tell you that. My Pap allus told me to be. It's hard to be a Republican here, but I stuck it out all my life. I still am a Republican. It don't mean you boys got to take up politics and fight ever time there's a election in this County. No sense in that."

"But you don't know, Pop, what I got to stand out there at

school. They ain't but two Republicans in the Deestrict. I am one. Jack Turner is the other. You know Jack Turner that stole them geese and carried that pistol. Well, he is the other Republican."

"They're all Democrats then."

"Yes, all Democrats. Even the teacher and he thinks it is funny when they call me a stinkin Republican. Damn his dirty looks. Hold my hand, Pop, and lead me. I can't see."

Mick Powderjay leads Shan. They walk up the leaf-strewn road. The Sexton boys come slowly up the road. It may be they are afraid of little Mick Powderjay. Mick stops and holds Shan's hand and waits for them to pass. "Jim Sexton, don't you know you are twice as big as my boy. Your brother West there is bigger. After he whopped West fair as he could be whopped then you went over and closed his eyes. I am goin to school tomorrow and if they ain't somethin done about this then I'm seein your father and if he don't do somethin, I warn your father, you and all the Sextons. You tell your father what I am tellin you. I mean every word I say."

"Well, I'll tell the old man—But he don't like a stinkin Republican no more than I do."

"What's the matter with Shan, Mick?—My Lord, what is the matter! What is the matter with that youngin's face?"

"Fit all over the corn patch down yander by that corner apple tree. I seen it all. He whopped West fair and square and then John Sexton's oldest boy Jim closed both his eyes. My blood biled. If old John had been down there I'd a landed on him I was so mad. My flesh and blood and your flesh and blood treated that way because he is a Republican."

"Well you know Pap never wanted me to marry you because you was a Republican——"

"Pity your Pap couldn't a had his way about it. Look what trouble it has caused me. Your people has been down on me because I was a Republican. My people don't like yours. It's a shame."

"Yes—come on, Shan, and let me hold some camphor to your nose and wash the blood off'n you and you'll feel better. Come in here and let me pour some water from the teakettle."

"Mom—be easy—oh, that is so sore, Mom. Wash it easier."

"What did he hit you with?"

"Hit me with his big fist. Hit me so fast, Mom, I couldn't count 'em. But I whopped West. I laid it on him. Jim is too big. I'll get him before my dyin day. Mom, I hate a Democrat."

"W'y, Shan."

"Yes, I do."

"W'y Shan, your mother is a full-blooded Democrat. She wants you to be."

"I'll never though—I'll never. I hate 'em all. Mom, you ought'n to be a Democrat. They're so mean all of them. They've called me every thing at school today and the teacher just laughed and laughed. I hate 'em all."

The blood is washed from Shan's face. His flesh is the color of a young potato plant. It is dark green under his eyes. His face is swollen. His hand is swollen. He cannot see. Mick Powderjay carries in the stove wood and draws water from the well in the two-gallon wooden bucket and puts it on the water bench. He does the work Shan is supposed to do. He comes in and sits before the blazing fore stick. The sap is runnin out of one end of it and the white-foam slobbers are falling onto the red coals and sizzlin. Mick sits down on a split-bottom chair. "You know this damned fightin 's got to be stopped. I don't aim to stand nary nother speck of it. The boy comes in every day with his clothes tore off'n him 'r his eyes blacked. Look at him, won't you! I don't believe in upholdin my youngins for fightin, but he ought to take a hickory club and brain 'em all. And I hope to see the day that he whopps 'em all and outlearns all that bunch out there. I hope to see my boy do it."

The red blaze from the green-oak fore stick lap their tongues up the chimney. It is a wonder they don't dirty their tongues with soot hangin to the rough-stone back walls like pods of green moss. The light flickers over the room.

"Mom, lead me on the outside the house. Leave me out there. Then come and get me."

"All right, Shan. Reach me your hand." Fronnie leads Shan

to the door—out into the dark night that is around the house—that the moon gleams peacefully through enough to show the color of the leaves.

"Leave me now. Then come and get me."

"All right. I'll be back atter you, Honey." Shan feels the wind against his sore eyes. He feels the cool October wind against the sore flesh on his face. He is in a world of blindness. He cannot see. Night is around him. It is the same as day. The world is dark to him. He can feel the wind and hear the dead oak leaves stir above his head.

"Ah, Mom—come and get me."

"I'm right here atter you, Shan."

"You know, Mom, it's awful to be blind—I'd hate to be blind forever."

"I'll bathe your eyes in warm salt water and work with them tonight so you can go back to school tomorrow. We aim to take you back if we have to put you in the express and haul you plum around the road and get you there."

"Wait till I grow up. I got just a few things I want to do. W'y Mom, they called me so many names at school today that I got so mad I cried. Then they laughed. They whispered them over the back of the seat to me. They called me a flat-nosed stinkin Republican. They called Pop one. I didn't tell him. The teacher laughed when they said smart things to me. I'll get him too. They said Republicans was all cut out of dead horse meat. A buzzard sailed up over Wheeler's field and they said it was atter me because it smelt me. Jack Turner's the only other Republican out there and they's sixty of us. Jack slipped off from school and said nobody could ever make him go back there and that just leaves me now. I got sick today atter they said all them things. I ast the teacher to go out under the shade of a oak and rest and he laughed and said: 'What's the matter, can't you take it?' He let me go. I set out there and watched a little black ant carry a load five times big as it was. The wind hit my face and I felt better. I watched the ants catch the flies and carry big pieces of bread and apples. I watched the jay birds carry acorns up into the tall oaks and hide them in the tops. I liked it out there a devil o' a sight better than I did in the house."

"Shan, don't you know how it is here? They ain't no Republicans. I used to think a Republican stunk. Pap allus said they did and when I married your Pa they nearly took the top the house off over home. Some places here in the mountains you don't find very many Democrats. It was caused by the War between the States way back yander. You ought to read about all that in your primary history. The Republicans here in the mountains are called the Lost Tribe of Israel. They are the only Republicans in these parts to amount to much. I am a Democrat and I wouldn't be anything else. My Pap fit back yander in the Rebellion and he hated a Republican worse'n a copperhead. W'y he turned on his own Pap who fit for the Yanks. Grandpap had a regiment of soldiers and fit right here among these hills. And my Pap, his own flesh-and-blood boy, fit with Morgan against his own father. And ever since the War we've been Democrats. Your Pa's Pap fit with the Yanks and that's why your Pa is a Republican. That war was awful here. Yanks had Rebels to climb trees. Then they shot 'em out. Rebels had Yanks to climb trees and they shot 'em out. Your Pa's people and my people all about got killed in that war. We ain't over it yet. But our children ought to be over it. They ain't no use to talk about it now. You go on and be what you want to be. Go to bed now and get some sleep."

Shan rolls under the heavy quilts. The whole upstairs is dark. He cannot see the moon throw its rays across the broad planks in the upstairs floor. He cannot see the dead leaves sifting down between the head of his bed and the moon—leaves in the strip of yellow moonlight. He goes into the world of darkness. The wind touches his face and moves the end of his pillow-case—rustles the stiff-starched blue curtains on the upstairs window.

"Just as I thought. Eyes not open. Well, he's goin back to school today. I'll see that he goes. I'm takin the mule and the express wagon and takin him right out there. I just seen the Sexton boys sneak by the house. I'm goin to see that they all get punished."

"Gear up the mule and hitch him up while I get ready and

get Shan ready. I'll have to get Vicey Martin to come over and take care of the rest of the youngins while I go out there. But I'm goin too."

Mick gears the mule. He leads him from the barn door—takes him to water. Then he backs him into the shafts. He hitches the traces and fastens the shafts—puts the reins over the hames and the check lines through the harness loops. Fronnie is ready. She has Shan ready. His face is swollen purple as a fire-scorched milkweed pod. He cannot see. They feed him breakfast with a spoon. They lead him to the express and lift him up into the seat. Fronnie climbs in beside of him. Mick takes the reins. "Get up, Barnie—Let's move along now, boy."

The wheels rip-raz the dead leaves. They crush them under the weight of the express. The wind blows. The wind is cool. It touches the white frost that covers every leaf, tree, deadweed, fodder-shock, panel of rail fence and briar. The world is white. The crows fly over the white-leafed world. The sun rises through a mist from a red bank of eastern hills. The wind slightly rustles the frosted leaves. Mick sits with his collar up high around his neck and his hands gloved. Fronnie sits with a fur collar up high around her neck.

"I wish I was on the ice this mornin. That's the way I like to go to school. I like to skate my way there—fall on the ice—break my lookin-glass. Get right up and go again."

Fronnie laughs. Mick is silent. He says, "Move along, Barnie. Move along!" Over the dead leaves—over the ruts. Around the road past the old Keyser house—over the low gap where the sand-briar leaves are red-steamin in the sun. The sun is coming up behind a golden cloud of leaves now—and a white stream of mist goes slowly swirling upwards toward the sky—mist spiraling as dry leaves spiral in a new-ground when the brush is on fire and the wind becomes heated and rises swirling toward the heavens with a load of leaves.

The hoofs of the mule click on the frozen ground. Now Mick says: "Hurry it up, Barnie. Can't you hit a few more mud holes. I believe you do it on purpose. Get up there, Barnie!" They drive past the old McMeans house—down the hill through a leafless apple orchard and out past Perkins' pig lot—

turn left—past the old worm-rail fence where the ground squirrels come out and "chee-chee" and dart back in their dirt holes again—The air is so good to breath now. They are passing the Wheeler pawpaw patches.

"I can smell the pawpaw patches, Mom. Smell like ripe pawpaws."

"Yes, Shan. We are passin them now."

"I can hear the ground squirrels, Mom."

"Yes, they run out on the rails and bark "chee-chee" at us and then they dart back in their holes again."

"Cowards, aint they? Just like them Sexton boys. They can't take it!"

Now they drive past the Wheeler place. Barns are all over the hill—a big house under the hill with a well in the front yard with a well sweep and water bucket chained to it. "Damned if I'd have my barn upon the hill above my well," says Mick, "I wouldn't drink that water."

The schoolhouse is in sight—just upon the hill past a lane that is lined on both sides with haw bushes. Up the lane. It is rough and rutty where the coal wagons and the cross-tie wagons have rolled over heavy loaded. The mule strains at the load and he is now choicy where he places his nimble forefeet. "It takes a mule to pull," says Mick, "they are the sure-footed things for these roads. I have had horses and mules and I know." Up the hill and past the hickory trees into the school yard.

"Get out, Fronnie. Let's help Shan out and you can wait till I tie old Barnie up here to this hickory tree." Mick takes Fronnie's hand. She places her foot on the brake block and he helps her onto the ground. Fronnie takes one of Shan's hands, Mick takes the other. They lift him from the express.

"I am at school now, Mom. Back at school. Old Jim is here. He blinded me, didn't he, Mom. Someday I'll put the cat on him."

"Forget that now. We're going to see the teacher. We'll attend to all of this." Mick has tied the mule to the hickory. The sun is getting up in the heavens now. A golden shower of hickory leaves rustle in the hilltop wind. The jay birds scold from the black-oak tree tops where they are laying away a winter supply of acorns.

"Well, come along, Fronnie. Grab his hand. Let's get out to the schoolhouse."

"Good mornin–This is Mr. Landon, the school teacher of Hickory Grove, ain't it? Well, I'm Shan's Pappie and here's his Mammie. We're bringin him back to school this mornin."

"Been fightin again, hasn't he, Mr. Powderjay?"

"Yes."

"Kindly looks that away, don't you think?" says Fronnie.

"Well, I should say so," says schoolmaster John Landon. "He's a bad boy to fight. I've had to correct him several times."

"Well I ain't come out here to start nothin, but I brought the boy out to show you what kind of a shape he is in and to tell you it's not quite fair for a boy of this size to have to fight two boys at one time the size of my neighbors–the Sexton boys. That's what happened. I was a eyewitness to it all."

"Is that right!"

"If it hadn't been I wouldn't a spoke it. They called the boy a stinkin Republican and that's what he fights over. I am a Republican and I don't care if God knows it or the Devil knows it or who knows it. He's a Republican because he has heard me say I was. Now that's what all this trouble is over."

"Can't he see a speck?"

"Not a speck. He's blind as a bat. Fronnie's bathed his eyes good last night. We'd a got a doctor, but we's so far away from town and it costs so much. We know the swellin will go down anyway."

The children turn around in their seats and stare at Shan. He stands holding the desk where the water bucket sets in the back end of the room. School children come to get a drink of water just so they can see Shan. They leave the room just so they can see him. There is a piece of a chalk box fastened by a twine string to a nail that is marked OUT on one side. When this is turned over and the word OUT is showing it means someone is out and no one is allowed to leave the room until this one returns and turns the board over where the blank side is showing.

"Well Mr. Powderjay, we'll do something about this. I'll call the boys back here and we'll thresh this thing out right here. Jim Sexton and West Sexton, will please come back here for a few minutes."

They rise from their seats—overall-clad, barefooted with big rusty-looking feet, they plod back to the desk where the water bucket sets. The schoolhouse is only one room where eight grades are taught by one teacher. Jim Sexton's big bear-claw hands hang at his side. He is a powerful youth to be in a grammar school. "Jim, did you close this boy's eyes and beat him up like this?"

"I did. He whopped my brother and so I whopped him."

"What started the fight?"

"I called him a Republican and he didn't like it."

"Tell the truth," says Shan, "you called me a stinkin Republican, and my Pop one, and said they's fit only to eat old dead horse meat and you know you said it."

Jim Sexton looks at the school children and smiles. He wants them to think he has done a big piece of work in closing Shan's eyes. Then he says: "I did say somethin like that. I hate a Republican. They are stinkin. My Pa said they was and you know, Mr. Landon, you told me once goin across the hill they was."

The color of schoolmaster John Landon's cheeks has flushed to color of a red-oak leaf. He cannot speak. Mick kicks his toe slowly against the wall and looks John Landon in the eye. "I am a Democrat," says Fronnie, "a full-blooded Democrat and not anythin else. Never voted any other way. But that is my boy. I ain't here to tear up a school and uphold for him, but I hope he cleans house with a few of you around here someday over the abuse he's had to take at this school. He'll not allus be a child, remember."

"No," says John Landon.

"What are you goin to do about it, Mr. Landon?" says Mick Powderjay.

"I am going to whip all three boys for fighting. Steave Brooker, you go up in the loft and get me a seasoned switch.

Better bring three along. Help him put the cedar pole up there, Tiny Literal, so he can get up into the scuddle hole."

Tiny and Steave lift a cedar sapling with branches trimmed off enough to leave a set of steps. They place the top of it in the scuddle hole and the heavy end on the floor. "Steady it, Tiny, and I'll get the switches."

Tiny holds the cedar. Steave scales up it like a cat. Nimble as a cat he darts into the scuddle hole. In less than a minute he is back with three seasoned honey-locust switches. His face is dust-dirty. "Here they are, Mr. Landon."

"Thank you, Steave."

The children are silent. Mick Powderjay is silent too. Fronnie says, "Shan, I'll lead you up there and you must take your whoppin like a man."

"I can take it, Mom. I've been whopped before and I took it."

"Jim Sexton, you come up the platform first."

Jim walks up the aisle between the girls' side and the boys' side of the house. Some of the children snigger at Jim as he goes past. The smile has left his lips. The platform is the place where the teacher has his chair. It is about a foot higher than the rest of the floor. The preacher often holds church in the schoolhouse and he preaches from this little platform. There isn't a church-house close.

"Turn around so they can all see, Jim."

John Landon turns Jim around so his back is to the crowd and his face is to the wall. "Take your hands from back there if you don't want them cut with this switch." Lap–lap–lap. The dust flies. John Landon steps back one more step so he can give more force to the switch. Lap–lap–lap. The dust flies. Lap–Lap––

"Oh Lordy, Mr. Landon! Oh Lordy–be merciful, Mr. Landon."

Lap–lap––

"Oh, Mr. Landon, you said the Republicans stunk–o-oooo-oooo––"

"Now go take your seat. Shannon Powderjay next."

Fronnie leads him up to the platform. Shan holds out one hand groping. Jim Sexton is crying at his seat.

"Oh–oh–oh–I'll bet my Poppie 'll get you, Mister Landon."

"Face the wall, Shan."

"Wait till I turn him the right way. He don't know where he is at. He don't know where the dark is or where the light is. He is blind. That boy is blind."

Fronnie turns Shan's back to the wall. Lap–lap–lap–lap–lap. Not a whisper.

"Give me a better switch, Steave. Yes, that one will do."

Lap–lap–lap–lap–lap–lap–lap–. Not a whimper. John Landon uses his left hand. Lap–lap–lap–lap–. Not a whimper. Now he uses both hands. Lop–lop–lop–lop–lop. The dust flies. Not a whimper.

"All right. Take him to his seat."

Fronnie leads Shan back to the water bucket. As he gets off the platform he says, "I'm still a Republican if I have to fight every day in the week and get whopped on Sunday."

"Come up here, West Sexton."

West Sexton walks up crying before he is whipped. "Turn around to the crowd."

"Lap–lap–lap–lap–lap–lap––"

"Oh my God, Mr. Landon, that is enough–enough. I can't stand it. I can't stand it. Oh my God, Mr. Landon–oooooooo-oo–ooo."

"Take your seat. Now I don't want no more fighting around here. Let this be a lesson."

"If you are through, Mr. Landon, I got somethin I'd like to say before I leave."

"Yes I am through and you can say anything you'd like to say."

"Well, I am a man to back the school, Mr. Landon. You ain't heard me say nothin about the school. I ain't got enough education to write my name. But I want my boy to come to this school and get a education, for it is somethin that no man can take away from him. He ain't but eight years old. Out here fightin around like this. If he just fights his books like he fights for the Republican Party or these other boys would fight their books the way they fight for the Democrat Party—then they'd all get some place in life. That's all I got to say."

"I got somethin to say, Mr. Landon, before I go," said Fronnie. "You know Republicans is scare as hen's teeth in these parts. I heard my Pap talk about the Lost Tribe of Israel and I didn't know what he meant for a long time. I thought it was a church denomination. But I found out he meant the Republicans in these parts. They's just a little band of them, where I growed up. They never could elect anybody, but they went and voted just the same. They voted the straight ticket. They don't get roads in their Deestricts. They don't get public offices. They don't get anythin. Yet they hold to their party, because their fathers held to it. I married Mick Powderjay. He is a Republican. I know how hard it is to be a Republican here. We can't get any place and our children can't. We have trouble all the time. Have rocks throwed at us. Slurs throwed at us. Just little dirty things. I am not a Republican. I am a Democrat and my people don't like it because I married a Republican. My own father said he'd never darken my door and he never did till he thought I was goin to die. Then he come to see me. We been Democrats since the Rebellion back yander. Mick Powderjay's people has been Republicans since the Rebellion. Our boy takes atter his Pa. That is all right. He has a right to be what he wants to be. I think he ought to be left alone and not have a lot of slurs throwed in his face all time."

"Mrs. Powderjay, I've had to correct Shannon Powderjay quite a lot for fighting. He can tell you. It was just the other day when he hit Henry Lewis in the nose with an apple core and blooded his nose."

"Yes, and Mr. Landon, he called me a stinkin Republican just what Jim Sexton called me. And the apple didn't hurt him much because I had took a big bite out'n it."

"Well, Shannon, I had to whip you for hitting Denver Wright with a stick."

"Mr. Landon, he throwed my straw hat in a briar patch goin over the hill and called me a stinkin Republican. And I hit him."

"Another evening you crossed the hill with the Crum children. You had a fight with them. I had to correct all of you."

"Dell Crum called me a old horse-eatin Republican. I hit him with a rock. Then his sister Martha run up and hit me with a old dead apple tree limb. I didn't know any more for a long time. They went on and left me dead on the hill. You know that, Mr. Landon. The time is comin. I'll get them that's got me and don't you think I won't."

"Let's go, Fronnie."

Fronnie leads Shan by the hand out of the door. Mick Powderjay takes John Landon by the hand, "I wish you a successful school year and soon as Shan can see I'll send him back."

"Thank you, Mr. Powderjay, and good luck to you. I am sorry for all that has happened." Mick walks toward the express shuffling the dead leaves with his brogan shoes.

The sun is up in the sky. The leaves swirl in the bright October wind. The jays scold from their high perches in the oak trees. The children look from the windows as the express wheels screak against the brake blocks going down the hill. Down the rutty lane between the haw trees and out past Wheeler's barns and farmhouse—past the rail fence and the saw briars golden in the sunlight—past the old well and round the turn by the apple tree where the fight started—and back to the log shack. And Shan says: "Oh, Mom I can see a little. Oh, I can see the chicken roost and the wash kettle and the smoke house and the hill. Oh, Mom, my eyes are comin open. Goody. Goody."

Shan Powderjay goes back to school again. He is whipped again by Jim Sexton. He is gotten down in the sand and his mouth poured full of sand. He is held under water at the deep hole by the beech log until the water bubbles. He was pulled out again and rolled on the bank and put in for more. He was thrown in a yellow-jacket's nest. He was stung until he was sick. He never whimpered. He was shoved into a hornet's nest. He was unmercifully stung by hornets. He laughed. Jim Sexton would say, "We ain't in school now. No teacher to whop us. Are you still a Republican?"

"I am a Republican," he would say. "I'll show you someday

what I am." One time he was put in a box with a ground hog because he would say, "I am a Republican," when they were trying to make him say he was a Democrat. He threw his body on the ground hog, choked it to death with his hands. It scratched into his belly with its sharp claws but not deeply. He choked it to death before it clawed him deeply.

"A ground hog is a dangerous damn thing. Hear about Mick Powderjay's boy fallin on that one some boys put him in the box with. He fell on it and took his hands and broke its neck. He's the fightinest boy in this country if he had a chance and didn't bunch on him."

"Ah, well he'll grow up atter a while and show 'em a few things. I don't like a Republican, but anybody likes a boy or a man that will stand firm. That kid's just about twelve years old now. Growin up like a bean pole too. Freckle-faced as a guinea."

"I got the best boy to work in this Hollow," says Mick Powderjay, "he just fights weeds in the corn from daylight till dark. He can take it like a man. He can stand more hot weather and do more work than any man in this Hollow. He's makin the best grades in his class too. He fights like a bulldog. He won't give up."

"I'm worried all the time about Shan when he is out. He's gettin up now sort of a man, you know, or thinks he is. He'll fight them Sexton boys to a finish if it ever starts again."

"Did you hear about Shan Powderjay? W'y he's the craziest boy I ever heard tell of. A blacksnake bit him over there in the strawberry patch and quiled and started to bite him again and he just jumped in and got that snake with his hands. He tore it into pieces with its guts hangin out. I wish you could a seen it. Snake bite never even stopped him from eatin strawberries."

"Witnessed one of the hardest fights I ever seed in all my born days a little while ago. It was down there on the sawdust pile. That Shan Powderjay just cleaned that Crum bunch of boys single-handed. He beat Dell till he was blue in the face and choked Oscar's tongue out and kicked Tim plum off the sawdust pile. One of 'em called him a stinkin Republican. And he says, 'I heard that too much when I was too little to do anythin about it,' and he bowed up his neck and went at 'em like a bull. I never seed such fightin in all my born days."

"I saw a funny thing while ago. I saw the pluckiest boy I ever saw in all my life. You know that guinea-freckled-faced Shan Powderjay—ugly and gangly as a half-trimmed bean pole. I saw him get into a yaller-jacket's nest. One crawled up his pant's leg and stung him. He went right in and dug out the whole nest and took his hat and a club and beat 'em all to death —He got seventeen stings. Cared nary bit for 'em. Fit 'em and the hot sun just a-bilin right down on his head and the sweat just a-runnin off'n his face. He didn't care."

A hornet hit Shan once between the eyes and knocked him down and stung him at the same time. He saw not far from him a big hornet's nest, the first one he had ever seen. He saw the hornets climbing all over the nest and preening the long whiskers together and saying something about him. "Plottin about me, are you. Surely you ain't found out that I am a Republican."

So, Shan gets two long poles, ties a wisp of dead grass to one end, sets the grass on fire and runs the fire up under the nest and burns it to the ground. "I hate to use fire on 'em, but they got the advantage on me—bein up in the air and so many of them. And they got wings. They can sting and bite all the same time and keep goin. Have to fight fire with fire."

The children crossed Radnors' pasture to school. That was the only way they had near enough to get there on time. Bill Radnor says: "They tear down my fences. I want them stopped from goin through here. The Law says they're entitled to a way to the schoolhouse and they have a right to cross my field. But I got the fightin bull John Plummer used to own and put him in there. I've warned them all not to come through my field any more."

"I'm not afraid of your bull," says Shan. "I'll kill him with a club if he ever makes a pass at me."

"He's paid for when you kill him, you freckled face smartelick you," says Bill.

"Did you hear about Bill Radnor's bull jumpin on the school

children the other mornin? He ought to be sent to the pen doin a trick like that. Got that bull a purpose to harm school children. Little Bessie Fials just got through the fence in time. That bull come nigh as a pea gettin her on his horns. Them kids have to go plum around the road to get to school–five miles around that way and just three across the hill."

"Mick Powderjay's boy killed Bill Radnor's bull. Did you hear about it? He pintly killed him with a four-year-old hickory club. Him and them Sexton boys was crossin the pasture the other mornin and here that bull darted out'n the bushes atter 'em and they all took to the trees but Jim and the bull got him on one of his horns in the seat of the pants while he was upon the side of the tree. It got him off and started to pin him to the ground under his horns and that Shan Powderjay nailed him by the horns and put his toes in his nostrils till Jim got up and West got down out of the tree and got a club. Then Shan jumps loose and grabs the club quick as a cat and piles the bull up in a heap. He's layin over there dead. Bill's goin to sell him for beef soon as he skins him this mornin. Lord but that's a game boy."

Shan sits by the fire on frosty nights now. He sees the blue flames leap from the fore stick–leap up the big-throated chimney and go into nothingness. And he says: "That is madness. It is nothingness. I hate to get mad and have to fight, but I can when I have to. And I fight like the very Devil when I have to fight. No use to go into it slipshod or any old way to get it over with–but go in to win it fair and square. If it's fire a body is fightin, fight it with fire."

Shan hears his father say before the fire when he is studying his geography lesson: "Pap said that war was somethin awful. He said they was a band of Democrats that heard about a Republican up in Winsor County and they started to get him one mornin. But this fellow was hidin out in the brush. And he had a muzzle-loadin rifle with him. He saw them come up to his house and ask his wife where he was. And she said he was gone and she didn't know where he was at and when he'd come in. Then they took all the meal in the house and broke the barrel up into staves and throwed them out the winder.

They cut up the feather bedtick and the white feathers just flew in the air. They throwed water buckets and chears out'n the house. They's about ten of 'em and when they got ready to leave they took the man's wife. A rifle cracked on the hill and the man that had tied her wrists with a piece of rope and was leadin her off against her will, he fell dead as a mackerel with a bullet in his brain. This man was their leader. The rest broke out in a run for the brush. The man come in off the hill, untied his wife. They hauled the dead man down by Little Sandy and buried him in the sand. In about a week a woman come there with a old bony horse hitched to a sled. She was ridin the horse and reinin him with the bridle reins. 'Did you kill my man?' she said. 'I killed a man, but I don't know whose man he was and care a damn sight less,' the man of the house said. 'He was tryin to take my wife. He had her tied with a rope by the wrists.' 'Well where is he now?' 'He's been in Hell for four days now. You'll find him buried down there in the sand with his feet a-stickin out.' The woman took the old horse and the sled and went down to the sand bank, dug him out and put him on the sled. He was stiff as a board and bobbed up and down on the sled like a pole o' wood. He had sand in his hair and eyes–was a sight to look at, but she said, 'He's my man and I want his remains.' So she got his remains and took 'em back to old Virginia with her."

And Fronnie says: "I remember bands of Republicans that used to come to Woodberry County and take the place. They was whole droves of 'em. And they wasn't anythin the people could do about it. They stole horses and killed and plundered the houses and took the cattle and et 'em. They captured Rebel Harry Meadows and told him if he'd climb to such and such limb on such certain tree that they would turn him loose. Well, he'd climb the sycamore tree up to that limb. Then they told him to go a little higher. He went a little higher. Then they said a little higher yet. Well, he went up just as high as he could get till the top went to saggin with him and then one up and shoots him out and says, 'Another ring-tailed coon hits the ground.'

"They left him there and his dog tracked him up and would

go back to the house and howl. And the dog led his people to where they had left him shot out of the tree. The dog had dug a big enough hole to bury him in. They hauled him out of the woods on a sled and buried him in that thicket on Wellman's pint. I remember the grave when I's a girl. I passed there a many a time. I remember seein a ground hog hole down into the grave and seein a lot o' bones work up out of the ground. One time two boys was goin to dig into the grave and see if he had any money buried with him. One of the awfulest rains fell that night that ever did fall in Woodberry County. It was just a token to leave the dead alone and let them sleep, Pap said. Well, they's a old man by the name of Rebel Bill Withe who said he'd clear the hills of the damned Yankees. So he hid in the brush and got 'em one at a time till he thinned their ranks. And one of Rebel Bill's men spied on him and told the Yanks his hidin place. So a Yank come one night when old Rebel Bill was in the bed under the kivers. He said, 'You old son-of-a-bitch I got you now.' And he shot old Bill in bed—walked back down the stairs. He didn't get old Bill. He missed him. And Bill crawled out'n the bed soon as the man got downstairs and Bill shot him. Killed him. I can show you his grave too. No stone there, but a wild cherry grows up through it. Well, no one never got old Bill. He died a natural death, but he died in much misery over killin so many Yanks. On his deathbed he would say: 'I see him in blue. Take him away. They've come atter me. I'm not goin.' And that is the way old Rebel Bill died. I wouldn't a been in his socks for his shoes."

"I am a Republican just the same, Mom," says Shan. "I am goin to whip old Jim Sexton sure as my name is Shan Powderjay. I'm goin to lay the cat on him soon as the next trouble starts. My mind is made up. This is the last year we'll be in school together. I'm goin to whop him before I leave that school. I'm goin to turn right around then and whop John Landon. He ain't done me nigh right. He's upheld Jim in every move he has made and thought it was funny to call me a stinkin Republican. I'm goin to whop 'em if it's the last thing I ever do. That's one reason I kept that bull from killin Jim. I am savin him to whop myself. I am a Republican and I don't care if God Almighty and the Devil knows it."

"Well, I got a lot of little tads in school. But I'll soon have one out. Shan finishes in January and I aim to send him to a bigger school summers if I can get the money. He's made the best grades in his class."

"Yes, but Mr. Powderjay, I heard that boy was a wildcat on wheels. I heard he'd fight like a wildcat–just claw and scratch and bite."

"No, Mr. Thombs. They pick on him all the time and they've made him that way. He won't start a fight until they call him a stinkin Republican. Then the fight allus starts. It's caused me a awful lot of trouble to be a Republican here in these parts, but like my own son I have stuck to the faith of my father."

"Did you know that Shan Powderjay said he was goin to whip Mr. Landon and Jim Sexton tomorrow, the last day of school? He said he was pintly goin to do it. Jim says he'll close his eyes closer than he did that time before. You remember way back yander when Shan was out of school so long. Jim Sexton closed his eyes then. That was the time old Mick and Fronnie Powderjay come out to school and they whopped all them boys. Lord, that Shan's tough. Can't make him cry. He's whopped all the boys over at Seagrave's watermill playin lap-jack. W'y they can cut the blood out of him with a long switch and they can't make him holler. He's whopped all that's ever fit him."

"And John Long, you must remember that he killed that bull of Bill Radnor's too. He's not so big but he's nervy. He might whop Mr. Landon."

"No, Landon is too much for a boy. He'll eat him up alive."

"Did you hear what happened today at the last day of school? The trouble all popped out soon as Shan Powderjay got his grades. He got the ribbon o' bein the best scholar in school and his poke of candy for treat. Then he got up and said, 'They's one thing I want to tell this school. First: I am a Republican. Now anyone who wants to call me a stinkin Re-publican just step out.' Jim Sexton stepped out with a great big grin on his face. Mr. Landon says, 'Here boys, we don't want no trouble.' But they went right into it. Shan throwed him on the ground and that big tooth of Jim's that pushes out from the rest in front cut plum through his lip. Shan beat him in the face and then he kicked him in the ribs. Mr. Landon run in and said, 'Stop that, Shan, right now.' And Shan says, 'You want some of the same medicine. I can give it to you.' And Mr. Landon struck at Shan and Shan ducked. Then he come back and hit Mr. Landon in the face and on the nose and the blood just squirted. The children started runnin home screamin. I stayed and watched the fight. He got Mr. Landon by the ear with his teeth and one of his fingers in his mouth too and told him he'd bite both ear and finger off if Mr. Landon didn't say he was a Republican and he made him say it. Then he let him up and Mr. Landon was a-bleedin all over. I was skeered to death. But atter Shan whopped 'em he got his books and says good-by to Hickory Grove forever. He jumped the rail fence and took out through Radnor's pasture for home."

"I ain't got nothin to say if he whops 'em all. I ruther make a old person mad as a child. It grows on a child. He never forgets. A old person does forget. They used to make Shan's life a misery for him. Now he can take his part."

Shan is sitting before the fire. He is reading. Fronnie is churning milk for supper. She says, "Son, what made you whop Mr. Landon?"

"He ought to a stopped them fights long ago. He didn't do it. Because he was a Democrat he let his feelins run for that side—the majority. I allus said I'd get even with that crowd. I feel all right tonight. I ain't got nothin against none o' em. I don't ever intend to fight one of them again. I've whopped all that old crowd now. They are my friends. I'm a Republican and they are Democrats. We don't mind. I'll be a Republican if they's not but one vote ever cast in this Deestrict."

"Boy o' yours, Mick Powderjay, must have some Democrat blood in him the way he's been fightin around here. All I got to say is I have never voted for a Republican in my life, but if that boy ever runs I'm for him for dog catcher."

"He's got the Democrat blood in him all right. He gets it

from his Ma, but he's a Republican like his Pa. He takes that fightin atter his Pa's people. Pap was allus into it, you know. He was captured twice by the Rebels. They liked Pa so well they wouldn't kill him. He was hung by the Yanks, the fellars he's a-fightin for. But he got out'n it some way and come back to these parts a-fightin the Gorillars. He killed 'em like you'd shoot a squirrel. They's the fellars you know, that plundered the country and killed men, women and children and wouldn't take no side in the War. Shan's like Pap."

"Well if he ever runs for anything let me know. I'm a full-blooded Democrat, but he's one Republican I'll vote for. I ain't voted for one yet. You can't fool me. It's the good Democrat blood in him."

"You are right, Vim Westbrook. He takes it all atter me, his Ma," says Fronnie and she laughs.

"Well, if he's to ever run for anythin and get the worst lickin in the world he'd take it for he's used to enough lickins. That's about all he's ever got all his life. A ground hog come nigh as a pea tearing his guts out and he never whimpered. Some crazy boys put him in the pen with one because he wouldn't turn over and say he's a Democrat. It backed up in the corner and growled at him and he lit on it and choked it to death. It cut the whole front of his shirt out and he told his Ma and me that he got it tore up in the head o' the holler on a swing."

"And he whopped the school teacher and a ground hog. Well, I'll be dogged. I'll give him my first Republican vote if he runs for Dog Catcher of this County and you tell him I said, "I's a stinkin Democrat."

THE SENATOR IS DEAD

“THE Senator is dead,” said Mae Marberry. “Senator Foulfoot has kicked the bucket. He has gone to the great beyond.” She drove her needle in and out of the crazy-quilt top and it clicked tin-tin each time on the battered thimble.

“Senator Foulfoot was a good man to the poor people too,” said Dave Marberry as he spit in the fire and it sizzled in the yellow flame. “Oh, they was a few things against the Senator. No man could trust him around where the women folks was. He was a bad ’n that way. He’s got children planted all over the County. His seed will never die. There will be more smart children springin from these hills than there ever was before.”

The wind whipped down among the February dead grasses that stood back of the smoke house with a lonesome sound. The clapboards flapped on the roof. The smoke-house door creaked on the rusty hinges. The glass jars slithered on the paling-ends. The dry dead grass caught between the slats of palings sighed in the wind.

“This is a bad night to have a settin-up with the Senator. It is such a lonesome time out. We ought to go over and show our last respects to the dead. I never did vote for the Senator because he was not on my ticket. He was a good man. I believe in payin last respects to the dead. Get your shawl and coat, Mae. Drop that needle. Let’s go over the hill to the settin-up. Martha will be glad to have us in a time like this even if we didn’t vote for her man. She knows we are not on that ticket.”

The moon is a yellow ribbon cut short. The stars are blotches of white silver in the sky. There is a handful of dishrag clouds that whips down among the spicewood twigs. The rabbits play in the moonlight. There are many rocks and roots in the cow path that leads to where the Senator lies now a corpse.

“What killed Senator Foulfoot, Dave, do you know?”

“I don’t exactly know, but I have heard.”

“What was it?”

"I heard it was his belly got too big."

"He got awful big before he died, all right."

"How much did he weigh?"

"Three-hundred and forty pounds."

"You remember when he got up and made that talk back in 1930, don't you, down at Hangtown? He told the people that they would have to use a corn knife and cut these Government expenses to the bone. Somebody in the crowd that didn't vote his ticket said: 'Couldn't cut you to the bone, Senator, with a corn knife. It wouldn't reach one of your bones for the fat.' And the Senator's big jowls just flopped when he laughed and he went right on talkin. Didn't stop for nary thing the people said to him."

"And his belly got him at last."

"Yes!"

"It was his own fault. It was the way he et."

"Yes."

"W'y I've heard about him stoppin at a restaurant and orderin up a beef stew. The waiter knew it was the Senator. He stacked his dish up high with big white potatoes and chunks of beef–and the gravy would just be floatin the potatoes. He'd eat that stew. 'Anything else?' the waiter would say. 'Yes,' the Senator would say, 'duplicate that order please.' He would hold up two fingers and the waiter would know what he meant. He'd eat that. The waiter would say, 'Anything more Senator?' The Senator would say, "Triplicate that order, please." He would hold up three fingers and the waiter would know what he meant. Then on top of that he would eat a whole pie, drink a couple of bottles of pop and a quart of buttermilk."

"No wonder the Senator is dead. He et too much for his own good. He was a good man. He got that road from Hampton to Jericho or we wouldn't a had a road that we could have rid a horse over. He got that schoolhouse upon Plum Branch. We wouldn't had a house to had a school in if it hadn't been for the Senator."

"I believe in payin last respects to the Senator even if we are out of place. We don't belong to his ticket. We'll be there after a while anyway and we will see how Martha and the Senator's children treat us."

"The Senator loved children, didn't he?"

"Yes, the Senator loved children. He kissed enough of them when he was runnin for office. He come to Tackett's once when a bunch of women was up there with their little dirty-nosed brats and the Senator kissed all them dirty-mouthed dirty-nosed children and give them a nickel apiece and told them he'd get them a school. And they took to the store with the nickels. The Senator got all the women votes there but mine, for they belonged to his ticket. They liked the Senator. They said they'd heard little things on him but he was a good man. He got Curt Hix's boy out of the pen for cuttin the Jones boy with intent to kill. He was sent for twenty years, but the Senator pulled the right ropes and got him out. Curt is a free boy today."

Here is where the Senator lives. See. The house is white. It is a big house at the foot of the mountain. It is weather-boarded. Here is the well in the front ward. Here hangs the bucket on the well sweep. It is blown by the wind. The pole suspended to the sweep swings like the pendulum of a clock and hits the limbs of a tan-barked peach tree at the well. This is the home of Senator Foulfoot.

"Howdy-do, Dave. Howdy-do, Mae. Come right in by the fire and take off your wraps. Get you some chears up closer to the fire."

"No thank you, Martha. We ain't a bit cold."

"That February wind blows pretty cold and mighty lonesome here tonight. It's awful lonesome the way old Shep howls tonight by the winder and the corpse in the back room. Mighty glad you come, Mae—you and Dave. Ain't a soul come in yet. Just me and the children here and the Senator's corpse is in the back room."

"Where is Thad and Dawson—Jack, Seymore, Bill and Lum —ain't they got here yet? They was always good friends to the Senator, wasn't they?"

"They appeared to be. They were good friends to the Senator when he was alive makin speeches and gettin things done.

Now he is dead. They are not here. No. They have not come."

"They voted his ticket too."

"Yes."

"And they don't come!"

"No."

"Well I didn't vote his ticket. I'll come and pay my last respects to the dead. I never did vote the Senator's ticket. I never will unless I do it in the grave when I don't know anythin about it. I don't have a child that will ever vote his ticket either. If one of my children does and I'm in the grave, I'll turn over in my coffin with my face down. I don't believe in the Senator's ticket. I forget that tonight. I am here to pay my last respects to the dead. We don't live forever and just to think I'll be right down there in the same graveyard with the Senator. I'll not be far from him and when Resurrection mornin comes, I'll be one of the first to shake his hand. Not in Heaven will I vote his ticket if he hasn't changed it by then."

"Shep! Shep! You get away from that winder. I can't stand to hear you howl like that. Funny a dog understands when his master is dead. Shep knows the Senator is dead."

"Has anybody offered to lay the Senator out?"

"No."

"Get me a razor, soap, mug and hot water. I'll shave the Senator and lay him out in his coffin if you women will help me do the liftin."

"We'll do our best."

"No. It is not right for you to have to help, Martha. It is not right for you to help lay out your dead husband. Not the kin shall put away the dead. But the dead's friends shall bury the dead. We'll get him ready and put him away. Somethin might happen to you if you have a thing to do with it. You stay out of this. Let Mae and me do the whole works."

"Give that dog some milk to lick from the cat's pan. Stop his barkin. His barks are more lonesome than the howlin of the wind tonight. Just everything seems to say: 'The Senator is dead! The Senator is dead.' I can hear it in the wind tonight. I can hear them words among the fruit jars on the palings. I can hear them in the dead grass in the yard and in the peach-tree limbs by the well box. I can hear: 'The Senator is dead. The Senator is dead!' Oh my God! Have mercy on me! What am I to do? The Senator is dead! And his friends don't come! The Senator is dead. They don't come. Men from his ticket don't think enough of him to come! A man from another ticket has come to lay him out. The Senator is dead and his friends don't come after all he has done for them! Got 'em out of the pen. Got 'em all the roads they've got. Got 'em a schoolhouse. Give 'em money and broke his own self and his family up. They don't come when he lays a corpse and help lay him out for burial."

"Be steady, Martha, and brace yourself up. Get me the hot water, the mug, soap and razor. I am ready to begin. Light the lamp. Turn the wick up so there'll be plenty of light and I can see in that room. I don't want to shave the Senator in a dark room."

The razor is not sharp, but it will do by stropping it on his pants' leg. The Senator's beard is a reddish saw-briar color. It is tough as blackberry vines for a razor to cut. Martha brings the hot water in a wash pan, the shaving brush, the mug and razor that the Senator always used. "Here they are," she said.

The dim lamp throws a yellow light on the Senator's white-clay cheek. There he lies in the bed with a sheet spread over him. He looks like a pile of white dirt that is big in the middle and tapers at both ends. There lies the Senator—with his face sandy with reddish beard.

Dave said: "Martha, you go out of the room. You are not supposed to lay out your own dead. Somethin might happen to you. I'll take care of the Senator."

Martha walks out of the house—out into the wind—out into the moonlight.

"Shep—Shep—Shep—you stop that barkin," she said. "I can't stand it. That barkin is lonesome as the wind."

Dead fat flesh is wobbly like flour dough and hard to shave. The lather is hot, for the water was just poured from the tea-kettle. The lather softens the beard as rain softens the willows in the spring. White lather on the face of a dead fat man in the yellow lamplighted room. The black sheets of night without with a little yellow moon lodged up in the sky. The night is lonesome and the wind whips lonely through the garden palings. The Senator is dead. Senator Foulfoot is dead.

"It makes me have cold chills to run up and down my spine to think Dave has to come in and lay the Senator out," said Martha. "He got them roads. He got them schoolhouses. He got them out of the pen. He kissed their dirty-nosed babies. They forsake him in death. Dave has to come in and lay him out. Man of another ticket has to come in and lay out the Senator."

"Take it easy, Martha," said Mae, "take it easy. Death has come and there is not anything a body can do about Death. Death comes to men like the Senator as it comes to men like my man Dave."

"But the night and the way old Shep barks–It makes me lonely here. I cannot stand to ever eat from this table again. I can't stand to draw water from that well or carry meat through that smoke-house door. The Senator sleepin up there on that hill. W'y I'm afraid I'll meet his speret out here on some dark night. I just can't stand to stay here. I'll go stay with my married children is what I'll do. I'll have to break up housekeepin. I can't even stand to see that wash kettle out there in the front yard. Just to think about the way the Senator used to come up there when I was makin lye soap from wood ashes. He'd come there and stand and watch me and tell me about his race–how he was makin big talks and gettin on with the people. He'd say: 'Now Martha, you watch that lye soap and don't let it get on your hands too long. It will eat your hands up. It will make them rough as a gritter.' And I can see him walkin out to the wash kettle right now. I just can't stand to ever look at that kettle again."

"The Senator is dressed, Martha. He made one of the prettiest corpse a body ever looked at. I put his speech-makin suit on him. He looks as natural as anybody I ever saw. He looks like he is standin up ready to say, 'Now Ladies and Gentlemen, if you want good roads vote for me.' That is just the way he looks. His lips are curved like he was sayin them very words. I never put him in the coffin. I left him under the sheet. He is big as a skinned ox to lift—too much for me and you women folks to tug our daylights out tryin to lift. Besides, you should never help bury your own dead."

"Now Martha, me and Dave are goin to have to leave you, for we left the children at home by themselves and we are afraid of fire you know. We got burnt out once this way. We don't want to get burnt out again. If there is anythin more we can help you do, let us know. We don't vote your ticket, but we're glad to help you in a time of distress."

From the weather-boarded house—out past the well box and the peach-tree limbs whistling in the night wind, Mae and Dave walk toward home. Dave sings:

"When you get married
And live over the hill,
Send me a kiss
By the whippoorwill."

The wind howls loudly and lonesome through the brush. This is the mountain toe-path Mae and Dave walked across. It is steep. There are rocks in it. There are stumps and roots. The moon is getting low and red. It rides low over the dark hills. The moon is like a copper penny set in a bowl lined with dirty dish rags.

"And the Senator is dead," said Dave, "come to the ground at last. I had the awfulest time layin that man out. His beard was hard to cut. He was dirty to wash even if he was a Senator. It was like puttin clothes on a barrel tryin to put that silk suit on the Senator. I rolled and tusseled and finally made it while you was out talkin to Martha. It was a job, I'm tellin you. The Senator is like a piece of lead to lift. I rolled him into his clothes. I know it was his belly that killed him. It is big as a small doodle of cane hay."

At the top of the mountain the lonesome February wind blows through the dead grasses in the graveyard and through the bare branches of the wild-cherry trees. One can see the white headstones gleam in the moon-lighted night. One can see white pieces of paper caught onto the graveyard saw-briars and holding there.

"It is here where they'll haul the Senator tomorrow," said Mae.

"Yes, Mae, it is here," said Dave.

"And this is such a lonesome place here. I wouldn't be buried here at all if it wasn't for my mother and my grandmother being buried here. Your Pap and Ma are buried here too. You and me will be buried here someday. Just think way up here in this lonesome place. We'll not be buried very far away from the Senator, will we?"

"No. I have just said that I'll greet the Senator on Resurrection morn. I'll tell him there that I won't vote his ticket if he's still runnin for Senator on the same ticket. I'll just be glad to talk things over with the Senator."

"Do you think the Senator will be in Heaven?"

"I haven't thought about it."

"I have thought about it, but I haven't said what I thought."

"The Senator was a good man."

"Yes."

"I never heard of him wrongin anybody."

"No."

"The Senator done a whole lot for these people."

"Yes."

"I hate to pass a graveyard at night. Let's hurry up and get past this graveyard. Listen to that fodder blade rattlin in the wind. See it hangin to that greenbrier! Look at them tombstones. See how they gleam in the moonlight. It will be lonesome for Senator Foulfoot upon this mountain top. They'll haul him here day after tomorrow with that big span of black horses they use for to take places the hearse can't go."

"Yes."

"I felt so sorry for Martha there by herself and the way that Shepherd dog howled and the way the wind blowed. It was enough to make anybody cry. And just to think, none of the Senator's friends come in to lay him out. That beat anythin I ever heard tell of."

"And Martha the way she talked about the Senator comin out to the wash kettle when she was makin lye soap. She said she never could get over that. Said she could never stand to see that wash kettle out by the wood yard again."

The path is rough going down the mountain. The moon hangs low. The wind whips through the saw-briars and the mountain-tea stems. The dog barks at the house below. It is old Lead barking. The house is empty and silent as a black autumn leaf weighted by rain to the wet earth. The night is black as a new leather shoe.

"The Senator is dead," said Mae, "and it is a good thing that daisies won't tell."

WALTER COBB'S wife invited us to the party. Walter's wife kindly runs Walter and the business though Walter is a prize fighter with a big mouth and two white rows of sound teeth. Never one knocked down his throat in the one hundred and sixty-seven fights Walter fought, one hundred and three wins, eight knockouts, seven draws and fifty-three fights lost. Walter would always hit his chest and say, "Not bad for a scrub fighter, is it?"

Walter's wife, Hessie, is an oo-bitsy little woman with a keen eye and commandin tongue. She has small white hands, but they are more powerful than Walter's big fightin hands. She runs the Walk Right Inn for Walter and the "herb stand" attached where men come and get herbs for stiff legs, for family sicknesses, for liver ailment and for snake-bites. I always kindly liked Hessie. But, God, I knew about her tongue and her temper. I've seen her jump a-straddle of Walter's back and claw him like a wildcat when he smiled at another woman. I used to think my wife Lona was bad enough, but I thanked God for the good woman I had when I saw the way Walter's woman acted. I was right proud of Lona because she didn't always try to find out my business. That's the kind of a woman a man likes these days.

Lona got ready for the party. Gentlemen, if I do have to say it I got the best-lookin woman in the Hollow. When my woman goes into the church house the old men rise from their roosts and look at her as she goes past. That's just the way I want them to feel about my woman. I want the prettiest woman in the country for my wife and I got the prettiest woman for my wife. Lona is a tall woman with light hair and eyes blue as clear winter water in the mountains. She has a smile prettier than any hound dog's bark that ever run a fox to the rocks. She's not all the time fussin around either. She laughs and laughs and I do too. We get along.

My wife looked like one of God's angels in Heaven the night last week we went to the party at Walter's. Funny thing

Walter didn't know anythin about the party. It was Walter's birthday and Hessie wanted to surprise him. She said the first eight years of his life when he was married to that pretty big red-faced Wessie Tremble that she never did have a party for him. Hessie hates Wessie and Wessie hates Hessie. They both love the same man. Wessie didn't like it because Walter used to smile at other women when he won a fight. So she used woman's ways against Walter and he took to other women for spite. She sued Walter and got a divorce. She always liked him after she sued him and separated from him. She liked his fine body and his pretty mouth lined with two pearl rows of teeth —she liked the skill of his big hands that keep them from goin down his throat in one hundred and sixty-seven fights. She married a big fat sheep butcher with five boys and she left her own with her mother and went to live with the sheep butcher and his five sons. But she liked Walter. She didn't like to hear about him throwin a party.

Lona and me went across the hill to Walter's. I had to go in front and part the briars so Lona wouldn't tear her stockins. I had to hold the barb wires apart so she wouldn't get her coat hung on a jagger. The moon showed all of the road except where we walked under the big oak trees on Furman Ridge. We hurried to the party. Lona is a tall woman and she can walk right along beside of me. God in heaven knows if there's anythin in the world I like to see in a woman besides bein pretty and that is to see one move. Lona can move. I'm in love with my wife if ever a man in this world is in love with his wife. I wouldn't take a million in spot cash for her. Walkin to a party in the moonlight with her, talkin to her, lovin her, settin before the fire stringin beans with her, slicin apples, talkin about the crops for next year and the farm and the timber—goin to a party with her. I kindly feel sorry for a good fellow like Walter to have all the trouble he has had with his wives. Both of them fight him like mad wimmen. I just couldn't stand wimmen like them.

We knocked on the door. "I'm glad we are here," said Lona, "long ways across that hill. Come here and the house is dark. I don't believe there's a party here." Lona knocked again. Then I pounded the door with my fist. The door opened. Hessie come to the door. She said, "Shhhhhh–shhhhhhhh–shhhhhhh–be quiet. This is a surprise party for Walter. We don't want him to know anybody is here." And she whispered deep in Lona's ear: "I want to throw the poor boy a party. He ain't had one in a lifetime livin with that other woman. I want to show him who loves him and who don't."

We slipped in in the dark. We could see people all around. We couldn't tell who they was and what trash had slipped to the party God only knowed. We could smell the tobacco smoke. I could smell burley leaf and taste-bud. I could smell the good old moon herb medicine that was made right below home. I know the brand old Jake Heaber makes. I know it like I know my feet and hands. I've drunk enough of it for my rheumetis to know. Hessie led us to a couple of chairs. We set down in the dark. Lord, that few minutes of waitin for the lights to come on. I hate the dark. I love the light. I thought what if Hell would be dark as this room and have people in it like was in this room. It would be enough of the Devil to just make us set and not roast us in a fire after we'd gone through with what we had on this earth. It's a funny thing to think at a party, but I thought it. The Devil could a grabbed my wife right there in the dark and I wouldn't a knowed a thing about it. Lord, it is a funny feelin waitin for the lights to come on.

"Walter is over in the 'herb room'," said Hessie, "I've kept him over there to keep him from seein who is here. I'll call him in here and light the lamp now. All the crowd is in. All this crowd will scare him to death. Just wait a minute. You people be quiet as you can be." Hessie went out of the room. She went to the herb room where Walter was sellin the boys herbs for snake-bites and stone bruises and the like.

We heard Walter's big tongue just a-goin and goin when he come out of the herb room. He was callin Hessie "Honey" and "Sugar-lump" and a lot of pet names just like there wasn't nobody in a mile of the place. Suddenly Hessie struck a match and popped the fire onto the lamp wick and a big yellow light flooded the room like moonlight. Here we set, a whole room full. It was like turnin the lights on in Hell to see who your next-door neighbor is. Walter turned white as a sheep. I never saw a body plagued so. And the party started. We all riz to our feet and started talkin. This was Walter's thirty-third birthday.

"Just the same age of the Lord when He was crucified," said Bill Higgins.

"Yes, but don't compare my age like that," said Walter, "I ain't done nothin in my life but fight and sell herbs. I sold them in the dry days. I'm still sellin herbs in the wet days. You know so many of our people get snake bit. So many have the rheumetis. We just got to have our herbs, boys. You know that."

Well, around and around the crowd swirled. Who do you think was in that crowd? Wessie and her fat husband, the sheep butcher. He was big and soft through the stomach as a barrel filled with goose feathers. Wessie had him by the hand. She looked from her apple-red cheeks with eyes blue as the sky. She kindly grinned when she looked at Hessie. I thought trouble was a-brewin for the night. I saw old Egg Hensley in one corner. He just couldn't keep his eyes off my wife Lona. I knowed him. I knowed there was goin to be trouble sure enough if we got too many herbs under our belts. It just takes women and herbs to start a war.

"Come and see your birthday presents," said Fennie Parsons. "Look at this pile of presents." Fennie stood there under lamplight grinnin. Maybe Walter hadn't had a party in his lifetime. He didn't know that he was to get presents on a birthday party. Walter come runnin over to the pile of presents. Every woman in the Hollow had bought Walter somethin and most all the men. It would a took a two-bushel coffee-sack to have held all the socks he got; a meal poke to have held the neckties; boxes of candy, shirts, plow handles, a hat, a suit of clothes (Wessie got them), herbs in padded boxes, cuff buttons, collar buttons, brass rings, pocketbooks, hair tonic, a razor, shavin mugs, a Smith and Wesson (an old one), and a bushel of turnips brought by old Seymore Smith Walter had let have herbs on credit a many a time.

Seymore didn't have money to buy presents. He had plenty of turnips and corn and potatoes.

"My God," said Walter, "I didn't know I did have this many friends after I shot Big-Man Howard. I thought I'd ruint myself."

"That's where you made yourself," said Seymore, "by shootin him. Decent women and respectable men was afraid of him. He was dangerous as a cocked gun. The Governor of this State ought to give you a medal. That's the best piece of work done in this County since Van Thompson shot them two chicken thieves right in his chicken roost a-usin the hot board. You got friends. Mark me down for that."

"Hurrah," the crowd shouted.

"Walter, we are all for you," said Ham Smith.

"Have a good time, my friends—every God-blessed one of you. Make yourself at home. Tear the old Walk Right Inn down if you want to. It's mine and paid for."

Wessie and her fat husband, Sheep Butcher Don, milled with the crowd. She had him by the hand lookin at Walter. He didn't like it. A cloud was on his dark face. His pole-cat black eyes were beamin hard as cold cat eyes in the winter dark. Egg kept lookin at Lona. He looked at her like a man does when he loves a woman. I liked for men to notice my wife, but not like Egg. I could tell. A man can just read sometimes what is in another man's mind.

"Come on in the back room, boys," said Walter. "Let's start the dance."

We went in the back room. Candles were fastened on the wall. A lantern was in where a strip of wind blowed out the candle fast as they lit it. Wildcat Bill Henderson and Jimmy Pratt and the rest of the boys were in the corner with their fiddles, banjers and guitars. "Let 'er go, Wildcat," said Walter. "Give us the works. We're a-rarin to go for a good old shindig."

Wildcat started the lead on the fiddle. The boys followed. Jimmy Pratt called.

"All together and promenade."

And we started the dance. Egg danced with Sarah Stone.

But when he come to Lona you ought to a seen him squeeze her and swing her. I could tell. He wanted my wife. He just looked like he wanted her. Sheep Butcher Don, Wessie's man, was too fat to dance. He set down on a split-bottom chair and went right on through it watchin the dance. Wessie wanted Walter. She danced with Dave Stone. When she promenaded to Walter you ought to have watched her swing Walter instead of him swingin her. I could see little Hessie's blue eyes twinkle. I know just exactly how she felt. I know how I felt. The dance went on. The dust come up from the floor and down from the ceilin.

Boys, did we dance! Around and around and the sweat dripped from the ends of our chins and the tips of our noses. The fiddle screamed. Blue Winters come in and said: "Say, Walter, the Law is snoopin on the outside. Reckon it is a raid."

"Raid hell," said Walter, "we got enough here to clean the Law tonight and they know it. They ain't comin in here. They can stay on the outside. That is fine. That is where they belong. On with the dance. On with the dance."

"Bring on the Law," said Egg, "bring the Law in here. I can take care of some of the Law." I did wish the Law would come in and get Egg. He's drunk so much licker he looks like a bottle of rot-gut. I can just see a bottle of rot-gut spelled right on his face. Them thin blue lips that just twist this way and that like a blackbriar in a winter wind. That mean glance his eye's got when he looks at a person. That little jerk he's got in his walk. The old sot. I don't see why he come to Walter's party. To tear it up, of course, before the night is over. He tears up every party we have. He comes and gets tight and then tighter and then tightest. Then the fur flies.

I knowed the bones in my fingers were not good or I'd a cracked him one when he wouldn't turn Lona loose. The bones in my fingers are brittle. When I pop a man without gloves on my hand my jints fly out of place. I broke my little finger once in two places hittin a fellow at a foot washin. If I hadn't hit him a deadner he'd a come back and whopped me in spite of all creation. I didn't have no gloves and God knows fingers out of place at the jints is something a man hates to suffer. It's awful to have brittle bones. God knows it is. It's hard to see somebody with your wife at a dance and won't turn her loose.

"Time out," said Walter, "after this set. Time out for the drinks. So step lively, ladies. Step on that fiddle, Wildcat, and give us 'Birdie.' We want mad music. We want to dance. Let 'er go."

I could see Wessie swingin Walter. I could see Hessie's blue eyes twinkle. I knowed she didn't like it. What could she do? Wessie weighin two hundred pounds and not a pound of it fat. It was her second man settin over in the corner on the floor that was fat. Not a chair in the house would hold him. No wonder he was a sheep butcher. About all he could do was kill sheep. They wouldn't resist much. They wouldn't fight back. I don't like a sheep butcher. Damned if I do. I like to see sheep on the hillsides eating green grass. If there's anything innocent in this world it is a sheep. I didn't like old Don. I thought of the poor sheep he'd killed. The big ugly Devil, why didn't he fight somethin like old Egg or say somethin to his wife for swingin Walter, her first man, the way she did? No. He wobbled around on the floor like a fat goose and let Hessie suffer. What did he come uninvited for? He was there because his wife fetched him. What was she doin there to tear up the party! She wanted Walter. Egg wanted Lona. I determined to make him leave her alone if my knuckles stayed in place. I would just get one lick on him and I wanted to make it a good one.

"Come let's have the drinks," said Walter.

We followed Walter into the "herb room." He had herbs of all kinds and descriptions. The walls were built up all the way around with shelves. The shelves were filled with herbs. I never saw so many in one place. There was enough good herbs in this room to float a cross-tie five miles.

"You are my friends. You are my guests. Now drink the kind of herbs you want. Drink and be merry. You know anythin might happen tomorrow. We live and dance tonight. Now drink, my friends! Drink!"

They can say all they want to about these Government herbs. But they ain't got the strength some of these home-made herbs is got. I took home-made herbs. Walter keeps both. The neighbors say home-made herbs is a lot better for men when they see snakes. I don't know. I ain't seen no snakes yet. I've been sorty brought up on home-made herbs and I hate to go against them much as I love the Government herbs. So I said: "Walter, if you don't mind I'll take home-made herbs made right here in the Hollow. I want to know what I am drinkin." Walter just forked me out a pint. I stood right there and killed it except the little snip I give Lona. I wanted courage in my bad fingers. I don't want a wife that gets stewed, but I want one to take a little snip with me. I hate to take somethin I don't want my wife to take. I saw old Egg gettin Government herbs. Lord, how he was loadin up on them. I knowed it would be between home-made herbs and Government herbs if Egg kept on and I kept on. I saw Walter takin on the home-made herbs and Don was funnelin down the Government herbs. That's one thing Don can do besides kill little innocent sheep. He can funnel Government herbs. Well, we stood around in the herb room till the sweat kindly left our faces. Wessie said, "Let's play games like we used to play, Walter."

"You are my guest," said Walter, "and what my guests want I want. If you want to play games, that suits me. Let's all go into the front room and start a game. What do you all say about it?"

"Suits me fine," said Egg.

"Suits me too," said Possum Radberry, "I'd ruther play them old-time games as to eat chicken when I'm hungry."

Walter walked in front as we left the herb room. There was a long line of us walkin in single file through the door from the herb room, through the little hall where the heatin stove was and into the front room where the fireplace was. Shirten McMahon built a fire in the fireplace while Walter and me put chairs in the room enough to hold the crowd. Hessie didn't put a fire there before. She wanted to keep the surprise party in the dark for Walter. Now the fire crackled and a yellow light lit up the room. There was the big spewin lamp that burnt ninety-five per cent air and five per cent coal oil. Just think! Burnin up the air! Plenty of it, though.

"Let's play Button, Button, Who's Got the Button," said Eif Hix.

"Won't do nothin of the sort," said Price Groves. "I played that up to Johnson's one night and everybody got in the dark with the wrong girl huntin for a button. And there's a lot of hard feelins over that yet. We ain't goin to play that game here tonight. If we do I'll take Manda and go home. Damned if I don't. Now I'm not a contrary man. But you understand well as I do somebody will get sore and there'll be hell a-brewin around here before this night is over. We ain't goin to play no Button, Button, Who's Got the Button."

"No. Let's don't play that," said Walter. "Let's play Fine or Superfine. What do you people say? It's a good old game we all know. Of course play what satisfies the most of you. The game that satisfies the most of you satisfies me."

"That's the game that satisfies us," said Wessie. "Me and Don likes that game just fine, don't we, Don?"

"Yes we do," said Don lookin at Walter. "I'd ruther play Fine or Superfine as I would to kill a sheep. I like to play it, Honey. You know I do."

"I like it pretty well," said Egg, his thin blue lips with that drunken jerk.

"All right. We'll play Fine or Superfine then," said Walter. "Now you people give me somethin to hold that you want back most. Somethin valuable. Hand it in right now. All you men and you women."

"My bottle of herbs to you, Walter. Wouldn't take a farm in Georgia for them."

"My watch to you, Walter."

"Here's my silk-embroidered handkerchief to you, Walter. Hold it for God's sake."

"My pistol to you, Walter. Wouldn't take anything for that old trusty."

"Get me a basket, Hessie, to put all this stuff in. I can't hold it in my pockets. Hurry, Honey. Let's keep the game goin."

"All right." Hessie goes out of the room to get a basket.

"My diamond ring, Walter." Wessie hands him her diamond ring.

"My gold-rimmed specks, Walter."

"A ten-dollar bill, Walter."

"My quart of home-made herbs, Walter."

"My pocket knife, Walter, that Grandpap give me two days before he died."

"My bracelet, Walter."

"Here's my weddin ring."

"Here's my gold watch."

"Here's my green fountain pen."

"Here's my pistol. I hate to pon it to you, but I guess it's the most valuable thing I got on me. It's a owl-head."

"Here's my silk scarf."

"Here's my leather pocketbook."

"Got about all the pons now, ain't I?" said Walter as he put them in the basket.

"Got a bushel basket full," said Egg, "looks like that's enough for a long game."

"You set down here, Hessie, in this chair. I'll stand over you and pick up one of the pons out of the basket. If it belongs to a girl it will be Superfine. If it belongs to a boy it will be Fine. When I pull it from the basket I'll say to you: 'Heavy, heavy hangs over your poor head.' Then you will ask me: 'Is it Fine or Superfine?' And I'll tell you. If it belongs to a boy it is Fine and if it belongs to a girl it is Superfine. And I'll ask you what the owner must do to redeem it. You can have them to make a telephone, measure three yards of ribbon, baa like a sheep, beller like a bull, chew a yard of string, play Post Office or do anythin you want them to do."

"All right."

"Heavy, heavy hangs over your poor head," said Walter.

"Fine or Superfine?" said Hessie.

"Fine," said Walter. "What shall the owner do to redeem it?"

"Measure five yards of ribbon with Fannie Spry."

"My Lord," said Bill Higgins, "measure five yards. Looks like you ought to a put it two or three."

They caught each other's hands and faced each other. Then they swayed to the right keepin their arms spread out like a hawk wings. They kissed at right at the tip of the arm's length. Then they swayed to the left and kissed at arm's length. They swayed back and forth five times until five yards of ribbon had been measured.

"Nice way to measure ribbon," said Egg. They all laughed.

"Here is your gold watch," said Walter. "It has been redeemed."

Walter reached down into the split-bottom basket. He pulled up a silk scarf. I knowed it belong to Lona.

"Heavy, heavy hangs over your poor head."

"Fine or Superfine?"

"Superfine. What shall the owner do to redeem it?"

"She must get down on her knees and go around to all the men and bark like a hound dog. If she makes them laugh she gets to kiss them."

"All right. Who does this scarf belong to? I don't remember."

"It's mine," said my wife Lona. "The scarf is mine."

I wanted to tell her not to redeem it. I wouldn't a been a good sport. And we was all feelin our herbs anyway. I just thought let her go ahead and live and learn. I just set there and pretended like I was a-laughin with the rest of the crowd, but I was mad as a wet hen. I saw old Egg just settin there in the firelight grinnin. He had one of them drunken grins on his face—his thin blue lips stretched from ear to ear. His mouth looked like a burnt milkweed pod.

Lona barked up in Sheep Butcher Don's face first. He let out the biggest laugh you ever heard. I knowed the ugly Devil wanted to kiss Lona. Wessie didn't care a bit when Don smacked her. Well, everybody laughed when my wife Lona barked like a hound dog. I knowed it wasn't that funny. They just wanted to kiss her. When she come around to Egg he just haw-hawed like a jenny and grabbed Lona and give her the maddest kiss you ever saw. And I was mad at myself for bringin my wife to such a party. I just couldn't hold myself. Walter laughed at all the rest laughin.

"You have well redeemed your scarf," said Walter as he handed Lona her scarf.

"Heavy, heavy hangs over your poor head."

"Fine or Superfine?"

"Fine. What shall the owner do to redeem it?"

"Make a telephone with Wessie."

"Who does this watch belong to?" said Walter.

"It's mine," said toothless Jim Preston.

"My Lord," said Wessie. She walked over to the wall with Jim. He put his right arm up against the wall. He bent his left arm around in front and over his right shoulder. Wessie took his left hand with her right and bent her left arm around and put it over her right shoulder. The telephone was started.

"I'll take Walter," said Wessie. Walter walked out grinnin and showin his teeth. Don set there on the floor like a barrel of flour. I could tell Hessie felt like I had felt. Walter took her left hand with his right hand and bent his left hand around and put it over his right shoulder. He called his wife Hessie and Hessie called Egg. Egg called my wife Lona and my wife Lona called me. I called Ossie Carttree and she called Bill Higgins and Bill called Fannie Spry—right down the line until we got 'em all but Stan Walker. He was drunk as a owl and smokin a cheap cigar he'd rolled out 'n taste-bud tobacco. "Put him out of the house," said Hessie to Walter. "He's drunk and tryin to tear up the party. Nobody wants to kiss that old thing."

"You keep still," said Walter, "he's one of the best customers I got. You treat him like he was the Lord come back to earth again."

Old Sheep Butcher Don was never called. He just sat there on the floor tryin to reach over the mountain of fat and brush his shoes. Jim Preston first kissed the wall. He groaned when he did. Then he turned round and kissed Wessie. She kissed Walter. Walter kissed Hessie. Hessie kissed Egg. Egg kissed my wife and she kissed me. I kissed Ossie and she kissed Bill and Bill kissed Fannie. We went right down the line with the kisses and old Stan run up and down the line blab-blabbin about all the kissin goin on and he didn't have anybody to kiss.

Walter told him to kiss Don. He lit right on Don and started to kiss him.

"Get off me, you damn drunk," said Don, "or I'll put you off."

"You ain't big enough to put me off nor nobody off," said Stan.

We kissed back up the telephone line to the wall. Jim Preston kissed cold wall again and groaned.

"Back to your chairs now," said Walter.

I saw Egg slip back in the pantry. I could see him huntin for a bottle while Walter reached into the basket for more pons. I saw him get a bottle. It had about a dram in it. He drained it to the last drop. Then he found another bottle. He drained it. He found another bottle. He drained a couple of drams from it. He killed all there was in six bottles. He brushed his pants legs and lifted his legs high. He walked back into the house. He jerked his thin blue lips. He was drunk as a owl. I knowed trouble would soon be brewin, for Egg would start it.

"Heavy heavy hangs over your poor head," said Walter.

"Fine or Superfine?"

"Fine. What shall the owner do to redeem it?"

"Get down and baa like a sheep to all the women in this crowd."

"The owner of this pistol, please."

Don got up out of the floor. He walked over and bent beneath Hessie. He baa-ed like a sheep. She smiled. Don kissed her. Walter looked funny. Don had his first wife. Now the big ugly sheep butcher was kissin his second wife. Don baa-ed to the rest of the women around to my wife. They held serious faces. Then he come to my wife. He baa-ed and baa-ed. He tried to make her laugh. If she had laughed I intended to let my knuckles fly. I didn't intend to save them for Egg. I intended to hit him right between the eyes hard as I could hit him. He just baa-ed once to all the rest of the women until he come to mine and he baa-ed and baa-ed to get her to laugh.

"Here's your gun, Don. You can't run very well and you might need it some time," said Walter.

Don took his gun. He set back down on the floor. Walter reached down in the basket. He pulled out a bracelet.

"Heavy heavy hangs over your poor head."

"Fine or Superfine?"

"Superfine. What shall the owner do to redeem it?"

"Chaw a yard of string with you, Walter." Hessie thought the ring was her ring. She had laid it on the mantle. She thought Walter had put it in the basket. Wessie got up. Walter walked out.

"Give us a string," said Wessie. "I'll show you how to chaw that string."

"My Lord," said Hessie, "but that is my ring."

"Yes, but I put it in the basket just for tonight. Get us a string."

Egg reached Walter a sea-grass string that had tied a bottle of herb medicine Walter got for a present. "Little hard to chaw," said Egg, "but you all want to chaw it slow like the cat did when he swallowed the mattock." Then old Egg grinned and stretched his blue thin lips. Walter and Wessie started chewin the yard of string. I looked at Don. Then I looked at Hessie. I had to laugh. It was so funny. They chawed and looked each other right in the eye. I thought: "My, the things they know about each other—the dreams they have had together under the same roof and here they are chawin a yard of string together. He's got the second wife and she's got the second husband. Wonder how they feel toward each other." Then I had to laugh. They just had the pleasure of chewin a yard of string together. Then a kiss. They used to belong to each other. My Lord. How things do change among people and cattle. Love one a little while and think you can't live without that one. Fall out. Marry again and find you made a better trade or a lot worse one. The world is funny. I wouldn't want Lona chawin the string with nobody."

They must a chawed that old tough sea-grass string ten minutes. Sea-grass is tough. We tied bundled fodder with sea-grass strings. It is good to use in jug handles too. Well, when they chawed that yard of sea-grass string up they must have kissed just as long as it took them to chaw the string. Don's polecat eyes got big as black peeled walnuts. Hessie's blue eyes danced.

"Heavy heavy hangs over your poor head."

"Fine or Superfine?"

"Fine. What shall the owner do to redeem it?"

"Chaw a yard of string with Lona Hailstrap."

Lord, I knowed soon as Walter raised the bottle it was the bottle that Egg had put in as the most valuable thing he had. He'd drained all the rest of the bottles in the pantry. He was dry now. He wanted to redeem his pon. He would do it by kissin my wife. There was no other way around it. I had saved my hand for one lick. I would paste him right on the cheek bone when he kissed Lona. Well, Egg jumped up and walked out with that drunk man's jerk he's got. He grinned from ear to ear. He got a sea-grass string. I don't know but I think it was the same one Walter and Wessie chawed. They started chawin the string. They had a yard to chaw. It looked to me like five yards of string. I wasn't seein just right. He chawed and chawed and looked my wife in the eye. Before he'd chawed half the string he run in and closed my wife. He hugged her and kissed her right there. He didn't turn loose only to say: "It takes old Egg to kiss you. Old Egg can kiss." And he started to kiss her again. I don't remember. I know one of the bones in my finger shot through the skin. I done it. Egg didn't come back. He lay sprawled out on the floor. My hand was gone. I couldn't hit another lick. My right fist was no good. I fight with my left. I took upstairs. Bill Higgins was after me. I run into the jelly press. Walter was after Bill. Wessie was thumpin Hessie and Hessie was pullin her hair. I could hear Wessie screamin.

"Oh, Lord!"

"My Heavens——"

"Thump, thump, thump."

"Left right. Left right. Left right."

We must a all been a-fightin. It sounded like the top of the house was comin in.

"I'll call the Law," said Don, "if this ain't stopped right

here. We've been framed. A yard of string. A diamond ring. Hell's fire."

"My God, you've broke my hip with that bottle."

Walter knocked Bill Higgins down the steps. I come out of the press. Walter put me down in a rockin-chair. He told Jim Preston to hold my heel up to about one foot above the floor so I couldn't get up. He did. I just had to set there with my finger bone run plum through the skin tryin to get up out of my chair. I couldn't. I could hear the screams below. It was like the house was fallin in.

"My God."

"Oh Lord, I'm hit with a bottle."

Then I heard Egg. He had come to. I heard him say: "Who hit me and what did he hit me with? I was hit hard. I chawed the string, didn't I. Where is the string? Where is the yard of string? And I remember the string, but I don't know who's got it."

I tried to get up from the chair. Jim Preston held my foot up. I couldn't make it. I just couldn't get up on one foot. I saw Egg. He stood down on the stairs. He said to Don and Bill: "You boys give me the empty bottles. I want to hold the bottles. The boys held them on me at the Red Onion the other night and you see behind my ear there where one of 'em busted a bottle around my head. I lived through it. I got a hard lick. I must a been hit with a bigger bottle tonight. Now I want to make a agreement with you boys that I hold the bottles and you drink what's in 'em."

"I got my wife," I heard Walter say, "Don can take care of his own wife. He didn't have no business comin over here nohow."

I heard wood splinterin, cowbells ringin, horns a-blowin, axes choppin and angels singin. I heard the house comin in over me. Jim Preston let my foot down. I got up. He led me to the back door. He led me out in the dark. Lona took my arm. We left. We went into the dark. I remember a little bit of moon in the sky. I wouldn't a remembered it or the yard of string if it hadn't been for the soft bones in my fingers. And I could see the white bone in the little bit of moonlight.

"ARE you ready?" Mose said to me.

"Not quite," I said to Mose.

"Hurry it up then. Don't you know the bus is out there waitin on you and me? I'm out huntin you up. It's time we's on our way to Chicago."

I grabbed my hat. I said to Mose, "I got a little bit of Kentucky herbs to take along if you'll give me time to run home and get them."

"Get on the bus. Never mind about the herbs. And never mind about your wife if you've got one. We got herbs on the bus. We got a-plenty. This trip is on me. I'm throwin this party for all my good Ohio herb customers. Get right down there to that bus."

Well, there was the bus. The engine was warmin up. I never saw such a well-dressed party. It was Mose Winthrop's party. Not a hoodlum among his herb customers. I saw old Jake Spradling on the bus. He was from Kentucky. I said hello to Jake. He said hello to me. I passed and repassed with everybody. But there was a lot of strangers on the bus. I saw four women. Eighteen men besides me and Mose. It was a big Greyhound bus that Mose had rented for the trip. There set the driver all dolled up in a gray clean uniform. The whole thing was tip-top. Everybody was laughin and talkin. Everybody seemed happy.

I took my seat. I looked down beside me. There was a gallon of herbs right by my seat. It was a white jug with a brown neck. That's the kind Mose Winthrop uses to deliver his herbs in. We know old Mose. Drunk a many a gallon of the herbs Mose delivers across the river into Crummit, Ohio. I am a Kentuckian, but I work in Crummit, you see. I live just over the river on the Kentucky side in Flickers, Kentucky. It is cheaper to live in Kentucky and row a john-boat over to my work. Mose doesn't have to work. He buys the sugar and the corn and runs a herb distillery. He has the Post Office and the store on Deer Creek and buys a few cattle on the side. He has a pull with the Law and gets the boys out of trouble when the Law catches them makin herbs. He just tells the Law to keep hands off and the Law does it. That is Mose. He takes care of his herb makers. He lets one get in the County jail sometimes. But never lets one go to the Pen. Mose is a big boy about helpin electin the Law. He's got the Republicans and Democrats organized on Deer Creek. They stick together. They have to if they make herbs and sell them. Their votes usually decide the election. They decide for the fellow who decides with them.

"Well, what's holdin things up?" said Mose. "We'd better be on our way."

"You left your sign in the bus station," said the bus driver.

"Run and get the sign," Mose said to me. "We need that sign."

I ran in the bus station. I asked the clerk, "Did Mose Winthrop leave a sign in here?"

"Yes," the pale clerk said, "right over there is the sign Mose left in here. Goin to have a good trip, aren't you?"

"I hope so."

"Well, you will with the Herb King of Kentucky. You fellows are bound to have a glorious trip out of it."

I could tell that clerk envied my trip. I could tell the way he looked at me. I looked at the sign on the run back to the bus. It said:

Hurrah for the Wildcats!
Hurrah for the Wildcats!
Wildcats beat the Bears!
Crummit Wildcats Beat Bears!

"Driver, put that up on the front of the bus," said Mose. "That's where it belongs. We want people to know that we are goin to follow our football team to Chicago. We are right with them."

"Are we goin to Chicago sure enough, Mose?" I said.

"We are right now headin for Chicago. You've got enough herbs, haven't you, for the trip? If you haven't we can get them. We'll go down here and fill up at the reserve herbs tank I've got in Crummit."

"Yes, I've got enough herbs."

"That's all I wanted to hear. The trip is all on me. I make the money. The people on the bus are my best herb buyers. They can tell you I put out good stuff and once a customer, always a customer is the way they deal with me."

"You're right," said the woman up front. She wore a black hat. She had blue laughin eyes. She was smilin. "When you once take a drink of Mose Winthrop's herbs you'll never buy 'em any place else. He makes the best herbs I ever put my tongue to, gentlemen. I don't know all the women I've told about his herbs. They're so much in demand among the women here in Crummit that half the time the reserve tank is empty and they can't get them."

"That is only when they catch a couple of my workers and lodge them over night in the County jail and I got to go after them. That don't happen often. You know that, Jenny Lovelace. Sometimes I can't get sugar. You know I buy sugar here and there. I don't buy too much in one place. I have eleven men workin for me. Nine makes. Two delivers. I run the business. I don't care for you people knowin. When I buy sugar I put in the expense row right then and there. Later when I sell I deduct this amount. I know I am hopin to sell and just how much I am goin to get. That's the way we work things out on Deer Creek. I am worth more money than a man holdin office in my County. They have tried to get me to run so I could throw some money in the ring—something besides me hat. I never wanted to get tied up with Law. I don't want the Law to work me for a livin. I want to work the Law for a livin."

Everybody talks on the bus. Everybody gets acquainted. Men shake hands. They say: "Old Mose is honest as the day. What he tells you about his herbs you can depend on it. He makes good herbs. You just can't beat them. I'd ruther have his herbs as any Government herbs I ever tasted. He makes good herbs."

"Old Mose is a good sport. Ever about his house? Got a

nice farm out there. The nicest on Deer Creek. He's got the store and the Post Office. He's got a lot of cattle. He buys and sells cattle. He makes money right and left. Big hunter. He invites his best customers out to hunt with him. Treats them right too. You just got to eat with him. He has plenty to eat too. I never saw as much grub in any one home in my life as I saw out there."

"When old Mose and me knocked down them eighty birds that day he had it on me. He was so tall he could just walk through the fields and step over the five-wire fences and shoot at the same time. He beats any man with a gun I ever saw. He gets more shots in than any man I ever saw."

"You wouldn't take Mose Winthrop for what he is. You'd take him for the Governor of a State. Don't he remind you of a Governor? A lot of people call him Governor. They say he can make as fine a speech as a body ever heard out at the Sheriff races over in Greenbriar County. I heard one fellow say he met with the Republicans out on a hilltop one night. Mose was there. And they said he got up and made the best talk that was made that night and they had a Senator from the deestrict there. They said Mose talked rings around him. He don't have to be no herb maker. That man can do anythin he wants to do. W'y he used to go to college. He went to the University of Kentucky."

The bus sped over the hard road. It was in front of us like a cow snake—a cow-snake-colored ribbon of road leadin us from Crummit to Cincinnati. The farmhouses where the Ohio River barns showed the people had plenty by their fat sides bulgin out with hay, ears of white and yellow corn showin heaped in the latticed corn cribs in the hallways. We saw clean meadows. Sheep standin around the haystacks and cattle feedin from haymows fixed in the fields in hayracks. But what did we care for the horns of plenty? We were goin to Chicago. Mose was givin us a party. We were speedin right along.

"A little faster, driver," said Mose. "We are just makin sixty. I can do this with my old Ford. Around seventy. We got to be in Chicago for the game by tomorrow at noon. Step on it. We got to go."

The driver stepped on the gas. We whirled past farmhouses fast enough to make you dizzy-headed if you looked at the sheep and the cattle on the farms and God knows I liked to look at fat barns and pretty cattle. I liked to see the clean-cut meadows and sheep eatin around a doodle of straw.

"Time for herbs, Gentlemen and Ladies," said Mose.

"You are right," said Jenny Mae Lovelace. "It is time for herbs. Let's every man and every woman to his own jug and try our capacities."

Everybody lifted the jug to his lips. Everybody supped. Everybody said: "A-a-ham. Good stuff." Everybody talked. Everybody laughed. Everybody was merry. We'd talked to each other, but we didn't know one another very well. We had to get acquainted yet. Anybody knows that if there is anything in the world that will bring on a quick acquaintance it is herbs. Drink herbs together and if you belong to one feud family and your partner belongs to another, you'll be friends long as the herbs last. After the herbs are gone you'll wonder why you two have been friends and get mad at yourself for bein so friendly and tellin your mind to your enemy and he'll be in the same boat and wonder why he's been so durn friendly with you. But herbs was the thing that put the old friendship there. If we didn't have herbs on this bus there'd a been a lot of grouches along. But everybody smiled. Everybody was happy.

"Comin to the big town, boys. Ain't this Cincinnati, Ohio?"

"Yes, Jake Spradling, this is Cincinnati. Have you ever been here before?"

"No. But I've heard of Cincinnati all my life. This is the first time I have ever been here."

"How'd you know it was Cincinnati then?"

"I've heard so much talk about how big it was. I just allowed we'd come to it. See the big house. See the smoke from the mills. A body can tell it is a big town. I purt nigh knowed it was Cincinnati."

Cincinnati is a big town when a person is in a hurry. Stoplights all the time red. Traffic in the way. Hard for us to plow through. People pointin to the sign Mose had printed and put in front of his bus. People laughin at the sign. What did we care. We'd not see Cincinnati for a couple of days. We'd never see these same people again. We had the bus and the herbs. They could have the laugh.

Out of Cincinnati. And was I glad to get through that town and get on the highway where we could move again. Soon we were on the ribbon of highway headin for Indiana. Mose said: "When you come to a pretty nice-lookin restaurant, Mister Driver, throw on your brakes. We want to stop. We need grub. We need to stop."

Well, I never can forget Mose. The way he rode in that bus. Pon my honor, he did look like a Governor. He is a tall man. He is about six-feet-five. He has a keen dark eye. He wears them little ribbon bow ties like a old-time speaker at the old-fashion barbecues like we used to have up on Beaver. He just set back there and puffed on a cigar like he owned the world. His eyes twinkled and his face was red. He was all rared back. In his coat lapel was a red rose Jenny Mae Lovelace had brought him from the hothouse. He just commanded the whole bus. We listened to him doin the talkin. He would say: "I was cut out to be the Governor of Kentucky. They lost the pattern they cut me out by when they got the Governor they got. They need old Mose down there at Frankfort. I'd show them how to run this State. I'm not jokin. Don't you think I couldn't run it better than it is run. I could just set there and do nothin and it would go on better than it is goin. You know you can do too much when you are the Governor of Kentucky. I've been on Deer Creek too long now, though, to be Governor of Kentucky."

"W'y, you are the Governor of Kentucky," said Ollie Spry. "We have the Governor of Kentucky right on this bus with us, Gentlemen and Ladies. We have Governor Randall Spoon. He is right with us goin to see a ball game in Chicago. This is the Governor's party and we are his guests. Lady Jenny Mae Lovelace, you are Tessie LaMore, his secretary. You are pretty enough to be a Governor's secretary."

"Oh, thank you, Ollie Spry," said Jenny Mae Lovelace. "I accept the position right now. I accept the compliments. May

I say, Ollie, that you are Lieutenant Governor S. M. Radnor."

"Smart woman," said Ollie and he continued, "Bill Dugan here is Secretary of State Hammonds Sizemore. Fred Kemp here is Attorney General Caley C. Rooten. That's about as big a party of State officials as we need. Sorry we can't make you all public officials. Who's a good Kentucky Colonel among you? Anybody got chin whiskers?"

"Fred Land here. He's got a nice set of chin whiskers."

"Make him Colonel Whitt then, famous drinkin Kentucky Colonel."

"Suits me."

"All right. We are all set," said Ollie.

"Do you reckon we're ever goin to find that restaurant, Mister Driver?" said Mary Snider. "My stomach's feelin hollow as a gourd. We got to find a place to eat."

"Comin into Indiana," said the driver. "See the car license. Won't be long until we'll be in Richmond, Indiana. We can find the good restaurants there. I used to work in Richmond. I'll take you to a good one."

"Okay. Just so we get to a restaurant."

Well, we pulled into Richmond. The party was gettin livelier now. The car was filled with tobacco smoke. Everybody had sampled his gallon of herbs. People on our bus were feelin just a little friendlier than when we left Crummit. People looked at our sign as we passed and pointed to our bus. We didn't care. The driver was takin us to his favorite restaurant. We pulled up and came to a halt in front of the restaurant.

"Here's the best restaurant in Richmond, Gentlemen and Ladies. Here is the place I used to eat when I drove bus through here."

"Do they know you in here?" said Ollie Spry.

"Yes, they do," said the driver.

"Do they believe you in here?" said Ollie.

"I'd think they would," said the driver.

"Well, you tell the manager that we have the Governor of Kentucky on this bus and part of his staff. You be damn sure you tell him that. Tell him to give us service. We got to have service. We got to be treated royal. We are the Royal House of our State not for two more years but for two days. We are the Governor's party."

"You are quite right," said Mose. "I want one more drink of herbs to act like the Governor and make speeches. I am already the Governor. Secretary, you work for the Ford Motor Company in Crummit. You know shorthand surely. You be ready to take down my speech if I make one along the road. Maybe one in this restaurant if I am called on. I may just get up and talk if I am not called on. I am the Governor of Kentucky."

Well, we got out. The driver pulled down the windows, fastened them and locked the doors. We didn't want anybody in Indiana to know the Governor of Kentucky had herbs on his party. We didn't care about the tobacco smoke. Anybody knows that's respectable and decent and expected that the Governor of any State smokes long cigars. It might be expected of the Kentucky Governor to take a little drink. But we wasn't takin any chances. We didn't want the people of Indiana to smell whisky on our Governor's breath.

The proprietor was standin back of the counter. He was a short man with a black handle-bar mustache. He was wipin a plate when we went in. He looked at our crowd and kindly smiled. Of course we didn't look very fresh after gettin off the bus for nearly a hundred and fifty mile ride or maybe more. The women needed to powder their noses and redden their lips a little. We needed to step out and wash our hands and faces and comb our heads. We made it straight for the washrooms. Our driver went over and shook hands with the proprietor. We saw him whisper somethin to him.

We got brushed up a little and walked back into the room. The proprietor had a serious look on his face. He was hurryin here and there. All the waiters were runnin. "The Governor wants the best dinner you serve for twenty-four people of his party and the bus driver," said Ollie. The Governor came out, tall and stately with his eyes twinklin. His conversation was fast and intelligent. The waitresses looked at him. I heard one whisper: "That is Governor Randall Spoon of Kentucky."

I wondered what we were doin stoppin in a restaurant quite

so small. No wonder the proprietor was mortally shocked. Just think of the Governor and his party stoppin at a restaurant unknown as one havin class for the royalty of any State. But the royalty of Deer Creek and Crummit was right there. The Governor of Kentucky and part of his staff, the rest his friends. "Gettin up there, aren't you, boy," I heard the proprietor whisper to the bus driver, "drivin the Governor of Kentucky around. Is he a football fan too? I know how all Kentuckians are about their horses. I know how the Governor likes horse racin. He must be some sport to like football the way he does."

"Our Governor is a sport. He's about the best sport you ever saw. He likes prize fightin and wrestlin. He likes shootin matches, baseball, pool, spittin at cracks and chicken fightin. Of course we don't put that out every place. But he's a sport. He's a big bird hunter too. He's a crack shot, that man is. He's another King Arthur when it comes to bravery and fightin. He's a Von Hindenburg when it comes to huntin. He's a Henry VIII when it comes to women. He's another George Washington when it comes to statesmanship for his State. Of course that's his limits you know, within the bounds of his State. Would you like to meet him?"

"I'd be tickled to death!"

"Governor Randall Spoon, I'd like to introduce John Farmer to you. He runs this restaurant and I've known him for years. He wants to meet you."

"I am glad to have the pleasure of meetin you," said the Governor. "Won't you be seated a minute?"

"No, Governor, I must hurry along with these plates. I wished I'd a knowed you was comin. You caught us not prepared for so many dignitaries. Just to think I've seen your picture in the paper so much, but I never dreamed about you ever stoppin here."

"Well you can't tell about the turn of things. No one knows just what fruit that time will bear. You just can't tell. I never knew that I'd ever stop here either. We are enroute to Chicago to a ball game—a pleasure trip combined with business."

"But you don't look like your picture. You are a much better-lookin man."

"Oh, thank you," said the Governor, "you are quite liberal with your remarks when you say I am a good-lookin man. The picture you see of mine in the papers is made from an old picture I had made after the worries of a hard campaign. You perhaps remember readin about that campaign. It was a bitter struggle. That Republican came nigh as a pea gettin it. They put out on me in Kentucky that I was against racin and good whisky. That nearly wrecked me. But we overcome all the propaganda. I got the election by a fairly conservative margin."

The proprietor went back to help with the plates of food. "That is where he belongs," said the Governor. "I like the common man, but I'm durn tired. I want coffee and grub. I am in a hurry.

"Well," said the Governor, "the smell of this food is just wonderful. The sight of it is appetizin. See that everybody is well fed. See that all the men that will smoke them get a good cigar after the meal. I must eat. I am hungry."

"The Governor of Kentucky," said one of the waitresses, "watch him eat. He is a hearty eater. He can put the food away. I've heard it said that about all big people head of the country are gluttonous eaters. I've heard it said there was a novelist come through Indiana once and he stopped at Halleck's Restaurant here in town. That he ordered a whole stewed hen. And when he took a piece of that hen he just run it through his mouth and threw the naked bone on the floor. He never stopped eatin like that till he finished that stewed hen and the rest of the grub and got up in a hurry—had to be asked to pay. He said, 'I'm sorry, I was about to forget.' The movies was a makin a picture of one of his novels."

"This is good grub," said the Governor, "you bring me some more coffee, please. I like your mutton chops. I like the sauce that goes with the chops. I like everything that you have. The food tastes fine. I was a very hungry man. I am not now, however, after all this food. Bring me a San Felice cigar, please."

Well, we put the grub away. Girls ran this way and that. They waited on us in a royal manner. It pays to be in company with the Governor of a State or some big name. Then you get service. But I wasn't asked to autograph any napkins. Thank goodness! They kept the Governor busy autographin napkins until he could hardly smoke his cigar. I felt sorry for the Governor. But he took his popularity with a smile. He said: "All this comes with bein a big man in affairs of the State. I am a big man and I expect all this. It sometimes takes a little of the joy out of life. But I don't mind. You pay for all you get out of this life anyway whether you are a big man in affairs of the State or a man diggin in the ditch.

"Secretary, find out how much the bill is, please," said the Governor. "Add in five dollars for service. I'll not write a check. I'll pay off in money right from my pocket."

"Twenty-five dollars even. The cigars go with the dollar meals."

"No sales tax," said the Governor. "They ought to have the sales tax. It takes the sales tax to turn the wheels of finance. Let a dollar turn over thirty-four times and it makes a dollar for the State. Not foolin me. Right here is the money."

Our driver said to the Governor: "Say, Mr. Farmer wants you to speak a few words while you are here. See, they's a little crowd gathered in here. Word is out in Richmond that the Governor is passin through here. Said he could have newspaper reporters in here in just a few minutes if it would be all right with the Governor."

"Yes, but you tell him that I'll speak a few words, but I don't want any newspaper reporters in here. This is not a publicity trip. This is a pleasure trip. Go right over there now and tell him what I said. I'll give them a little talk. I'll get up right now and give it to them and we've got to be movin on toward Chicago."

The driver walked over to the Proprietor. He whispered somethin. The Governor got up from his chair, brushed the gray ashes off the end of his cigar. He laid it down on the edge of his plate: "Ladies and Gentlemen and Fellow-Citizens: I am just passin through your beautiful State, I've come up from a sister-State of yours as you well know, the State of Kentucky. And I want to say even on this trip of pleasure, it is a part of this pleasure trip to speak a few words to you of Indiana. I have looked your people over in Indiana and you are so much like us Kentuckians that I can't tell you apart. There is not any way of knowin. (Laughter.)

"In our State we have a few things you do not have. But we are about the same people after all. We have our horses down there and we love them. We have our hills and our blue grass and our mountains. We have our little specks of trouble as any State will have. As Indiana will have, Ohio will have and West Virginia will have. And we have some things that other States don't have. The pioneer spirit of this nation still exists in the people of Kentucky. People have to be guarded at the polls on election day with soldiers. We take our religion and our politics seriously. And why not? Aren't they both vital pillars in this Constitution of ours? Aren't they strong pillars to hold Old Glory up to flutter in the breeze over the land over America?"

The Governor of Kentucky spoke for twenty minutes. He let the words fly. People stood with their mouths open. Our secretary took down the Governor's speech. When the Governor closed he said: "Ladies and Gentlemen, I beseech you, one and all, to stand as pillars—to stand as mountain rocks under this Government of ours for support. Let us stand as oak-tree sentinels for Democracy and keep Old Glory free to wave from coast to coast, over the Land of the Free and the Home of the Brave. I thank you." (Applause.) (More applause.)

But Governor Randall picked up his cigar and walked out. He said, "Good-by, Indiana. We'll meet you at the Kentucky Derby. Good-by, Mr. Farmer. Hope to eat another good meal with you sometime."

The driver unlocked the door. We got back on the bus. We took our old seats. The motor hummed. We started through Richmond on our way to Chicago. We felt much better. The

Governor was a success speakin to the Indiana people. "I'll speak again when we stop," said the Governor. "I like it. I like to be Governor. Every man now and every woman to his own jug. Help thyself to the herbs. We are out of the city now. Drink and be merry. You don't know about tomorrow. You don't know what tomorrow holds for you."

Well, we helped ourselves to the herbs. Now when one man starts on a gallon of honest-to-goodness mule-kickin herbs it takes a long time to kill it if one drinks moderately. We tried to take our herbs moderately goin. Comin back didn't matter so much long as the driver didn't get any herbs. We didn't intend to give him any herbs. We intended to keep his hand on the throttle and his eye on the rail.

We passed through Muncie, Marion, Logansport and into Hammond. We had been jostled down. We were ready to eat again. It was dark. We were gettin tired. It was in the evenin. "What do you say, Gentlemen and Ladies, we stop and eat and relax before we get into Chicago?"

"Suits me," said Ossie Spry. "I'm feelin like it's bean time again. I am ready to eat. I am a hungry man. What do you say, Governor, that when we get in front of a nice-lookin restaurant that you let me go in and ask the Whole-Cheese what he would take to fix a steak dinner for the Governor of Kentucky and his party which includes several of his staff?"

"Suits me fine," said the Governor. "It lets them know in advance who to expect. That is a bright idea. I'll be thinkin of another speech to give at partin."

"What shall it be, Governor?"

"Fair Women, Fast Horses, Honorable Herbs!"

"What a talk! What a talk! Can you handle that subject?"

"Can Rubinoff play his violin?"

"Here is a nice-lookin soup house," said the driver. "You want me to stop here, Governor?"

"Why not?"

"Let me out, you people. Get your feet up square around until I get out and make arrangements for a meal for the Governor of Kentucky and his party."

Ossie walked down the aisle. He went out the bus door. We

saw him enter the restaurant. We saw him talkin to the Head-Cheese. We saw him motion, "Bring 'em on." They all wanted the honor of havin the Governor of Kentucky. No one would turn us down. They really couldn't turn us down. It put them on the spot. Not us.

"Come on, all of you," said Ossie, "he said it was a pleasure for him to have the honor of feedin the Governor of the State. That it would increase business for him. That he would name the restaurant Spoon Restaurant for the honor of havin fed the Governor of Kentucky. He wants the Governor's picture to put up in the window. He wants his autograph. He wants his napkin autographed. When he runs his ad in the paper next week he is goin to say: 'We feed many notable celebrities. The Governor of Kentucky and the majority of his staff dined with us Saturday evening last.' Boy, he really wants you, Governor of Kentucky."

"Well, he can have twenty-five hungry people just in the minute. Herbs in place. The door locked and the windows down, driver. Let's eat. Come on, everybody. Come on with your Governor!"

We walked into the restaurant. Waiters ran quickly. The Proprietor came out and said: "This is the Honorable Randall Spoon of Kentucky, isn't it?"

"Yes, this is he," said Mose. "Yes. I am the Governor of Kentucky."

"I am glad to welcome you and your party into my restaurant. I hope we can serve you to your satisfaction."

"I think you can all right," said the Governor.

"If I had just had word that you were comin and could have fixed for you. You caught me unexpectedly. I never dreamed of seein a Governor here today. We'll do our best by you."

"That's all a mule can do," said the Governor laughin. "Just take it easy. We are not hard to please. We are very tired, hungry, and in a hurry. We are en route to Chicago and we have been delayed by motor troubles or we would be in Chicago now."

"May I call a newspaper reporter in and give him this story? Let him interview you? I'd like to."

"Yes, but don't do it. This is a pleasure trip. We are on our way to see a football game between the Bears and the Wildcats tomorrow. And I have a little business in Chicago to fix up tonight. I don't have time to be interviewed, though."

"I am sorry then, Governor."

"That's quite all right. I appreciate your thoughtfulness. I hope you understand my position. You know the affairs of State are many and large. It is not often the Governor of a State can slip out like I did this mornin early. Not a paper reporter got that I was takin this trip. Just to think every time you go out even to see a neighbor it is strealed in all the papers. You've seen my name in your papers here many times. You have seen my picture. Thank heavens I'm out tonight just with my staff members and my friends. No reporters askin me questions and sendin it out to all parts of the country."

We went to the washrooms and got ready for dinner. The Governor was delayed talkin to the proprietor. But the Governor just walked away to the washroom. They were carryin hot dishes of steak dinners to our tables white-clothed and big enough for four. The Governor, Attorney General, Secretary of State and Lieutenant Governor ate at the same table. I was at the table with the Governor's Secretary, the Kentucky Colonel Whitt and another not of the Royal House but just a friend of the Governor. His name was Ely Hunt. Did they carry the grub to us! We started carvin the tender steak. The Governor's table got the most attention. Our table was the second to be recognized.

The waiters nearly fell over each other carryin food to our table. "More coffee," Mose would say. They went in a run to get coffee for the Governor. He would sit back, his red face beamin like a winesap in the autumn sun. His eyes would twinkle like two liquid stars set against a sky of red. He would eat and his shoulders would twitch. He was serious.

"How is the food?" asked the proprietor.

"Couldn't be any better," said the Governor. "You have real food here. We are enjoyin it."

"Write that down with your name here on this napkin, Governor. I'm glad to hear you say that."

"I don't very often do this. But I'll do it for you. Secretary, ask for the bill, please," said the Governor. "Include smokes for all and ten bucks for service. Now," said the Governor. "I'm ready to say a few words and we got to be goin. I hope he asks me to speak."

"We'll see that you get to speak, Governor," said Lieutenant Governor S. M. Radnor. "You must speak before you leave here, Governor. You can't miss givin that three-point publicity speech on your State. Remember what you said in the bus."

"Bill is nothin. Not a thing," said Secretary Tessie LaMore.

"I won't have that," said the Governor. "He must take his pay."

"No," said the proprietor, "I won't have it. I won't have it. I won't have a thing. No use to insult me by askin me to take it. I just won't do it. You have helped me more than all the ads I could put in the paper. Your presence here has helped me. Your signature will help me. Do you have a picture of yourself with you?"

"Sorry, but I do not have."

"Quite all right. Do you reckon you could send me one?"

"Surely."

"Do you have somethin to say before you leave? You see some people have gathered in here. They heard you was in here and they've heard so much about the Governor of Kentucky. They want to see him in person and hear him. How about a few words, Governor?"

"Citizens of Indiana," said the Governor of Kentucky, "It is a pleasure to speak a few words to you while passin through your most beautiful State and sister-State of Kentucky. It is a pleasure indeed to note the progress your State is makin. I could go on and on and speak to you of your own State. I have kept a close observation on the State of Indiana for years. Her people are so much like our own people. Just crossin the river one can't tell a Hoosier from a Corncracker. (Applause.) God has been good to Indiana by looks of the fat barns over the countryside. (Applause.) Now if I make a talk here this evenin, my previous Indiana friends, citizens of one of these great States of America, I choose to call that talk, 'Fair Women, Fast Horses, Honorable Herbs.' (Laughter and applause.)

"You know we got the prettiest women in the world. We got them in the mountains and we got them in the bluegrass. Our State is shaped like a plow point. We got fair women all over the old plow point. Check any place you please. They are tall in the bluegrass. It is the lime in the food products from the soil that makes the bones grow in the women same as in the horses and men. They got the stock in them too. I have been warned about the importation of so many canned goods into this fertile section of our State. That practice, Ladies and Gentlemen, must be discontinued. If you want fine-lookin women, fair women, come to Kentucky. (Laughter and applause.)

"There is no need for me to tell you about our horses. There is but little left to say after all that has been said. The world knows about our horses. We love a horse, us men do, better than we do our wives. (Shouts and applause.) Our women, though, Ladies and Gentlemen, love the horses better than they do their husbands. (Shouts and louder applause.) We bury our horses with ceremony. We name our churches for our horses. We put up marble tombstones at their graves. Let me tell you about a scrub horse once. He came from a farm back in the hills. He won every race he was put in—just a old scrub horse. He wouldn't work at nothin. People thought he was a work horse. The truth was found out about his mother's breedin. She'd jumped the fence and got to Satan, that famous horse of the turf. Satan was the father of this plug that swept the race track and focused the eyes of the nation upon Kentucky. That just goes to show you we got the horses with the blood in them.

"Now, Ladies and Gentlemen, last but not the least thing in our State, we are very proud of. That is herbs. (Laughter and whispering.) You may not know what we call herbs. You may have another name for herbs. You, perhaps, up in this section of the United States call it 'moon' or 'white-mule.' But the real name of it is herbs. (Laugher and applause.) We call it 'herbs' for it is good herb-medicine for snake-bites, chills and fevers and a lot of things I could go on here and enumerate until mornin. That would be useless, my good Indiana friends. When one of our citizens has made 'herbs' that is no more than his duty. Our fathers have made them for generations. You know about all of us like our 'herbs.' When I was a Judge I never sentenced a man for makin herbs. Now I have the chance to go one further. When he is put behind the dark walls—all it takes is my name to fetch him out into the light and make him a free man. Honorable herbs, Ladies and Gentlemen! W'y, do you think I'd degrade a reputable man's reputation by puttin him in a buggy jail? No! I'd take him home with me if I could to the Governor's mansion and give him a decent feather bed! I feel for humanity! God turned the water into wine! Didn't he do it? Then what is wrong with Honorable Herbs! When you come to our State don't forget our herbs. (Applause. Applause. More Applause.) So, good-night, Ladies and Gentlemen, and may God bless you." (Applause. Applause. Applause.)

The Governor of Kentucky walked out the door. We followed him to the bus. He made a stirrin talk. People ran up with napkins, papers, whisky-bottle labels and asked for the Governor's autograph. He hurriedly scribbled, "The Governor of Kentucky and so on." He was tall and stately as a pine tree on a Kentucky hillside. He had the military bearin of a Knight in search of the Holy Grail. He smoked a cigar and blew the smoke out into the cool Indiana air. We loaded in the bus as the motor hummed. We roared away to Chicago.

"I'll take some Honorable Herbs, boys," said the Governor liftin the jug to his mouth: "how about you, Gentlemen and Ladies?"

"Suits us," said Ossie. "I love my herbs. Chicago is not far away. Better take them now. Dry country, you know. Maybe the time will come when the people will crave herbs and vote them back. But Government herbs don't come up to these herbs."

The bus went by leaps and bounds. Ossie gave the driver a

swig of herbs. That had been what was wrong all the time. He just started drivin now. We were just a matter of minutes from Chicago. Each person took a little dram of herbs. The bus roared on. We passed everythin on the road. Our driver would say: "Lay over, road hog. Lay over before I knock you off the road." And we droned right into the Chicago Loop.

"Are we goin into the Big City, boys?" said the Governor. "Looks like a lot of town here. Seems like we've come over Hell and half of Georgia. Hurrah for the Wildcats! Hurrah for the Wildcats. Wildcats scratch the Bears! Paw them Cats! Scratch their eyes out! Hurrah for the Wildcats!"

Boom–Boom–zzzrrrr–Motorcycle cops whizzing past us.

Clop–clop–clop–Mounted police!

Zzzzzzzzzzzzzzzzzzz–Police cars.

"STOP!" One pulled in front of us with a growl.

Uniformed men stepped forth from all sides. Our bus had been stopped! What was wrong? Herbs? Surely not.

"Open the door, driver," said the Governor.

The driver opened the door. A uniformed policeman stuck his head in at the door. He said, "Consider yourself under arrest."

"What for?" said Ossie Spry.

"You are goin in the wrong way on the Loop. That's what for. You know better than this, driver."

"You can't do this," said Ossie. "We got the Governor of Kentucky on here and part of the House of Representatives. We got part of the staff. We are already due in Chicago at the Mortfield Hotel!"

"Pardon me, gentlemen," said the policeman, "if your Governor is on that bus. Go right on. Go right on. Go right in on this side the Loop!"

"Thank you."

"Say, officer, don't you want to meet the Governor!"

"I'll be delighted."

Our Governor from Kentucky stepped out where the police could see him.

"Yes, I am the Governor of Kentucky. I am glad to meet you, Gentlemen. I am sorry my chauffeur made this mistake.

Very sorry. Gentlemen, you know I am a law-abidin man. I assure you nothin like this will happen again and if you gentlemen will be so kind I'd be happier if you wouldn't mention it. You understand! Well, Good-by, Gentlemen, and good luck."

"Good-by, Governor, and good luck to you."

One said: "My lands, but isn't the Governor of Kentucky a big scamp? He's a good-lookin man too. Surprised me. I thought from his picture he wasn't so hot-goin from his looks. W'y he's a fine-lookin man!"

We drove in on the wrong side of the Loop. People dodged us and razzed us. We were tired out. We were goin to the Mortfield Hotel. I don't know whether it was because we were on the wrong side of the Loop the reason why people razzed us or the sign on the front of our bus.

"Just soon as we get in front of the hotel, women and men, get your herbs in your luggage. You know people are on the lookout these days for good herbs. Put your herbs away. Get your reservations. The Governor pays for your rooms and your meals while you are here. Remember, driver, take that sign off soon as we light in front of the hotel."

The porters ran out. A whole swarm of them, blue-uniformed with rows of brass buttons up the sides. "Say, what's the sign doin up there! Comin up to beat us, are you?"

"That's what we've come for. Just a friendly match in sports," said the Governor. "We have come to give you a tussle if we don't give you a sound beatin."

"Uh," said the porter.

"Say," said Ossie, nudgin the porter with his elbow, "you don't know who you are arguin with. You should know better than this long as you've been a porter. You are arguin with the Governor of Kentucky. Ain't you never heard of him? Stand there with your mouth open! Don't drop my grip."

Then it was whispered: "Governor of Kentucky is on that bus. He's the big, tall, fine-looking man. See him there. Look at him!"

Each porter tried to get his leather bag. One nabbed it. The Governor didn't pay any attention to them fightin for his leather bag. He had the affairs of State at heart, and the affairs of Chicago at heart presently. We had to get rooms for the night. It was late. We were tired.

The hotel manager met us: "Is the Governor of Kentucky here?"

"Yes. This is he."

"My name is James Hampton. Glad to know you, Governor. Welcome you to our hotel."

"Glad to know you, Mr. Hampton. Glad to be a guest in your hotel for tonight."

"We'll have your rooms just in a few minutes. I know you must be tired."

"We are," said our Governor of Kentucky, "we're tired out. We have come since early this morning. You see it's late now. I've made two talks on the way. The only thing, Mr. Hampton, I ask of you, is not let it be known we are here. I don't want any newspaper reporters here. I want rest. Hear me!"

"I do, Governor Spoon. I'll see you are not disturbed."

I don't know who stayed with the Governor. I know he went to bed. He didn't stay up and discuss the affairs of the State. I went to bed. I roomed with the Lieutenant Governor. I don't remember. I needed sleep. Look what a place we were in. Chicago hotel with the Governor of Kentucky. Only this mornin we started as just ordinary folks. We were goin fast up that ladder of celebrities. You become a celebrity overnight when you get into affairs of the State.

It was nine o'clock Sunday morning. The telephone brought me out of bed.

"The Governor wants you downstairs in the dinin-room to breakfast, Sir."

I dressed and went downstairs. The Governor was at the table already with nearly all of our party. We just had Ossie to wait on before we started breakfast. Table was dressed the best it had been for a long time. It was dressed for company. "Ladies and Gentlemen," said our Governor, "here's each of you a complimentary ticket to the game between the Bears and the Wildcats."

"Thank you, Governor."

"Yes, thank you, Governor."

"That's nice of you, Governor."

"Can't thank you enough, Governor."

"Waiter," said the Governor, "bring us two-for-a-quarter cigars, please. Good as you got and that's the best you have for I got one this mornin. It's the Pince-Pete Cigar. It's a jim-dandy."

We had breakfast. We smoked. The women took to cigarettes. They held them properly in their fingers and poised them beautifully when they weren't between their red-bought lips. We had a crowd of dignitaries all right. I felt proud to be with the Governor of Kentucky. I'd remembered old dates with him, the prize fights, the bird hunts, the fox hunts, the square dances, the political rallies, at the herb reservoir, at the chicken fights. The Governor was at home any place you put him. He had dignity. He could make a speech. He could buy cattle, farm, hand out your letters at the Post Office out on Deer Creek. He could get men out of jail. Demand them of the Law. Why couldn't he make a good Governor?

Well, we got a section of seats—box seats where we could see the Wildcat-Bear football game. If ever the Governor enjoyed himself it was here. He pounded my hat in once when the Wildcats scratched the Bears for a long run up the muddy field. He hit Ossie on the ear with a quirt and made it bleed when the Wildcats intercepted a Bear pass and made a fifty yard run. It was a hard game. Just a few minutes to play after the long struggle when neither side had scored. One of the Bears kicked a field goal and then the whistle. We lost. The game was over. We made for the gate, and to our bus. We had to return to the hotel to get our luggage and settle our bill.

Our rooms were four dollars for each of us. The Governor's room was a little more. "But the bill was light," the Governor said. "One good reservoir of Honorable Herbs will pay that little bill of $142 plus tips."

We loaded on the bus. The motor hummed. The Governor was delayed. We were waitin. He ran down the steps: "Step on the gas, driver. Newspaper men wantin to interview me. I don't have the time. We must be gettin back to the affairs of State. Be damn sure you go out the right way on the Loop. Our trip has been a success. We've got a few herbs left, haven't we? All right. Help yourselves to the herbs. When you run out we have a reserve amount of herbs on this bus. If you get by with a gallon to the man and a gallon to the woman, why not? Remember we'll have our herbs."

We smoked. We sang songs. We talked about affairs of the State. We breezed over the ribbon of white road. Back into Indiana. Back to Hammond. Back through Marion, Muncie, Richmond. We stopped at a new restaurant. It was night. Darkness had covered the level Indiana countryside. "Now," said Hattie Ogles, "I'll make a speech here. I want to talk."

"Don't let the herbs be too much your guide," said our Governor of Kentucky, "but speak from the heart if you say anythin and not too much from the herbs."

We stopped at a midnight restaurant. "Lunch for twenty-five soon as you can fix it," said the Governor. "We are in a hurry. Do it quickly as you can."

Our driver slipped over and said somethin to the little restaurant keeper. "What," said the restaurant keeper, "this time of night?"

He hurried about. His waitresses hurried. We didn't have to wait twenty minutes for a midnight meal. We were tired out. We were hungry. We needed food. The owner came over. He said: "I heard the Governor of Kentucky was here among you. Is this the Governor of Kentucky?"

"Yes," said Mose, "I am the Governor of Kentucky. How did you know I was the Governor?"

"You look like some great man," the fellow said foldin his thin hands and squintin his eyes.

"Thank you," said the Governor. "It is very nice of you to hand me such complimentary remarks. I appreciate them to the depths of my heart. I am the Governor of Kentucky and a few of my friends and I have been to Chicago on a combined business and pleasure trip. We are gettin back late. I must be servin my State tomorrow. I am in a hurry."

"Just a minute, Governor, and we'll be ready for you."

Food never tasted any better to me in my life. It was a midnight lunch. We got buttermilk and sauerkraut with lunch. I ordered that. Some got coffee. I took buttermilk. My stomach was in an uproar. We had better than one hundred and fifty miles. It was now near midnight. We had to get in before daylight. The Governor had to be on Deer Creek by that time. He must get in before daylight.

We finished the food. It was fine. We lighted our cigars and started to push back from the table. "Ladies and Gentlemen and Our Most Honorable Governor of Kentucky," said Hattie Ogles, "I have a few words I'd like to say before we move on where our party will disband, each to go to our respective duties, the Governor go to his affairs of State and his Staff Members go with him—I want to say that as an outsider, not a native Kentuckian, but one from a sister State, that I have never been with a more loyal group of people nor better sports than with this group of Kentuckians. I have had the most memorable trip in my life. (Applause.)

"Kentucky has one of the greatest Governors of all the Governors in these United States of America. He is a sport above all. He is a man of the common people—the Governor for the man of the street you people have heard so much talk about. Kentucky has produced her Breckenridges, her Clays, her Lincoln, and Ladies and Gentlemen, she has produced her Randall Spoon, our most worthy Governor of Kentucky with you at this minute." (Applause. Applause.) ("Full of Honorable Herbs," whispered Ossie. "Get her down if you can.") "He has come to the people of Kentucky in a time of need. We were goin in debt by degrees. He has given us a tax that is honorable for all men alike. He will bring our State to the front. It is comin there already. After his services to his State and then to the world. He is a man for the country. He is bigger than his State. Ladies and Gentlemen, this is all I have to say and for the privilege of sayin these words, I most heartily thank you."

Our Governor stood and knocked the gray ashes from his cigar tip with his long index finger. He was the man of the hour. He bowed to the crowd in the restaurant. He walked out. "Good night, Gentlemen," he said.

We walked out into the cold air. The moon was racin through some big cold gray clouds. "I believe I am the Governor of Kentucky," said Mose. "If I'm not I'd make a good one. I could be the Governor of Kentucky. Now. Just think, tomorrow, I won't be anything but a postmaster, a storekeeper, a cattle buyer, a good sport, a handler of good Honorable Herbs. It's hard to fall to that after this trip. Get in the bus, my friends. Get in the bus and us move on toward Crummit. You know my wife has left me once over stuff like this. You remember that trip to Columbus that filled all the papers that time that I had such hard time gettin out of. I couldn't handle the Ohio Law like I did the Kentucky Law. You know I'm rooted in Kentucky and it's a pretty damn good dirt for the roots to grow in too."

We loaded in the bus. We got our seats. "The herbs are gettin low, Mr. Governor," said Fliam Flannery, "mighty low. Mighty low. Mine is down to the very dregs. But here's to you all!" He turned the jug to his lips and emptied it stone dry, dregs and all went down.

"I love my herbs," said Mose, "and here's the last. My jug is emptied. My herbs are gone. All gone. My friends are all here. We have had a good time together. Sing 'The Old Ship of Zion.' Sing. Sing. Sing."

We sang "The Old Ship of Zion." The bus plunged on through the darkness. The stars were bright balls of fire glued in the blue above us. We could see the bright lights boom past us on the highway. We overtook and passed each car we got sight of. We moved. We gave our driver herbs and told him to step on the gas. He did his best. We made seventy. We made all the bus would do. We made top speed around the curves. Three o'clock Monday mornin and Crummit!

We shook hands. We parted. Men shed tears. Spirits in us were high. We had finished our honorable herbs. Those of us who had not finished, Mose told to take the jugs home but be damn sure and save the jugs for he needed them. It was a sad partin.

I went with Mose to get his car and ride to Kentucky. He had left it parked in Crummit. The Crummit policemen had picked it up. It was in their custody. We were informed by a policeman we asked to search for a stolen car and gave him our number. We had to go to the police station.

"Yes, Mr. Winthrop, we have your car. We thought we would take care of it for you. Next time don't leave it out in the street."

"What's the bill of fare to get it?" said Mose.

"Not a thing but your good will. You understand."

"I do," said Mose.

"Good night, Cap."

"Good night."

We got in the car and breezed across the bridge. The toll collector was asleep. We needed the time more than he did the money anyway. I lived near Deer Creek.

"Now if I can just get by the old woman good as I got out of that w'y I'll be on top of the world. My worst is yet to come. And I got a date with a woman at four o'clock in our barn this mornin. It's goin to be just one more trial. Pray for the Governor of Kentucky. Don't let his spirits fall."

I left Mose. I got out near home. I'd have to slip in at the window to keep from wakin my wife. I heard a chicken a-crowin. Soon would be day. What a night! What a trip! What a party!

"When I got home," said Mose, "I put my car away and run down to the barn. I was supposed to see that sweet little Claire County widow down there at four o'clock. Well, she was in by the manger. I pulled her up in my arms. I kissed her. I called her Honey. And she answered and said, 'W'y Mose. You do love me, don't you.' And I'll declare if it wasn't my wife I'm a liar by the clock. She had come to the barn early to see about some young chickens. And I said, 'W'y yes, Honey, I love you. I've always loved you!' And we hadn't spoken to each other in two months. We made up right there."

WHATEVER I am or ever shall be, school teacher, tiller of the earth, poet, short-story writer, upstart, or not anything–I owe it to my own Kentucky hill-land and to my people who have inhabited these hills for generations. My hills have given me bread. They have put song in my heart to sing. They have made my brain thirst for knowledge so much that I went beyond my own dark hills to get book knowledge. But I got an earthly degree at home from my own dark soil. I got a degree about birds, cornfields, trees, wild-flowers, log shacks, my own people, valleys and rivers and mists in the valleys–Scenes of a fairyland childhood that no college under the sun could teach me.

I have learned from walking through the woods in W-Hollow at night where the wind soughs through the pine tops, I have learned where the big oak trees and the persimmon trees are; I have learned where the blackberry thickets are; where the wild strawberries grow; where the wild crab-apple trees blossom in the spring. I have learned where the large rocks are in the fields; where the crows build their nests; where the groundhogs den; where to find the red fox and the gray fox; where the squirrels keep their young in the hollow tree tops and where the quail hides her nest. I know the little secrets of Nature, of the wild life that leads me to these things. I have tried to write about them in my humble crude fashion. I have enjoyed doing it more than I have eating food, visiting people or cities. My love is with my own soil and my own people and may I truly say the land is a land of log shacks and lonesome waters.

Last night I came home from teaching school. I am teaching school twenty miles away from home on the Ohio River front. Though in the background on the Kentucky side of the river one can see the hills lined back under the Kentucky skies whence cometh the students that make up the majority of our school enrollment. Across the river from where I stay I can see the sky on fire by night and pillars of smoke by day from the mills. The blasting rattles my windowpanes and makes me nervous when I get in bed. I wish that I were far enough away that I could not see fire from the mills. I wish I were back in W-Hollow where the only light I could see would be sunlight, moonlight, starlight; where my windowpanes would be rattled only by the wind. I wish often that I were back where life is quiet as a floating cloud and where there is poetry in the wind, the skies, the moon and the stars, the people and the good earth. It is true, where I am, I board on a fertile river farm. I eat products direct from the farm. The earth about me supplies the table with food. But the land is a level land. There aren't any hills but the river banks. This river land will produce per acre three times as much as my own rough acres. But that is not it. My land is hill. We have only one hundred and two acres of land. Only two are level and one hundred are rough. I long to return to my own land, because it is my own and I know every foot of it.

Our house is not on a highway where we can hear the drone of motors. It is in the head of W-Hollow and only a rough wagon road leads to it. It is impossible for an automobile to reach us. We have lived hereabout in the Hollow for three generations. The children have gone out beyond the Hollow, but they have come back. There are seven of us children, two of our group sleep eternally out of the Hollow, for there is not a cemetery on the creek. The two married plan to return to the Hollow, the two who have gone out to further their education will return to the Hollow and this one teaching school returns when chances permit.

Last night I returned. The night was dark. I left Riverton, Kentucky, for the Hollow. I had about three miles of mud path to go and carry a load of books, typewriting paper, a small typewriter and my clothes. The mud was yellow and heavy. It stuck to my feet. It was hard to walk through it, but it was good earth mud to me and I didn't care. Sweat trickled down my nose. The white November rain henpecked my face softly and mingled with the sweat. I was happy to get back to the Hollow—back where it was quiet, back where I had roamed the hills at night and had written poetry out alone with the trees, the earth, the stars and cold blue skies and the small gurgling streams. But this night the skies were low and dark. Rain clouds hurried across the sky like long racing greyhounds. I walked up Academy Branch and touched the high hill that led over into the Hollow. I walked up this path, crooked as a snake twisting through a briar thicket. I could smell the storm wind bearing the splashes of rain from the pines. I could smell the ripe shoemake leaves. I could smell the earth. I could see the bare outlines of the leafless twigs etched against the dark racing cloud background. I saw a rabbit dart across my path. I heard the quails calling in one of our desolate winter cornfields. It was a covey getting together after they'd been fired into that day by hunters. They were getting together again to roost in the tall dead crab-grass.

When I reached the top of the hill, I laid my load down and looked into the Valley. I could see an outline where the Ohio River ought to be. I could see below me the bare outlines of hills covered with barren timber—etched against the sky. It made my heart beat fast to be back where I could write poetry, where I had written poetry, where I could live my own life with the trees, the wind, the water, the storms—the night, the day and the people in the Hollow. I could run wild with the dogs over the old hills now November-desolate and forsaken. I could write poetry. I could live poetry. I could feel poetry in the November wind and hear it in the pine tops. I was back where I could hear the lonesome waters. I could hear the falls at Little Sandy just over the backbone of bony ridge from W-Hollow.

I looked out into the space. I could feel the wind and it seemed with hands tearing at my coat tail. I could feel the cool November wind against my hot face. I picked up my load and crossed the fence onto our own good one hundred and two acres of land. I walked down under the oak trees. There are still bundles of dead leaves clinging to their tops that will not leave regardless of time and tide until next spring when these oak trees put out new buds. Then the dead leaves fall from these oak twigs. I heard the wind pleading for these dead leaves. They resisted the pleas of the wind and they held to their tree of life. I stopped in reverence under the oak trees and uttered my words for reverence for my earth beneath my feet that I would never leave, my earth that feeds me bread from the old stubble fields that are so desolate and wind-swept in late November. I sat on a rock beside the path. I said: "Creator of the Universe: Make me as solid as my hills. Give me the solidness of my stones. Let me still see beauty in the stars that hang above my land. Let me see beauty in the night and hear music in the wind. Let me gather poetry from the wind and from the night. Let me gather poetry from the lonesome waters that I can hear above the wind and rain tonight. Give me life close to the earth. Let not my feet stray too far from what is my own. Let others laugh if they will. Give me fists big enough to fight my own battles with, a backbone big as a saw log. Let the white rain hit my face. Let me feel the teeth of the wind. Give me the right to live, the power to live, as my people have lived before me. Let me be buried when the power to live, the right to live is over in the land that has cradled me. Let me lie back in the heart of it in the end. I ask these things, Creator of the Universe in Your presence, these and daily bread."

I cannot sing tunes that great men have sung.
I cannot follow roads great men have gone,
I am not here to sing the songs they've sung,
I think I'm here to make a road my own.
I shall go forth not knowing where I go.
I shall go forth and I shall go alone.
The road I'll travel on is mud, I know,
But it's a road that I can call my own.
The stars and moon and sun will give me light.
The winds will whisper songs I love to hear;
Oak leaves will make for me a bed at night,
And dawn will break to find me lying here.
The winy sunlight of another day
Will find me plodding on my muddy way.

THE END